Jerzy
MAN WITHOUT A COUNTRY

RICK BURR

OMNI
PUBLISHING

What early readers are saying:

"...my tears flowed freely not just from the grief the characters experienced, but also for the depth, triumphs and love shared in this story."
~ Ravinder B.

"...it certainly holds your attention & is a page turner ...you want to know what comes next & you tell yourself, "Just one more chapter!"
~ Karen A.

"WOW! That was intense!"
~ Elaine R.

"I loved the book, and will be honored to share it once it's in print! My emotions were all over the place while reading it."
~ Alicia W.

"It is a wonderful story, and I am telling everyone I know about it!"
~ Linda R.

Dedication

This book is dedicated with heartfelt gratitude to Elaine Rooks and Linda Wild Reed, whose insights, encouragement, and unwavering belief in this story kept it alive. Without you, it might never have reached the final page. I cannot thank you enough.

Contents

PART THREE

Part One

One

The Top Dog

Lublin, Poland
 Spring, 1939

The children were running from every direction all over town just to watch sixteen-year-old Jerzy Czaplicki die. They were yelling and laughing, urging the others to hurry to the empty lot behind the old movie theater, for that was where it was going to happen.

Soon, the lot began filling with spectators whispering to each other and staring in awe at the self-appointed executioner, Boguslaw Owiti, the only nineteen-year-old still in the school's ninth level. He was a commanding presence, pacing, pounding and grinding the knuckles of one tightly-fisted hand into his other open hand, anticipating the pain he was going to inflict upon Jerzy, the hurt he intended as payback for being laughed at. Boguslaw was the most feared student there... a hulking Neanderthal who lived only to taunt the younger boys into submission, a calling to which he succumbed

3

with immense glee. He was especially merciless in his harassment of Jerzy. Experienced by his attacks on so many other boys, he had become vicious, yet sly about it; he knew how to wait for just the right opportunities, sometimes flicking his middle finger hard against the back of Jerzy's ear when he was not looking, just enough to irritate him, or maybe waiting until Jerzy was carrying all of his books, and then tripping him. And when the boy turned to see who sabotaged him, Boguslaw would just smile at him, showing off his yellow teeth, and not even pretending innocence.

But Jerzy was far from his only target... the more boys Boguslaw intimidated, the more secure his position as top dog in the whole school. Of course, he was also the oldest boy in the school, but nobody dared point that out. It was not his fault that those stupid teachers kept holding him back, just like it was not his fault that he was bigger and stronger than all the other kids.

The crowd continued to grow. They all figured that if they came to witness this event, Boguslaw would see their attendance as an act of devotion to him and leave them alone. But they were wrong. He glared at the rapidly growing crowd of onlookers, already wondering which of them would be next.

As Jerzy walked to his doom, the boy had a look of helplessness in his watery green eyes, which stared into the nothingness ahead of him, knowing that any escape was futile.

"What did I ever do to deserve this?" he said, opening and closing his fists.

"Jerzy... listen, you do not have to go," said Nikodemos, his best friend since forever.

"Of course I do, you idiot."

"Look, maybe he will not even show up. Maybe he is sick. Or maybe—"

"He will be there, and my sorry ass will be history."

Normally, Jerzy was good-natured despite the incessant hunger that gnawed on his bones, but today his heart was as empty as his stomach, and he just walked on silently with his head down, not thinking or feeling, but just walking, and entering into the rhythm of his legs as they slowly measured off the distance between him and his funeral, rhythmic and predictable, like a heartbeat.... a rhythm that he would hear no more as each step brought him that much closer to his final moments. He wished he was already dead.

His pants were weathered and torn, the cloth flapping against his skinny legs as he walked, and he was barefoot, as always. He even went to school barefooted. It was a look that nobody could imitate, for he was the end result of beautiful, but poor parents, and years of deprivation. The other kids understood; at least the poor ones did. It was the rich kids, the ones whose fathers held government jobs, the ones who never had to worry about the Great Depression, who gave him a hard time, as though their money made them better than him.

"Nik, I will be the first to admit that I am scared, but I have to do this, otherwise I will be laughed at for the rest of my life, and you know that. I have no choice." Jerzy looked up at a passing plane. The sky was brooding, with dark ominous clouds that seemed to follow him, and a deep rumbling that shook the air, announcing a large storm ahead. Naturally, he thought. Then he felt the wind behind him gaining strength, pushing him, urging him forward.

"You are on a suicide mission, Jerzy. Only the insane would actually fight Owiti. That guy is a machine, and he is going to crucify you."

Jerzy winced. "Do you seriously think I want to do this?" He had seen school fights before, however he had never actually been the star in one. But there was no way he could back out now, not with half the school there to watch him. Nothing, absolutely nothing was worse than being branded a coward. The least he could do would be to die bravely. "What time is it?"

Nik proudly pulled out his pocket watch. It had been a present from his father, who had been given the watch from his own father. He held up the forefinger of his left hand while staring at the treasured timepiece in his right, and waited seven seconds before answering, nodding his head at each tick...

"There... it is exactly 3:45, my friend."

Jerzy trembled... it was close now. He was not a fighter and he knew it. Built like a small fencepost, he much preferred to think of himself as a lover. Or more honestly, a potential lover. His unusual eye color made him a favorite among the girls at school, but he had no experience yet with the ladies, so he was extremely shy and awkward around them.

Right now, however, that did not matter... these were his last moments, and he trembled with that knowledge. Why is there so much pain in life? And why do we have to die? His own mortality was a difficult thing to acknowledge, and he wondered why he had even been born. He had been brought up as a Catholic, but the stories always felt more like fairy tales to him, so he was not a strong believer, especially with the miracles.

"What a shitty life," Jerzy said as he walked to his ending.

The sky rumbled again, as if in response to the boy.

"Yeah," answered Nik.

"And it is all my fault. Everything was fine, you know? At least it was until this morning, when Boguslaw picked on me again and I lashed out at him in the school hallway, like a stupid jerk."

"What in the world did you say to him, anyway?"

"He was giving me the usual crap about me being poor, and I was thinking that that cabbage-head should already have graduated, but just my luck, he is a big idiot, and is still here."

"Jerzy, what exactly did you say to him?"

They stopped walking and just looked at each other.

"Nik, I just could not take any more, so without even thinking, I... sort of yelled at him, saying, 'Well at least I was not kept back three times, Booguslawww,' and then I made it even worse by laughing real loud, right in his face."

"Ouch. And what did he say to that?"

"Oh man... first, he leaned forward, and brought his face so close to me that I thought he was going to bite my nose off... then he looked straight into my eyes in a way that scared the crap out of me, kind of like the devil was looking right into my soul, you know? And then, he spoke slowly, but loud... I think he was making sure everybody around us heard, and he said, 'After school, poor boy, four o'clock, in back of the movie theater... then everybody will see just how funny you really are.' And right then he slammed his big hairy knuckles into the wall right next to my head before he turned and stormed off. He made a hole in the wall, Nik, just from one punch, and I could not stop staring at it. My head is next."

"Glad I am not you."

"It is not funny." He felt faint.

"I know... sorry."

They again continued walking, but more slowly now, more thoughtfully. Jerzy looked down, slowly shaking his head.

"I should have just kept my big mouth shut, especially in front of the others," he said in a whisper. "Now I have really had it." He spoke in the barely audible voice of a boy under intense physical strain, and he felt sick to his stomach with regret.

The rumors about this impending fight had spread throughout the school, just as Boguslaw wanted, like a bad case of poison ivy, without mercy and impossible to ignore: He was going to kill Jerzy... and it was common knowledge.

Jerzy hoped for a quick death... at least that way he would not have to suffer the embarrassment of losing what little self-esteem he had left.

At almost four o'clock, Jerzy and Nik approached the old brick theater, and as they began walking towards the empty dirt lot in back, Jerzy could hear the excited voices of his schoolmates. There must have been at least thirty of them there, maybe more, kids of all ages and levels, to witness his destruction.

The wind was picking up now, blowing dried leaves and cigarette butts across the usually vacant lot as though they had their time in the sun, but now it did not matter. Nothing mattered, for the curtain was closing. Near the edge of the field, a dog was peeing on a few tufts of grass.

Jerzy lowered his eyes, trembling anew as he neared the crowd, which hushed at his approach, quietly opening up a path for him to walk in, a sacrificial path to his doom at the feet of the school's mighty demon. The rumbling in the dark sky grew louder.

When Boguslaw saw the boy, he smiled... a slow, slithering smile that reeked of obscenity. His usually dull eyes now lit up with anticipation.

"Now I am going to show all the school what happens to anybody who dares to laugh at me," he whispered to no one in particular. "Today is payday." He opened and closed his knuckles, one finger after another, as though trying his huge fists on for size, all the while glaring at the younger boy.

Fighting was a raw urge to Boguslaw, a calling as old as humanity, man against man, a measure of brute force repeating itself since the beginning of time, ancient and indomitable, an apotheosis of the raw spirit of masculinity, at once hostile and majestic, but conquering... always conquering... and void of morality. It was the savagery that called to him personally.

As soon as the combatants were face-to-face, the path closed like a giant pincer, or perhaps a mouth, preparing to chew Jerzy up and spit out the crushed bones.

A factory whistle blew, as though proclaiming the beginning of the bloodbath. Boguslaw smiled, then both boys began posturing with fists raised, glaring into the squinted windows of each other's souls. Slowly circling each other, they alternated their fists in and out, bobbing and weaving, looking for just the right opening, Jerzy, ever so wary of Owiti striking first, and Boguslaw taking his time, just wanting to give his fans something to talk about. The witnesses strained to watch every move, every nuance of every move, lest they miss the crucial moment of Jerzy's demise.

But because no punches had yet been thrown, the opponents looked more like dancers than fighters, which frustrated the onlook-ers, who could not wait for the real action to begin. So, the crowd taunted them, egging them on... they were spectators after all, and even though this fantastic entertainment was free, they wanted raw violence, and they wanted it now.

What really frustrated Jerzy, though, was that everybody was rooting for Owiti. Nobody even liked that jerk, he thought, but they were scared to cross him, so they pretended, acting like they were best friends. It hurt to feel so extremely alone, but he understood, never-theless. Understanding, however, holds little comfort when you feel that you are being tossed under a truck.

"Come on, you stupid shithead, hit me right here," Boguslaw said with his teeth clenched and jaw tight, pointing to his large angry chin.

"I dare you, poor-boy." He sneered, seriously wanting to kill Jerzy, but he knew that would put him in prison, so instead, he would settle for merely crippling him for life. "You thought it was soooo funny that I was kept back, maybe you even think you are a genius, but I think you are a scared little mouse, and I am going to have the last laugh, poor-boy."

Jerzy, breathed quicker now, noted Boguslaw's large, Neanderthal knuckles, but said nothing... he remembered the entire year with a stunning clarity, thinking again about the hole Owiti made in the wall when he punched it right next to Jerzy's head.

"What's the matter, Girlie? Are you afraid I will step on your naked little girlie toes? Are you going to cry? You better be scared... plenty scared, because I am going to rip off your head and drink out of your skull."

"Ooooooooooo," said the crowd in unison.

He threw several sharp jabs at Jerzy's head, backing him up, backing him up again, and again... threatening the big one, "The Haymaker," he called it when bragging to his friends, all of whom wanted to see it in action. He had been talking about it for the past month, and a demonstration was long overdue. Jabbing yet again, but harder now, he caught Jerzy on the forehead, snapping his head way back, and crossing the boy's eyes. The lights in Jerzy's head twinkled off and on.

He swayed, but then shook his head and managed to pull himself together long enough to refocus his eyes. Then, still backing up, he tripped on the foot of one of the idiot spectators who had his foot out too far, and started to fall backwards, but the others caught him and propped him back up on his feet again, pushing him forward, nearly launching him into Boguslaw's lap. This is such a gift, Boguslaw thought. He almost wanted to say, "Thank you," as he launched a hard uppercut into the boy's gut, pushing his diaphragm so far up that it whooshed all the air out of his lungs.

Jerzy was bent over, trying hard to breathe... just a little air into his lungs... that was all he wanted, just for a second. His eyes were watering, but he still managed to catch a glimpse of Boguslaw's famous Haymaker heading his way. He trembled again from somewhere deep within, not planning any kind of strategy, not even thinking, but rather just reacting and hoping that that he could live to see another day... not that his days were great. Especially this one.

Then, out of sheer panic, he was somehow able to suck in a huge gulp of air, and at the same time, throw his head back and to the side, causing the Haymaker to just graze his face. It whooshed by his head, and there was a loud crack of thunder as the skies grew darker. And at that same moment, Jerzy lunged forward with every ounce of terror trying to escape through the pores of his skin, throwing a punch that was more than a punch, which landed smack in the middle of Boguslaw's nose, accompanied by Jerzy's most intense scream, born of raw emotion.

The loud crunching sound was unexpected by all, especially Boguslaw, and with that unforeseen turn of events everyone stopped talking as the blood came pouring, gushing, from the scrunched-up nose. It was as though a major dam had broken. Boguslaw, his eyes bugging out and watering, put his hands to his face to stop the flow, but the blood continued pouring out between his large fingers, splattering on anyone close enough, and so a few boys near him began to yell and run, while the girls just screamed.

"Oh shit," Jerzy mumbled to himself... "Now he is really going to kill me."

But he knew that apologizing would be seen as an act of weakness, so he maintained his fighter's stance, still trying to catch his breath properly, with trembling fists out in front of him, yet he could not help but stare at the blood gushing out, like a rarity of nature.

It was beautiful.

Boguslaw had never bled like this before... never... and it would not stop. The fear of bleeding to death became bigger than his biggest fear, which was about what his father would do to him for losing a fight, especially against a smaller, younger opponent. A real man never lost a fight.

But, he finally conceded to himself, bleeding to death had to be worse than the severe beating his father would give him. It just had to be. So, he pulled off his shirt, popping a few buttons along the way, bunched it up against his nose while glaring at Jerzy, and ran home, yelling for his mother.

Jerzy was stunned. Had he actually won this fight against the mighty Boguslaw Owiti? Watching his enemy disappear in the distance, the boy finally dropped his shaking fists, his legs buckling beneath him as he sank to the ground, on his knees. Head bowed, he felt the tears welling behind his eyelids. He was still alive.

The other kids, awed by the magnificence of what they had just witnessed, slowly approached Jerzy before leaving, each of them silently patting him on the back. They had no words for what they just witnessed. It was a miracle.

Nik, who had to rush home to get there in time for supper, took the time nevertheless to also pat his best friend's back. "So, my hero, my champion boxer, what excitement do you have planned for tomorrow?

Jerzy never heard him. His heart was still pumping intensely, not understanding what just happened.

And then the rain came, gently at first, but then a little harder, washing the blood off the ground, purifying the remnants of fear from Jerzy's body as he finally gathered himself together and walked home, slowly, his clothes soaked right to the skin, but it did not matter, for he was lost in deep thought.

He realized that the school would know all about the fight. He did not know how, but they always found out, and they would contact his parents about it. He also knew that he was supposed to just walk away from fighting. His father had told him over and over that fighting would just get him in trouble, big trouble, and Jerzy trembled at the thought of what he had done, but his father did not understand what happened to cowards. "I cannot let Papa know about this," he said aloud, even though there was no one around to hear him. Of course, to prevent that, he needed to keep the school from telling his parents, and he had a rough idea of just how to do that.

* * *

When Jerzy awakened the next morning, he looked out the window, but had no energy. All he wanted was to just to sleep all day, however, he had important business to take care of, and it had to be done this morning. Part of his exhaustion was from all the tension that had filled his day yesterday, and the other part came from worrying about his parents finding out about the fight he had been in. He could not shake the memory of his father telling him that fighting was the mark of an uncivilized man, and that talking was the best way for men to settle their disputes, no matter what they were about. Intelligent men could talk about their differences. Men needed to listen to one another, he said... only then could the fighting end.

But Papa did not know about Boguslaw Owiti. This was an idiot who did not listen to anybody because he cared only about himself. And he was not just an idiot... he was a mean idiot, an intolerant idiot, an idiot with no sense of empathy whatsoever, so if he decided he wanted to fight you, there was no discussion to be had. There would be a fight, whether you wanted one or not. But Papa was just as stubborn about such things and would not listen. He had made that clear a long time ago.

As a result, Jerzy was scared awake for most of the night, thinking and planning and revising, until his idea began to germinate, which he nourished with details, until finally, it evolved into a solid plan. It was, in fact, the only solution he could come up with, so he had no choice. He was too scared to even consider that it might not work.

As the sun rose, he sat up and looked out the window at the airplane factory. At one time, he thought, everybody believed that flight was an impossible dream, but now look... since the airplane was invented, even ordinary people take flight for granted. I know this idea can work, too, he thought. It has to.

Since only the rich families had phones, and his family was far from rich, he knew that the only way the school could contact his parents would be with a note carried by another student, so... instead of going back to school that morning, Jerzy's idea was to wait in the bushes about a block away from his home for the messenger and then, just intercept the note, then go hide somewhere while school was still in session, and finally to come home after school let out. It was a work of genius, he thought.

After all, I beat up the toughest boy in the school, so who will dare challenge me? he thought with confidence.

And so it began, that very morning, a beautiful sunshiny morning with the birds chirping and the browning leaves departing from their homes in the trees, when Jerzy supposedly left for school. He let the front door slam closed, just to make sure they heard him go to school. "BYE," he said loudly to the house. Now he just had to hide and be patient.

Sure enough, less than one hour after classes began, he saw a smaller boy from the school walking towards his home. The boy was younger, maybe twelve or thirteen, and walked unknowingly toward the trap Jerzy had set. Running quickly to his hiding spot behind the bushes, Jerzy waited. A bee buzzed next to him, and he gently blew it away. Then he felt something tickling his arm. He looked down and saw a small dog, sniffing him as though he was a juicy kielbasa. "Shoo... scram... go home, dog." Then he pushed the mutt away as hard as he could without hurting it, but hard enough to let him know he needed to get out of there. The dog lowered its head and started to come back, so again, Jerzy told him to go away, and to convince him that staying was a bad idea, he lightly slapped the dog's rump as he scolded him. The dog curled back to look at his back end up close, then turned his head to look again at Jerzy as though waiting for an explanation, but the boy merely pointed at where he wanted the dog to go, and said, "Go." That worked.

When the school messenger got close, Jerzy leaped out from the bushes, trying to look intimidating. He grabbed the kid's shirt with his left hand and made a fist with his right.

"Do not hit me, please do not hit me," the boy said. He was shaking.

"I will take that," Jerzy said, curling the upraised fingers of his right hand open and closed as though calling someone closer.

"Take what?" said the kid, whimpering.

"Look, do not play stupid. I know the school gave you a note for my parents, so just hand it to me and I will not hurt you." He held his other hand open, waiting for the note.

The boy trembled. "But I will get in big trouble if I do not give this to your parents. Please..."

"Then do not tell anybody and there will be no trouble," Jerzy said, shaking the kid while motioning with his fist. "Besides, you are already in big trouble... you want to continue living, yes?" Jerzy stared at the kid's eyes, showed him his teeth and growled to look as fierce as possible. He gestured again with the fingers of his right hand to give him the note, while shaking the kid roughly with his left hand, still tightly clenching his shirt. Of course, it was all an act, but he needed to make it look convincing.

The kid trembled at the memory of that fight. He saw it for himself... so much blood... nobody had ever done that to Boguslaw. Nobody. His shaking hand went into his front pants pocket and pulled out a sealed envelope addressed to his father and stepmother, which Jerzy quickly snatched out of his hand, then let go of the kid. He had what he wanted. That was when the boy turned around and ran for his life, back the way he had come.

"He must think I am like a bull," said Jerzy, now smiling. "This is turning into a superb morning after all, so maybe my luck is finally changing. In fact, since I am already out of school today, I think this would be a great time to go fishing."

He walked almost a kilometer to the pond that he and his friends used as a swimming hole, and it appeared to be the same as it always had, probably looking the same since the beginning of time, with the sun reflecting on its surface like sparkling jewels, catfish swimming lazily in the shallows, and wildflowers preparing to fight the oncoming winter. The birds were trilling, and the insects buzzing their greetings to Jerzy as he picked up a flat rock and skimmed it across the water for no reason other than the pure joy of doing it. Even the splashing of the water was sheer delight.

Jerzy looked at the ground and wondered if there was a spot, just one spot around here that nobody had ever stepped on? Virgin territory, a place unmarked by a single human foot, ever? Wouldn't it be great if I was the first human in all of history to ever step foot on such a place? He sighed.

The day promised to be long, and he wondered how best to fill his remaining time there. Then the boy remembered... Nik was not the only one with a neat hand-me-down once owned by his grandfather; Jerzy had a beautiful pearl-handled jackknife in his pocket, given to him by his own grandfather shortly before he died, and there were plenty of long, stiff branches nearby, branches that he could whittle into great fishing spears. His grandfather had loved to whittle, and he used to sit down with Jerzy and show him some of his carvings, explaining how he did them. And this knife was the one he used. Jerzy really missed him. Unlike Papa, Dziadek would have understood why he had to fight Boguslaw.

Oh crap, the boy thought. How in the hell am I supposed to cook the stupid fish? I forgot to bring matches. Damn it—what an idiot I am sometimes. His stomach rejected the thought of eating them raw, and there was nothing else edible out here. At least, nothing he could eat uncooked. Well, I guess there is no point in even fishing, then, he thought. And if that is the case, there is also no point in making any spears.

But... there is plenty of wood to whittle the time away. And so he looked, and found, a fine piece of wood to turn his attention to, sat down with it, and pulled out his pocket knife, his only connection with the man, besides Papa, he loved for so long with all his heart, and the boy then proceeded to drown out the rest of the world with his carving.

When Jerzy figured school was letting out, he stayed just a bit longer, just to be safe, then took off for home again, hoping that nobody came to his home from a different direction with a note from the school, but everything seemed normal, so he began to relax. Having had no food all day, his stomach rumbled deeply in protest. But still, he could not tell his parents, so he ended up with nothing to eat. His stomach continued to protest, and loudly, but fortunately, his parents did not notice. They were too busy with other things.

The next morning, the boy woke up with his stomach rumbling even more. It was partly from hunger, but it was also because he stayed awake for half the night thinking about his situation. He got away with it yesterday, but then he realized that the school would try again today since his parents did not respond to their note, which meant he had to stay out again. But how could his parents respond, since he had intercepted the correspondence? Rats. That meant he would need to stay out again, and again and again, until...

His thoughts raced, and he found himself looking at various possibilities of this situation, as though examining different facets of a well-polished gem. He turned it this way and that, then he saw a facet that caught his attention... it virtually gleamed.

Wait a minute... he thought. Eventually, they will just think my parents do not care, and the school will give up sometime—they will not keep on sending messages forever. Sooner or later, they will have to stop. I just need to be patient.

So, Jerzy, believing he was onto something significant, went into hiding in the bushes again, deciding to ambush other kids as the week progressed. And, starting right now, he also vowed to remember to grab some matches before he left the house so he could eat some of those fish that were so lucky yesterday.

By the time he got to the swimming hole, Jerzy's hunger had reached epic proportions, so the very first thing he did was to quickly carve himself a fishing spear and catch a nice, big catfish. He waded into the water, holding his spear like he imagined his ancient ancestors must have done some thousands of years ago, and moved quietly... slowly. Seeing a fish nearby, he was excited, but the fish was on his left side and he was right-handed, so he had to turn around. Unfortunately, the fish saw him move and quickly scooted away. Jerzy again took up the hunt. At first, he saw nothing, but out of the corner of his eye, he spotted a big one, lurking among to roots of a tree that had long ago fallen. Despite the hunger that bit into him, Jerzy exhibited remarkable patience.

Finally, the fish slowly came out into the open, not knowing that a hunter stood waiting for him. As he approached striking distance, the boy slowly reared back with the spear, closer... closer. Finally, Jerzy lunged, piercing the fish cleanly and then raised it out of the water in triumph. He ran out with his catch onto dry land, not believing his good luck. The boy breathed deeply, and stood there staring at his trophy. The fish stared back at him. He had to have been at least five pounds.

Preparing the fish was always difficult for the boy, not because he lacked the skills, but because his empathy was always so acute. He never really cared for fishing. Even with worms, he always empathized with the night crawlers as he skewered them lengthwise onto the hook, torturing them, and would find himself wondering what it must have felt like, thankful he was not a worm, but hating himself for this act of betrayal to a fellow creature. He knew that like him, the worm just wanted to live.

He continued to look at the fish, wriggling on the spear and trying desperately to breathe as he held it out of the water, and he felt for this creature, who continued to stare back at him as though asking, "Why?" The animal had done nothing to him, and certainly nothing to deserve such a cruel fate, yet there it was, fighting against impossible odds to continue its existence. Jerzy wondered how much pain it was in, and if his own fate would someday be similar because of this. When the fish stopped moving at last, the boy reached out to remove it, but when it felt the boy's fingers, the fish surprisingly fought again for its life, wriggling desperately on the stick, perhaps hoping its fanatical maneuvers could somehow propel it back into the water. How could it have survived so long without air, he wondered.

Finally, after a couple of last twitches, the fish was dead at last, and Jerzy was able to take it off the spear so he could clean it. This was another task that repulsed him, yet it had to be done. While cutting into his catch, he felt as though the fish was still staring at him, but he knew it was dead, yet the feeling would not go away. He solved that difficulty by immediately cutting off the head and throwing it back into the water before gutting and scaling it so it could no longer make him feel guilty. Now at least he could finish cleaning the fish, and finally the fish no longer resembled the living thing it came from. It just looked like food. He walked over to the water again to clean off his knife, then wiped it dry against his pants and returned to cook his meal at last.

Once he got the fire started, and the meat held by another stick, it crackled above the open flame, and threw out a magnificent odor that made Jerzy's stomach dance with anticipation. Cooking it was fast, and eating it even faster. And big as it was, he was able to consume the entire thing.

Finally gorged, Jerzy lay on the grass, looking up at the sky through the overhead branches and thought about how his life had changed since the fight. He absentmindedly picked up a piece of straw to chew on, and realized that one problem still remained. What if one of the messengers tells the teacher what happened? But so far, that had not happened. He thought back to the fight itself, and remembered that he was more scared of being branded a coward than he was of being killed. Perhaps it was the same with the note bearers, and none of his classmates would admit to being so scared of Jerzy that they would not fight him, so no one knew that an ambush was waiting. It had to be like that. He was counting on it.

The coming days followed the same pattern, and it became almost like a ritual.

* * *

After a week of this, Jerzy walked in the front door of his home after school was out, only to find his stepmother and father staring at him. This was not normal.

"How was school today, Jerzy?" said his father.

"Oh, you know, the usual stuff, Papa." He wondered why they were looking at him that way.

"The usual stuff? Did I actually hear that? Nothing new?"

"Um... not really." He shrugged his shoulders, looking at his father hopefully.

"Well son, surely they teach you something. Either you already know all they have to teach, or you are not paying attention in class... so which is it?"

"Papa, please... it was a lot of work today, and I am so tired from all the lectures that I honestly do not want to even talk about it." He turned to walk away.

"Hold on, son. Honestly? You honestly do not want to talk about it? Jerzy, you know how I feel about honesty... and about liars."

"Papa, what are you talking about?" This was not at all going the way the boy would have liked.

His parents looked at each other, then at their teenage son. "Your principal came to our home today at lunchtime... our home, Jerzy, and he told us about the fight, and all the notes they wrote to contact us, notes that we never received. And he told us that you have not been in school all week. He was worried about you."

The boy swallowed hard. "Papa, I — "

"No, Jerzy. School teaches you how to think, but clearly, you are not even coming close to that, so I am going to help you think better thoughts... the kind that you can be proud of. The kind we can all be proud of. And you are going to help me to do this. I want you to go out in the back yard and cut off a branch from one of the birch trees for me. You know what kind I want. Now GO."

The boy knew that a train was coming through the tunnel and he was sitting on the tracks. There was no way out, and as with the fight, he just had to accept it like a man. He went outside, where he considered running away, but knew that was a stupid idea... besides, he was getting tired of eating only fish.

At first, he thought maybe he could bring in a lighter branch, one that would not hurt so badly, but he also knew that his father would never accept that, and would just send him back out for a heavier one and whip him even harder.

Jerzy reentered the house, walking with his head down and holding back the tears as he handed the branch to his father. He was defeated, like a dog about to get whipped. And get whipped, he did... his father gave him a shellacking that wore the bark right off the branch.

Quietly watching all this through a small opening in the doorway, Jerzy's brother, ten-year-old Ruslan, smiled, then turned to join his mother in the cooking area.

Two

Klaus Boellman's War

Second Lieutenant Klaus Boellman, newly graduated student pilot, looked all around. Three planes were high in the sky, practicing maneuvers, while a fourth was lifting off from the runway, and yet another was making its landing approach. All were synchronized in preparation for a singular act of aggression that promised to have a major impact on the fears of the world for years to come. The base was alive with non-stop activity.

The German airfield was new, and loud with the unmistakable scent of pines and cedar freshly cut from the surrounding woods to build it. The entire base was almost pristine, suggesting an air of innocence, but that was not to last.

A deer stood off against the surrounding woods, watching all the goings-on with a momentary, but absolute curiosity. Nobody noticed, or if they did, they paid it no mind.

Walking to his hanger, Klaus could not stop smiling; soon, he was going to participate in the making of history. He again looked around the airfield, in awe of all the preparations required for the big day, and it made him feel like a child on the night before Christmas. "I am so lucky to be a part of this," he said to himself. "No, I am more than lucky... I am proud to be a part of this."

Another soldier, an enlisted man walked past him and saluted. Klaus returned his salute without thinking about it, without even losing his train of thought.

It is still hard to believe that this is actually beginning. But then, Poland really does deserve it. How can they have so many Jews living in their midst and not see what they are doing? And where is this incessant and insultingly anti-German rhetoric of theirs coming from? I have no idea who these Polish dogs think they are, but we will fix that little flaw right away. Oh yes, we will.

He smiled, then stopped to take out a pack of cigarettes, tapped the pack against the edge of his other hand, and selected the one that poked out the furthest, then tamped it down on the face of his "Good Luck" watch. Klaus, who finished his training just last week, was glad he stuck with it. Now he could make history and help to reshape the world.

This must come to pass... there is no other way, he told himself. *Poland has way too many Jews, all of whom need to be eradicated, like rats, if the planet is ever to right itself, and this is the perfect time to begin. What happens tomorrow must stand as a symbol to the rest of the world, and they will one day recognize the necessity of what we are about to do and follow suit. I am certain they will even thank us. Then, once under the supreme leadership of Nazi Germany, the world will be a better place. A much better place, indeed.*

Klaus lit the wooden match, scraping it with his thumbnail, then protected it against the breeze by cupping it with both hands as it flared up to light the cigarette. The odor of sulfur drifted up his nostrils, and he closed his eyes against the sting of the smoke, greeting it instead as a gift from the gods of adulthood.

Born in 1915, he was just a baby during the Great War, but now he was a young man of twenty-four, primed and ready to help the Motherland once again realize her greatness. He was a German after all... the very pinnacle of humanity. And best of all, this would make his father stand up and take notice, at last.

Das Generaloberst, as his father was called, had fought in the Great War as a highly respected officer in the cavalry, and lost his arm to a Polish soldier, a nobody who came out of nowhere to ambush him. It was a miracle he even lived, but a quick-thinking German officer was with him and applied a tourniquet immediately, which held him until they could reach a field doctor.

And now it was up to a new generation to set right the wrongs inflicted upon his nation by those ignorant fools who actually believed themselves to be superior to the German psyche. This war to come was Klaus Boellman's war, his generation's call to a greater destiny. He was a highly skilled aviator after all, not too old and not too young, which meant that he was born at exactly the right time... another sign that he was destined for something big... something important.

It was so hard to believe this was actually happening at long last. The tension of the day was energizing, and he relished the excitement as he paced all over the German airfield, electrified with anticipation, and mentally going over and over the flight details. He knew each word of his instructions forward and backwards, yet he insisted on mentally rehearsing all of it again and again until knowing he could perform every last detail, every nuance, automatically, without thought. In his mind's eye, he could see the rudder control as he reached for it, and he felt the forces of gravity and inertia play upon his body with every move. And he played and replayed every possibility until he knew he could do it automatically, without thinking about it. He knew that an eagle took down its prey with strength and agility, but he also knew that superior instinct was key. He wanted to hunt down his prey as though he had been born in the air. He wanted to be an eagle, lion of the skies... the most feared and respected bird on the planet.

Klaus also played and replayed his mission to himself with the same fervor that would make him an ace pilot. He was attached to the southernmost route of a giant pincer movement flying into Poland from the west, entering just south of Krakow, and while some of the planes from his unit were to veer north, between Lodz and Warsaw, his group was to continue flying even further west, then northwest, where he and two other planes were assigned to soften the city of

Lublin, especially focusing on the electric company and airplane factory, destroying them completely before they knew what was happening. Surprise was everything. In addition, any possible means of defense in Lublin were also to be obliterated, any signs of weaponry, chemical production, and railroads, along with any and all forms of communications and manufacturing. Germany needed to make the advances of their ground forces run as smoothly and effortlessly as possible. This would be the fastest warfare ever performed, surprise was its cornerstone, which was henceforth to be known to the world as Blitzkrieg, or lightning warfare, a way of combat such as never seen or even heard of before.

"After that, my official job is finished, which means that I will be free to wreak havoc on the unsuspecting Polacks, avenging my father at last by destroying those sub-human dogs who dared to think themselves as good as Germans," he said. "I will give them much to remember." Deep inside, though, Klaus found himself hoping that at least one Polish pilot, hopefully their best, would somehow make it to his plane and challenge Klaus in person. It would be the perfect opportunity to prove himself to all, and establish his future role in the lore of military aviation.

The breeze picked up, and Klaus closed his eyes to better feel it. "It is a good day to be alive," he said. "And it is a wonderful day to be a German. But best of all, it is a fantastic day to be a Boellman, especially if your first name is Klaus, and you are an aviator in Adolf Hitler's prestigious Luftwaffe."

But as good as Klaus felt and performed with his newly honed skill, his father was a man of means, and a perfectionist; as such, his ego flew high, so nothing that his son ever did was good enough. Klaus was never fast enough, never strong enough, never even smart enough. It was as though his father wanted the boy to become some kind of super person, and maybe then he would be worthy of being loved.

Yet Klaus loved his father anyway. He had only to demonstrate that he was good enough to get the approval of this hero... this man-god who wanted his boy to be every bit as special. Germany had lost the Great War, and his father had lost an arm in combat, which he never let Klaus forget. His enemies were his son's enemies, and now, Klaus could at last avenge him. He, Klaus, would join the highest of the high... not just as a pilot, but as an ACE pilot... the kind of man everybody talked about in whispers... because they were awed by his very presence. The kind of man legends grew from, and his would be among the finest.

Walking on, he heard other planes flying above, practicing formations and bombing runs. He knew each plane just by the sounds it made, as though each one had its own personality. Watching them, Klaus could picture the blitzkrieg already in his mind's eye. He saw the smoke and destruction, the Polish dogs' screaming and running in every direction with nowhere to hide. And he saw his own plane, diving and bombing, twisting, feeling his plane turning in small arcs to give chase in between buildings where the space was too small for ordinary pilots to travel, then flying above the smoke and carnage triumphantly. When he envisioned the glistening war bird in action, he could feel his chest swell with pride. He was sure the Nazi victories would be celebrated afterwards with accolades and parades, and he wanted to salute the entire world for honoring him.

The enemies in this war were inferior forces, and they deserved whatever Nazi Germany could dish out, especially after the way they flaunted their victory following the Great War, the way they rubbed the German noses in the mud through their incessant demands for reparations and other such outrageous foolishness.

But now the game was changing... he could feel it in the blood pounding through his veins in a hungry anticipation of revisions needing to be made. Historical revisions. "Herr Hitler is right... German history has been darkened and must be corrected," he said. His great nation must stand at the forefront of the world, not meekly on the sidelines as though they did not matter. This was not just pride, but a matter of what is right.

Their supreme leader promised those who were ready that he would lead them to victory, and Klaus was ready. More than ready. In anticipation, he practiced every element of his role in the upcoming activities over and over until he was certain he could fly this mission in his sleep. Indeed, he did fly it in his sleep, so much so that it was sometimes getting hard to discern when he was sleeping and when awake. All that remained was for the mission to begin. Just one more day, he thought.

Mesmerized by the smoke of his cigarette as it curled up to the heavens, he saw within it a myriad of Polish battle corpses, along with the debris of his slain enemy's cities, and that thought alone evoked a huge smile. Adolph Hitler was giving him a chance to shine, a golden opportunity to walk, like his own father, among the gods, and he was more than anxious to begin.

The ground crew was watching him, many of them wishing they could be just like Klaus, for he looked every bit as sharp as he felt. He had thick reddish hair with tight waves, and even though he felt plain looking, his uniform was always clean, starched and ironed, his insignia and shoes polished to a high shine, and his salutes were crisp, demonstrating a confidence that was evident even in the way he wore his dress hat cocked to one side.

Klaus dropped his cigarette butt onto the tarmac and ground it out with his foot, then carefully picked a piece of lint off his pants. The man had learned a long time ago to make every action of his count, to do nothing unless it was deliberate.

He looked around and saw that the entire airfield was a beehive of vibrant activity. *I was born for this mission, and the others to come. And there is no doubt... I am going to be an ace pilot... I can feel it. Father will be so proud of me.*

He entered the hanger where his plane, a Ju-87 dive-bomber, was being readied, and he stared at it in awe. Each man there had his own area of expertise and was working hard at it. Two men were loading the bombs, another was cleaning and polishing the glass, yet another painting a large swastika on the tail, and a few remaining men loading armaments into the cannons and machine guns, or assisting in whatever ways they could. It was like a family event of supreme importance, and each crew member wore his dedication like a badge, proud with his head held high.

The engineers who designed this plane were brilliant. It was a bomber, yet it was also maneuverable, like a fighter. Klaus loved flying the Stuka, and he could not wait to see those stupid Polacks running from sheer terror when they heard the ear-piercing scream of the siren attached to the plane's wheel carriage as it dived down on them. He could picture its wailing victory in his glorification any time now.

"Herr Hitler is a true genius," he said, patting the siren.

The mechanics grinned in acknowledgement.

He called the crew over to him. "Soon we will begin to cleanse the world for the glory of our Fuhrer, and for all of Germany," Klaus said to the Hauptgefreiter in charge of the ground crew. "Make sure she is washed and polished... I want her looking like new in combat, shining and pure," he said to the rest of the crew. "I want the Polish dogs to see her gleaming body emerging from the smoke and flames of our attack like a giant Phoenix, glistening pure and untouchable from the ashes of Hell itself. I want them to stare in awe of our supreme majesty before they die. And I want those who manage to survive to always remember, and to tell their children and grandchildren about the end of their world as they witnessed it firsthand, and to warn them of the mighty power held in the fist of Nazi Germany."

The ground crew did not understand his talk about the Phoenix, but they got the general drift, and they believed in Klaus, in every word he said, because he was educated, and he looked so damned good in that uniform, plus he was an officer in Hitler's elite Luftwaffe, so he must know what he was talking about. His excitement was contagious.

Still smiling, Klaus was about to turn when he saw Colonel Schwartz enter. He abruptly snapped to attention and gave the Wing Commander a sharp salute in recognition of his rank, even though he thought the man was not as dedicated to the cause as he should have been. If he had truly been committed, he would have been an ace pilot by now, unless maybe he just did not have the skills. Either way, he should not have been a Wing Commander, but in time, and with patience, perhaps that would change.

"Ready for Operation Case White, Leutnant?" said the Colonel, with a concerned look on his face. He had been observing Klaus since the lieutenant started training, and though he said nothing yet, he saw a disturbing tendency in this young pilot to take unnecessary chances with his plane, acting as though he was indestructible. He had done so more than once. The Colonel had seen this in a few other pilots earlier, and he watched them self-destruct, but enough was enough. He did not want to see it happen again, especially not now, when so much was at stake. Germany could not afford to waste another pilot, let alone another perfectly good plane.

"Jawohl," said Klaus through his never-ending grin, as he snapped his heels together sharply. "Tomorrow, I will show the world what happens to insignificant little mice who try to bite the mighty wolf."

The Colonel calmly leaned his head in close to the pilot's ear, putting his face right next to him, and the lieutenant saw a reflection in the Colonel's eyes, he saw himself, larger than life, and he reveled inwardly at this vision, his smile almost bursting.

"Leutnant, this is not a game, and you are not in this by yourself. After the mission is complete, we need every Luftwaffe pilot and plane back again in one piece. Do I make myself clear, Boellman? No working for yourself. You are a good pilot, but you have no combat experience yet, so just stick to the plans... nothing else. And wipe that stupid grin off your face."

"Jawohl, Herr Oberstleutnant," he said, the smile gone. He wanted to scream at the Colonel, to tell him that he was unfit to be in command, and that soon, he, Klaus Boellman would be a household name, like the Red Baron, and when that happened, he would see to it that the Colonel was replaced by someone more fit for this kind of command, someone more like... well, himself. But now was not the time... not yet.

Satisfied, the Colonel stared at him a moment longer, then turned and walked away.

But the Colonel is wrong, thought Klaus. The chant in his soul began to beat yet again to the rhythm of war, and it was getting stronger. *This IS a game... a game of the finest kind, and I am going to win it, no matter what.*

The smile began to creep back.

Three

In the Beginning...

Sitting in his favorite chair after the boys had gone to bed, Kaspar Czaplicki laughed quietly about his older son's antics. He reached for his tobacco pouch and being mindful to not waste any, tapped out a small amount into the bowl of his pipe, which he then tamped down, but not too tightly, in order to get a better puff. He scraped a wooden match on the bottom of his shoe to light the tobacco, and sucked contentedly on the pipe in short draws. Watching the smoke curl, he quickly shook the match out and thought back to a time when his first marriage was new, before the Great Depression, even before Jerzy came along. Things had definitely changed since those days.

Life back in 1922 Lublin had been perfect in every way. Kaspar was a dapper-looking young man, possessing a boyish charm that was natural to him. He wore a thin, neatly trimmed mustache on his broad face that gave him an air of regal sophistication, contradicted only by his warm, contagious smile. And his beautiful newlywed, Llona, was equally alluring.

Everybody loved her. They told him how lucky he was to find

such a beauty in both heart and soul, and this amazingly good fortune always left him asking himself what he could possibly have done to deserve such a treasure.

When she bore him a son seven months later, he was beside himself with happiness. The three of them spent many moments of spontaneous laughter, often dancing together for no reason other than the pure joy of it, roaming through the cooking area, the parlor, wherever and whenever the mood struck. They did not even need music... they made their own, and it was always wrapped in the magic of their mutual love.

He had it all back then and he knew it. Despite his lack of any formal education, Kaspar had a good job as a machinist, owned his own home, even had extra apartments that he rented out, and lived with the two people he most adored.

But like all else in that world, it was not to last. The downfall began when Jerzy was five, and Kaspar's beloved wife became sick with a cough and fever. But instead of getting better like she normally did, she got worse. Much worse. Her cough became blood-tinged and she developed night sweats.

Llona insisted that she would soon be better, but when her ailment would not abate, Kaspar sent for a doctor anyway, pacing endlessly until his arrival. He heard a heavy rain outside and kept looking out the window, worried about the doctor being delayed. Seconds felt like days, minutes like years. Finally, he heard a loud rapping from the heavy brass knocker on the front door and he ran to open it. A well-dressed gentleman with thin-rimmed spectacles stood there, dripping from the heavy rainstorm that slowed down traffic. Kaspar noted his large black leather bag, wondering what marvels of modern science he kept in there. To Kaspar, that bag was a curious mix, a blend between the precision of science and the magic of a shaman, he thought, the place where miracles happened, shrouded in secrecy, and he desperately yearned to have his Llona back again, would do anything, pay any price, to help bring that about.

"Mr. Kaspar Czaplicki?"

"Yes, yes, you must be the doctor. Come in, hurry, do not just stand there. Quickly. Follow me... my wife is in the bedroom. I think she is getting worse by the minute."

As they entered the room, the doctor turned, gesturing to the bedroom door. "You will wait outside, please. If I need anything, I will call for you."

"But—"

The doctor merely gestured for him to leave, so he could examine his patient without being disturbed by incessant questions that hindered his analysis.

Kaspar wanted to yell at the doctor, to tell him that this was his home and his wife and he would damned well go wherever he damned well pleased. But he was afraid. He did not want to take any chances with Llona's welfare at stake, so he merely stared at the doctor, and when the physician approached his patient, Kaspar left the room with his head down, quietly closing the door behind him.

He could hear small bits and pieces of conversation in the bedroom, mixed with that scary cough of hers, and he could picture the blood in her spittle. All he could do was pace back and forth, letting his imagination dictate the mood.

He looked down at his son, who played on the floor, totally unaware of the impending drama going on around him, but knowing anyway that something was wrong. For the past week, his Mama had not been in to hold him before bed like she always did before, and in his insecurity, he needed her to comfort him. Despite attention from Papa, the boy was feeling lonely like never before. Kaspar bent over and picked him up.

"Hey Jerzy," he said. "It's just you and me, kiddo." But the boy squirmed to be put down. It was the hugs of his mother he wanted and he could not understand what she was doing that was keeping her away from him. Kaspar put him down and the boy ran off.

The man renewed his pacing, unable to stop the incessant thoughts from bubbling to the surface. *Surely, she will be alright,* he thought. *After all, she is young and strong. She is probably just tired and caught a bad cold she cannot shake. Perhaps I need to hire someone to help her manage the house, that is all.*

He wondered what was taking so long. He was not a church-going man, but on this day, he gave serious thought to praying.

When the doctor finally came out again, he closed the door softly and signaled for Kaspar to talk with him, away from the door.

Kasper's face was white. "She is going to be all right, yes? Tell me."

"Kaspar, I am afraid that your wife has caught the tuberculosis," the physician told him quietly.

Kaspar stared at him again.

"Unfortunately, there is no cure."

"No! Doctor, you must have made a mistake. She has never been sick, not one day... she is young and filled with life. Maybe if I can get her to eat something, she will gain some of her weight back and be stronger so she can fight this thing. Surely you can fix her again. I will give you whatever you want"

The doctor merely shook his head.

Kaspar was crushed. He sat down, unable to even think, and stared into the emptiness.

"...What can I do, doctor? I will do anything," he whispered at last.

Putting his hand on Kaspar's shoulder, the physician repeated what he had already said to countless others during the past few months: "All you can do, Mr. Czaplicki, is try to make her as comfortable as possible. If you are lucky, she will live for another week or two. I am so very sorry." There was nothing else he could say, so he then patted Kaspar gently on the shoulder, turned and let himself out.

Kaspar just stared at the empty space where the doctor had stood when he so calmly pronounced his wife's death sentence. She meant more to him than all the rainbows and the stars... more than life itself; *how could she be dying? Noooo...* The tears began welling up inside of him, but he would not let them out, not in front of his son, and especially not in front of Llona. He loved her too much to tell her the truth, but he had to see her right now, had to have every moment possible with her, every second. He went to her, wanting to run, but not wanting to scare her. Letting himself into the bedroom quietly, he saw that her eyes were closed. As he approached the bed, however, she

31

somehow knew he was there and slowly opened her eyes to gaze upon the love of her life.

He stood next to her, and took her hand in his. "Llona, my beautiful beloved Llona, you will be alright," he lied, while softly caressing her cheek and temple with his other hand. He smiled while gazing into her tired eyes. A desperate part of him actually believed his own words, needed to... but even though he said this aloud day after day, he knew better. Somewhere deep inside, he knew better.

And so did Llona... but she never let on. Not even at the end.

* * *

His beloved wife was only twenty-five when she died, and the actuality of her death devastated Kaspar. She had always held his world together, and without her, he no longer cared, so it all began to crumble; he had lost that most important part of himself, and now he could not focus on anything. Even Kaspar's work suffered from his taking so many days off to care for her, along with the funeral after, and as a result, the company he worked for had to let him go.

"I am sorry, Kaspar." That was all his boss had to say. And it was a good job, too. One he took pride in. But jobs were scarce, especially for formally uneducated men like himself, so he found himself needing to go out each day to look for work, even if it was only day jobs. Work was work, so he took whatever he could find.

He also needed someone to care for Jerzy while he went out, but because work was not steady, he could not even afford a nanny. And even though he had a few tenants in his house, they also were unemployed, and he did not have the heart to evict them. One of them, an older woman, watched the boy whenever she could in exchange for her rent, but she was getting old and could not do this every day. "I wish I could do more, Kaspar," she said. "I am sorry."

Everybody was sorry, but none of it helped. Kaspar closed his eyes, not wanting to face any more of the world right now. "I understand," he said.

* * *

The five-year-old boy was disconsolate with the loss of his mother, the one person who held his heart in her own, and finally he could not take any more. Why did she not come back to him? Crying himself to sleep every single night, Jerzy finally ran away a week after her death to look for her. Kaspar went crazy trying to find him. At the end of the first day, he notified the police, who promised to do everything they could.

Three days later he was brought back home by his Uncle Frydryk, Llona's older brother. That little boy had somehow found his way to his uncle's farm, over thirty kilometers away.

Jerzy was everything to his father, who worried about him endlessly. He knew that the boy needed someone sensitive who could tend to his emotional needs, as well as keeping him clean and dressed as nicely as possible... someone who would find imaginative ways to create meals, even if the food was sparse, and to keep their home neat and clean. Kaspar had no imagination for cooking, and like most men, he was blind to dirt. Above all else, he missed coming home to a wife and lover. But he had no choice. For his son's sake, at least for now, he had to find a way to endure.

And then, just two months after Kaspar buried his wife, a close friend and former coworker, Konstancjusz Porczyński, seeing Kaspar's loneliness and utter despair, wanted to help, but he was at a loss so he told his wife about Kaspar, asking if she had any ideas. As she was a friend of the widow Yevgenia Kananowicz, the wife decided to play Cupid by inviting both her and Kaspar to dinner at their home, without telling either one about the other coming.

* * *

It was a difficult time for both Kaspar and Yevgenia. Kaspar missed Llona deeply, and Yevgenia was empty inside. She, too, had gone through an emotional tsunami, and it crushed her entire world.

As with Kaspar, she had experienced a married life that began beautifully. Yevgenia was a striking woman with an almost aristocratic face, which sat upon a long, slender neck, and she had found her true love early. After her first year of marriage, the two of them became three as she gave birth to a beautiful son, who had quickly become the center of her life... she loved him more than she loved herself, and would do anything for him.

Her husband's chest would swell with pride when he watched the two of them. "That is my family," he would brag. He was a farmer, a proud, hard-working man, but after a couple of years of unusually bad weather, he began to lose money, and the pressure of holding the farm together got to him. He became agitated, searching endlessly for other ways to bring in some income. He was the man of the house after all, and it was his responsibility.

Eventually, he learned, from a friend, that it would be really easy to build a still and produce some home-brew to sell. It would require a small initial investment, he was told, but that would quickly pay for itself, even in these hard times.

He built the still, produced the mash, and carefully produced his first batch of liquor. In an effort to avoid legal troubles, he called it his medicinal recipe. And every time he brought a new bottle to his lips, it became truly medicinal... at least to him.

Sales were slow in the beginning, but as word spread, sales began to pick up, although it was sporadic, so he again began to lose confidence in himself. And so it was that temptation got the best of him, and he began taking his own medicine, just a little at first, enough to take the edge off, but later taking it more and more frequently. Inebriation became his friend, consoling him when miserable in ways no person could, not even his wife. When sober, he was a good man, but when he was drunk, he became a self-absorbed narcissist and could care less about the rest of the world. Even the chickens were not amused, as he would often forget to feed them.

Then one day, it happened... he drank himself into a stupor on some exceptionally strong home-made brew, as had become his habit, and he accidentally drove his tractor backwards over their young son, killing him instantly, and emotionally destroying his wife.

Yevgenia forgave her husband many things, but not that. Never that. Her wailings rolled across the town like an endless wave, echoing in the empty night air. She thought she would go mad. She was out of her mind with grief, and filed charges with the police, who arrested her husband. At the trial, he was convicted of negligent homicide and given the death penalty. He cried, not because of his sentence, but because of the burden of guilt that he shouldered. He felt such remorse, for there was no other peace to be found for him... that even his death was not punishment enough.

She washed the broken remains of her boy's little body herself, preparing him for the funeral she never expected. Children should never die before their parents. It was not natural. She would not allow anyone else to touch him, but in the end, despite her screams, she had to let the town doctor remove the body to be buried properly in the local cemetery.

On her part, there was no protest over the sentence, nor even a hint of sorrow... she just did not care anymore. All the love she once felt for her husband had died along with her son, and life no longer held any meaning.

Word spread quickly. Eventually, the entire town knew about what had happened, and Yevgenia was shunned. For women like her, a second chance would have been impossible, as men generally would not marry a second-hand woman, and especially not one so cold, so savage that she would have her husband convicted over the accident, no matter the circumstances.

After that, Yevgenia had no hopes for any kind of future — she knew what most men were like. They all wanted only one thing from widows, which was not marriage, and so the possibility of love became a foreign country whose language she no longer spoke. So, she was prepared to automatically say no to all potential suitors, but there were none. Behind her back, though, most of the community called her, Czarna Wdowa... the Black Widow.

Four

Nightmares

Ruslin lay in bed, scared to close his eyes, but you would never know it by looking at him. His expression never changed. He had dark, brooding eyes, a rather long nose, and below that, full, pouty lips that rarely smiled, and tonight was no exception. Why should he smile after all? There was never anything to be happy about.

It had been this way for an uncommonly long time, although just lately he became convinced that something big was going to happen... something vague... undefinable. He could not quite put his finger on it, but whatever it was, it was not arriving in a good way... nothing definite, but he could feel it nevertheless. It was as though a heavy cloud was slowly covering the sun, and the beauty of what his life should be like was becoming darker each day. Especially in his sleep.

He had been suffering almost every night from weird dreams he had been having for the past two weeks, and he was exceedingly tired. As a result, staying awake was becoming ever more difficult with each sleepless night. This night was no exception. He tried with all his might to stay awake, but finally, he could fight it no longer, so he gracefully dozed off, and like the seasonal rains, the visions came again, and the frightening dreamscape along with them.

Each night he saw in his sleep that the entire morning sky was falling on him, the firmament filling itself with all forms of ponderous darkness, complete with malevolent twinkling that would not stand still, along with dark storm clouds hiding an angry light inside, and it was loud and he knew it was heavy, way too heavy for his head and neck to support, but it was coming specifically for him anyway, wailing his name over and over, only it was not speaking so much as sounding like a small animal being tortured in unimaginable ways.

But then he realized that the animal was him, and try as he might, running away from it all proved impossible. Every step took him nowhere. And every night, that same sky came back, like a living, breathing presence to taunt him with images about his mortality as it hovered above, always above, and always threatening to crash down on him. And he tried all the harder to outrun it, the wailing growing ever louder with each step, yet it always caught up with him anyway. And each night, just as the sky again began to fall down on him again, he awakened instantly, hairs on the back of his neck standing at attention like little swords, and he bolted upright, screaming his unending fear into the world.

When Jerzy heard his brother, he also bolted upright from his own deep sleep, his heart pounding, despite the nightly repetition of this intense drama.

"SHUT UP, RUSLIN... STOP YOUR SCREAMING... YOU ARE DRIVING ME CRAZY, NIGHT AFTER NIGHT AFTER NIGHT. STOP IT, STOP IT... AAARRRRGH." And he slammed himself back down again, throwing the covers over his head, and sticking his index fingers into his ears to drown out the din.

Then Ruslin's mother came running in, slamming the door open in mortal fear for her son's life, she would not lose another child, and she enfolded her son in the warmth of her arms, like the wings of a guardian angel, comforting him, brushing his hair back with her hands, and shushing him with all her love until he calmed down again. His breathing slowed and he snuggled against the calming warmth of her breast, when he suddenly trembled as

37

though he was having an aftershock from the trauma of his nightmare.

"Shhhhh... it was just a bad dream, baby," she said softly, kissing the top of his head. She knew that his incessant night-scares were probably because of his being so alone all the time. She could not understand why his older brother would not let Ruslin tag along with him and his friends. Yes, they were older than her son, but he needed friends, and Ruslin just was not interested in any of his own classmates.

She glared at Jerzy, remembering when she first met him after she and his father were wed. After the wedding, Yevgenia tried everything she could think of to befriend Jerzy, but he seemed determined to not like her. She cooked his favorite foods, made sure to keep him clean, clothed as nicely as possible, and even tried playing games with him that her own son had loved, but all to no avail.

"Jerzy, I once had a son, and he was very much like you, but then I lost him, so I know just how you must feel without your Mama," she said.

Is that what happened to my mother? he thought. Did she lose me? No, the words of this stranger rang cold and false, so he said nothing. He could feel her emptiness toward him inside his heart, and could respond no other way. After all, she was not his real mother, and if she lost her own son, she would lose Jerzy as well, maybe even faster. So, he simply remained silent, not even looking at her. And it felt like the harder she tried, the more he fought her.

In time, she became pregnant and when Kaspar told his son that he had a new brother or sister coming, the boy became even more isolated. Kaspar tried more than once to talk to Jerzy about this, but he did not want to force the issue. Given enough time, he was sure that his son would come around. And having a brother could not help but bond all of them as a family.

But no one counted on the intensity of Jerzy's stubbornness. His mother was gone, and that was that. This other woman could pretend to be his mother, but she could never take her place. Eventually, Yevgenia resigned herself to the inevitability of a distant relationship with her husband's son.

When the baby was born, it was a boy, and she named him after her first son, for she saw in him her second opportunity for the meaningful life of a mother, and she watched over her new son like a woman possessed. Yevgenia had been cheated out of her first chance to see her boy grow up... there was no way she would let anything happen to her second. She knew better.

* * *

Yevgenia saw that Jerzy was still asleep, so she could not help muttering. "My baby is obviously much too mature for children his own age," she said to him, her voice soft, a barely discernible whisper. "He needs someone older to be friends with. When you were younger and had no friends, you paid attention to him, and it was good. Ruslin mattered in those days, like a brother should. But now, all you want are your friends. You are just a very selfish boy, Jerzy; you always have been."

Unknown to her, Jerzy heard every word. He winced at her last comment, but said nothing, preferring instead that she think he was asleep. But he remembered her words as they churned inside of him like ice picks, eating holes in his gut.

When she thought Ruslin had fallen back asleep, the mother quietly kissed his forehead and slowly laid him back down, feeling that his pillow was wet with his sweat, so she lifted him again to flip the pillow over before laying him down for the night. She quietly left the room, hoping that he would sleep the rest of the night, but unknown to her, Ruslin also was still awake, pondering his mother's words.

He thought back a few years, remembering a different Jerzy, the one who cared about him. Ruslin's thoughts went back to when his older brother was about twelve, and he was six or so, and in those days, the government was issuing food to help out those who were the hardest hit from the Great Depression. That was when his one household chore was to walk with Jerzy every day, every single day, bringing the family's government-issued ration cards to the nearest soup kitchen, about one-and one-half kilometers from the house, just to fill up the kettle with soup for the family. The pot was large, with a handle on each side, and it was heavy for them, plus there were many obstacles along the way to watch out for, such as dogs who caught a whiff of the contents and followed them all the way home, or things to trip on, sometimes even the weather, and they were always wary of anyone who might want to steal their soup, forever watchful, but though they struggled, they both took great care to not spill a single drop no matter what, for this was more precious than gold, and each time they arriving home with their cargo intact, their little chests puffed up with great pride—the pride of grown men over a job well done.

Those times felt really good, just knowing they were doing something important for the family. They were helping, and by working together, they shared the experience, as real brothers. They were a community unto themselves in those days, but that was the closest they had ever gotten to each other.

"And now, Jerzy acts as though I am poison," he said to himself. "I just do not understand."

As he lay in bed, Ruslin tried hard to figure out why it was so different now. He could not sleep with all the noise his thoughts were making, nor did he want to sleep anyway because of his incessant nightmares. His head was spinning, the thoughts tape-looping like his dreams, and when he could take this no longer, he sat up in bed quickly, his words bursting free on their own with the force of a small volcano.

"Jerzy, why do you not like me anymore?" he loudly asked his brother. "What has changed? It is not like I am a thief or a murderer," he said.

His brother rolled over onto his side, opened his eyes and stared at him. "No, you are such a good brother, filled with love, which is why you do things like putting snakes in my bed."

Ruslin had forgotten all about that. It was just a stupid garden snake, but when Jerzy felt it under his blanket, you would have thought it was the deadliest anaconda from the bowels of an African jungle.

"Well, you deserved that for all the rotten things you do to me."

"I do nothing bad to you. Ever," he said.

"Oh yeah? Well, how about when you made me stick my tongue on that frozen light pole? Or when you poisoned me with that really big fart of yours, and then held your blanket over my head and squeezed it there until I almost died from the stink? I bet you forgot all about that."

Jerzy had forgotten about doing those things. The tongue sticking to the pole so quickly and with such force really was a surprise. He had heard it was possible, but did not really believe it. So like the good brother he was, he tricked Ruslin into trying it.

As for the gas attack, money was tight, so the family had been eating beans all week, and after five or six days of that diet, he was more than ripe... he was primed. Of course, letting one rip in front of Papa would have been suicide, so he held in what he could, at least until bedtime. And by that time, he was seriously ready to explode, but he knew it was going to be a whopper, just too big to waste, so he thought that sharing it with Ruslin would be the proper thing to do. Calling his little brother over to his bedside by promising to show him something he would never forget, he quickly threw the blanket over his head and let himself go full boogie. The noise alone was amazing... it was incredibly long, almost like a symphony. He felt it was one of his greatest creations. And visually, Jerzy could have sworn that the blanket actually puffed out a little. Too bad, he thought, that nobody was recording such moments for the history books. Events like that would be so much more interesting to study than learning about Polish kings and war details and all that fool-ishness.

He really wanted to smile at that memory, but instead, he chose to ignore his little brother, giving no sign that he even heard him. But that was not the real problem.

Jerzy knew that if he allowed his brother to tag along with him and his friends, nobody would be able to talk openly about the stuff that really mattered to them, so they would ultimately resent Ruslin, eventually extending that resentment to Jerzy for not being "man" enough to insist on him hanging out with kids his own age. No, Jerzy could not allow his mother's favorite to drag him down to his friend-less level. It just was not fair for him to be put in such a spot, but he could not explain it to his stepmother, for he knew she would never understand.

Ruslin wiggled his eyebrows up and down in a desperate attempt to make Jerzy laugh. Nothing. That used to work, but now... completely stone-faced.

Jerzy wanted to laugh. Hell, he would love to be nice to his brother, but then he knew damned well that Ruslin would again beg to hang around with him and his friends, and that was just unacceptable. No, easier to just make him want to stay away. Far away. Besides, his stepmother's hateful words still hung in the air.

Ruslin lay back down again. "Maybe it would be better if I was dead," he said quietly, but loud enough for his older brother to hear.

Again, Jerzy ignored him. Stupid kid, he thought. Why can he not find his own friends, kids his own age? Does he really think he is so special that he needs to be around older people? I do not see anything so special about him. I think maybe I am doing him a favor, and this will force him to start playing with his own classmates, then we will all be much happier.

Jerzy tried to get back to sleep, but he had a hard time getting comfortable, so he kept flip-flopping, causing his pajama top to keep riding up until the neck felt as though it was going to choke him, even with the top buttons undone, so finally, he sat up and removed it. Why do mothers insist their kids wear those stupid things anyway? The room was a little chilly, but he knew that the air under the blanket would soon warm him with his own body heat, and all would be well again.

Meanwhile, surprising himself, Ruslin found himself actually wishing that he really was dead. The thoughts brought some satisfaction as he saw in his mind's eye Jerzy's regret after he was gone, all because Jerzy had been mean and ignored him just to please his stupid friends.

Ruslan even began dreaming up ways to end it all. I could always do something dramatic, like burning myself in oil, he thought, but that sounds really painful, and so does jumping off the roof or playing on the train tracks. It needs to be quick and painless. Hanging is probably easy, but also scary. I do not like the idea of choking to death. I cannot use a gun because guns cost big money, and poison might not work, even if I knew what kind to take. I suppose I could stab myself, but that would hurt like crazy, plus it would make a big mess that Mama would have to clean up. But the biggest problem, though, he finally admitted to himself, is that I am just too scared to really do it. And besides, if I cannot be around to see how sorry Jerzy feels afterward, what good is it?

Tossing and turning as these thoughts tortured Ruslin, he felt something sharp, like a tiny needle poke him in the face. "Ow," he said aloud. His pillow was filled with goose down, and every night a handful of quills from the feathers inside poked through the pillow casing and jabbed his face, so he carefully pulled out the offending feathers one at a time, as though he was plucking demons from their secret hiding places in his pillow and banished them forever from their hiding places there, letting them float to their new home on the floor. With each new offender, he spoke to it, saying the same thing, like a mantra... "Stupid feather," and watched it float down. When he had finished, he ran his hand across the entire pillow one last time, just to be sure that was all. Once satisfied that no more dangerous quills were going to poke him tonight, he rolled onto his side, and looked out the window, where he saw a wall of blackness coming up beyond the distant hills, merging into a series of moving shadows, sort of like the scariest part of his dreams.

It is probably going to happen again if I go back to sleep, and then Jerzy will just be mad at me for keeping him from sleeping and he will never ever let me go anywhere with him and his friends. I really wish I was brave enough to kill myself.

While Ruslin was entertaining all his thoughts of suicide, Jerzy was wrapped up in his own concerns.

He stared at the wall, which became a sort of screen for the movie of his thoughts. Usually, he found great pleasure in contemplating the mystery of girls, and of how they were changing as they became young ladies. Why do girls become women faster than guys become men? he wondered. It was exciting, yet wrapped up in such mystery; he did not understand why all the fascinating details were being kept from him. The girls all acted like everything was so secretive and the whole process was incredibly dramatic, and all the adults knew what was going on, too, yet the boys were apparently not important enough to be brought in on all the mystique.

He knew that his world was changing, and that his feelings were somehow wrapped up in these changes. He felt different now when thinking about his female friends. It was not because they no longer seemed interested in playing ball with the guys. Now, they all seemed more delicate, as though they might break. They were no longer shaped the same, either. He would give anything for just one small peek. And the older they got, the more they talked about things like love and marriage and having babies. And as they matured, he felt ever the more insecure about them.

How do you know when you are really in love, for crying out loud? For that matter, how do you even get a girl interested in you? It all drove him absolutely crazy sometimes.

But as maddening as that was, another mystery, an even bigger one, was also brewing these days. He could not pinpoint exactly when it started, but he could feel the shadows of it somewhere deep in his bones. Try as he might, he could not articulate the creeping of this fear, this growing sense of dread coursing through the very marrow of his bones, like a fog, vague, yet settling on everything. All he knew was that the adults all around him often spoke in hushed tones, whispers, hiding something from him, but though he knew not what, he could feel a growing intensity, as though it was going to turn into a primordial monster and eat the entire town.

This was not even something he could discuss with his friends. How do you explain a vague feeling? Especially a scary one. Everybody would just laugh at him and tell him to go crying to his Mommy. No, he could not talk about this to his gang. Not even jokingly. But it worried him nevertheless.

He was becoming a man, but he never felt more like a boy.

Five

Sixteen

The days turned into weeks, and Jerzy's punishment became a thing of the past. Boguslaw never went back to school, his father saw to that. It was too embarrassing for the old man to be among his drinking buddies with kids of their own going to the same school as Boguslaw, and listening to the stories they told their fathers about the fight, and about how well their boys were doing with their studies. So, he pulled his asshole embarrassment of a son out of school and made him get a factory job, working with him. He would make a man out of him yet.

But even though he was no longer living in the world of children, Boguslaw did not forget. Every time he thought of Czaplicki, his face went red with anger. Because of him, his father had given him a horrible beating. Because of him, he lost his status as top dog in the school. And because of him, he would never have a high school diploma.

Of course, it was just as well he was no longer in school, because all the kids saw him get beaten, and once the word got out, nobody was afraid of him like before. He was not invincible after all... he knew it and they knew it. And it was all because of Jerzy.

"Someday," he vowed, "I will pay that skinny little bastard back, and I will pay him back big." He did not yet know how, nor when, but it was bound to happen. It was inevitable.

Vengeance was a beautiful dream to Boguslaw; it made him salivate and he held onto it tightly, knowing that it was only a matter of time.

* * *

Many German Jews began arriving in Poland, fanning rumors of Hitler's hatred for what he called the Jewish problem. Within a month, people were speaking anxiously about the inevitability of war to correct the wrongs inflicted upon German pride after the Great War. There was talk of big tanks, airplanes, and even the gassing of soldiers, like before. Many of the people spoke of a German military build-up, but then others thought that was absurd.

In Poland's schools, the teachers felt the rumors needed to be addressed to keep the fear-based stories from panicking the students.

"Many people feel that Herr Hitler is gearing up for another war," said Mr. Bodenheimer, Jerzy's world history teacher. Since this was a teacher who had been born and raised in Germany, the students felt that he understood the recent changes happening there far better than anybody else, so they listened.

Gesturing with his chalk in the air, as though he was poking the students, Mr. Bodenheimer looked around the classroom at his young charges, whose eyes were opened wide. He sported a large beefy mustache, not unlike that of a walrus, and unless he was talking or eating, one was never quite sure when his mouth was open, or when it was closed. It was fun to guess.

When asked about the rumors, he spoke slowly and deliberately. "Such people are ignorant and let their fears talk for them. They talk about Herr Hitler's sudden alliance with Stalin, the military buildup, even his anti-Semitic philosophy... but they do not understand... it is all defensive. He has no reason to declare war. Why should he?

Germany signed an armistice at the end of the Great War, and with the reparations and rebuilding of their own economy, Germany is in no position to start another war. Nor is there a reason. Hitler has already made substantial changes for his country, as is his great right to do so. The improved economy alone is just short of a miracle."

Jerzy listened to all this with Nik, but the constant talk of politics bored him. It always had. Jerzy was just an ordinary guy and he felt it was far more important to devote all of his energy toward learning how to talk to the girls, unlike his best friend, who had no problems with the ladies.

Nik had a full head of sandy hair, wavy, yet it was always mussed up just a little bit, sitting atop a face that was salted with freckles. He had those rugged good looks that made the girls melt, yet he was so passionate about politics and philosophical ideals like equality and fairness that he hardly ever gave the young ladies any thought. And right now, this speech on Germany had his full attention.

He rubbed one of his ears, then raised his hand. "Mr. Bodenheimer, what about all the threats Hitler has been making against Poland?"

"Ah, Mr. Zworski... the purity, the innocence of youth. You are mistaken, young man... those are not threats. Herr Hitler is merely trying to protect his loyal German citizens who live here, in Poland. And he is also worried about Poland attacking Germany, as there have been some serious threats made lately by certain Poles who do not agree with his politics. But do not worry about such things... your lives are just beginning and you must enjoy them now, while you still have so much youthful exuberance at your command."

The last bell rang, and the students all ran out to officially greet the end of the school year, like a herd of lemmings that just discovered a giant stash of seeds.

"What do you think, Jerzy?" said Nik putting his books in his locker.

"I think it is amazing how fast a school can empty itself out when the year has ended," Jerzy said, turning in his textbooks. "I do not know why school is mandatory when almost all they teach us is useless foolishness. When in my life would I ever need algebra? Now if they taught a course about girls, then they would have my undivided attention."

"Come on, Jerzy, you know what I am talking about. This whole thing with Germany gives me a bad feeling."

"I do not know, my friend, and do you know what? I do not care," he said, turning about and heading for the airplane factory, which was just across the street from his house, about two blocks down the road. Nik ran to catch up.

"How can you not care? If Hitler attacks, this could totally change our lives... our futures, everything we have been dreaming about, all gone. Maybe we will even have to fight... and die, before we have lived." He thought about all the lurking menaces to his promised life. He had not even had sex yet. Not with another person, anyway.

They stopped walking and looked at each other. "Look... if it happens, it happens," said Jerzy, staring at his friend's freckly face. "And we cannot do a single thing about it either way. We are not yet men, Nik. Yes, we could be killed. All who are born must die someday, but until then, I want only to be young and foolish, and to learn about the sensual music of love. It calls to me, and I am sick with desire because I do not know how to answer. And if war is knocking at the door, the urgency for love is all the greater."

As Jerzy walked away, Nik stood there, just staring at his friend, and wondering if they even lived in the same world. He found it difficult to believe that his best friend did not care about the horrendous dangers that Hitler posed.

Soon summer vacation was over, then on September first, something unexpected happened. Jerzy and his classmates were supposed to enter the tenth level of school, but to the surprise of almost everyone, a "no-school" announcement was made. Schools all across the country were being shut down, completely stopping the children's formal education, maybe forever. The adults were extraordinarily hush-hush about the Nazi invasion of their country, in the hopes that Germany would be defeated by the Polish army before the fighting reached Lublin.

But despite the mysterious closing down of his education, Jerzy was unconcerned, for life was still full of promise to him. He felt like a sapling, with its strong roots entrenched firmly into the ground, yet supple in even the strongest winds. And he was filled with the energy of youth, feeling immortal, as does all life in its beginnings.

At home, though, the boy was beginning to feel stifled. Yevgenia was always after him to take his brother along with him, but Jerzy said no, that he could not do this. Ruslan, with his deep blue eyes and jet-black hair was way too young... and Jerzy just knew that his friends would hate him for letting his baby brother tag along with them, and he would be embarrassed.

"I cannot, Momma," he would always say. No explanation, no apologies.

Jerzy saw how his stepmother always catered to Ruslan first. She said it was because he was the baby, but Jerzy knew better. It was obvious to him which boy she really loved. So, Ruslan learned to play alone while Jerzy spent time with his friends.

* * *

Like always, Jerzy and his friends, his gang, he called it, mostly spent their time by musing about their imagined futures, or talking about girls while watching the planes take off and land from the small airplane factory across the street from Jerzy's home. And what a gang it was. There were five of them, including Jerzy, who hung around together... boys, learning how to be men.

Always scheming, Gerwazy, whose father died last year from too much drinking, was the oldest, so he had become the father figure, the protector of the group, and the others looked up to him. All the adults loved his dirty blonde hair with strong natural waves, and that helped to give him an air of confidence.

Everything he did, he did as if he was paternal to the entire gang. It wasn't enough for him to smoke his home-made cigarettes as the others did, pretending to be grown up and sophisticated like the movie heroes... real macho men... no, he smoked his in a long, slender cigarette holder, like FDR, suave, sophisticated, with chin held high. In the same vein as Roosevelt, Gerwazy even had a bad leg, but not from any disease; he broke his right ankle at the age of seven playing ice hockey with the big boys. The blade on one of his skates got caught in a rut on the ice, and he twisted the ankle hard enough to separate it completely from his leg bones while trying to stand quickly. The snapping sound it made was the talk of the school for the entire week. It took a few months to heal, and never totally recovered, yet today, he was the only member of the gang with a job.

Then there was Czabor, the romantic idiot bullshit artist. Two years earlier, he fell in love with the idea of getting a horse. Since then, he discovered girls. He wore his hair slicked back, like Valentino, and sported a mustache (he said it tickled the girls), telling everyone his goal was to be a honest-to-God cowboy, because, as he put it, "Everybody knows that all the real ladies love cowboys."

"Czabor, I saw you staring at Karynia yesterday," Gerwazy said. Tapping his cigarette holder lightly, his eyes narrowed with anticipation; he loved taunting Czabor this way. "When are you going to ask her out, boy?"

"Gerwazy, you know I have no money... how can I ask her out?" He looked at all of his friends, hoping somebody would understand, and maybe even come to his rescue. "Jobs are too hard to come by."

"Well, you had better do something... she is becoming a juicy tomato, and I think her womanly curves are driving you crazy."

"Gerwazy..." he said in a quiet voice, "...maybe you could loan me some money?" He did not want the others to hear.

"Mmmmm, such a waste... perhaps I will ask that fair maiden out myself," Gerwazy said loudly enough for all to hear, looking lost in thought, but grinning all the while.

"No," Czabor said, standing up fast. "No, my problems are temporary. I will attend to my love, do not worry... I will find the money somehow, and in the meantime, you just leave her alone. Besides, she is too much woman for you... for any of you," he said, trying to stare everyone down. "So... just leave her to me," he said, his thumb pointing to his chest, head held high. "I know how to please such a beautiful creature," he added, smiling. "Just one touch of my lips and her socks will fly up and down in anticipation of more."

Everybody moaned, but it was good-natured. Czabor drove Jerzy crazy with all his phony swagger, but the other guys seemed to like him, and he lived only a few houses away, so Jerzy found it easier to keep his mouth shut and just tolerate his idiotic behavior. So what if he thought he was God's gift to women everywhere?

Lukasz, a tall brunette, with drooping eyelids, was just the opposite of Czabor; he never spoke unless he had to. Like Gerwazy, he, too, lost his father the year before and had to work after school to help support his family. Because of his quiet nature, the gang thought he was a deep thinker, so it did not matter what he said, no matter how idiotic. When he declared that life was like a scrambled egg, which was his favorite expression, everybody thought he was a genius and his thoughts radiant, so they all just nodded in agreement, as though they understood.

Lukasz's face was thin and young-looking, except for all the facial hair... he had been shaving since he was twelve, so he was now trying to grow a big, bushy beard on his face and jaw to look like a lumberjack, or someone who spends a lot of time alone in the woods, thinking about life. Jerzy thought he already looked more like a tree fell on his head, but he would never say so aloud.

And of course, there was Jerzy's best friend ever, Nikodemos Zworski, who he had pretty much known since birth, and the two of them had become nearly inseparable. He felt more like a brother to Jerzy than Ruslan did.

"Okay everybody, put whatever tobacco you have into a pile on this sheet of paper so we can roll our cigarettes," said Gerwazy.

They made their cigarettes from the loose tobacco they found in old discarded butts, and they wrapped the tobacco in newspaper, and sometimes, with a good puff, the paper would burst in flames, but that was all just part of the fun. The bigger the flame, the bigger the laugh.

When smoking, the talk generally turned to serious stuff, however... man stuff, and when it did, they all made their voices go deeper, like real men, talking of their dreams and the promises of tomorrow, as did every generation before them, and those before them. This was the ritual of their gender, after all, of boys finding their place in the world as men, an ancient ritual going back, perhaps even to primordial times, to the cave in preparation for the hunt, for they were soon going to join the hunters, the providers, as did all men before them. It gave them a male bond, a sense of place within the community.

They watched the planes, mostly the older biplanes, being tested in flight for a while, each boy dreaming it was he in the cockpit, and bragging about what he would like to do with the plane if he were piloting it, the stories growing ever bolder with each retelling. Sharing their bravado was expected, and applauded. The drone of each propeller as it left the ground incited them... it spoke of continuity, which they expected as a birthright, but it also it spoke of adventure. With a plane, one could go anywhere, and that appealed to the ever-growing wanderlust of their youth.

Finally, the whistle blew at the factory, signaling the end of the workday. There would be no more flights to entertain them today.

"What do you all want to do now?" asked Gerwazy, arching his eyebrows.

"Hey, you guys want to catch some frogs?" Nik said. "I have a couple of straws..."

Everybody grinned. They were not kids any more... they were all sixteen now, but somehow they understood that this would probably be the last summer when the gang would have a chance to amuse themselves this way. So, they walked to the great pond where Jerzy spent his time hiding from the school after his fight with Boguslaw. They could hear the bullfrogs everywhere, as though the creatures were calling the gang to join them, at least until the boys arrived, then they shut up.

The gang went to work, all bent over, looking at the different places where a large bullfrog might hide. It had to be of sufficient size for what they had in mind. They looked under some of the larger leaves, inside hollowed out logs, and along the edge of the pond, where Czabor grabbed a water snake by accident, then threw it into the middle of the pond while screaming and trying to escape from it.

"Hey, I found one," Jerzy said, picking it up. It was a nice, big one, hiding ever so quietly behind a large rock.

"He is a beauty, alright," said Czabor.

The boys held it still while Nik carefully pushed one of the straws up the frog's butt. The frog's eyes got big. Then they all flipped a coin. Three tails, one head.

"The honor is all yours, Nik."

He blew hard into the straw, and the boys watched the frog inflate, hoping it would not explode, but moved back just in case. When he finished, Nik put his finger over the end of the straw to hold the air in while Jerzy helped him put the now-round frog into the water. He floated beautifully. Then Nik pulled the straw out, and they all rolled on the ground in laughter as the frog shot across the pond much faster than usual.

It was good to be sixteen.

Six

Birth of the Blitzkrieg

The day began like any other, the sun rising slowly, gently calling life out of its warm slumber. Jerzy had not yet arisen, and the stillness in the room beckoned for him to stay, but outside, the animals were fidgety. The boy heard his father calling for him to wake up, but at sixteen, he valued his sleep more than anything... except perhaps food. His stomach always made rude noises, but that was nothing new. Food was so precious, and to waste it was not only a sin, it was unimaginable. The rumbling of his empty stomach had become his constant companion long ago, and he knew its every trick.

In the years before this one, school would begin in just a couple of hours, he thought, and then he would be able to start his day with a real breakfast given to those students who could not eat properly at home; he would have received a slice of dark bread with a cup of warm milk to wash it down. Just the thought made him drool. But now that school had been cancelled, there was no meal to start the day.

Then, in the quiet of the early morning hours Jerzy thought he heard the faint rumbling of aircraft. The sun was just rising. As the

54

noise grew closer, the boy wondered why the aircraft factory was testing their planes so early in the day, when he heard a ferocious screaming. A second wail joined the first... then yet another.

Leaping out of bed, Jerzy ran to his open bedroom window and witnessed the fury of a man-made storm erupt upon his city. He saw the electric power plant across the street and the airplane factory behind it explode in giant balls of flame as three planes swooped down from the sky in a steep dive, each one screaming as though it came from a cat being skinned alive, until reaching the bottom of their dive, where they unleashed a series of bombs, molesting the living and non-living alike, then each climbed back up into the clouds again and circled, like buzzards in search of prey. He stopped breathing, frozen by this vision of death and destruction, stunned by what he was witnessing. A bomb exploded right in front of their house, causing Jerzy to jump backwards. It was not just a loud crashing sound, like in the movies. This was more of an ear-piercing BANG, sharp and frightening. And it created a shock wave that reverberated deep in his stomach.

"Holy crap," he said, running backwards, away from the window.

"Boys... get in the basement, NOW," yelled their father, who was already running to the cellar doorway. Jerzy sprinted after him and was almost at the door when he turned his head and saw Ruslan in a corner of the cooking area, squatting in a fetal position, his thumb in his mouth, and rocking forward and backward, eyes wide open and glazed.

"Rus-"

Just that moment, an ear-piercing scream followed by a loud series of crashes, like a locomotive smashing through their home at full speed shook the house and a part of the ceiling crumbled, as did a part of the floor directly beneath it. The impact threw Kaspar sideways, off the bottom stairs, where he landed on his side, a little bruised and a little shaken, but basically unhurt. Instinctively, Jerzy turned and bolted down the cellar stairs, almost falling himself, his young heart pounding and ready to burst in the confusion of still being alive, pieces of plaster and other debris in his hair and eyes; he could taste the thick, acrid air as he tried to breathe. He coughed and wiped his eyes with the bottom of his palm. Debris was still floating in the air from the floor that had partially collapsed above them. And explosions, even though more distant now, continued to rattle the basement windows.

"Papa,—"

Kaspar looked around quickly. "WHERE IS RUSLAN?"

Jerzy, his thick, curly hair matted with white dust said nothing, but he hugged himself as he stared at the upstairs door. His lips moved slightly, but nothing came out.

The bombs continued to fall, some shaking the building more than others.

Kaspar, telling his wife to stay there, raced back up the stairs, pushing hard against the door, slamming his whole body into it to get it to open enough for him to squeeze through, yelling for his youngest son while throwing large pieces of debris aside as he moved from one area to another. "RUSLAN... RUSLAN," he shouted. "Where are you? Answer me..."

Kaspar grew frantic, searching under the debris with a renewed fervor born of desperation, his senses on fire. He saw a large hole in the ceiling above his head, one above that in the second floor, and daylight from the hole in the roof. There was also a hole in the floor they were standing on, directly below the other holes, and Kaspar walked carefully around it to a pile of debris on the far side of the room.

His wife, hearing his shouting, felt her stomach lurch as her trembling legs leaped up the stairs, squeezing through the doorway just as Kaspar was struggling to move a huge large block of plaster from a corner of the cooking area. Careful not to fall through the hole, Yevgenia stumbled over the rubble in an effort to help her husband move it just as Jerzy reached the doorway. And it was there that they uncovered their youngest son, his neck cruelly twisted. Yevgenia wailed in her knowing, trying to grab the lifeless body, but Kaspar stopped her, holding her tight in their shared horror and grief. She broke free and falling to her knees, wrapped her arms around her beloved son, cradling his flopping head to her bosom with her head tilted and resting upon his, her tears running down her cheeks and unto his head.

"No, noooo... no, not again." And she wept loudly, rocking him and holding him in her anguish. She would not let go... could not let go. She had carried him in her womb, sheltered him from all of life's hurts, nurtured him. No, she would never let go.

None of them noticed the unexploded bomb that had crashed through their roof and the floors beneath, the bomb that came to rest in a pile of debris in the basement, not twenty feet away from where they had sought shelter.

Jerzy had followed his parents. He wanted to scream, but he could not. Looking at them, and at the lifeless body of his half-brother, he thought about the resentment he had harbored for so long, how he avoided Ruslan just because he was his mother's favorite... but now it ate a hole in his heart.

Ruslan actually was not so bad, Jerzy thought, not bad at all... but now he was gone, and it was too late to tell him that. Too late to tell him anything. Jerzy could not bear to look at his parents.

They could still hear explosions in the far distance, but from the sounds, Kaspar knew that even as the planes were receding, ground troops were coming. He figured that all of Germany would be heading their way.

Kaspar tried to take the body of their son, but his wife held him even tighter.

"Yevgenia, listen... the Nazi troops will be coming to finish what they started. It is too dangerous for you to stay. Go with Jerzy to his Uncle Frydryk's farm in Urszulin. He is the brother of my first wife, and was an army officer in the Great War; he will protect you both."

"No, Papa, I want to stay with you."

"Jerzy, you must go with your mother."

"No, Kaspar..." said Yevgenia. "I need to be with Ruslan, I ne-"

"Yevgenia, you must leave now. He was my son, too... I will take care of Ruslan. Please... go now, before it is too late."

He gently took Ruslan from her.

"Kaspar..."

"No... you must go now. Jerzy, it is your job to be a man now and protect her. Promise me."

"Papa — "

"Promise me."

Jerzy was silent, his father glaring at him.

Then finally, "...I promise, Papa, he whispered."

"Then it is good," Kaspar said, his hand on Jerzy's shoulder.

"Kaspar, you will come later, yes?" his wife said in between sobs, her tear-stained face buried in her hands.

"I will do what I can," Kaspar said softly. "Now go -- hurry."

Jerzy pulled her away gently. Miserable and disconsolate, they each gathered what few possessions they had and would need, and left in silence, both of them looking back at Kaspar holding Ruslan close to him, his head nestled against the boy's, and crying quietly as they left.

* * *

When the barbershop had opened that morning, three men had been waiting outside; Boguslaw was among them. He walked quickly to the chair, pushing Lazor Ruzicki, the town jeweler, who was but a slightly built Jewish man, out of his way so he could be first.

"And how are you today, Mr. Owiti?" said the barber with a slight tremor in his voice and a forced smile on his lips.

The barber, Wielhelm Dabrowski was a thin, middle-aged man, a romantic, and unusually sensitive. His eyes were glamorous, but small, like pebbles. Unlike Boguslaw, the barber honestly cared about people, and as a result, he was nice to everyone, although Boguslaw was one customer he would be happy to never see again. But a customer is a customer, so he mentally prepared to do what he knew best.

"Just cut the hair, Dabrowski, and make it pretty... I want to impress the ladies."

Wielhelm took great pride in his work. He picked up his brand-new Wahl electric clippers that he bought just two days ago and started trimming his customer's head when the screaming of the bombers began, followed by a series of sharp explosions. At the first

WH-BANG, Wielhelm jerked and the clippers rode across the top of Boguslaw's head, from front to back, cutting and even ripping some of the hair out as he created a major road right down the middle of the young man's scalp.

"Stupid shithead," Boguslaw yelled, leaping off the chair and running his hands to the pain at the top of his head. A large clump of hair was still embedded in the head of the clippers.

They stared at each other when they heard more explosions... WH-BANG... WH-BANG-BANG-BANG. They could feel the vibrations in their stomachs as the percussions shattered the large plate glass window in front of the shop, and rattled the building, knocking most of the bottles down off the shelves.

The men all wanted to run outside to escape this insane tempest, but there was nowhere safe, so not knowing any better, they crouched down low, hiding behind their chairs, as though this would somehow protect them. At the same time, Boguslaw caught his reflection in the large mirror just before it crashed to the floor.

"Aaarrrgh... I will rip your balls off," he screamed at the barber, who cowered in a corner of the room.

Otto Pastula, another customer, was watching all this. "Boguslaw, shut your mouth," he said in a gruff voice. Four inches taller and thirty pounds heavier, he was a commanding presence. He tired of listening to Boguslaw's endless threats, and his mustache bristled with anger.

"Your hair will grow back, asshole, but right now, look outside. We have bigger problems," he said.

Boguslaw blinked and slowly turned his attention to what was going on, as it finally dawned on him that something else was happening, something bigger than the road going through his hair. He walked outside, pushing through the door that was hanging by only the top hinge. It looked as though a tornado had ripped through Lublin, tearing apart everything in its path, and fires appeared sporadically, trails of black smoke winding their way to the sky as testimony to the ferocity they endured.

Walking aimlessly through the rubble, Boguslaw just stared at the carnage. It reminded him of all the anthills he loved kicking down, and when enough ants came scrambling to the surface, he would always squish them with his big feet, stomping and grinding them back into the ground. Doing this made him feel like a mighty god, pulverizing the minions of his domain, those who were less than he, and therefore did not deserve to live. Only the strongest survived, and he was a king. Until today. Now, he was one of the ants, and he needed to find his way back to the surface. Staring at the carnage, he slowly turned and began walking, not going anywhere in particular, but feeling a need to explore all this.

He heard his father's voice and he turned, looking, but he could not see where the voice was coming from... *Only the strongest survive, you chicken shit... You hear me, girlie?* Boguslaw stumbled over the debris, hearing that ever-angry voice again.

Be a man, you worthless piece of crap. Toughen up, and stop your damn whining or I will give you something to whine about. He heard the whistle of his father's belt coming to eat his skin, and he cowered.

You let a sixteen-year-old break your nose? Stupid shithead... What kind of a girlie are you? Boguslaw thought he felt the back of his father's hand coming at him. "I am sorry, Pa — "WHACK... WHACK...

Be a man, you little turd. TOUGHEN UP.

Boguslaw looked around for his father but could not see him anywhere. Instead, he found an injured puppy lying on the side of the street, whimpering quietly. He walked over to it and squatted to better see.

"What is the matter, little doggie? Why are you whining?" When the dog whined again, Boguslaw stood up...

...and kicked it. The dog yelped, so he kicked it again. Just in case, he kicked it yet again... and again. Finally, the puppy was still. Very still.

"There now... I gave you something to whine about," he said, smiling.

As he walked on, a movie played in Boguslaw's head—a parade of all the faces he had beaten up over the years. He looked up, as though it was being projected on a giant screen in the sky. He saw each kid, and beat them all up again, one by one. The more he was kept back in school, the bigger he got, and the smaller the kids he beat up. And just when the movie got to Jerzy's stupid face, he remembered the humiliation he felt from having that stupid blood vessel in the back of his nose slit open by the cartilage that little asshole broke. And he yelled with rage.

It was just then that he felt something splat right on the bald spot, the new road on top of his head. Looking up quickly, he saw a black crow, which had made the deposit.

"Aaaarrrgh. Stupid shhhiiiithead," he screamed, quickly picking up a brick and throwing it at the bird. He missed, and the bird flew away, a little lighter, and a little happier. Boguslaw reached up and wiped the white stuff off his head, with his bare fingers, then flicked it off his hand as best he could, and wiped his hand on his pants.

Maybe I should buy a dress for you, huh? WHACK. Toughen up, I said... WHACK... WHACK. I'll make a man out of you yet, girlie, even if I have to kill you.

He covered his ears, and looked around again, but his father was not there. Unknown to Boguslaw, he was busy at home, beating up his wife. He would give her something to cry about.

Boguslaw finally decided to head west, toward Germany. He had been awed by the brutality and the raw, vicious power displayed by the Nazi Luftwaffe.

And he wanted to be a part of it.

* * *

There was an old Polish expression favored by the womenfolk that said, When thou hast leisure, say thy prayers, and when thou hast none, get thee a good friend. Poland was a country filled with Catholics, and today nobody had time to pray, but many new friendships were forged.

By noon, pretty much the entire town seemed to be on the move, many heading towards the large field of sugar beets outside the city. That was the direction in which Jerzy and Yevgenia were heading.

A woodchuck stopped his toils long enough to watch the spectacle of humanity parade past his home. The wind carried the sound of hundreds, perhaps thousands of weary feet, along with the rattling and creaking of old wooden carts with large wagon wheels, being pulled by oxen or horses as they made their way through the debris of the smoke filled town, fires raging out of control, people yelling and running every which way among all the refuse. Those who stayed made way for the procession, crossing themselves, many in tears and asked, "Where are they going?" But there was no answer.

The exodus looked like a slow, but relentless volcanic eruption, torrents of people pouring out in rivulets, like lava in search of level ground. They stopped once in a while to catch their breath, but they did not dare stop for long; they could still hear explosions in the far distance. Each moment slipped by, never to be seen again.

"Mama, I am tired," said Jerzy.

His complaint was greeted with silence, and more silence when he complained again. She did not even look at him, and so he looked down at the ground, thinking about his brother again, and how his stepmother must feel the pain from his death a thousand times worse than the pain Jerzy felt in his feet. And so he said nothing more, plodding on, one foot after the other, feeling the soft dirt sliding under his feet as he walked, and wishing he had been a better brother.

After about two kilometers, they were in the center of the sugar beet field, when a Nazi warplane passed over their heads so low that they felt that they could reach up and touch it. Their clothes flapped in the wind of the passing fighter, and the roar of the plane made them duck. Nobody realized that after passing overhead, it was coming back to play with them.

Seven

Becoming an Eagle

Klaus Boellman was having the time of his life. From the moment they lifted off early this morning, everything had gone exactly as planned. No, it was even better. Every pilot had done his job without flaw. Both the primary and secondary missions were a complete success, and now he was flying free back to Germany. But seeing the steady flow of fleeing Polish civilians on the outskirts of town, he thought perhaps he could at least get in a little badly needed target practice.

He did remember what his wing commander said to him about sticking to the plan and not going off on his own, but he just as quickly dismissed the thought.

"Aargh, that is foolish," he said. "Nobody is even shooting back out here. The commander is just an overcautious fool and he knows I am a star, and capable of shining far brighter than he ever will. Besides, there is no way I can become an ace pilot unless my shooting is perfect, and for that, I need practice. He should know that."

He squinted from the reflections of the afternoon sun on the glass canopy surrounding him. The plane was new, but he had practiced many hours in it, and knew every dial, every switch and the pedal as though he had been born in the cockpit. It had all become second nature for him.

Klaus had flown exceptionally low so he could delight in the destruction they had laid on the town, when he had unexpectedly flown right over the fleeing civilians, and the possibilities it had offered looked lip-smacking good, but he knew better than to get his hopes up. "They had to have seen me and are wary, but... if I can turn and fly back much higher, approaching them again from behind, perhaps I can surprise them."

Licking his lips, he gripped the controls firmly, banking hard, then diving and turning the plane around to line himself up for this new sport. He could not tell where he began and where the plane ended... it was as though he and the plane had become one, so how could he not break the rules of lesser men?

As hoped, he soon found himself approaching the dog-weary, but intact column of displaced civilians, and not believing his luck, a grin crept onto his face as he strove to see how many undesirables he could eliminate for the pleasure of his Fuhrer. He almost forgot to breathe.

"Now you are all mine," he said, chuckling. "A new day is dawning and there is no room in it for the likes of you."

He flew past the rear of the column, then banked the plane swiftly to line up for his first attack on the unsuspecting civilians, climbing a bit just so he could dive for full effect before strafing them. "Just a little closer now... I must be patient."

Nearing the refugees, he dove hard, the plane's siren screaming as the pilot began squeezing the triggers, unleashing the rapid-fire bullets from his machine guns without warning, tatatatatatatatatatata... tatatatatatatatatatata, an avalanche of fear and death erupting out of the quiet.

"DEATH TO THE POLISH WAR PIGS," he shouted, even though he knew they could not hear his voice.

The air was filled with a cacophony of screams and yelling as everyone tried to duck or run in a desperate attempt to live, but cover was far away from the position of the largest part of the fleeing refugees in the middle of the beet field.

"Holy crap," said Jerzy, as he ducked to make himself a smaller target. Remembering his promise to his father, the boy grabbed his stepmother's hand and pulled her between two large boulders nearby, hoping they would offer enough protection. She tried to stand, but Jerzy was strong enough to keep her down as the plane flew past them, two of its bullets hitting the rock behind them.

So many targets... it is almost as though they want to be shot, Klaus thought.

He shifted the angle of his fighter back to attack the others again with his machine guns, shooting continuously until passing the entire column. He was becoming the eagle.

Knowing that the survivors would now scatter, Klaus grinned even harder as he banked his plane and turned for another pass from the opposite direction.

Jerzy and Yevgenia stayed put.

Tatata...tata...tatatata... tatata.

"Now this is more of a challenge," he said, almost laughing, and he was more careful this time to not waste any bullets. "Herr Hitler will be so proud of me," he said. "So will Papa. Not so many this time, but nevertheless, it will help me to sleep tonight."

And at the end of this pass, he banked once more for a final attack.

A parish priest, Father Szel, who traveled with the procession, was now on his knees, holding a rosary in his left hand while making the gesture of the cross with his right, trying to administer last rites to as many victims as possible when the plane came rising up again from the hill right behind him. He never felt the plane's bullets. But the effect of its volatile firepower excited Klaus to no end.

When the pilot was finished at last, he gracefully, almost merrily tipped his wings, first one side, then the other, as though saying goodbye to old friends, then turned away, heading back to Germany. He was getting low on ammunition, and perhaps there was bigger game somewhere along the way that he had missed earlier.

Seconds after it left, another plane followed in his tracks, then... silence.

Just as suddenly as the maelstrom had begun, it stopped. Such absolute quiet was frightening in its intensity – not even the crickets dared to interrupt. The plane that attacked them was now a distant spot in the sky, harmless and no longer fearsome. The group stayed hunkered down anyway, just in case he came back.

In the continuing silence, Yevgenia rose to her knees, shaking her helpless, dirty fist at the retreating warplane and screaming at it. "Why do you torture us? Damn you, we did nothing to you... we are not soldiers... it is not even our war... and you killed my baby, you dirty cowards. BASTARDS."

She wept uncontrollably, pounding her fists onto her thighs, head bowed in the knowing that the pilot never heard a word. Finally, she was able to cry, both for herself, and for the loss of her special child, her Ruslan.

Jerzy watched in guilty silence as her tears touched his heart. Why did it have to be him? He could have treated Ruslan better, and he knew it. She was right about him all along. How could he have been so unfeeling? So selfish. If only he had been killed instead of his brother, everyone would have been better off. "Ruslan is gone now, and I am still a nobody," he said to his shadow.

Then Jerzy was awakened from his self-absorption. From somewhere within the deep silence came a low, agonized moan from those whose flesh had just been so violently ripped apart; their sounds, from the bowels of Hell, all that existed in the aftermath. He looked around, and saw a dead man lying across a boulder near the woods, as though it expected the large rock to carry it to safety. A seven-year-old boy climbed up on the rock, but when he saw the body, he stopped and just stared at it, not able to take his eyes away. It appeared that he intended to speak, but nothing came out of his mouth. Finally, the boy's father, seeing this, walked over, silently picked his son up, and carried him away.

The field was littered with the dead, and the cries from the dying rose up in a clamor of pain and anguish spreading into the sky, all bearing the larger question of "Why?" A few of the victims still alive, but without doctors, all anybody could do was to hold each other for comfort and warmth, and try to bandage the wounds with torn clothing as best they could. Some could not even be bandaged; their wounds were so large and brutal. One young man was shot badly from the waist down, yet he was still alive, trembling as he tightly held the shirt of his grandfather, who was himself in shock and was barely breathing. The young man, knowing he had been hit, but not daring to look down, whispered, "Is it bad?" All he wanted was to live. That was all.

Another victim, a young woman, died without a wound of any kind on her. Not a single mark, but her heart and lungs just stopped anyway, as though they decided that living in this kind of world just was not worth it.

The survivors had no shovels to bury the dead, so they covered them as best they could with rocks, praying and crossing themselves quickly, then moved on.

Fearing another attack, Jerzy sat in the shadows of the setting sun. He cursed at first, cursed the Nazis for their brutality, cursed Ruslin for dying, and cursed himself for having had the audacity to even be born. But then the profanity of the attack broke him. He looked at the carnage, the violence, and wept for everybody. When no more tears came, he felt the gentle touch of another hand on his back. He turned, and seeing a small girl looking so sad and lonely. He reached out to hug her, wondering what she thought of all that took place today, wondering how anyone could possibly explain it all to this sweet child, this sensitive soul, in such a way that made sense to her. And he realized in the embrace that this girl had somehow cleansed him a little. Instead of him comforting her, it was the other way around, as though she was his guardian angel.

"Thank you," he said softly, brushing the top of her little head and kissing her forehead. She smiled softly and walked off, never to know the goodness she brought to another soul.

Getting up, he moved toward the trees, and as he neared the edge of the clearing, he stumbled on a broken wagon wheel, but was able to steady himself with a hand on the closest tree, feeling a scar in the tree's bark, where a bullet from the plane had nicked it.

"We need to get deeper into the woods," he said.

And again, Yevgenia was silent... instead of commenting, she just stared at nothing, as though her soul was empty. Filled with remorse, Jerzy looked down at the ground, his eyes squeezing shut to hold back new tears. He cursed at first, but then remembered his promise to his father, and he resolved to be the man in Papa's absence.

Jerzy raised the collar of his jacket against the cold as the sun started to go down. "We must go now," he said quietly to his stepmother, and the boy led the way, not daring to stop for long. The days were getting shorter, and there was no time to waste. They followed ancient paths in the woods, paths that spoke of times long forgotten, when man and animal spoke the same language of fear and respect, and each day was a hunt for food and survival, times when endurance was revered, for it alone ensured life. And they felt the massive sense of loss that towered over them all.

They continued without speaking, walking endlessly, still carrying their few possessions despite the aches in their muscles and the blistering of their feet. They also carried their fear, their sorrow, and their memories; despite the weight of such a burden, they did not know how to put it down.

Even though now well outside the city limits, the smell of gunpowder was still in the air. They walked on nevertheless, all day and all night and all day again, stopping only long enough for short naps, for it was too cold to sleep, and sometimes, they could still hear artillery in the background.

Each step was becoming a ritual... a baptism into the church of loneliness.

Eight

Where is Yehuda?

Benvenuto spent the night in the home of the Abramowicz family. Ben had become like one of their own, and they loved his visits, for he was filled with sunshine, and always treated them with the utmost respect and courtesy. They even learned long ago to overlook his Catholicism... after all, nobody was perfect.

The next morning, they woke up early to loud, piercing screams that sounded like they came from Hell itself, followed by glass-shattering explosions... WH-BANG... WH-BANG-BANG-BANG. The women in the house screamed with every concussion, while the men grabbed them and the children and ran for the basement.

Most of it came from the other side of town, where the airport and power company were, but some of it hit here too. WH-BANG-BANG. They turned out the light and huddled together in a corner, trembling anew at each explosion. They knew they were safe there, unless a bomb landed right on top of their heads, and even though the odds were small, they still feared it.

When the bombing finally stopped, Benvenuto turned to look at

Emil's grandfather, the family elder of Zion, Yehuda Abramowicz. By tradition, he was the policy maker and made all important family decisions.

"Look folks," said Ben, even though he was specifically talking to Yehuda. "I have seen first-hand what the Nazis are capable of, and we really need to leave here now. Those bombs are a present from Adolph Hitler. I was not worried about him until after his stupid alliance with Mussolini, then I started paying attention and discovered the degree to which Hitler hates anything Jewish, and to put it bluntly, if we are here when their tanks arrive, they would just as soon kill all of you as look at you." He stopped for a moment, looking quickly at everyone, one person at a time. "I have grown to love this family deeply, all of you, so please, let us leave here now, while we still have a chance."

They all began to talk at once, generally agreeing with Ben.

"Everybody, please calm down," said Yehuda, who had his hands in the air at shoulder height, palms down, gesturing a short, pushing-down motion. "Do not worry, young man," he said slowly to Ben, "... it will not be so bad, because God will protect us. You must have faith. He will watch over us, just as he has for centuries. Come, let us pray." He paused, and urged all to hold hands in a circle, as he recited an ancient Yiddish prayer. Ben knew better, but despite his fears, he could not abandon this family that he had grown to cherish as his own.

During the prayer, he silently snuck in a few of his own Catholic prayers, the Hail Mary, the Lord's Prayer, and especially his favorite part of the 23rd Psalm, ... Yea, though I walk through the shadow of the valley of death, I will fear no evil, for thou art with me. He said those words for himself at first, but he offered them up to God for his friends as well.

In the tranquility that followed, they each lost themselves in the silence. The quiet lasted for only a short while before the ground forces began shelling the town with massive blasts of artillery. Part of it came from large cannon fire, and some from tanks.

The Polish army had heard many rumors about the German military, and one of the more interesting stories said that Germany could not afford the steel to build their tanks because of all the reparations they had to pay to other countries for losing The Great War, so they built them out of cardboard. As a result, it was rumored that part of the Polish Cavalry attacked the tanks on horseback, trying to halt them by stabbing and slicing at them with their sabers, but this was not true. They were not idiots. Nevertheless, the Polish cavalry, brave as they were, did not last long.

Many civilians, especially veterans from the last great war, went into the streets and tried to engage the Nazis in hand to hand combat, but they did no better than the Polish Cavalry. They never got close enough for hand-to-hand anything. Those with weapons fought valiantly, but ammunition was in short supply, and handguns do not fare well against tanks.

The rout was complete before the sun went down. Within a few more days, the Nazis had confiscated all the weapons, and all the records in the town hall, including birth records, certificates for all deaths, marriages, and papers for anything or anybody requiring a license. From that point, they searched every house, like extermina-tors, looking specifically for Jews.

When they came to the Abramowicz residence, the doors were locked, so the soldiers pounded on it with their rifle butts, and the lieutenant in charge shouted, in perfect Polish, that if the door was not open in ten seconds, they were going to create their own door with a tank.

The Elder Abramowicz slowly opened the door just enough to show his face, but that was enough for the Germans to push it wide open and barge in, knocking Yehuda flat on his back.

"Where is Yehuda Abramowicz?" the German lieutenant said.

"He is on the floor, where you knocked him over," answered Emil. "He is eighty-five years old and very fragile." He bent over to offer his grandfather his hand to help him up, but one of the soldiers hit Emil in the head with his rifle butt, knocking him down to join his grandfa-ther. His mother screamed and went charging after the soldier who struck her son, but before she could reach him, the lieutenant took out his pistol and shot her at point blank range. Ben had yelled at her to stop, but she was a mother enraged and totally ignored him.

Her husband threw a lamp at the soldier who shot his wife. The lieutenant ducked, and two other soldiers quickly raised their rifles and shot Emil's father, lifting him right out of one of his shoes.

Benvenuto dropped to his knees. "Nooooo," he said, looking down at his friend and his family.

"And who are you?" asked the lieutenant. The records for this house do not show any other residents."

Ben looked up at the soldiers, glaring hatefully at the lieutenant.

"I said, who are you?"

"My name, he mumbled... is Benvenuto Lombardi, and I come here from Italy to visit my long-time friends." He looked at his friends on the floor, and at all the blood. "You killed them," he said between sobs. "Why? They did nothing to you."

"It does not matter, Lombardi... they are Jews, and do not deserve my spit. But what about you, are you a Jew too? Or maybe just a Jew lover?"

Emil's head began to clear, and he got up on his hands and knees so he could move to where his mother lay. One of the soldiers saw him and kicked him, hard, in the ribs, which sent Emil to his side.

"Where do you think you are going, Jew?" Another soldier kicked him in the back. He moaned in pain, but his life had become meaningless. The lieutenant grabbed him by the shirt and picked him up, only to punch him in the stomach. It was like a feeding frenzy among sharks, all of whom smelled blood and joined in, mindless of any sense of humanity. They beat him without mercy, beat him with pleasure, laughing at their victim, seeing him only as subhuman slime, and they continued to beat him, over and over, until finally, he died.

When they were done, they turned to Benvenuto, who was bent over, crying.

"Feeling left out, Jew lover?" The lieutenant slapped him on the side of the head. Then Ben felt a fist slam into his lower back, maybe on one of his kidneys. And they proceeded to beat him, too, but they didn't beat him up quite as badly as they did Emil. Part of that may have been because Italians were German allies, and they were being kind to him. Or it could also have been that they were just too tired from the beating they just gave to Benvenuto's long-time friend. He could feel the blood running from his nose, and one eye was swollen shut, but surprisingly, his teeth all felt intact. As for the rest of his body, he thought it could not be any better than if a train had hit him.

"Throw him in the truck," their leader said. "Since he is an Italian alley, he can work for us. Colonel Heisinveld says he wants healthy captives to help out in Germany with our war efforts, and I will bet this Jew lover cannot wait." The others laughed as they lifted Ben off the floor and dragged him outside, where they threw him into the back of a transport truck.

Nine

Medicine for the Soul

By the time they hobbled into the farm, both Yevgenia and Jerzy were exhausted and could barely stand. Although his farm had not been touched by the invasion, Uncle Frydryk had been aware of the rumors from days before, and later heard the explosions and artillery. He was a veteran and knew what was happening, so he was not afraid so much as wary... he had fought the Germans once before, in the Great War, but he was older now, and this was a different kind of war. It was unbelievably fast. Faster than anything he ever experienced.

Hearing the approach of someone on his front porch, Frydryk instinctively grabbed his old army rifle and cautiously approached the window, from the side. He slid the curtain aside just enough to peer through the opening, tightening his grip on the rifle, which had served him well in years past. What he saw though, instead of Nazis approaching, was his own family from Lublin, looking the worst for wear. Quickly putting the rifle down to rest against the wall, he pulled the door open and ran unto the porch. There were hugs and more hugs, and Jerzy's uncle held the boy's shoulders at arm's length, taking a good look at this nephew, whom he had not seen since Jerzy ran away from home when his mother died. How in the world that little boy had ever found this farm when only five years old was beyond Frydryk. Only his beloved sister could have produced such a lad. He shook his head with wonder and amazement.

"Where are my manners? Please, come in, Yevgenia... Jerzy... come in and sit by the fire. You must be half frozen." He looked around, confused. "Where are Ruslan and Kaspar?"

Jerzy looked down, but Yevgenia began to weep. "They killed Ruslin, those bastards. He never hurt a fly, my baby, and they killed him, like he was nothing. But he was something... he was braver than all of those Nazi bastards put together."

"Oh my God," he said.

"Papa stayed behind, Uncle Frydryk," said Jerzy.

Frydryk nodded to the boy, closed his eyes and sighed. "I am so sorry, Yevgenia." He knew about her first son, and even though he could imagine her anguish, he struggled nevertheless to find words of comfort for her.

She just stared off into space, sobbing, and numb to her present surroundings.

"Please, both of you sit down and take off your shoes. I cannot believe you walked the entire way."

As they removed their footwear, Frydryk saw the skin from their broken blisters mixed with small puddles of blood inside their well-worn shoes. He shook his head and got up to bring them each a basin of water in which to soak their feet. He mixed this with some black tea to slow the bleeding. Then feeling a chill in the air, he noted the dwindling flames in the fireplace, and added more logs. The crackling of the wood was soothing in the quiet room. They all sat, just staring off into the emptiness.

The uncle was a kindly man who sported short white whiskers that were betrayed by his darker eyebrows. But the brows held a few long white strands which would soon enough spread. His shirt was buttoned to the neck, and even the wrinkles that graced his forehead and around his gentle eyes... his father called them laugh lines... could not hide the loving soul behind them.

There was a rustling on the porch, followed by a knock on the door. It was more refugees, seeking shelter. Frydryk accepted without question all who came for safe shelter, away from the brutal Nazi onslaught, and they gratefully slept in the barn, or anywhere else they could find an unoccupied spot. But in the morning, they moved on, not knowing where they were going, just understanding on a gut level that they would know it was the right place when they got there.

Jerzy and Yevgenia stayed, making this their new home. All Frydryk asked for in return for a roof over their heads and food in their bellies was some was help with the chores, which they gratefully provided, after the time it took for their feet to heal somewhat.

* * *

Back in Lublin, six-year-old Karina Zajac sat crying on the floor of their small attic, staring at the space where a brick wall used to be. Now there was just rubble and one hell of a view, along with the bodies of her mother and father who had been watching the war from the only window up there. Unknown to Karina, the floor she sat on was beginning to sag badly.

* * *

Rich Wolski stood in the open doorway of his tailor shop, hands holding the sides of his head as he stared at the carnage. One window had dropped down at an angle, like the Tower of Pisa, and debris lined the sidewalk outside his business. Even his overhead sign had come crashing down.

All he could think of, was, Who is going to clean up this mess?

* * *

Boguslaw's mother, Henryka Owiti, the only bright spot in his life, never got to see more than a few hours of WWII. Her husband beat her to death because a button fell off his shirt.

76

* * *

Twenty-four-year-old Krystyna Rutecki was at home, delivering her first baby when the attack began. One bomb fell right outside the bedroom, killing both the midwife and her husband who was bringing water. Krystyna delivered the baby herself, cut the umbilical cord, and cleaned the child as best she could. Afterward, she and her baby lay clinging to one another throughout the rest of the initial invasion.

* * *

After the fighting had stopped, any people found on the streets, even if they were trying to leave the city, were searched by Nazi soldiers, many of whom took an especially long time frisking the beautiful young ladies. Anyone trying to stop them was shot immediately, and the girls forcibly taken away to more private locations.

* * *

One man was hanged right outside the doorway to his home, and his body left there. A week later, he was still there. A sign was attached to his belt; it said only one word: Judas.

* * *

For Jerzy and Yevgenia, life on the farm was like medicine for the soul. The hours of toil were long, sore, and heavy hearted, but this helped Jerzy to forget some of the guilt he carried with him constantly.

The boy learned how to feed and yoke the oxen, turn the soil and rotate the crops, depending on the acidity or alkalinity of the earth. And he learned how to care for the few cows his uncle owned. Eventually, he could even predict the weather just by feeling the tightness of the spring in his dark, curly hair. His uncle had been watching him.

"Jerzy, you seem to understand about the crops better than most people. How is it that you know so well without growing up on a farm?" he asked.

"When I was in school, Uncle, we had a science teacher who understood that many of us were poor, so he would teach us all about growing food. He brought in many different kinds of seeds for us to plant. There were tomatoes and cucumbers and squash, and he gave us some potatoes and carrots and each one of us had a little space of our own in a garden in the woods just outside the school. And whatever plants grew first, we would bring them into class and we would study them. We learned all about how they reproduced and which vegetables used up what minerals in the soil and about why the crops had to be rotated. But the best part came when we had finished learning about any of them... he let us eat our studies." The boy smiled with the memory.

"That is a good man," Frydryk said. "I would love to meet him some day."

Jerzy nodded.

* * *

On Sundays, the boy's job was to care for his uncle's two horses. And Jerzy immediately discovered a difficulty that drove him crazy—any time he held one horse to clean it, or brush it, or do anything else with it, the other horse ran off. This happened no matter which one he held. He wanted to ask his uncle how he got the horses to cooperate, but he did not want him to think he was an idiot, so instead, Jerzy just sat down and stared at the beasts. Unfortunately, the longer he stared, the dumber he felt. But inspiration had not given up on him totally. He remembered a movie he had seen when he and a friend snuck into the theater one day. It was a Tom Mix film, one of his favorite westerns, and in this movie, Tom had used a rope to tie someone up.

Jerzy laughed. "Of course," he said.

That next weekend, Jerzy spoke to one of the horses. "Well now, Mr. Horse, if I do this right, you just may not think that running away is such a good idea." Then he took the rope he had brought with him and proceeded to wrap the animal's two front legs together, below the knees, then above them, then below them again, then above them again. Not too tight, but not too loose, either. He figured that just the front legs would be enough.

And he watched that horse carefully, determined to not let him run away again.

Sure enough, as soon as he grabbed the reigns of the other horse, the one he tied up tried again to run away, but this time it was different... the mighty horse had to hop like a big rabbit. The creature snorted and dipped his head low, only to rear way up high, as though he was going to come down again slamming his front hooves hard onto the ground in an effort to break free of his binds, but that did not happen. No matter what that horse did, he could not free himself, and it did not take too may hops before he tired of being the farm's biggest bunny.

Jerzy heard a chuckle and turned around, where his uncle was holding his stomach, laughing behind a large pine tree.

"Nephew, I wondered how you were going to handle those beasts. They can be as stubborn as mules, and just as persistent, but I guess they finally met their match." He looked seriously at his nephew.

"I am proud of you."

Jerzy smiled and his chest stuck out.

"Just be sure you put that rope back when you are finished," Frydryk said.

And so it was that Jerzy slowly became a Polish cowboy.

But not every job brought him a sense of accomplishment. His most difficult lesson in that place was in what should have been the easiest job there... learning how to milk a cow. It looked simple, but every time he sat down on the stool, he would come up dry. Instead of doing her job, that cow would turn her head and look back at him with those huge eyes as though wondering about Jerzy's mission on Earth.

"Miss cow, I have tried everything," he said, sitting back on his milking stool. "I talk to you. I sing to you. I promise you extra food if only you will cooperate. I pat you like a dog. I even beg, and I hate to beg, but every time, every single time I pull on those useless udders of yours, all I ever get for my trouble is dust. And I know you have not dried up—my uncle can milk you on any day with ease... you are just a stubborn cow who does not like me, that is all."

The cow, which was watching him intently as he spoke, blinked once, turned her head to the front, and then raising her head, gave a great big moo, as though agreeing with his assessment.

* * *

In general, the pace of life on the farm was slow, conversations were minimal, and they worked hard, from dawn to dusk. There was no theater, no newspaper, and no radio.

The leaves fell, and they became accustomed to their new lives. The Nazis bothered them very little, partly because the farm was in an isolated location, but mostly because the German army collected most of the crops on a regular basis and they saw no reason to harass the farmers.

Hiding whenever any German officials were nearby, Jerzy felt helpless. He did much thinking there, now starting to regret that he could not go back to school.

Often he would lay down under a tree, just looking up at the clouds and pondering what kind of future he had to look forward to, thinking about his home in Lublin, wondering who was still alive and who was not, whether the school would ever reopen, worrying about how his Papa was doing... and he was sad with not knowing.

Early one day, about six months after Poland had been invaded, Frydryk looked intently at his nephew, as though coming to a decision.

The boy saw him staring and was certain he was in trouble for something. Perhaps I forgot one of my chores, or maybe I am going to be thrown out for not getting any milk from that stupid —

"Jerzy... I am going to take the horses and wagon into town this morning for the open market. Would you like to tag along?"

The boy's eyes grew large.

"Are you serious? Yes, please, I am soooo bored... let us go right now. Can we? Please?"

"Yes, yes, we will leave, just as soon as your stepmother finishes packing a lunch for us. Now let me tell her to pack an extra meal while you get the horses harnessed and the wagon ready."

Jerzy had just finished cinching the last harness when Yevgenia brought them a basket with sandwiches and drinks.

"Be careful," she said. She always said that, as though it was a law of some kind. "And do not forget your hats. It looks like it may rain." She handed each of them their hats.

They climbed up on the buckboard and Frydryk flicked the reigns to get the horse moving. The other horse was tied to the back of the wagon. It was a nice, leisurely pace, with only the gentle clippity-clop of the hooves to listen to, and the quiet was soothing. As they rode, Jerzy became lost in his private thoughts of growing up... he would be seventeen soon, but his world had been flipped upside down so quickly... and of course he thought about careers and girls, wondering if he would ever get the chance to experience either, and he was so immersed in his daydreaming and so comfortable in his inner world that the need for chit-chat became unnecessary. Frydryk, too, was lost in thought as he often was on these trips.

As downtown of Urszulin approached, Jerzy began to take notice of his surroundings. It reminded him of his home in Lublin, only smaller. This was where his biological mother was born. He tried to remember her, but it was becoming more difficult as he grew older.

When they reached the center of town, they pulled the wagon over, and just sat there, waiting. Jerzy looked at his uncle, but knew better than to question him. After a short time, a man walked over to them. Pointing to the horse in back, he said, "Hi, folks. That creature for sale?"

Looking at Jerzy, Frydryk said in a low voice, "No matter what happens, just let me do all the talking."

Jerzy slowly nodded, not sure what his uncle was going to do.

"Could be," he answered the stranger.

The man slowly walked over to the horse, checking him out from top to bottom, carefully examining his mouth and pulling the gums away to see all his teeth, then checking his stomach and legs, and even looking under his tail. Jerzy had no idea what the man expected to find there that might be a surprise.

Finally, without taking his eyes off the horse, the man asked, "How much?"

Frydryk looked very seriously at the creature and said, "That is much horse, but for just ten dollars, he can be all yours."

The man was outraged. "There is no way I will give you that kind of money for this sad creature," he yelled. And he carried on, raising all kinds of hell, and when Frydryk said nothing, the man walked off in a huff.

Jerzy just looked at his uncle, but the older man was not bothered in the least.

A little while later, the potential buyer returned. "I will tell you what. Even though I would be taking a loss, I will give you five dollars for this broken animal." He punctuated this by then slapping Frydryk's hand.

Frydryk just shook his head sadly. "This is a fine specimen, and I am selling him only because I need the money to build a new barn. But I will tell you what... you seem like a nice person, so for you alone, I will let this beautiful animal go for only nine dollars."

At this, the man took off his hat and threw it on the ground, yelling that there was no way he was going to let himself be robbed like that, and he again stomped off in anger.

But, Frydryk remained undisturbed, and again, the buyer returned later.

"Six dollars, and not a penny more," he said.

"Eight dollars, and you walk away with the best horse in town."

After three more trips back and forth, the two men finally agree on a price of seven-fifty, whereupon they shook hands, had a smoke together and went into the tavern to celebrate the sale with a drink.

Afterward, Frydryk and his nephew rode home slowly, basking in the afterglow of excellence. It was a good day. No greed, no contract, no taking advantage of anyone... just the satisfaction of a job well done, leaving everyone room to brag afterward.

Ten

Colonel Heisinveld

It had been a long time since Colonel Wolfgang Heisinveld had been in Germany and he expected it to have changed, but unlike the vivid destruction experienced by the rest of Europe, the physical changes here were more than inspirational... they left one with a sense of awe.

The architecture alone was magnificent, reminding him of drawings and photos he had seen, hinting at the size and splendor of the greatest of ancient cultures such as Rome and Egypt. He saw Nazi flags everywhere, with the power of the bold swastika proudly declaring its might to the world, just beneath the glorious German eagle, reminding the citizens every day of the grandeur, the magnificence they were now a part of. The pride of being a German citizen glowed inside of the Colonel, burning within him like an eternal flame. Hitler's fervent speeches, the huge military parades, fantastic new weaponry—all larger than life, making him so incredibly proud to be a Nazi, to be a part of this rebirth, this emergence of Germany's Golden Age. And so it was.

After all, does not Germany lead the world in modern warfare techniques? The blitzkrieg was a German invention, as were the V1 rockets and the widespread use of chemical warfare. Our technology is second to none, leading the world, as does our precision. Ingenuity at its best, and this is just the beginning, he thought.

The sun was just coming up as the Colonel stood in front of the Farbenfabriken Bayer chemical factory in Leverkusen, and he marveled at its size and complexity, a monumental testament to German imagination and drive. It was a symbol, not only of the will to live, but of the will to dominate, to reign supreme.

Heisinveld began to walk down the street. The city had not yet come to life, but on this cold morning, the warm glow of the early morning sky called out an invitation that was hard to resist.

Herr Hitler... a man after my own heart, he thought.

He walked on thoughtfully, hands clasped behind him, his chin held high, his chest inflated. Even his monocle seemed to sparkle brighter.

All the rest of Europe had felt the roar of Germany... in city after city he saw collapsed buildings from Nazi bombings, rubble everywhere, some buildings still burning, bodies being carted off for burial elsewhere, and people crying. Like animals, they did not have the capacity to understand that it was all necessary and unavoidable; a new world order was being born after all, and the death throes of the old regimes were normal and to be expected.

Heisinveld closed his eyes and realized he was living a dream. He inhaled deeply and was filled with the soul of a new Germany, his patriotic heart beating with a rhythm he could march to forever. He breathed it in and felt it was all as it should be. It was destiny.

And now, because of his commitment and success in reorganizing Lublin, Colonel Heisinveld's new orders brought him here, where he was to bring in some new Polish workers and reinforce security. Production was lagging, and with so many foreigners, there was fear of saboteurs among them.

But he also knew that he must be ever cautious, for he, Colonel Wolfgang Heisinveld, would have the distinct honor of answering directly to Himmler, himself, and every precaution needed to be taken to assure success. Mistakes were inexcusable... and deadly.

"Enjoying the day, Colonel Heisinveld?" asked another Colonel who was approaching from behind. Heisinveld turned and looked intently at the stranger, wondering how the man knew his name, cocking his head to one side in an attempt to see if a different angle might make him more recognizable.

The stranger laughed. "Forgive me, Herr Colonel. It is the monocle that gives you away. I am Colonel Heinz Rupprath, Kommandant of the Farbenfabriken Bayer complex you are looking at, and I have been expecting you."

Relief washed over Heisinveld. "Ahhh, a pleasure, Colonel," he said, then shook hands. He again turned to the buildings, leaning forward and placing both hands on the railing in front of him. "A magnificent enterprise... I am truly awed, Herr Kommandant."

Colonel Rupprath beamed. "I have enjoyed running this operation, but I am concerned. Have you had a chance to read my last report?"

"I have read it, and I find myself wondering what could possibly have produced such a sudden change in your production output. Do you have any ideas?"

"At first, I found myself thinking that perhaps there were hidden saboteurs among our workers. But there has been no sign of such activity, and in all honesty, I do not think any of them are capable, so now I am thinking that perhaps it is just the stupidity of the more recent slave laborers we are importing," said Rupprath. These foreigners are all so inferior, don't you think?"

"Of course... but now I am curious. Do you find them more unable or more unwilling to do the work?"

"They are just too ignorant, if you ask me," said the Kommandant. "And their attitude is deplorable. Very lazy, even dirty. They take no pride in their work whatsoever."

"Perhaps. But if I may ask, what determines who is assigned to what job?"

"Needs, Colonel. At first, we just placed them anywhere, but six months ago, because of labor shortages, we began placing the newest arrivals where they were most needed. But you see the results."

"And that was when your production levels began to fall?"

"Yes, yes... do you see?"

"Then we must change that method of placement immediately."

"By putting them where they are not needed?" said Rupprath. "That makes no sense at all."

"Herr Kommandant, let us start with basics. I will soon be bringing in many young workers from Poland. But I first will be screening them in accordance with the kind of work they have been doing there, and their success, or lack of it. Instead of merely placing any person to do whatever jobs you need, as before, I would like to begin by changing the placement process, emphasizing an alignment of each worker's skills with your specific needs. Those with mechanical skills and experience, for example, will be assigned to mechanical duties. Those better suited for physical labor will be assigned to those types of work, plumbers will work on pipe maintenance, and so on. This will give the workers more knowledge, hence more confidence in their jobs, along with enough satisfaction to help in avoiding stupid job-related mistakes while simultaneously speeding up production."

The kommandant's face lit up. "Yes, of course," he said. "How did I not see that?"

"Can you give me a list of all the jobs here, along with a description of each one?"

"I will see to it right away, Herr Colonel. Is there anything else I can get for you?"

Heisinveld just smiled. "Just get me the kind of production that will make our Fuhrer's eyes light up with delight, Herr Kommandant," he said. "I will supply the rest."

Eleven

Mr. Roszkowski's Pigeons

When the German occupation of Poland was complete, Yevgenia went back to her husband in Lublin, but she insisted that Jerzy stay on the farm, for his own safety. What she really wanted, though, was time alone with her husband.

The first snow had fallen, but it was just a dusting, yet it made the world look fresh again, as though it had been born anew. Jerzy missed his Papa terribly, but he got along well with his Uncle Frydryk, and he still carried guilt over the death of his brother, so he did not object to his stepmother going alone.

By spring of 1941, Jerzy had been living at the farm long enough that it began to feel like his home, until one special evening when he was sitting by the fireplace, watching the flames flicker, and was quietly enjoying the rich aroma of the freshly burning wood when the front door opened. It was Kaspar.

"Papa," Jerzy said, jumping up and running to hug his father. "I have been so worried about you."

They hugged each other tightly.

"You have nothing to worry about, son," Kaspar said. "In fact, I am working again. I am now a fire engineer," he said, his chest puffed out. There was pride in Kaspar's voice... "Ah, to finally have a job again. It is what a man was meant to do... to provide for his family. When a man cannot do this, he feels incomplete, like he is less of a man. It is like being a lion that cannot roar"

Jerzy noted that his father now stood straight. It had been a long time.

"Hello, Kaspar," said Frydryk, who also had arisen to greet him. They hugged, whacking each other hard on the back or the shoulder in that odd display of masculinity all men must demonstrate to differentiate their hugs from those of the weaker sex, then sit down. "Good to see that you are still in one piece. I hear things are pretty rough in Lublin."

Kaspar swallowed, not knowing where to even begin.

"Papa, have you heard from any of my friends?" said Jerzy. Right then, the burning wood in the fireplace crackled loudly, as though to accent the importance of his question. The two looked long and hard at each other.

"Kaspar," Frydryk said, "... you look as though you are wrestling with your thoughts. Jerzy has already seen much death and destruction. Perhaps it would be best to be truthful."

Kaspar looked at Jerzy carefully. "Your friends are alright, son," Kaspar said, "...except for Gerwazy. Those Nazi sons of bitches have been taking our young men to send back to Germany for slave labor. Gerwazy was called for this, but because he had no father, he was worried about his family surviving without him to provide for them." Kaspar slowly sat down again, as did his son, who was silent for a moment. "He knew that the inductees needed to be checked by a doctor before being sent to Germany, and another friend, I do not know his name, advised him to fail the physical. They told him that all he had to do was make a beverage, like tea, out of tobacco and hot water, then drink it the night before the exam." Kaspar looked off in the distance, his eyes beginning to tear up. "He did this, and when he went to be examined, he had developed a fever, so he was sent home. His family was so happy... but later that night, his fever got worse.

Much worse. And the next day... the next day, he died." Kaspar looked at his boy.

Jerzy said nothing; he did not have to. His pain was in his eyes.

"I am sorry, son. He was a good friend to you, and I hate to bring such bad news, but I think this is an omen from God, a warning. Jerzy, those Nazi bastards are still looking for more of our boys to send to Germany. You must remain here, with your uncle. Stay hidden... at least for a while longer."

Jerzy cried. He cursed God and cried for the loss of his friend; he cried for the loss of his brother; and he cried for the loss of his freedom. He sobbed until he was empty, then cursed God again, not understanding why good people had to die like this.

Days became weeks, and weeks became months. One morning in the autumn, Yevgenia came to the farm for a visit, looking weary, maybe even scared, and the boy overheard her talking to his uncle in the kitchen.

"Kaspar is in trouble, Frydryk. The Nazis have been badgering him to tell them where Jerzy is hiding, and he always says he does not know, but he thinks they suspect otherwise." Yevgenia grabbed his arm with both hands, eyes pleading. "You were a soldier and understand these things. Are they going to kill Kaspar?"

Jerzy stood by the doorway, and was sure his heart skipped a beat. How could he continue to stay on the farm, knowing this?

Frydryk stared at her terrified face, knowing that nothing he could say would help her climb out of the deep pit of despair she was trapped in. All he could do was draw her in closer and hug her while she sobbed.

Jerzy knew that he could no longer hide. His innermost thoughts had always been a good companion, but now they lashed out at him for thinking only of himself. He was scared to die, but he knew deep inside that that only he could save his father's life.

That evening when he and his uncle were alone Jerzy told him they needed to talk.

"Uncle Frydryk, I must go back to Lublin. I miss Papa badly."

"We all miss him, Jerzy, but you heard what he told you."

"No. Uncle, you were an officer in the Polish Army, and you know that any soldier or saboteur caught hiding will be executed, along with his entire family."

"You do not have any papers, Jer—"

"Then I will get some," he said. "But in the meantime, do you honestly think I am safer here with you? A decorated military veteran? No, I have made up my mind, Uncle. I am going back... with or without your approval."

Frydryk looked around the room, as though help would come from somewhere... anywhere. He knew the boy was right, but he was torn between the promise he made to Kaspar to protect Jerzy, and his nephew's needs.

"Alright," he finally said. "You want to take on a man's obligations, so I will treat you like a man. Go saddle up one of the horses. We will ride into town together. I will drop you off just outside the city, and bring the horse back here afterward. You will then be on your own."

Jerzy hugged his uncle quickly, then turned and ran to saddle the horse before Uncle Frydryk changed his mind.

They left when darkness fell, riding all through the night, quietly and slowly, often going through the woods that bordered the main roads so as not to attract any undue attention. The night was still, the air foggy. It was exciting to finally be doing something, yet it was also sad, for the boy had grown close to his uncle. When they arrived, Frydryk stopped his horse. Jerzy, who had been riding in the rear position, climbed down. The sun was just thinking about rising... it was that small space between the night and early dawn, and they could hear the city slowly coming to life.

"Be well, Uncle, and thank you for everything." He spoke quietly, almost whispering.

"Take care of yourself, Jerzy... and remember, stay hidden until you get papers. May the angels go with you."

The boy nodded, lightly slapping the horse's flank, and watched as his uncle turned and disappeared into the early morning mist. Sighing, he turned, and walked into town, keeping to the alleys and hidden paths he had learned so well in his youth, and being especially careful to not show himself on the streets. The soldiers were everywhere, and Jerzy began to wonder if he had not made a mistake in coming back after all. But then he remembered what he had overheard about the Nazis pressuring his father to tell them where his son was. He could only guess what they would do to his father if they discovered he was lying.

"No more... I cannot go on letting Papa risk his life over me," he said. "I just hope they do not catch me."

It was right then that Jerzy saw someone coming out from the back door of the automobile repair shop to put something in a trash bin. He ducked quietly behind some nearby bushes, watching carefully. He did not even dare to breathe. But then the person turned, and in the moonlight, he could see the features of his best friend, Nikodemos.

"Nik," he whispered loudly from behind the bushes. "Nik... over here." He waved his arms wildly.

Nik saw him.

"Jerzy, is that really you?" He grinned from ear to ear, looked around, and ran over to greet his lifelong friend.

Nik was only seventeen, the same age as Jerzy, yet, because he had started working part time, a year before the invasion, he was already repairing automobiles like a professional. European cars had been coming in, damaged from the war, and the job was no easy thing because spare parts just did not exist, so the mechanics here had to manufacture all their own parts. Everything.

"Nik, you look great."

"Missed you, my friend. Oh, I am so happy to see you again. So happy to see you are alive and well."

"Thanks. My father told me about Gerwazy."

He looked in his friend's face for a reaction, but Nik merely looked down at the ground and nodded.

"Nik, I miss my father very much, and you and our friends, and I want to stay here, but I have no idea of how to do this. Do you know of a way to get papers and a good place to hide in the meantime?"

"Jerzy, I would love for you to live here again, and do you know what? Your timing is excellent. We need a new mechanics' helper to work here." He looked at Jerzy and scratched his head. "Of course, without experience, you would have to start off by just carrying around the mechanics' toolboxes for them and watching to learn how to repair stuff, so the pay is not so high, but as you learn, you can advance, and I am sure that with the promise of a full-time job here, we can get your papers made right away. If you are interested in this, I will vouch for you, so there should be no problem."

"Oh boy, that would be so fantastic. Are you sure, Nik? I do not want to get you in any trouble."

"How could I say no to my best friend ever?"

Jerzy grabbed his hand, pumping it up and down, almost maniacally. "Oh Nik, thank you so much."

Nikodemos added his other hand atop Jerzy's.

"You do not have the job yet," he said, smiling as he spoke. "But come back first thing tomorrow morning and I will tell you how it goes."

Jerzy left the way he had come, making his way back to the building he grew up in, the place he always thought of as his nest. He probably thought of it that way because of his old neighbor, Mr. Ruszkowski, who raised pigeons. The man even looked like a pigeon. Ruszkowski had a prominent nose and his eyeglasses were huge, each lens like a thick window. And he was old and balding on top, with gray hair on the sides and even in his eyebrows, but he had the most contagious grin that Jerzy had ever seen.

His pigeons kept him young... they were like his babies. Calling them high-flyers, he kept all his birds in a large wooden crate on his flattop roof, and allowed Jerzy to help him each day after school.

The boy remembered one day in particular... Mr. Ruszkowski had just released one of the birds, when suddenly the old man froze, pointing to another bird in the sky.

"Jerzy... Jerzy, watch this," he said, pointing upwards. "That, my boy, is a hawk," he said, still pointing with one hand while shielding the sun from his eyes with the other. "Watch what he does."

While the boy watched, Mr. Ruszkowski elbowed him.

"See how that hawk just flew under the pigeon, Jerzy? He is flying in small circles, but he is flying higher and higher each time, forcing the pigeon to also go higher."

When the birds were so high they could barely be seen, the hawk shot out, away from the other, and when it had gone far enough, it turned, and that hawk then flew back at full speed, charging at the now defenseless pigeon with a single-minded devotion to its primeval hunt, pure instinct, raw and savage, yet also beautiful... like a dance of the universe preparing to explode in a crescendo of life and death.

And then, impact. The feathers flew out in every direction, and Jerzy just stared in wide-eyed wonder. The boy thought Mr. Ruszkowski would be upset over the loss of one of his treasured birds, but instead, he merely said softly and with awe in his voice, "That, Jerzy, is the natural world."

* * *

And now the sun had risen, and the boy was carefully returning to his own nest, even while the Nazis were still hovering over the streets, not unlike the hawk that hunted Mr. Ruszkowski's pigeon so long ago. The boy was anxious, but moved quietly.

And suddenly, there it was... the house he knew so well. Many repairs had been made, but even broken, it was the most beautiful sight he had ever seen.

When he thought the way was clear, he slowly meandered to the back door, but unlike in the days of his youth, the door was locked.

"Crap," he said. His father must be at work already, but where was Yevgenia? He did not dare knock for fear of attracting unwanted attention. "It would be hell to get caught now," he said. Before the invasion, people always left their doors unlocked... apparently trust was no longer in the air. Looking around, Jerzy wondered what he could do to while away the hours until his father returned.

Then he remembered the old fishing hole. It was in the woods, and it was isolated. Perfect, he thought. No matches, but it is just as well. If I started a fire, the smoke would probably be seen and I would be caught, so this is best. A little hunger will not kill me; after all, I am no stranger to this. When he got there, he sat at the edge of the pond, skipping an occasional pebble across the surface and watching the sunlight dance on the ripples. It was even quieter here than on the farm, and he found it soothing. Every now and then he spotted a huge, lazy catfish swimming near the surface.

"Mr. Fish, this is your lucky day," he said.

When the sun finally started to go down, Jerzy walked back to the house, again staying off the streets, and again approaching it from the rear. The door was still locked, but this time he knocked, lightly, just in case. No answer. He knocked again, a little louder. He heard the latch click, and the door opened just enough for the eye inside to look out.

Then the door suddenly flew open, and Kaspar, recognizing his son, grabbed the front of his shirt and pulled him inside quickly, shutting the door behind him and latching it securely.

"Jerzy," he said while hugging him. Then he pulled away, grabbing his son by the shoulders and shaking him. "Are you crazy? What in the world are you doing here?"

"Listen, Papa... I know about the Germans threatening you for hiding me, so I am going to stay here."

"Jerz-"

"Papa, please listen. I have seen Nik, and he is going to get me a job in the garage where he works. Once I start, I will get papers and I will be able to stay here and the Germans will leave you alone."

"You damned fool," he said. But he looked again at his son, and for the first time, he saw him as a young man, accepting a man's responsibilities. And he hugged him again.

"Where is Yevgenia, Papa? Is she alright?"

"She went to stay with her sister for a while. Things have been difficult with us."

"Well maybe now that I am back, the Germans will leave you alone and things will get better."

"Maybe," Kaspar said. And he looked at Jerzy thoughtfully. "I am so happy to see you again, son. But you must stay hidden until you have papers. This is very serious."

The boy looked around. He saw that some indoor repairs had been made from the bombing, but the building was not in the same condition as before the war. But then so much of the city was rubble when he left. He said nothing. "It is so good to be home, Papa... to finally be with you again." Kaspar grinned.

"Are you hungry?"

"Starving... I have not eaten all day."

They went into the kitchen and Kaspar heated up some leftover soup. After Jerzy had filled himself, they both decided that it would be best to shut off the lights and go. No sense inviting trouble.

The next morning, Jerzy flew out of bed before dawn and walked unseen to the garage even before it opened, and he waited in the early sunrise in the bushes behind the building for his best friend to arrive. Hearing someone approach, Jerzy was about to stand when something stopped him. Peering in the direction where he heard the footsteps, he could finally make out the figure of a German officer emerging from the early morning mist. Walking next to him was somebody he had not seen or even heard from in a very long time... someone he did not want to see ever. It was Boguslaw Owiti. He and the Nazi continued on past the garage, laughing like old friends. Boguslaw was dressed in a suit jacket, complete with hat and tie, looking the part of a highly successful businessman.

They stopped not more than six feet from the bush Jerzy hid behind, and both men looked around, as though somehow knowing he was there. Jerzy trembled. Finally, they walked on, again talking to each other... something about production.

Ten minutes after they left, Nikodemos finally arrived, the first worker there, and as soon as he opened the back door, Jerzy looked around, and seeing no one else, he ran inside.

"Nik, please tell me I have the job..." his eyes were big, pleading.

Nikodemos just stared at him with a serious face, not saying a word.

"Oh no," said Jerzy.

Finally, Nik laughed. "My friend... you are now an official mechanic, starting today. Your starting pay will be seven cents an hour." He whacked Jerzy on the shoulder in congratulations.

Jerzy breathed again, and hugged his longtime friend in gratitude. He could not believe his good fortune... seven cents an hour... he felt that he had finally hit the big-time. He would give most of his pay to his family for room and board, and maybe even buy his father a pouch of tobacco on occasion.

And so it was that Jerzy began his new craft. All was right with the world.

Twelve

Ekaterina

Sixteen-year-old Ekaterina Ivanovich Tikhonova had never had a boyfriend, so she was enthralled when Viktor asked to see her early last month. They went to school together, and he was the most handsome boy there; she could not believe her good fortune. They had been keeping company since then, but for a teenage girl living from one emotional moment to the next, a month was a supremely long time.

Viktor Roman Aleksandrov was eighteen, a tall young man with wavy brown hair piled high atop his head, as though he was wearing a permanent hat, brown eyes to match the hair, and a strong body from working on his father's farm. His ears poked out a bit at the top, but that was easily overlooked because of his other fine qualities.

Everybody knew that he had some experience with girls. He bragged about it often enough, but Ekaterina did not care, for she knew how men were, and she loved him with all her heart. Besides, she knew that he loved her as well, and she could not wait to be married so she could devote herself to him completely. To be a wife and mother was the natural way of things, and she knew Viktor would be a good provider.

Ekaterina lived with her grandfather in Minsk, where she had moved after Stalin's thugs killed her parents six years earlier, in 1935. Both parents had been college professors, and their education posed a supposed threat to Stalin's new regime, but her mother's father was merely an uneducated furniture maker, and so, not being a threat to Stalin, he was allowed to live.

The grandfather mourned the loss of his own daughter and her husband, and had endured many sleepless nights with murder in his heart, but there were so many others like him; he eventually found some comfort in their shared grief, and in his work. It also helped him greatly that he had a granddaughter to care for. She was a beautiful girl, and in many ways reminded him of her mother.

"Grandfather, please sit down. I made some nice, hot soup for you. It is getting colder outside now, and this will warm your bones," she said. He looked at her with gratitude, sunning himself in the glow of her gentle love and understanding.

Then she turned to the grandfather's loyal wolfhound, who had followed him to the table, where he laid down next to him, but it was mealtime, and the dog looked at her with hope in his big eyes. Grandfather had gotten him as a companion for his granddaughter when she first came to live with him at the tender age of twelve, and she loved that dog from the moment they first met. She was still mourning the loss of her parents, and the dog sensed her sadness, nuzzling against her in an effort to provide some comfort. He slept by her bed each evening, and his constant companionship was the difference to her between just existing within an eternal sadness, or living a life which held love and even laughter.

"Oh, come on, Korzhik, how could I forget to feed you, too?" she said. The dog thumped his tail on the floor rapidly, as though he understood, then he got up and followed her over to where his bowl sat. He was quite hungry, but also well trained. She gave the signal for him to sit, her palm up and raised, as though lifting something invisible, so he sat obediently, knowing this was a small price to pay for the juicy reward he was about to taste. Grandfather had shown her years ago how to train the dog, and she learned as fast as Korzhik.

Then she commanded him again. "Stay," she said, her vertical palm facing him, while she put his bowl on the floor, a nice bone with some meat still on it, but he looked only at her the whole time, just waiting oh so patiently, yet with great anticipation, for the word. She stared at him, paused a few moments, knowing he could smell the meat, and when she felt he had shown the proper amount of obedience, said, "Okay," and signaled with her hand that it was alright to eat now, whereupon he dove for the food like a dog possessed.

Grandfather smiled. He cherished these moments, for life had become difficult since Stalin's rule began. His own wife, Ekaterina's beloved Babushka, had died many years earlier and saw none of the suffering, nor the hardships her husband and granddaughter had to endure. He still missed her, but was glad she escaped their misery.

He finished his soup, but then put on his old sweater and jacket, for he had to go out again right away. He kissed his granddaughter on the forehead and promised to be back before sundown.

"Thank you, Sweetheart, for another wonderful meal," he said. "I will see you soon, my beautiful pateechka... my sweet little bird."

She watched him go out the door, and smiled in contentment, feeling the love of the only family she had left. She was lucky and she knew it.

Like all Russian laborers, the Grandfather worked hard and took great pride in his craft. Much of his beautiful work was carved by hand, with ornate decorations that separated his art from the plain furniture that was being mass-produced in the modern factories, and today was market day in the neighboring village, where he had gone to sell his ware. Many people knew of his beautiful furniture and were anxious to see his newest offerings. They knew he would not try to take advantage of anyone, despite the wonder of his creations.

While there, he had left Ekaterina to her chores.

She had just finished sweeping when she heard a knock on the door. Wondering who it could be, she opened it just enough to peek at the visitor.

"Viktor... what are you doing here?" She opened the door a little more... just wide enough for her head.

"Katya, I could not stay away. You haunt me — everywhere I go, I hear your voice, and your beautiful face is always on my mind. Not being with you drives me crazy."

She looked all around behind Victor. "I cannot invite you in - my grandfather is away and nobody is here but me."

"Then I shall stay for a while to keep you safe," he said, pushing the door open wide and brushing past her into the house. It was small house, but comfortable.

"Viktor, I have my chores to - "

"Just for a little while, my sweet Katooshka. Please sit with me here on the sofa for just a few moments and fill my heart with happiness." She loved him so much, and when she saw his eyes pleading with her, she could not say no.

"Alright Viktor, but just for a few minutes, then you must go."

She sat next to him, and he put his arms around her, and they hugged, whispering those words of endearment that all young lovers share.

"Katya," he said, kissing her lips deeply, then on the length of her neck, her long hair swept to one side. "You are so beautiful; you drive me crazy."

She understood what he wanted, but it was not proper now. "Oh Viktor, when we are married, I promise I will please you in every way. But we must wait until then."

He was filled with passion, kissing her and roaming with his large hands across her back, brushing the sides of her breasts, and she was on fire. She knew that she should stop him, but her feelings ran deep.

Then his hand went lower, down between her thighs, insistent on more, but she was not yet ready. They needed to be married first.

"No..." She pushed against his chest, but he would not stop, his urgency rising to the surface, getting rougher.

"No... stop. Please... STOP."

But again, he persisted. What was wrong with him?

She fought him as hard as she could, but he merely grabbed both of her wrists and held them over her head. "I will show you how a woman should be handled," he said, grinning. Some women just needed to be shown who was the boss. That is all. He lifted up her dress with his other hand, and ripped it, along with part of her undergarments.

Out of desperation now, she somehow managed to free one hand and clawed at his face, scratching him. He backhanded her face.

"Crazy bitch," he said.

"Stop it," she pleaded.

"You are crazy," he said.

He pushed her to her back, and she tried to knee him, but he was too strong for her.

All she had left was her teeth. Panicking, she bit into his arm, and this time he punched her face, bloodying her nose. But still, she would not stop writhing wildly in an effort to free herself.

Enraged now, he put both hands around her slender neck and squeezed.

Fighting for breath, her arms flailing blindly, she touched the wrought iron base of a lantern on the end table next to the sofa, and desperately grabbed it with what little strength she had left. She lunged at his head, but from the corner of his eye, Viktor saw it coming, and blocking her, he ripped it from her hands, throwing it down to the floor. She inhaled quickly and again fought, this time with her entire body, kicking, scratching, biting, whatever she could manage. Angrier than ever, he renewed his efforts to choke the life out of her. He would teach the little slut... nobody said no to Viktor.

He squeezed her throat with both hands, until she could no longer breathe. Her arms stopped flailing and froze for a moment in mid-air, dropping slowly as the lack of air took its toll. Her eyelids fluttered.

Caught up as he was in the throes of his anger, Viktor never saw Korzhik, who had been restlessly watching the struggle unfold, whining anxiously every few minutes. Finally, even though he had not received the commend, he was unable to restrain himself any longer, and silently lunged through the air like a cannonball toward the one who was hurting his young human. His instincts did not allow for thoughts of right or wrong.

Viktor had time for only a short scream and a shorter fall to the floor, where he now tried to choke the dog, but the hound would not hold still long enough to be gripped. He grabbed a handful of the dog's long hair, but that seemed only to make Korzhik angrier. Then Viktor spotted the wrought iron lamp he had just moments before thrown on the floor, but just as he was reaching to grab it, the dog saw his opening, found Victor's throat and eagerly lunged, sinking his teeth into it. The sudden spurt of blood made the dog jump back, but he was ready to lunge again if necessary. The enemy did not move.

With her tormentor finally off of her, Korzhik whined again and leaned forward to stretch out his head, anxiously licking Ekaterina's face. Her eyes snapped open and she grabbed the couch, gasping, desperately struggling to inhale in an effort to live again. She screamed the scream of one whose entire world just came undone in a matter of moments. Korzhik sat at her feet, waiting to see how she would react to what he did to the man. But hardly able to see through her tears, Ekaterina had no idea that Viktor Roman Aleksandrov was dead, his throat ripped wide open.

She struggled to stand, and holding her ripped dress together, ran out of the house, terrified, still gasping for breath in between sobs. When she was outdoors, she ran down the road, looking around for someone, anyone... but except for a few chickens and a goat, there was nobody else. The dog cautiously followed her, unsure of whether she was alright.

Not knowing where to go, she ran on, crying, gasping, and struggling to find her way through the tears until she came at last to her neighbor's small farmstead, about a half kilometer away. There, she saw the farmer's wife, Olga Mikhailovich, hanging laundry on the clothesline in back of the house. Ekaterina stumbled over to her.

Olga immediately threw her clothespins back into the half-filled laundry basket on the ground, and ran over to her bruised and crying young neighbor. "Katya, what happened to you?"

Ekaterina was sobbing too hard to answer, but when Olga saw the ripped dress, along with the bloody nose and red marks around her throat, she had a pretty good idea. She just did not know yet who to hold responsible, but she would find out, and there would be hell to pay for the filthy parasite who tried to defile this sweet young girl.

Olga cradled Ekaterina in her arms, soothing and comforting her as best she could, and as her sobs quieted down, in the emerging silence, they faintly heard the first of many distant explosions from the invading German army.

Thirteen

A Need for Revenge

The months came and went, and in that time, the boy learned about what made cars go, about the electrical and fuel systems, about the transmission and how the gears worked, the exhaust system, about the hydraulic system in the brakes, the steering linkage, and he learned many useful skills along the way, including body repair, welding, painting, and even glass repair. Making all of your own parts was an art in itself, and everything had to be precise, so it was equally a science. It was difficult, but the knowledge gained was invaluable.

Jerzy had been working at the garage for almost six months when Nik failed to show up one day. This was not right... Nik was always at work. He loved this job, and was even hoping to own the garage one day. Unknown to anyone except Jerzy, he was putting a little of his pay aside each week, hoping that someday he could buy it. Even Nik's mother did not know.

Jerzy asked around if anybody had heard from him, and finally, Jedrik Pyrzyce, another mechanic, who lived next door to Nik, said he needed to tell him something, but in private. Jedrik had been acting strangely all day, and Jerzy needed to know what was going on. They went into the supply room, where they could talk in private. Jedrik sat down, putting his face in his hands. Then he sat up straight, as though resolved to tell his story.

"Jerzy, I am scared to tell you this... it is horrible."

"What are you talking about?"

Jedrik paused, looking around first, then spoke. "Late last night, the Germans showed up at Nik's home, shouting and making all kinds of racket. The noise woke me... probably woke the entire neighborhood. So, very carefully, I peeked out the window, leaving the light in my room off so nobody could see me looking. My apartment is on the second floor, you know, so I could see and hear everything, especially at that time of the night, when everything is normally so quiet."

He looked around again to make sure no Germans were listening in the supply room. "And now, I really wish I had never woken up."

"Alright, what happened? C'mon, you know that Nik is my best friend." He had a bad feeling about this.

Jedrik stared off into the empty space in from of him, slowly shaking his head, back and forth, over and over. His lips were moving, but nothing was coming out. Jerzy angrily grabbed Jedrik by the shoulders, and shook him. Jedrik finally looked back at him, and his voice returned.

"The bastards were at his front door, Jerzy, and they were pounding on it with their rifle butts, yelling, 'ROUST... ROUST,' on top of all the banging. It was like they wanted the entire neighborhood to hear.

"When Nik opened the door, six soldiers grabbed him and took him and his mother forcibly to a nearby field, where many other citizens had been brought, men, women and children, and most of them were crying from the noise and being dragged out of bed. I could hear everything because my window was open a little bit. His mother was begging the Nazis to let her boy go, and Nik was begging them to let her go.

"Anyway, the soldiers made the men dig a long, deep trench in that big field to the left of Nik's home, you know the place, and everybody was ordered to stand in front of it."

"Oh no," Jerzy said, realizing his worst fear.

At this, Jedrik began sobbing. Jerzy patted his shoulder, waiting patiently for him to calm down enough to finish. "Nik and the others all knew what was going to happen, Jerzy, and the women started crying and begging the soldiers to let the children go, some of them were just babies, and the parents were begging, and hugging their kids."

Jedrik cried some more, then staring at the floor, took a deep breath and wiped his eyes with the sleeve of his shirt. Between sobs, he continued.

"Once everybody was lined up, a Nazi lieutenant read something aloud to those friends and family members who were brought along and forced to watch. I cannot remember the exact words, but basically, he said, 'Let it be known that last night, a brave German soldier was murdered by an unknown Polish coward. Such acts from your underground traitors have gone on long enough. From now on, beginning immediately, three hundred of you will die for every German patriot who is killed.'

"Jerzy, it was awful. A firing squad was lined up, and at the signal, Nik and the rest of them, even the young children and little babies, were butchered, without conscience and without mercy. The bullets knocked them all backwards, into the trench. Well, most of them... there was one guy who was wounded and somehow ended up sitting on the edge. He was crying, looking down at all the bodies, and one of the soldiers pulled out a pistol and walked up behind him, holding the gun about an inch from his head and pulled the trigger as though he was swatting a fly. Some of the people lay there in the trench, moaning because they were not all killed, and the soldiers walked over to the edge and fired down onto the bodies repeatedly, making sure none of them lived. And the worst part... the worst part, Jerzy, was when they were finished... some of those bastards were laughing.

"Then the Polish witnesses were told to go home and tell everyone what happened. After the crowd left, some of the Nazis went back into Nik's home and came out with some of their stuff, laughing some more and showing the others what they just got.

"And I can still smell the gunpowder, and the sound of all the mothers crying, begging for their babies' lives, and three hundred tortured souls screaming into the cold night air, and that sound, along with the sharp bang of every bullet fired echoes in my head and refuses to leave."

He paused, just staring into the emptiness in front of him. "Nik never said a word, you know? He was so brave, Jerzy, and I was so helpless... so totally helpless... and scared to death." And he sobbed again, hiding his face in his hands, his shoulders heaving.

Jerzy's fists clenched and unclenched as he listened. First his only brother, now his best friend. And for what? He wanted badly to kill the Nazis himself, he could taste his need for revenge, but his awareness that such an act would only end in the death of three hundred innocent people for each German he killed was exactly the deterrent the Nazis counted on. Besides, he did not know if he would actually have the courage to kill another human being. It was one thing, he realized to think about it. But it was quite another to be face-to face with a person and deliberately end his life. Everybody, no matter how evil, must have people who love them, people who would cry at their loss. What gave him the right? But then, if he did not, would the person whose life he spared kill him, or even worse, someone he loved?

The boy was young, but he realized the ferocity of the beast that was upon him and all of the people he cared for. It was a demon, brutal and heartless, controlling Jerzy's world, salivating at its own greed and insensitivity... but complete obeisance was Jerzy's only choice.

Fourteen

Goodbye

On the first of February in 1942, Jerzy was bleeding the brakes of a Hillman Minx, a British sedan that had seen better days. What it was doing in Poland was anybody's guess, but he had learned long ago not to ask too many questions. Lying on the cement floor under the car, Jerzy was focused on watching the brake lines for air bubbles in the fluid while fellow mechanic Idzi Warzinski sat in the driver's seat, pumping and holding down the brake pedal. The metal wrench was ice cold, but Jerzy had gotten used to this, and now paid little attention to it. Out of the corner of his eye, he saw his reflection on the toes of two spit-shined black boots standing next to his face.

"Can I help you, Sir?" Jerzy said as he slid out from under the Hillman. He found himself looking up at a German Officer, and shot to his feet immediately. "Begging your pardon, sir... I did not know..." he said, wiping his greasy hands on his overalls.

The Official was wearing his sharp and crisp dress uniform, and standing with his chin up in the air, looked important. He wore a monocle over his right eye, and had a neatly trimmed mustache. His face was stern looking... right on the edge of mean, and Jerzy thought he looked as though he smelled some bad cheese.

"Are you Jerzy Czaplicki?" he asked. His Polish was impeccable.

"Jawohl, Sir." Jerzy looked straight ahead, not daring to upset the officer before him, but he suddenly felt sweaty.

"I am Standartenfuhrer Heisinveld, a Colonel with the SS. I see that you are a hard-working young mechanic. Good... good. We need strong, capable young men like yourself.

"You are to go with the men waiting for you outside for a medical examination." He turned his head to face the window, and Jerzy's eyes followed the officer's, but one of the other mechanics walked between Jerzy and the window, so he saw nothing. "If you pass, you will be sent to Germany to aid our noble cause by working in one of our factories."

"But sir, I have —"

"Be glad, Czaplicki... this is an honor for you."

Jerzy's heart sank as his head began spinning. "Jawohl, Herr Colonel." He again looked out toward the large front window, only this time he saw three soldiers waiting outside the door.

"Well, do not just stand there... schnell, Czaplicki... SCHNELL," he said more loudly.

Jerzy quickly put his wrench down and grabbed a rag to wipe his hands as he ran to meet the soldiers who were waiting to escort him. The other mechanics heard the exchange and stared at the colonel, but when he slowly turned to meet their gaze, they quickly went back to work. One of the soldiers outside looked back through the window, and the Colonel gave him a small, almost imperceptible nod.

As Jerzy walked down the street with his three escorts, he saw that no one, other than the soldiers, would even glance at him. Perhaps they were all afraid to look, he thought. They probably figured he was going to be shot and if they were caught looking, they would be made to join him. Fear was in the air... everywhere.

One soldier walked on each side of him, a third in back, as though Jerzy was some tough cookie. Maybe they heard about his big school fight and they were not taking any chances, he thought. The idea brought a small smile to his face, but then his grin disappeared just as quickly when he realized that he could be a world champion professional boxer and that would not matter against their weapons.

Walking on, they came to the old building that was once used for public bathing, and he was ushered inside. It smelled musty now. The lights were dim, but once his eyes adjusted, Jerzy was surprised to see two of his old friends, along with about a dozen other guys around the same age. The soldiers who brought him remained outside.

"Lukasz," said Jerzy... "and Czabor... you too?"

"What is this all about?" asked Lukasz.

"They are sending us to Germany to work for them," said Jerzy quietly.

"I do not care," said Czabor. "I just hope that wherever they send us has some beautiful woman, or I will die, I swear." Jerzy rolled his eyes. Some things never changed... but he was also glad for that.

A door opened from the back of the room, and two people came out. One was a German SS officer, calling everyone over to where both of them were standing. The other was a solid older woman, maybe forty-five or fifty, stern looking, wearing a clean white medical coat. Her blonde wavy hair was formed into a neat bun on the back of her head, and her narrow-framed glasses sat halfway down her nose. Behind those glasses, her eyes were blue, but piercingly dirty and dark, as though her soul had been dipped in tar.

The officer spoke first: "Gentlemen, this is Doctor Brunhilda Kruell, and she will be giving you your medical examination." Jerzy saw that she was holding a long stick, which he thought to be a strange tool for a doctor.

"But first," said the officer, "you must remove all of your clothing."

"Everything?" asked Czabor, eyes wide.

"I said ALL... are you deaf? SCHNELL," said the officer.

After they quickly undressed, each of the boys were completely dusted with delousing powder by three soldiers. Even their faces were covered.

As they gazed at the doctor, she screamed at them, "NOW, LINE UP QUIETLY IN TWO ROWS AND LOOK STRAIGHT AHEAD." She stared at the group, as though trying to decide which of them to eat, then casually walked over to Lukasz, who was next to Jerzy, on the far-right side of the front row, and with her stick, she lifted up his genitals.

Jerzy quickly glanced at the doctor, whose eyes were now bulging out, as though threatening to leave their sockets. All he could think of was Katherine the Great, of Russian fame. He had once read a book about her, before the town library had been destroyed. According to his favorite legend, she had quite the sexual appetite. But no matter how many lovers she took, her amorous thirst could not be quenched because none of her lovers had equipment in a size large enough to extinguish her hungry flames, so in the interest of brevity, she began physically examining each new lover before going any further.

Jerzy glanced down quickly at his own equipment, wondering what the doctor might be looking for, when she saw his eyes and screamed at him to look straight ahead.

Oh crap, Jerzy thought, as she slammed her stick loudly into the palm of her other hand. She again slammed the stick into her palm, louder, and stared at him, as though daring him to move his eyes just a fraction of a millimeter. He did not dare to even blink.

Suddenly, Jerzy felt the stick slowly lifting his own privates, then almost tickling him with a few short strokes, and his eighteen-year-old body began to react in a most embarrassing way. Was she? Oh, please, God—nooo... he said to himself. He quickly began picturing all of the ugly, painful things he could think of to distract his traitorous body. She seemed to be taking an extremely long time. His eyes closed in misery, and all he could do was wait...

Oh please, God, let this stop and I will give up every bad habit I ever had, I will stop swearing, no more smoking, I swear, I will even go to church every day if that helps... please, please, and although she stopped stroking him with her stick, she continued to stare at him, as though coming to an important decision. And then without moving a muscle, she suddenly shifted her eyes to gaze at the next boy.

As she finally moved on, Jerzy almost collapsed with relief, fully intending to keep his promises to God.

When the exam was over, everybody put their clothes back on, and was told that they had all passed and would be moving on to their new assignments first thing tomorrow morning. They were to be ready and waiting here at 6:30.

* * *

His job as a mechanic had come to an end, so he walked home, lost in thought. "This is going to kill Papa," he said. "But what else can I do? If I refuse, or try to run away, the entire family is in danger. Crap, I must go... there is no choice."

Sauntering home, he looked at the other citizens walking about on their own business, and wondered what secrets they were hiding from the world. "What are they feeling?"

Finally reaching his nest, he just stood on the front stoop, staring at the door, trying to build up the courage. He slowly turned the doorknob, and entered with his head down. His father was sitting quietly in his chair, and Yevgenia, who had finally decided to return to Kaspar, was in the cooking area, peeling potatoes for supper. Surprised by his son's arrival, Kaspar looked up.

"Jerzy, what are you doing home so early? You did not get fired, I hope."

"No, Papa. Worse."

"Jerzy, take off your shoes in the house," said Yevgenia. "You know better than that. And wash your hands."

The boy just looked at her, not believing she interrupted his important news for that. Saying nothing, he removed his shoes, and took them over to be placed next to the door.

His father just stared at him, waiting to hear what could be worse.

And so the boy told his father all about Colonel Heisinveld's visit at the garage, and what he had ordered Jerzy to do. Out of embarrassment, he left out the details of the medical exam, telling him only that he had passed and was to leave in the morning. Kaspar just stared into empty space, saying nothing, but his eyes betrayed his heart. Yevgenia heard this news from the next room, and stood still, her own heart filled with emptiness. The boy who denied her and would not give the time of day to her own son--his leaving meant little to her.

Jerzy looked up at his father, but did not know what else he could say.

"Did you wash your hands?" Yevgenia asked.

Jerzy rolled his eyes upward and went to the pump outdoors to loudly wash his hands, making sure the whole world knew how clean they were.

The food was brought out to the table, and the three of them sat together silently to eat their last meal together, as a family, yet they all felt very lonely, with only their private thoughts to keep them company. As they ate, all that could be heard was the clinking of forks and knives against the porcelain dishes, and now and then, Jerzy saw the faintest sign of a teardrop threatening to leave the eyes of his father.

That night, Jerzy went into his father's bedroom to say goodbye, but Kaspar just lay there, silently. He looked at his son, yet it was as though he was staring at nothingness, unable to even speak his own goodbye. Jerzy took his father's hand in his own as he sat on the bed next to him.

"Papa, I do not wish to go, but I have no choice. This is not your fault, and it is not my fault, either. Still, it is ripping me open on the inside. Please do not be angry with me. I will always love you, and I promise to write whenever I can. I am sorry... if I do not see you in the morning... goodbye, Papa."

Jerzy could again see tears forming in his father's eyes even as he felt the water in his own. He squeezed his Papa's hand, turned and felt something deep inside of himself begin to shatter as he walked away.

Fifteen

Poor Boy's New Job

The next morning, Colonel Heisinveld, who still looked as though he was smelling bad cheese, picked up Jerzy and six of the other boys in front of the building where they had their medical exam. Neither of Jerzy's boyhood friends were in the group... apparently, they had different assignments. The boys were herded into a military convoy truck where they were then driven to the train station.

This was Jerzy's first time on a train. As he climbed aboard, he saw many other young Poles, apparently from neighboring towns. Once at the door to his assigned section, Jerzy needed to go to the bathroom right away, and was told to go between the cars, within sight of the guard, but on the opposite side from where everyone was boarding.

"Make it a good piss," the guard told him. "This is going to be a long ride, and you will not be going again."

When Jerzy returned, he quickly entered the car and saw an empty seat next to a window, and as he was squeezing through that small space in front of the two passengers between him and the window, the train started up with a lurch that caused Jerzy to lose his balance and accidentally step on the toes of a man in the middle seat.

"Ouch... be careful, you idiota," he said. He was older, maybe thirty-five or forty, dark, raggedy hair and complexion, and sporting a short goatee.

"Sorry."

The train lurched again, but this time, Jerzy managed to flop into his seat. Then the locomotive began to move in earnest... slow, lumbering moves with a pulse of its own, the wheels straining to pull the large cars, heavy with passengers, to somewhere else, some mysterious destination that only their captors knew about.

When the boy looked up, he saw Colonel Heisinveld standing at the head of the car, staring back at them. Jerzy looked away.

"Any idea where we are going?" he said to the stranger.

"Why you not just keepa you mouth closed, huh? It makes no difference... they bring us where they want, and that is that."

The boy stared at this sour grape, but he said nothing.

Gradually, the train picked up speed, and the rocking motion, along with the rhythm of the engine was soothing. Nobody spoke.

After a short while, the man sitting next to Jerzy looked down at the floor, as though lost in thought, then turned to him at last.

"I am sorry for my rudeness... this has been a distressing time for me. Recently a close friend of mine and his family were beaten and killed by these Nazi bastardi, all for nothing, and I was powerless to help them."

Jerzy nodded. "I understand," he said. "I, too, have lost people who were close to me because of these monsters."

The stranger stared at him, as though evaluating his character. "Benvenuto Lombardi," he finally said, offering his hand. "Call me Ben. My pleasure to meeting you."

Jerzy noting his accent, shook his hand. "Jerzy Czaplicki... you are not Polish."

"I come from Italy," he said. "When Mussolini sign this stupid Pact of Steel with Hitler, I decide to get out while I can. Who wants to be inna army and have people try to kill me all the time? So, I come to Poland to visit my old friend... the one I speak of earlier, when the

Nazis attack and grab us. I think maybe they want to kill me, too, but when they find out I am from Italy, they decide to let me help them in their German factories instead, like a good Italiano ally." He said this contemptuously.

Jerzy looked up and saw Colonel Heisinveld, still staring at them.

The train moved on, stopping at Warsaw to pick up more workers, then eventually continuing on to the cities of Berlin, Wolfsburg, and Cologne. A few travelers disembarked, but most of the passengers were foreigners and not allowed to leave until reaching their final destination.

The ride felt surreal. After having lived at home for the last several months, Jerzy's sense of belonging was gone again for the first time since moving to the farm, and the uncertainty that replaced it made him feel nauseous. The few friends he had were nowhere in sight, and even among so many others who shared his fate, the boy felt totally alone. Seeking comfort, he began to mentally reminisce about home, remembering every detail about the three room apartment he grew up in... all the chips and cracks in the plaster that he used to trace with his finger, the crude heating system where the house was warmed by a coal-fed fire located in a roughly hewn wall opening... the stone well in back of the house from which they would lug water in a pail to be heated atop a cast iron stove and used for washing and bathing... even the straw filled mattress he slept on and his little pillow, stuffed with pointy feathers that would poke his face until he pulled out the offenders, one-by-one. He even thought about the winter mornings when he would wake up to see a thin layer of ice on the inside of the windows, and how he would sometimes draw figures in the frost with his warm fingertips. And that would make him realize that he needed to go to the outhouse, but it would be so cold that he would shiver like crazy the whole time. It was not a rich man's home, but it was still his nest, and he loved it.

Instead of comforting Jerzy, however, the memories served only to give him a feeling of emptiness somewhere deep inside, a longing for something that should have been there, but was not. He could not recognize this new feeling... he was somewhere, yet he was nowhere. He felt suddenly old... very old, and abandoned. But the train was indifferent to all this, and it continued on its journey, gently rocking, lulling Jerzy into a badly needed sleep. He closed his eyes.

Eventually, they arrived in Leverkusen, where they were herded off the train by Colonel Heisinveld, and brought by military transport truck to a huge chemical factory. Benvenuto was still with him. They stopped in front of the main building, where they were told to get out.

"This is where you will be working," said the Colonel, gesturing toward the industrial complex, as though they could not see for themselves. "You will first be shown your sleeping quarters to put away your belongings, then brought into the work area where you will receive individual assignments." The barracks were arranged by nationality, so all of the new workers were separated into the proper groups and brought to their new homes.

"You will all later be assigned to what we feel would be the right job for you. In the meantime, you will find a bed for yourselves and put your stuff away."

The first thing Jerzy noticed was that the barracks smelled like piss and sweat, so Jerzy quickly selected a bed next to a window.

All the new workers were then marched to what the Germans called a staging area, which was basically just a large, empty room. Jerzy found that someone who looked important was waiting for them. He had his back to the new arrivals, clasping his hands behind him, and was staring blankly out one of the windows, as though sadly waiting for something.

Turning to an older worker who was there to help keep order, Jerzy quietly asked, "Who is that?"

"That, son, is the camp commander, Kommandant Rupprath, and I strongly suggest you be careful around him." Just then, the commandant turned to face the new workers.

"Why does the Kommandant look so depressed?" asked Jerzy.

"He just found out that his nineteen-year-old son is serving on the Russian front, and I guess the fighting has been pretty rough out there."

Jerzy wondered if his own father was thinking about him right now.

The commandant looked at this newest batch of workers and wondered if any of them would prove useful before they died. "Welcome to the Farbenfabriken Bayer Chemical Factory. In a little while, you will be brought, one-by-one into another room, for a personal interrogation to determine what kind of job you would be best suited for."

Jerzy raised his hand. "Sir, do we have any choice in what our jobs will be?"

The Kommandant stared hard at him, as though memorizing his every feature.

The boy swallowed hard and wished he had kept his mouth shut. But he could not undo his stupidity.

Ten minutes later, a young soldier came in calling the name of one of the new workers, and they walked out together. After just a few minutes, the soldier came back for another worker, and then another, and yet another. Finally, Jerzy was called. On the way, he asked the soldier how long he had been assigned to this job, but the soldier ignored him.

Jerzy was brought into the interrogation room, where he once again encountered Colonel Heisinveld, and thought that maybe the Colonel was watching everyone to see who should be allowed to live, so he was careful of what he said and even how he said it.

"Jerzy Czaplicki?" said the interrogator.

"Yes sir," he answered, knowing full well that they knew it was he.

"The Colonel here says that you have worked as an automobile mechanic."

"Yes sir."

"He also says that you were a good worker."

"I guess I was," Jerzy said, shrugging.

"Well, I am certain the good Colonel knows what he is talking about. And since you have a keen mechanical aptitude, I am going to assign you to a chemical quality control unit, where you will help monitor the variables that go into each mixture, such as temperature, pressure, and so on."

"Sir, I know nothing about chem —"

"YOU WILL BE TAUGHT, Czaplicki," he shouted, slamming

his fist down on his desk. "Report to work at 0700 hours tomorrow." Then he turned to the soldier at the door, and said, "Next."

Okay, that went well, Jerzy thought. He walked out to re-join the others, and after everyone had been processed, they were all brought on a tour, where he noticed that the factory workers he encountered all seemed to be subdued, as though preoccupied with something important. No joking or laughing... they just did not speak to each other. They did not even look at each other.

"What has happened to them, that rips out their very souls?" he whispered aloud.

Nobody replied, but the newcomers all looked around at the other workers more carefully now.

At the end of the tour, they were brought to a window where they formed a single line and were each given a small bowl filled with boiled sauerkraut and sauce. They were also given a tin can of coffee with their meals. Actually, they merely called it coffee... in reality, it was burned wheat. It was the closest thing they had to coffee, so they drank as much as they could, just to fill their rumbling stomachs.

That night, when his shift was over, the boy went back to his barracks, which was broken up into four sections, each of which held eighteen men, divided by nationality. In the center of each section was a large barrel-type stove, but they were not allowed to confiscate any wood. Not even scraps.

The beds were without mattresses... just boards covered by a large straw-filled potato sack. Even the pillow was filled with straw, which scratched Jerzy's raw skin. He wished he could have his pointy feathers back from the pillows of his childhood. The older workers explained that the straw was changed only once a year, so it had bugs in it, all kinds, creeping and crawling silently. And lice were every-where, even in the walls, but the worst bugs were the big, brown bloodsuckers, which swarmed on everybody and feasted every time the lights were turned off. Nobody slept that first night. Jerzy took stock of his life, short though it was, and it made no sense to him. He thought about the different creatures, and realized that each life survives by eating other lives. No exceptions. Even plants absorbed whatever the remnants of any plants and animals that died nearby. All of life continued only by nourishing itself with the dead bodies of other creatures. What kind of maniac dreamed up that one, he wondered.

* * *

When Jerzy left for work the next morning, he realized for the first time just how massive this complex was. He saw two-story-tall storage tanks on both sides of the isles. And everywhere he looked there were miles and miles of pipes, along with gauges, valves, and other gadgets whose function he could not even begin to guess.

It was as though he was inside a giant mechanical beast, a creature with veins and organs that erupted in steam and pulsating noises, alive and unfeeling, ready to do battle with any and all intruders. And the din... he became aware of a roar composed of several separate noises: the hissing of steam from the valves being opened and closed, air knocking in the pipes, chemicals slurping and whooshing from within the giant vats, the sound of large metal wrenches clanging against giant nuts and bolts, and orders being shouted in German, all merging into a cacophony of raw power, totally devoid of feeling.

Great clouds of mist floated in the highly saturated air, threatening to drown out his view of this vibrantly malignant panorama. As he rounded a corner, the boy saw that the entire factory was a crying mass of men reduced to slaves serving the machine, subordinating themselves to the mechanical exhortations of this giant beast as though it alone was worthy of being kept alive. And now he was going forward, to the heart of the creature.

Was he actually going to help these monsters who killed his brother and destroyed the only home he had ever known? If any of his friends or family back home could see him here, they would see a worm. In his imagination, he felt the scrutiny of his loved ones, and he felt more alone than ever before, cast down by his own judgment upon himself, and he tumbled headlong into an abyss of a nature he had never before known, a hole of guilt and despair that left every cell of his body in agony. He groaned from somewhere deep within and went toward his new assignment, staring in painful awe at the beast.

He thought it impossible for things to get any worse. And then he heard a voice from behind...

"Czaplicki, take a good look," said the voice, which sounded oddly familiar. Jerzy turned, his eyes wide.

"Boguslaw," he whispered slowly, his heart skipping a beat, and then he did not know what else to say, or even what to think. He noted that Boguslaw's nose was just a little bit crooked. That scared him even more. "What are you doing here?"

Boguslaw smiled. "I am your boss here, Poor Boy. Your boss," he said slowly... "How does that sound?"

How does that sound? How could that idiot cabbage have accomplished this?

Staring at his old tormentor, Jerzy could feel his heart pounding as he tried to think... he could not run, nor could he stay... crap, he was as trapped as a person could get.

Boguslaw fell in love with the moment, and turned to admire that portion of the mechanical monster he cared for. Following the gaze of his old nightmare, Jerzy turned again, staring at the complex beast. He trembled visibly, for it was threatening to devour him.

"Your past has caught up with you, Czaplicki," said Boguslaw, as though reading his mind. "We were just students then, you and I, and I had no real power. Now, though, just look at me... I run this whole part of the operation," he said, his arms outstretched, as though wanting to hug it all. "The Germans trust me, and I will not ruin that. They like me, you know? I turned in my own father to them... said he was a traitor... a Jew-lover. Just think how much more I can do with you." He snickered with delight over that thought. "But not yet." And then he smiled the smile of a cat that has just discovered a nice, juicy mouse, and he wanted to play with it for a while.

"First, let us put you to work. Those tanks you see are all used for mixing the chemicals. They might hold paint, explosives... whatever the Germans need. Your job... poor boy... will be to watch the level in this tank." He patted the side of the huge tank lovingly. "When it drops, you will turn off the valve here, go back and fill the barrel with ammonia, then turn the valve back on. Simple."

And it was simple, however, Jerzy had no mask, and the fumes choked him. "Damn that Boguslaw." Jerzy learned quickly though to hold his breath, turn off the valve, breathe, go back and fill the barrel some more, never breathing while filling, and repeat this over and over, all day long, knowing all the while that he would do this day after day after day. He never before realized just how much he took normal breathing for granted.

When the shift was finally over and Jerzy was able to leave, Boguslaw breathed a sigh of victory as he looked out the window framed by blackened red brick. He was waiting for Jerzy to walk by just so he could look at him and gloat. It had been a long time in coming; too long, he thought.

"But now, his ass is all mine, and I am going to rip it apart, one small piece at a time."

Then, rising above the other noises, he heard his father's voice and turned quickly, his throat knotting up.

What is the matter, girlie? Are you still scared of the little boy?

He put his hands over his ears and tried to clear his head, but there was not much he could think about that did not draw his throat taut.

Chicken shit.

"No, you are dead. I saw them shoot you, so shut up."

Chicken shit...

"Noooooooooooo..." he screamed, his eyes squeezed shut.

* * *

Jerzy wanted to run away, anything rather than this slow torture, but he was scared to die, and he was so young. He was thinking about how he had not even kissed a girl yet, let alone all the other stuff. And the thought of helping these bastards was just too much.

He knew... at that moment, he just knew that he had to escape somehow. But his stomach and his heart both decided to wait for the right time... this was not it. Besides, the Germans would be watching the new arrivals closely right now.

The noon bell rang for lunch. "Jeez, I need to eat before I do anything. I am so very hungry," he said. Going to the same window as the day before, he was given a bowl with some kind of green stuff, sort of like ground up seaweed... maybe it was spinach... it was difficult to tell... floating in water somewhat like soup, but with no meat, no other vegetables. Each day, the meals were almost the same. Now and then, perhaps a paper-thin sliver of meat, maybe only two inches square, was thrown in. It could have been pork, but nobody knew for sure because it was eaten so fast. Or it could just as easily have been horse meat.

At lunch the next day, Jerzy saw that the subdued workers now came to life, wolfing their food down quickly, like sharks in a feeding frenzy. Like everybody else, Jerzy now wrapped his arm around his bowl, covering it between bites with his body, just in case anyone had ideas.

On the end of the third work day, as they returned to their barracks, each worker was given a small loaf of bread, one cup of sugar, a slice of liver sausage, a grayish-yellow stick of margarine, one spoon full of jam, and a little bit of cheese. All the new workers were told not to touch anything until it was all handed out.

"In addition to your meals, this food supplement is your allot-ment for the next three days," said the German handing it out. "Do not eat it all at one sitting, because no more food can be spared until the next allotment."

After the foods were all dispersed, they each slowly cut their bread into precise thirds, then divided their sugar the same way, followed by the rest of their supplements.

That was when the arguments began, starting with one of the old-timers speaking to the newer workers.

"I will bet that your food does not last the three days."

"And I will bet that it lasts longer than your big nose," said one of the young men who stood up to punch him.

They tried to fight, but neither man had the energy to throw any hard punches, and eventually, they tired of this bickering, and apolo-gized to each other.

But that night, Jerzy and the others were unable to sleep. Their stomachs were rumbling from emptiness, and they keep worrying about their food.

Laying in the dark with his eyes wide open, Jerzy thought, "What if someone else takes my bread while I sleep? What if it goes bad? Maybe it is already too late... I had better check for myself, just to make sure." But after checking the contents of his locker, he saw his three days of food and thought, Well, I see that it is all here, but maybe I should eat part of it, just in case.

The others heard Jerzy eating, and they decided to check their own supplies. Fearful of the worst, everyone's entire three-day supply was gone before the night was over. The next day, all that was available to eat was the meal of sauerkraut, which was already beginning to attack their intestines.

For variety, they sometimes received a meal of yellow mush... maybe squash... something normally used for feeding the pigs, but despite the variety, they still felt hungry.

And every now and then, whenever Hitler enjoyed a big military victory somewhere, the workers were given a big treat... in the spirit of celebration, they were allowed a spoonful of macaroni mixed with tiny chunks of meat, along with a little sauce. But it did not matter. At night, the hunger remained, and when lying down, their rumbling stomachs could be heard across the room.

The food filled them, yet no matter how much they ate, it left a bottomless void chewing on their stomachs with an ever-expanding intensity. Each meal was a gesture only, a cruel pretense, mocking the very act of eating, offering the promise of nutrition, yet withholding it, always withholding without giving. Eating had become a slow death, merciless, yet nonjudgmental, offering its lies to all.

The next night, because they no longer had any food to distract them, they were more aware of the insects than ever.

"These bugs are driving me crazy," said Jerzy.

"Me too," said another. I have no meat on my bones, yet they chew on me anyway."

"There must be something we can do," said another.

"Hey," said one of the guys. His name was Tomasz. "I have an idea. We will all get undressed like always, and I will turn out the lights but I will stay next to the switch. After a few minutes, when these little demons all come out to eat us, I will turn the lights back on and we can squash them back to the Hell they came from."

"That is an excellent idea, my friend. Top quality thinking."

And so they all removed their clothing, climbed onto their straw mattresses, and waited. Jerzy could feel the bugs coming out from their hiding places, squirming all over his body. He could barely control himself, and just when he was ready to scream, Tomasz hit the switch, flooding the room with light, and before the bloodsuckers could hide, everybody began slapping and yelling like warriors in battle, killing and cursing as many of them and their mothers as they could. When the slapping stopped, they all looked at each other and then someone noticed the odor; the stink turned their stomachs, but the battle was worthwhile. For now, nobody dreamed of food.

Sixteen

Danke Shön

Jerzy's first days were filled with learning, some of it the job itself, some of it ways to survive. After finishing with the ammonia tanks, he learned how to shave a wax-type product with a lathe, checking his accuracy with a micrometer and making adjustments as he went along. Then he would fill the barrels with this product by dropping it down from the floor above.

"What is in this stuff?" he asked another worker.

"Do not question anything... ever," he was told. "It is better not to know."

* * *

One day, Jerzy discovered that workers were allowed, once in a while, to take a day off and go into the city. He wanted this badly, hoping against all hope that the solution to his food problem could be found. Other workers occasionally came back from town with a bit of food they smuggled in, but they would not tell him where or how they obtained it without ration cards. It was as though they were afraid somebody would steal their only food supply. Maybe they were right.

The emptiness he felt was no longer isolated to his stomach alone; it washed through his entire body like a tsunami, depleting his life force, his very essence. His need to go into town took on a life and death urgency.

The only condition to going outside the factory was that he must wear his patch, an embroidered "P" visibly on his outer clothing. He had always been proud of his heritage. He knew, though, things were different now, that to wear this patch was to wear a symbol, which limited his mobility here, in Germany. It was a cultural castration, marking him as an inferior, even though deep inside, he wanted to feel that he was not.

When the day finally arrived, Jerzy was ready. He had befriended a guy who had a girlfriend working in a different part of the plant. The Germans tried to avoid men and women working together because it created too many problems. But through this guy, Jerzy was able to get a small sewing needle, which he hid under the lapel of his old, worn out suit jacket, and a little bit of thread which he kept in his pocket. Once outside the gate, he asked the first person he saw, an elderly man, "Sir, where can I catch a bus into the city?"

The man looked at Jerzy's patch, then deeply into his eyes, as though trying to find his very soul, and Jerzy was preparing to run when the man finally spoke... "I am afraid that no bus comes here, son, but you can catch a trolley car over there," he said, pointing with a trembling hand to a bench a half a block away.

Thanking him, Jerzy walked on, and along the way he saw a small cluster of trees, which he cautiously walked over to. Hiding within, he carefully removed the razor blade he had hidden in the lining of his jacket and used it to cut off his patch, which he then put inside his pocket. With this new freedom, Jerzy now walked to the trolley car, pondering along the way just how he might get some food. He had learned a few words of German since arriving, but not enough to hide his Polish origin, so, fearful of getting caught, his senses were heightened to a keen edge.

When the door to the trolley opened, Jerzy saw a police officer standing in the doorway, so pretending he was merely passing by, he continued walking until the trolley disappeared, then he doubled back, hoping for better luck with the next one. It was eleven kilometers to the city — too far to walk, for Jerzy was weakened from the food deprivation, so he could not go for long without having to stop and rest.

The next trolley car looked good, so he hopped on board, hoping for the best. Everything was new to him, the city so clean and neat compared to his bombed-out home in Lublin. When he walked off the trolley car, he first scanned the area, looking for police again, and only when he thought the area to be safe did he allow himself to feel any hope.

He felt lost among the crowds of people, all knowing where they were and where they were going. Jerzy knew neither, and it struck him as odd that the more people he encountered, the lonelier he felt.

It did not take long to find a bakery. His sense of smell had intensified during his captivity, and now it was working like radar for him. Like a runaway dog, he cautiously allowed himself inside. The odor alone filled him with remembering, and his stomach trembled in anticipation. Bread and cakes and cookies and all things from his dreams came to life, and his eyes began to fill with tears of a life long gone. He was so captivated, all he could do when asked if he wanted something was point to a loaf of dark bread, inhaling deeply all the while.

But it was now against the law to sell food of any kind to anyone who was not a German citizen, and that, of course, was controlled by the ration cards. The baker knew what was going on, but she was afraid of getting in trouble with the German police.

"I need to see your card," she said.

Jerzy pretended to get one from his pocket, and when it was not there, he looked surprised, frisking himself all over. He looked at her as though wondering where it might have gone, then shrugged, using his hands as a signal that he had no idea where his card went.

"Out," she ordered, shaking her head and pointing toward the door.

Jerzy looked at her as though he could not believe this, then looked again at the bread and took in a huge breath through his nose, as though filling his lungs with all the nutrients he so badly needed, turned, and walked from the building, slowly and dejectedly.

On the sidewalk again, people walked past him as though he were invisible. They seemed somber in mood, yet prideful at the same time, waiting for their grand destiny of a new world order to unfold.

But Jerzy was not a part of this German Utopia. His was a world beneath this one, a world where he was but an outcast fated to survive only through subterfuge and cunning. It was a world where he, and people like him, did not matter because they had no value. He was a shadow now, and shadows were not to be trusted, for their very vagueness made them suspect.

At the same time, though, Jerzy was also glad in a strange way that he was so hard to see; the last thing he wanted was to be noticeable to the police, and interrogated at every turn.

By the time Jerzy had reached a third bakery, he doubted that anyone in all of Germany had a heart, so he merely stood outside staring through the display window at the offerings, and imagining the most wonderful of daydreams. He imagined himself frolicking among the pastries, dipping his fingers into the cakes and hugging great rolls of bread, immersed in a cerebral foodscape, complete with odors and tastes and textures that were more real than reality, and he wanted to stay there forever, but instead he was snapped back to reality by a sudden rapping on the window. It came from within; when the last of her customers had left the store, the owner peered through the glass, looking all the way to the left, then just as far to the right, and back again. Seeing no police, she pointed to the door and beckoned for Jerzy to come inside. As he ambled to the door, the owner opened it, holding something behind her back, and again looking to make sure no one was watching. When she was sure it was safe, she produced from behind her a small loaf of bread, beautiful, real bread, which Jerzy gratefully took in his now-shaking hands and beheld in a reverent silence, just staring at his fortune. He started to thank her, but she said, "Now go, quickly," and turned her back to him as she hurried back inside, fearful of getting caught. He stuffed it under his jacket and left, almost delirious with happiness.

Jerzy wanted so badly to taste this ambrosia, but he was scared of being spotted and having it taken away... he could not bear such a thing, not now, so he carried it hidden under his jacket, all the way back to his barracks. When he arrived at the guard post, he sucked in his gut to hide the bulge, but there was very little gut to suck in, so he doubled his efforts until it felt like the front of his stomach was touching his backbone. Fortunately, the guard did not notice, so Jerzy finally had something wondrous to share with a few of his closest co-workers.

That night, he dreamed about going back to that same bakery again and again, but smuggling opportunities were limited, so he and the other workers were forever hungry for something, anything that might sustain them just a little longer.

They never saw milk, fruit, or eggs. The only vegetable was the occasional small piece of cabbage leaf, floating at the top of the water they called soup. To get either a tiny piece of meat or cabbage leaf was euphoric, like winning a giant game of poker.

It did not take long before the skin under their nails began turning red, as did their hair, and their faces became pale, like ghosts. They ate what they had, worked as long as they could, and in between, argued with each other over whose recipes were best, even though they never had the ingredients necessary to try any of their recipes out.

One day in the early part of spring, Jerzy decided to explore the outskirts of the city some more, and he went into a small village nearby. Wandering aimlessly, he noticed a small cottage with an older woman digging in a new garden she had made in her yard. She was a chunky little creature, and had twinkling eyes, like shiny buttons. Obviously winded, she stood, leaning on her shovel to catch her breath, and wiped her brow with the other forearm. This gave the boy an idea.

"Good afternoon," he said nervously. His German was improving, but still lacked finesse, yet he went ahead anyway, hoping she would understand. "And why is such a beautiful woman working out here in this hot sun?" He puffed out his chest to impress her with his masculine strength. "You should have a man to do this hard work for you. A man like myself."

"Oooh... you want to help me?"

"Oh ja, I would like to do that," he said.

"Good, good. What is your name?" He decided to tell her the truth. "Jerzy," he said.

"Oh, Jerzy," she said with a laugh. "Danke shön, danke shön." She handed him a gardening fork, saying, "Continue this digging here... dig right here," she said, pointing to where she had been working, then turned, and walked back toward the house, taking the tiniest of steps with her little plump legs, looking as though she would never arrive anywhere.

Even though she never asked how much he wanted for the work, he was desperate to impress her anyway, so he dug harder than he had the strength for, harder even than he had ever worked before, because he was so very hungry. A half hour later, she looked out the door to see his progress.

She smiled, and said, "Jerzy, come here, come here." She liked to say everything twice.

When he entered the house, she told him, "Take off your shoes. Off, off. And wash your hands... wash them."

Jerzy wondered what was going on. Her bossiness reminded him of his stepmother.

"Sit down, sit, sit," she said, gesturing toward her kitchen table. And there, sitting in the middle was the most amazing sight he could even think to behold... while he was working, she had prepared a large bowl of vegetable stew, with beautiful rings of fat floating on top. It had no meat, but that did not matter. The smell alone was intoxicating. His stomach began talking.

Jerzy picked up a spoon almost as soon as he sat, but his hand was trembling... and his eyes began to water. It had been so long... so very, very long.

"Eat... eat," she said merrily in her little singsong voice, offering him bread to go with the stew.

He could hardly see the bowl through his teardrops, but that did not stop him. "Ja, very tasty," he said between mouthfuls with his limited German, shoveling the food in as fast as possible, one bite after another, hardly taking time to breathe before she changed her mind.

She refilled his bowl before he had finished, and again, he attacked the food, devouring anything that came close to his mouth.

He stopped for a moment and just stared at her, wondering where this angel had been hiding. Laughter filled her heart and her soul, and her food filled his.

She understands, he thought. After he finished the second bowl, he continued to sit at the table, reveling in the afterglow of such heaven as the world could not possibly know. He still felt hungry, but did not want to say anything.

The silence, however, eventually became uncomfortable, and finally, he said, "Well, I have to go now."

"Oh... oh... come again," she said, lightly touching his arm. "See me again tomorrow."

He wished so badly that he could... he nodded, and then he got up, thanking his hostess, and slowly walked out the door.

Seventeen

Meeting Her

In 1944, a new camp had been built on the other side of the factory, and the word spread quickly. Jerzy heard about it from one of his coworkers, Wieńczysław. "It is for girls only, Jerzy, and I heard it houses about five thousand females from Belgium, France, Poland, Russia and Czechoslovakia... everywhere except Germany, of course. You know, we owe it to these poor, lonely women to at least introduce ourselves."

Jerzy had not thought about any girls since the war began, so he found this new development exciting. "That is a superb thought, my friend... Yes, we must check them out immediately, before everyone knows they are here." He grinned.

The following Sunday, Jerzy finally had the opportunity to go there and see this divine place for himself. Males were not allowed inside their camp, but they could speak to the girls through the chain link fence. And the females, like the men, were allowed out once a month.

When the big day finally arrived, many men were already there, which Jerzy found discouraging. Some secret this was. Looking at all the men and women with fingers entwined within the links evoked a longing within him, an emptiness that had no name. Why did he even bother? He knew he could not compete, and was just about to leave when he noticed a girl, maybe seventeen or eighteen, sitting alone on a wood bench, about twenty feet from the fence, just staring off into the distance. She was thin, as they all were, BUT... he thought, ...this is the most unbelievably beautiful girl I have ever seen. Her eyes were sharp, but feminine, with long lashes, half-closed in that sexy way that reduced men to a puddle, her lips full and just begging for attention. And she had long, brunette hair that flowed gently down almost to the middle of her back. To Jerzy, she was a young goddess, but he saw that she was not talking to any other guys. He wondered why not.

Summoning up every ounce of courage he could find, he called out to her. "Heyyyy..." he said. She looked up, shyly, and he gestured with his hand for her to come over to the fence.

She looked around, then back at him. "Me?" she said, pointing to herself.

He nodded, gesturing again. He could not take his eyes off of her.

She had large doe eyes, and overall was tiny with hunger, and delicate like a twig, moving slowly, cautiously, as though the slightest misstep might snap her in half. She seemed to him a lamb of innocence, uncorrupted and not even understanding the delicacy of her own condition. Her helplessness brought out some kind of protective instinct in Jerzy, making him want to hold her gently and somehow shield her from the cold hunger that feasted upon them all, body and soul.

"Hi," he said quietly when she had reached the fence. "My name is Jerzy." He saw that her eyes were a beautiful shade of brown... almost golden. "What are you called?"

"I am Ekaterina," she said, shyly.

"Do you work here?" he said.

She merely nodded, looking down at the ground.

"I work way down at the other end of the factory," he said.

She looked at him with curiosity. "You are from Poland."

"Lublin," he said. "Yes, I am. Are you Polish?"

"I am from Minsk, in Russia, but my mother was born in Warsaw, and from her I learned some of your language. She and my Papa were killed in the purge by Stalin when I was just ten."

He nodded, feeling her hurt. "I understand. My younger brother was killed during the first week of this war, and a couple of close friends were killed later." He was silent for a moment. "It still hurts," he said.

She looked at him, trying to understand the ways of this new world. "First, it was the Russian Revolution, then the Great War, now this..." Her eyes looked as though seeing a sad memory. "You are a man... why do men always feel the need to kill each other?"

Jerzy looked down. "I do not know, Ekaterina. But not all men feel that way... I do not feel such a need, and I never have."

She nodded. "For now," she said... "maybe that is enough."

He looked in her eyes and saw a kindred spirit within, a soul in search of compassion, and an emptiness yearning for companionship. He found a hope that maybe this was an omen of a possible romance, a future with meaning, and his heart began to beat anew with the song of promise.

He heard Ben calling him to go back.

"Listen, Ekaterina..." Jerzy nervously ran his fingers through his hair to brush it away from his eyes. "I cannot stay here, but I would really like to see you again. Next Sunday, would you meet me at the Rhine River? Please?"

She hesitated. "I do not know you, Jerzy. You seem nice, but how am I to know that you can be trusted?"

He could feel himself deflating rapidly, but then he had an idea. "Ekaterina, if I trust you first with a secret of mine, one that would get me in big trouble if the Germans found out, would you then feel better about trusting me?"

She thought about this. "Maybe," she finally said, with a softness in her voice.

"Look," he said, as he removed a razor and needle from their hiding places in his jacket and held them out for her inspection. "Whenever I go into the city, I use this razor blade to remove my Polish emblem that the Germans make us wear, and then I sew it back on again when I return. Ekaterina, I have never shown this to anybody before, not even my closest friends, but I am trusting you to keep my secret. Can you trust me as well? Please?"

Her eyes filled with admiration for his bravery and cunning, and she looked at him with a new respect. He was different than Viktor Roman Aleksandrov. This was a sensitive man, an intelligent man with feelings and consideration for others... this was a man she felt comfortable with. Besides, she was older now... almost nineteen, and more cautious.

"Okay, I will trust you, Jerzy," she whispered. "And I will meet you at the river on Sunday afternoon, perhaps next to the bridge?" She had been there before with a few of the older women, and knew that others would be in the area, in case she was wrong about him.

He could not help but grin. "Two o'clock," he said, almost exploding with happiness.

As Jerzy turned to go back to his barracks, he looked back at her and tripped. She saw this and laughed, but it did not matter to him. All he could think about was her eyes... her smile... and the way she made his heart skip a beat. Seven days would be an eternity.

Once in bed, he wondered about these strange feelings he was having. Was it love? No, it was too soon... too fast. All he knew was that sleep would be a long time coming, for no matter what, he could not get Ekaterina out of his mind, so he tossed and turned until, finally, the blackness came.

That night, he dreamed that he was walking by a bakery when the odor of newly baked bread stopped him in his tracks, and he deeply inhaled in order to fully absorb this delight. Suddenly the door opened and the baker thrust two beautiful giant loaves into his arms. They smelled sooooo good, and in all the excitement, Jerzy woke up. But upon realizing that the bread was not real, he closed his eyes again in the hope of finishing his fantasy. Even fictional food was better than the incessant hunger that gnawed at his bones in real life. "Wait for me, bread... I am coming back for you," he whispered.

And again, he dreamed, but this time it was images of Ekaterina that filled his mind. She was tickling his face with her long hair, making him giggle like a small boy... but something was wrong... her breath was foul, and she began growling deeply.

Jerzy's eyes snapped open, and when he could focus, he beheld a growling beast with fangs just inches from his face. It barked loudly right in his face. He scrambled back quickly, and the guard dog, a German shepherd, went to lunge after him, barking again, even more fiercely, but it was held firm by an SS soldier. Behind him, partly hidden by the darkness, was another man wearing a trench coat, and he peered at Jerzy as though trying to rip out his very soul through his eyes. Stepping forward, he bent down so that his face was right in front of Jerzy's.

It was Colonel Heisinveld. His monocle reflected a sparkle of moonlight from the window, which in the dark of night sent a cold chill down Jerzy's spine, and even Heisinveld's hair, slicked back with grease, looked threatening. He pulled a wrench from the pocket of his overcoat and held it inches from Jerzy's nose. "Do you see this, Czaplicki?" Putting his nose right up to Jerzy's ear, he said, "We found it in one of the barrels you processed today. Did you throw it in there?"

Even if I had, did this monocled turnip think that I would say yes? "Of course not," he said. "Why would I do that? Maybe it fell in there."

"And just exactly how could that happen?" he said, slapping his other palm into the side of Jerzy's head.

"Ow! Well... sometimes tools are placed on the edge of the barrels by the workers," he said, rubbing his head. The boy's eyes were huge now, and he saw the dog staring at him, as though wanting a taste... a big one.

The turnip looked intently at Jerzy's face, perhaps trying to decide whether he should live or die, finally pushing him back with contempt. "We will be watching you, Czaplicki. We will be watching you very closely."

After the SS left, Jerzy looked at the door and saw Boguslaw standing in the shadows, looking at him in the dark. He was smiling, and Jerzy's blood ran cold with understanding. Sleep felt impossible after that.

* * *

At 4:30 the next morning, one of the workers came into the barracks, looking for the boy. "I am looking for Jerzy Czaplicki." he said loudly, waking everyone.

"I am right here. Why do you wake me, and so early at that?" It was an hour before he normally got up, and he feared that Boguslaw was setting him up again in some way to cement his guilt in the minds of the SS.

"Sorry, Czaplicki—orders from the commandant. He wants to see you right away, before you start work"

"Crap... last night was not enough." Now what do they blame me for?

Jerzy put on his clothes quickly and walked as rapidly as possible to the commandant's office. He did not dare to run, for fear of knocking down a worker, or even worse, for knocking down one of the foremen, but he also knew that the Germans frowned on being kept waiting.

A young guard saw him hurrying and stopped him. "Hey - where do you think you are going in such a hurry?" he asked.

"The commandant wants to see me right away," Jerzy said.

"A likely story." He did not want to be the one responsible for letting a saboteur get away.

"Look, if I do not get there right away, it will be your fault, and I would hate to be in your shoes when you explain to him why he had to wait. Now let me go."

"Hmmm... I will go with you," he said, grabbing Jerzy by the forearm.

When they reached the commandant's office, the guard pushed Jerzy roughly inside, where there was a young officer sitting behind a desk in the waiting area. "Heil Hitler," the guard said, saluting the officer. "Sir, I caught this worker running in the factory. He claims that the commandant wanted to see him right away, but I —"

"Are you Jerzy Czaplicki?" the officer asked the boy.

"Yes Sir."

The officer turned to the guard. "That will be all, Gefreiter."

"Yes sir," said the guard.

The Captain looked at Jerzy, and knocked lightly on the door behind his desk before opening it. "Herr Commandant, the man you wished to see, Jerzy Czaplicki."

"Thank you, Hauptmann... that will be all. Come in, Czaplicki."

He entered cautiously. "Sir?"

The Colonel stared at him." Do you know a Kaspar Czaplicki in Lublin?"

This was not the question he had expected, and his stomach began to knot. "Yes sir... that is my father."

"Then I am afraid I have some bad news. I received a telegram that he came down with Typhoid fever... there has been an epidemic in Poland, you know. And he was not able to recover."

"Sir, no... are you saying that my father... has... died?" Jerzy could feel the teardrops threatening to fall, but he knew that the Germans would see this as a sign of weakness.

"I am sorry, Czaplicki."

Jerzy just stared into nothingness. Finally, he asked, "Sir, may I have your permission to attend his funeral in Poland?"

"I will see what I can do. In the meantime, I need you to report back to work."

Jerzy nodded, turned, and walked out, oblivious to everything except for the loss of his Papa, and the memory of the last time they were together.

* * *

Sunday came, and Jerzy still had not heard anything about going back to Poland, so he decided to meet Ekaterina at the river, as they had discussed. She was the only bright spot in his increasingly dark world. His thoughts had been pretty much equally divided between her, his father, Boguslaw, and food.

He arose early, shaved as neatly as he could with the same razor blade he had been using for the past three months, then quickly got dressed in the shirt and pants he had just washed the night before... the only ones he owned... and set about on his date.

He was about to get on a trolley when he noticed a policeman standing on board, so he pretended to be more interested in the German newspaper he was holding, and waited for the next streetcar. Fortunately, the second trolley was police-free, so he clambered on board. At their first stop, a different policeman climbed onto the car, and Jerzy climbed off just as quickly. He was now becoming suspicious of nearly everyone.

The next car, however, was police-free and took him into the heart of the city. At the first bakery he came to, he went inside and approached the young clerk, looking for any sign of compassion in her eyes.

"I have a girlfriend... and today is her birthday," he said. "Can I please buy a cake?"

She stared at his puppy-dog look, knowing that he had no ration card, but sympathizing with his plight. Except for her and the boy, her shop was empty. Finally, she decided... even though it was against the law, she gave him a loaf of dry bread, and even included a small box of cookies.

"Thank you," he said, his hands shaking. He offered her the money, but she would not take it.

"Just have a good time with your girlfriend," she said.

He stared at her, then nodded, walked out the door, and went in search of the bridge. With the bread and cookies hidden under his jacket, he felt rich, for he was able to provide something for them both, and with Ekaterina in his heart, he felt blessed. Today promised to be a day among days.

He found her sitting on a bench near the bridge, their eyes lighting up at the joy of seeing each other. He extended his hand and she took it, rising to join him in a walk that went nowhere and everywhere. Touching her hand was like holding wings of gossamer; he marveled at the softness, the delicacy, and he was afraid to squeeze even a little. He looked at her face, and his heart pounded. He could not stop staring at her in awe of her beauty.

Eventually, they came to a park where they saw some German teenagers at a small distance, both boys and girls in costume, singing teasing songs to each other. Jerzy and Ekaterina did not want to get too close to them, so she put on her eyeglasses, and finding a closer bench nearby, they stopped to listen.

"Do these make me look ugly, Jerzy? Please be honest."

Her pupils were huge... and so very captivating. "Ekaterina, nothing could make you look ugly." And he meant it.

She blushed, and he felt taller somehow.

"I have a gift for you," Jerzy said during a lull in the singing. "It is not much." He pulled out the bread from under his jacket and her eyes grew huge. Then, before she could say a word, he reached in again and pulled out the cookies.

"Jerzy..." she said, awed at this treasure. "How did you ever —"

"Ssshhhh," he said. "Please, just enjoy, okay?"

Her eyes watered up... "I do not know what to say."

His heart melted. "Do not say anything," Jerzy told her. "Just open your mouth for food, and we can talk afterward."

She laughed, and leaned into him while Jerzy broke off a piece of bread for her. She looked so poor, so undernourished... but despite her hunger, she ate slowly, with dignity. Watching her eat was heaven; they ate and laughed together, wiping crumbs off each other's faces, and loving the feeling of being cared for by another. Words were not necessary.

Being young, they were both filled with energy, so after their food was gone, they went strolling along the bank of the river, first walking hand in hand, then arm in arm.

All too soon, it was time to go back, so they left together, taking the same trolley, and all they could see during the ride was each other. There was a small park just a few kilometers from the factory, and they went there so Jerzy could sew back the patch on his jacket. Finding a spot under a tree, in the shade, they sat together, and Jerzy pulled out his patch, along with a sewing needle and some thread.

"Jerzy, would you let me do that for you?"

"Okay, but do not make it too good, because I will just be cutting it off again."

"I know," she said. "And the next time, I will do mine as well."

They smiled.

141

When she finished the sewing, she asked Jerzy, "How does that look?"

"Almost as beautiful as you," he said, smiling.

They looked in each other's eyes, and remembering a movie he had once seen, he reached out with both hands and slowly removed her eyeglasses, put them down on the grass, then leaned in and with his forefinger, lifted her chin and kissed her softly. It was his first kiss, and it was even better than he could have imagined. They looked at each other again, smiled, and touched foreheads. But it was not to last.

The air raid siren began screaming, men were running everywhere, and the young lovers were both rocked by the sharp concussion of the nearby German anti-aircraft gun firing at the American bombers directly overhead. Jerzy and Ekaterina just looked at each other.

"Oh crap," he said. Taking her by the hand, he pulled her toward a nearby ditch he had spotted earlier, which was partially covered with timber and some dirt. He guided her in, following right behind her, both of them going in deeply and hiding as best they could. Jerzy was feeling highly protective and pressed himself against the back of her body to shield it.

Then they felt the whole planet tremble as the Germans again unleashed massive antiaircraft fire, the giant guns sending shock waves through the ground as well as the air. POW! POW-POW-POW... BANG!

She turned to face him, wrapping her arms tightly around his neck, and he felt her shake, and he hugged her closer, whispering, "Shhhhhh... shhhhhh... it is okay, I am right here... I will not let anything happen to you," and he kissed the side of her head. And then another POW! She held on even tighter, trembling all the while.

I have been dreaming since forever about a date like this, and now the war is giving me a chance to hold this angel from Heaven close and comfort her. Perhaps this war is not so bad after all.

He peeked through the planks of wood at the planes flying through the flak, then he again felt the arms of this girl wrapped around his neck, and her trembling body pressed up close to his own. Wow! Even her natural scent was intoxicating.

And so, filled with fear along with the mystery of love, he closed his eyes to soak in every second of this experience.

When everything calmed down, an all-clear signal was issued, and the young couple walked back to look for her glasses, but it was getting dark outside, and no matter how hard they looked, the glasses were not to be found. Jerzy knew they could not be replaced, and he felt terrible, but Ekaterina put her hand on his arm.

"It is okay... you took care of me, and that means more than you will ever know. Please do not feel bad. I had a wonderful time with you, Jerzy. Really."

They took another trolley and when they disembarked, he walked her back to her camp, where they said goodbye, promising to see each other again soon, agreeing that every other Sunday would be best. She hugged him one last time, and gave him a quick kiss to hold him over until then. Then she turned, and walked past the guard at the gate, back to her barracks and the emptiness it provided.

Eighteen

Dreaming of Rabbits

The next Sunday, Jerzy went alone to Mülheim, about eleven kilometers west of Leverkusen. The day was cool, but not cold. He was wondering where to go to find food when he saw two women digging hard in their garden. The house was on a street corner and the women were in the back yard. One of the women was older, with long gray hair held in a bun. She had a kind face, but the many broken lines on it spoke of intense hardships. The other woman was younger, her daughter perhaps.

"Well, it has worked once for me," the boy said to himself... "perhaps it will work again." He crossed the street to where they were digging, and knew immediately from his work on the farm with his uncle that they were digging up potatoes. His stomach rumbled... hunger now doing most of his thinking for him, along with much of his talking.

"Good afternoon, ladies. I have been watching you both, and I am wondering why two exquisitely beautiful creatures are doing such hard work out here." He saw himself as a knight in shining armor, but the women just looked at him, then at each other, then at him again. Perhaps his armor was getting rusty.

They continued to stare, saying nothing.

He was getting uncomfortable, and was starting to turn around to leave, when they spoke to him at last.

"What is your name?" said the older one, ignoring his overblown compliments.

"Karl," he lied. "Ladies, may I please do this hard work for you? I could not live with myself if one of you was hurt while I sat nearby, knowing that I could have helped." He knew how cheesy it sounded, but a part of him sincerely meant what he said.

"Ah, Karl. That is a good name. And you would like to dig these potatoes up for us, Karl?"

"Ja... oh, Ja," he said, nodding his head vigorously as if to emphasize his eagerness.

Again, the women looked at each other, as if reading the other's mind, then the older one turned to Jerzy and spoke. "It is very hard work, and we appreciate this, Karl. But we have not yet talked about price... how much will you charge?"

"Do not worry, ladies. I could not take any money from such beautiful women. I would ask though, if you could spare a bite to eat... that would be more than enough."

The older woman agreed to let Jerzy dig for them, signifying this by handing her shovel to him. "Karl, that would be no problem. We have a deal, young man. Just come to the door over there when you have finished, and knock." She pointed to the side entrance he was to use.

Jerzy smiled, knowing that soon he would be fed and would live a while longer. In the meantime, he grabbed hold of the shovel and dug like a madman, even before they left, eager to demonstrate what a hard worker he was. Although he was weak with hunger, this meant food, and just the thought gave him the extra strength he needed to complete the job. He was no longer a boy... he was a man on a mission, a quest to survive, and he needed to demonstrate this.

The women turned and went back indoors, but the daughter returned a few minutes later with boots and coveralls for him to wear. No words were exchanged. He nodded, then put them on and resumed his digging, working up a sweat, even though the weather was cool. The potatoes were plentiful, and he put them in the large burlap sacks the women had placed on the ground. When he could find no more potatoes, he hefted the sacks onto his thin back and carried them, two at a time, up onto the porch. It took him three trips. Wiping the sweat off his face with his forearm, he knocked on the door. The younger woman let him in.

"I hope I have them all," he said.

"Oh, that is plenty, Karl," said the mother. "Please take off your boots and coveralls, then you can wash in the sink over there and come in to join us at the table." He saw that it had already been set for three.

Jerzy could smell the food... and he became dizzy with hunger. It forced him to steady himself by holding onto the counter for a brief moment, but thankfully, nobody noticed. Just as he was looking where to sit down to eat, his stomach began making rude noises, and while looking up to see if they heard, he just happened to glance at the far wall near the front door, where he spotted a German military helmet hanging on the hat rack. His hunger immediately dissolved in a vortex of fear. Oh great," he thought... The clever rabbit has just walked into the fox's lair.

As the boy stood there, he tried to think of some excuses for leaving, but the odors of that food made his stomach rumble so badly, he told himself maybe his luck would hold out until he had at least a few delicious bites. The odor alone was almost worth dying for.

They showed him where to sit, then joined him at the table. When he picked up the spoon, his hand was trembling uncontrollably. Part of that was from his extreme hunger, the other part from the effect the strenuous digging had on his muscles. But all that mattered right now was the food.

The boy was chewing his first mouthful when he heard the front door open and close. He looked up, but nobody was yet in sight. Then Jerzy heard each footstep of the hard military boots on the wooden floor as they slowly approached the dining room. He stopped breathing. Oh crap, he thought. I am dead meat. He slowly brought his spoon down to the table, aware of every breath and heartbeat, and waited for his life to come crashing down.

When the officer finally appeared in the kitchen doorway with a German Shepherd, Jerzy stopped breathing, watching the dog scrutinize his every move. The boy was like a statue.

"Hello, Darling," the woman said. "We have a guest. This is Karl... he helped Brigitte and I in the garden today. Karl, my husband, Hauptmann Rottenberger. This fine young man worked very hard, Dear, so we invited him to dinner."

Jerzy stood. Looking straight ahead, he bowed slightly, saying, "An honor to meet you, Sir."

The captain had a hard face, with eyes of cold steel, and they stared hard at the boy, as though seeing all his secrets. He silently walked closer to the lad, not taking his eyes off of him. The dog also examined him, with his nose.

Jerzy began to tremble, afraid that the dog would pick up the scent of his fear, but before he could run, the captain smiled. "Thank you, Karl, for helping my wife and daughter with digging out all those potatoes. You have some experience with this kind of work?"

"I worked on a farm with my uncle for a while," he said.

Leaning in, the officer brought his face close to Jerzy's. "Good... then you will appreciate this. Let us go outside for a quick moment... I would like to show you something," he said.

Of course, thought Jerzy. Shooting me inside would make a mess that his wife and daughter would have to clean. He will shoot me outside, and then maybe the dog will eat my body and everybody will be happy. He nodded, but his throat closed up, and he followed the captain outside.

They went to a place opposite from the garden. There, they came upon a large wire coop, where the officer extended his arm out to show Jerzy his pride and joy. "These, Karl, are my rabbits," he said with his chin raised. There were a few dozen of them, all fat. "I raise them for food. They are very tasty."

Jerzy stared at them. I feel like we are in the same cage, rabbits, he thought. Except you have more food to eat than me.

He thought about those rabbits all day, and when he slept that night, he did not dream about eating them... he dreamed that they were his family.

Nineteen

The Hug

Work continued, as did the war, but Jerzy's hunger never took a vacation, and his need to survive constantly pulled at his every thought, always rising to the top. He was still seeing Ekaterina as promised, but now he had to get into town again. Summer was over and the weather was getting too cold for gardening, so he needed to find a new way to work for a free meal.

On his next Sunday alone, he again left the factory in search of food. He saw more police than usual, and with his fears of discovery growing, he got on and off the trolley more than he normally did, but eventually he made it into the city. As he began his walk, a big gust of wind blew hard at his face and chest, so he wrapped his jacket tighter about him and hugged himself. Ahead of him a horse whinnied, and when the boy looked, he saw a coal wagon being slowly pulled by two Clydesdales, so he decided to follow it, hiding now and then behind trees so the driver did not see him. The street was lined with two and three-storied buildings, and he thought perhaps he could offer his services to shovel the coal for someone once the wagon unloaded it in their yard in exchange for a meal.

The boy saw the wagon stop, and he peeked from behind a tree as the driver climbed down and walked onto the porch of a three-story tenement building. When the man rang the doorbell, a window on the top floor opened up and woman's head appeared, yelling down to him to unload the coal into the yard, then the window closed again. While he was unloading the coal, the woman came downstairs to sign the delivery receipt. After he left, she wandered over to examine her new pile of coal, scratching her head as if to wonder how she was going to shovel such a pile into the basement bulkhead. Jerzy saw his opportunity.

Quickly crossing the street, he approached the woman. She looked to be in her mid-forties, and a flowing mane of beautiful white hair contrasted against her darker olive complexion.

"Good morning," he said. "It looks as though you could use a hard worker to shovel this big pile of coal for you." His hands were in his jacket pockets, partly because of the chill in the air, and partly because he did not want her to see his crossed fingers.

She examined him carefully, looking deeply at him, but it was a non-threatening look, the kind made by people you just know you can trust.

"What are you called?" she said.

She looked like she had a kind heart, so he felt no need to hide behind lies.

"I am named Jerzy, and I work for the Farbenfabriken Company, but they do not pay me the thousands of marks that I deserve, so every once in a while, I look for nice ladies such as yourself to help out. All I ask for in exchange is a free meal."

Her eyes scrutinized his own, feeling for his motive. "This is a lot of coal, Jerzy."

"And that is why I wish to do this for you. No woman should have to do a man's work."

"I have worked hard all my life."

"And today you have a strong young man offering to take this one burden off your shoulders." He smiled warmly, and that single gesture found its way into her heart.

"Alright," she said returning the smile. "One home-cooked meal coming up. The shovel is over there," she said, pointing to the back porch, "...and here is the chute. Ring the doorbell when you have finished."

As he shoveled, the boy found himself warming, but with his rumbling stomach, all he could think about was the meal. He could not stop daydreaming about what it would be, but it did not matter because anything would be better than a bowl of water with maybe a cabbage leaf in there somewhere on a lucky day.

About halfway through the job, the upstairs window opened up, and the woman stuck her head out, calling Jerzy, but with the scraping of the shovel on the ground and the noise of the coal going into the chute, he did not hear her.

"JERZY," she called again between scoops, louder now. This time he looked up. "Come upstairs—your meal is ready."

"But I have not finished," he said.

"Get up here now." And she closed the window.

Putting the shovel down, he trudged up the three flights of stairs and knocked at her door. She opened it just as he was breathing on his hands while rubbing them together in a vain attempt to unthaw them.

"I wanted to feed you while the food was still hot," she said as he stepped inside. "It is getting cold outside and all you are wearing is this thin jacket. You must be freezing."

"The work keeps me warm," he lied, while ogling the food.

"Well, shoveling a hot meal into your mouth will keep you warmer. Dig in... please."

He could not stop staring at the food. And the odor filled the entire room, making his stomach create more noise than a symphony. She heaped the food upon his plate, and Jerzy wasted no time in filling his mouth. Oh my God, he thought. This is what Heaven must be like.

He ate with his arm wrapped around his plate. It was a habit he did not realize he had. The woman looked long and hard at him, and her heart melted.

When he had finished eating, he stood to go back outside, but she stopped him. "No, Jerzy. Rest awhile and let your food digest a bit before going back to finish."

He looked in her eyes and saw such compassion there, like he had not seen in a long, long time. Her hair was pure white, as though something had once frightened her, but her face was of a kindliness he had never before experienced. She stared into his eyes.

"Excuse me for one moment," she said softly, getting up from her chair and leaving the room.

I need to get back to the barracks before it gets too cold out, he thought, considering the possibility of just sneaking out while she was gone... but he finally decided to wait, if only because she had been so nice to him. When she returned, she was carrying a heavy wool jacket, along with a pair of new slacks, gloves, and a new flannel shirt.

"These belonged to my son, who was a soldier and was killed last year. He was about your age, even your size, and I could not bear to throw his things away... but it pleases me to give them to you," she said, holding them out to him.

Jerzy stood up to accept them, then put them down in the chair he just vacated and hugged her as though this was his long-dead mother. "Thank you," he said. Then he grasped her shoulders and stepped back so he could look at this living angel, but he could not see her through his tears.

* * *

A month passed, and his job might have been almost tolerable, were it not for Boguslaw, who taunted the boy almost daily. It was just like it had been back in school, only deadlier. That, along with the incessant starvation had worn him down little by little; it was so hard to always be aware of the constant danger. He was exhausted, and sometimes it was all he could do to just keep his eyes open. One good thing about his hunger though was that on days like the one he was currently having, the rumbling was so loud it kept him awake.

As the boy walked into his work area, his boss approached him wearing the latest in sinister smiles.

"Hey, look at this, poor-boy" he said, almost giggling. He was carefully holding a small bottle. "Watch carefully," he said. Working the cork stopper slowly and carefully out of the neck, he held the bottle chest-high, slowly tipped it so that a single drop came out, right over Jerzy's foot. Not knowing what it was, but thinking maybe it was a powerful acid, and knowing Boguslaw's hatred of him, Jerzy moved his foot back quickly, before the liquid could hit it, but it never got that far. Instead, the single drop of this liquid exploded into a ball of flame before it finished dropping. Just the friction from the air was enough to set it off.

Jerzy leaped backward. "Holy crap," he said.

"Isn't that amazing, Czaplicki? And just think... you are going to help make this stuff. Of course, it would be such a shame if there was an accident and anything happened to you, so I hope you are very careful, my friend. Very, very careful." Then he giggled again, as though privy to the world's biggest joke.

Twenty

Bombs Away

By November of 1944, many allied planes were flying over the factory, at least four or five times a week, but they never dropped their bombs on it, and that puzzled Jerzy. The allied forces were dropping their big, beautiful bombs all over Germany, all around them, in fact, so why not here? He looked around, and saw one of the older Polish workers that he had befriended.

"Stefan, why is it that this factory never gets attacked?" he said. I have been here now for almost three years, and not once has this place been bombed.

"You do not know?" He looked around to be sure no Germans were listening. "This company is international, and it makes much money for some very important people, so nobody dares to blow it up."

"I do not understand."

"Think about it, my young friend. There is good money to be had in any war. Somebody has to make the bombs and tanks and planes. And somebody has to make bullets and mines and hand grenades and other things that go boom in the night. And somebody, Jerzy, somebody is getting rich off of our cheap labor, too. And they do not wish to bomb their golden egg."

Jerzy stood there, lost in thought.

"Who?" he finally said. Who would kill people by the thousands just to make money? That is crazy."

"Oh really? Well, I overheard the Kommandant last week talking to some German Colonel about how happy the company investors were over the improvements in production since he got here. Then I heard them list some of those investors... two of the biggest were American industrial leaders, names known to everyone. And they said there were over two hundred international corporations operating in Germany, and not just here. Many of them make tanks and planes, engines, radar, high explosives, and many other things the Nazis need for their war. And many of them were using slave labor from the concentration camps to work for them for free."

"Is this true?" Jerzy said.

"Why would I lie to you? Especially over something like this."

"Crap... I have been helping these bastards make money from this stuff that they use to kill other people? And I never once questioned what I am doing. Damn it, Stefan. A handful of people are getting rich while the little people, the weak, helpless people like you and me are suffering, bleeding... even dying. If that is true, then those monsters make the Nazis look like decent human beings." He looked hard at his friend. "What is wrong with me? Hell, what is wrong with the world?"

Ironically, the moment he said that was the moment the siren for an air attack blasted, and like usual, everyone headed for shelter, but because they had never been bombed, the workers had become complacent, almost casual about it, so they moved slowly.

But not for long. The first explosion rocked the building where Jerzy worked, taking everyone by complete surprise. It was almost as though the allies knew exactly where to strike. Other explosions followed, and the running for safety now began in earnest. One of the bombs hit a gasoline storage tank, which sent up a series of fireballs. This resulted in a roaring wall of flame that stretched to the heavens.

There was mass confusion, the men were covered with a rain of steel from the debris and flak thrown up by the Nazi anti-aircraft, and struggled to breathe within the new atmosphere of hot, poisonous air. Concussions traveled in waves, shattering glass and eardrums alike. One of the walls in Jerzy's section began to collapse.

"Yes... YES," he yelled, smiling his biggest smile all the while, but nobody could hear him over the din. "Do you know what this means, Stefan?" He grabbed his friend's upper arm. "Do you? It means that there is still somebody good out in the world, somebody who cares, and has enough power to make these Nazi bastards pay for what they have done."

He was ecstatic, even laughing, and dancing in circles, then he ran to end of the building and out the heavy steel door to the porch landing to see his saviors. The flames had not yet come this far. A military guard was also out there, watching the sky, which was black with allied planes. There were so many, the soldier just stared up at them, oblivious to all else. He wore a rifle over his shoulder, but the planes were way out of his reach, so he merely gripped the metal handrails and watched the anti-aircraft guns fire at the American bombers.

Boguslaw saw Jerzy go outside and followed him. He ripped open the door. "WHAT ARE YOU DOING?" he screamed. "WHO TOLD YOU THAT YOU COULD COME OUT HERE?" He grabbed Jerzy by the arm and threw him back inside with all the flames and chemicals, and took his place on the porch. "Zakuta pala," he shouted, slamming the door in Jerzy's face and smiling with satisfaction at the way his world was unfolding. Soon, he thought, ...that little asshole will be as dead as my father, and I will mount his head on the wall, or even better, make a punching bag out of it. The image brought a smile to his face.

Jerzy cautiously moved deeper toward his work area, shielding his face with his forearm over his eyes as he tried to find another exit. The flames sounded like a freight train going full steam, heavy smoke was everywhere, making him cough, so he instinctively pulled his shirt over his mouth, and as he bent closer to the floor in an attempt to find breathable air, he saw a worker on fire, screaming and running without destination, as though he could somehow outrun the flames that were consuming him, running until finally he dropped in agony, writhing on the floor, his body smoldering even after the flames went out. That burn victim never saw the man running after him with a blanket, trying to catch him to put out the flames.

Jerzy knew right at that moment that he had to get out of there, and with all the current confusion, there would never be a better opportunity than right now.

He heard a loud bang which sounded like it was just outside the exit from which he had just been thrown back inside. It sounded like a car slammed into the building at high speed. He ran all the way back and with difficulty, pulled the heavy steel door open. The first thing he saw was Boguslaw hanging over the twisted rail, so sliced up that his innards could be seen still pulsating, as though waiting to be told by his brain that he was dead so they could stop moving. Jerzy stared at him, not able to tear his eyes away. He should have been sickened, but instead all he felt was relief. Looking around, he could not see any sign of the guard, then he looked over what was left of the handrail, down on the ground and found him there. Most of him, anyway.

The entire landscape was filled with explosions and smoke, and the sky was black with allied planes, with bombs still falling everywhere. When Jerzy ran down the stairs, he saw another friend who signaled Jerzy to follow him to a good shelter he knew about. Running after him, Jerzy saw that there were fires and people running everywhere amid the massive debris from the allied bombing. This is crazy, he thought as he ran. Nuts. The friend ran to a tall smokestack, and stood in its doorway, gesturing to Jerzy, yelling for him to hurry up.

Jerzy followed, but stopped at the last second without knowing why, and ran toward a different shelter instead, and as he was running, he heard a whistling in the air. He turned and saw something dropping right into the center of the giant smokestack he almost went into. Out of the corner of his eye, he also spotted a small hole amid some concrete rubble ahead which he dove into and covered his head to protect it from the chimney bricks as they filled the sky overhead.

When things quieted down, he climbed out slowly and looked around at the massive destruction, shaking his head as he remembered his earlier conversation with Stefan. "This is wrong... this is all wrong. Why in the hell have I been working for the Germans? What good did I think I was doing? No, no more. No more. I would rather die than continue."

He was sickened by the thought that he had become a traitor to his own people. "I need to return home, now... immediately, and I need to bring Ekaterina with me."

Finally, the bombing stopped as the allied planes had delivered their entire payload, but Jerzy did not notice it because there was no absolute quiet to be found as the fires roared on in the still exploding factory. Fire trucks screamed their calls of urgency, and men scurried here and there, like ants responding to their own collapsed architecture, yelling directions to each other, each going about his own business as though it alone was of the utmost importance. Jerzy stood cautiously, dusting himself off while he looked around at all the turmoil, trying to decide what he should do next. He thought about his dead father, wondering if he was watching over him, thinking that maybe it was he who kept him from going into that smokestack, and Jerzy cried inside for the love of his Papa. And so it was that he found himself walking toward his barracks, wearing his sadness as the only vestige of what it meant to be human.

When Jerzy got there, the room was almost empty. He quickly removed the tattered clothes he had on, put on his only clean shirt and pants with his one jacket and simply walked out of there, never turning back, and never saying a word to anybody he ran into. Not a word about how he felt he had betrayed his own people, nor the decision he had just made to skedaddle on out of there and set things right, as they should have been from the beginning. Not a word either about the man who was on fire or the close call he had with the exploding chimney. Nope, he was leaving this God-forsaken place now and forever, and that was that. Once in a while, he heard a new explosion, but he did not care. He was going home.

Twenty-One

Punishment Camp

When Jerzy arrived at the women's barracks, he saw much turmoil, the females busy everywhere. This portion of the complex somehow escaped with minimal damage, but they had lost electricity from the bombing and fires, so it was dark and the air filled with smoke. Many of the women were trying to help the workers who were wounded. Jerzy looked for his girl, but could not find her in all the confusion. He spotted one of her friends, and ran over to talk to her. "Have you seen Ekaterina?" he asked. The woman was kneeling on the floor, wiping the blood off the face of a wounded man who was lying amid the debris. Without saying anything, she merely pointed to a place where more wounded were being brought in, and there he saw her at last.

Jerzy ran to her. "Ekaterina, we need to leave here. This is our best chance to escape, while everything is so confusing. Please, let us go quickly." He took one of her hands, but she pulled it back hard.

"Ekaterina..."

"No, Jerzy, I cannot," she said. "No."

"Please, we must go now."

"No," she said again, shaking her head to make sure he understood. "I am scared, Jerzy. I cannot... not now, anyway. I am not ready. Besides, many people have been hurt and I could not live with myself if I just left without doing what I could to help. But you go... please. Go, and come back for me later. Will you do that?"

"Ekaterina..."

"Please?"

"Then let me at least say goodbye to you properly." He looked into those gorgeous big brown eyes and just shook his head sadly, then gently hugged her. "I do not want to leave you," he said.

"But you must... go while you can. I will be all right... the older women care for my needs as though I am their own daughter. Just promise that you will come back for me... that is all I ask."

Jerzy looked down, and finally nodded. "I will," he said firmly. "Nothing will stop me."

He kissed her quickly, and then turned to walk away while he still had the will to do so.

"I love you," she yelled to him. "And I will wait forever."

He turned. "I will be back for you," he answered. "Do not forget me." And he continued on. He did not dare to look back again... if he did, he knew he would stay.

Jerzy decided to take a train to Warsaw. He needed to get home. Badly. The telegram about his father's death was in his pocket, so he was hoping that if he was stopped along the way, he would be treated with compassion.

He removed his patch and threw it away, then took a trolley to the train station. According to the schedule, the first stop had a two-hour layover, so rather than just hang around, he left the train station because he knew it was always watched by the Germans for suspicious activity. The last thing he wanted to do was arouse anybody's curiosity.

He had heard that the Germans were giving furloughs to the French, so with the little money he had, the boy bought a French newspaper and a beret, hoping he would be left alone. He also picked up a small pouch of tobacco as a gift for his uncle.

Jerzy boarded the train again, his newspaper under his arm, but before the train left the platform, two SS agents stopped him.

"Where are you going?" one of them asked.

"France," Jerzy said, hoping that his one-word answer would not display the wrong accent.

"Then you are on a train that is going the wrong way. Your papers?" he said, holding his hand out.

Jerzy knew that all he had left was honesty, so he reached in his pocket for the telegram, and as he was handing it over, he said, "I have none, but my father has died, and I was hoping to visit his grave." He looked at the agents hopefully.

"Come with me," he said.

I have no idea where we are going but with some luck, perhaps he will help me, Jerzy thought. They left the train, then walked down into a tunnel. It was long and dark. The boy could feel his heart beating faster. When they emerged, they approached a place surrounded by a fence with barbed wire on top. This was not looking good. The agent pulled a cord and moments later, the gate opened. Jerzy followed him inside, where he was brought to a room with two men. One was a military officer, the other a civilian, about the boy's age. The SS agent whispered something to them.

They turned and stared at Jerzy. "Where were you going on that train?" the officer said to Jerzy.

"To Poland, to visit the grave of my Papa, who died while I was working here." He answered immediately because he knew that the Germans did not like it when you hesitated.

"What are you called?" the officer said.

"Jerzy Czaplicki."

"And where are you from, Czaplicki?"

Jerzy hesitated a moment too long, and the civilian kicked him with his hard-tipped shoe. "Answer," he said in a loud voice.

"Owwww... I was born in Lublin."

"Did you parachute in here?"

"No, I have never even been in a plane."

The officer stared hard at him. "Empty out your pockets. SCHNELL."

Jerzy removed what money he had left, along with a few photographs. His hands were visibly trembling.

"Anything else?"

"No," he lied.

"Put your arms on the edge of this desk, and spread your legs out." They patted his pants legs, his shirt, and his jacket pockets, and there they found the tobacco.

"I THOUGHT THAT WAS EVERYTHING," the officer screamed.

Jerzy cringed, hoping that the purple-faced officer would have a heart attack right then from all that yelling. Instead, both men attacked him, working him over with their fists all over his head and body, and when he fell to the floor, they kicked him, yelling at him the whole time.

"You are a poor excuse for a human being, Czaplicki," they yelled, punching and kicking him over and over again. "Why were you even born?"

Jerzy asked himself the same question. They continued their attack, with the boy covering his head instinctively, and finally they were winded and had the guards throw him in a large shed with about fifty other people. They carried him over, swung him through the entry where he slid onto a dirt and gravel floor on his side, landing finally in a fetal position, with his arms still covering his head. And then everything went black.

When he came to, a fly was buzzing in his ear, and he knew from that and his own moaning that death had eluded him. Both eyes were swollen shut, but he wanted to know where fate had brought him. He moved his arms slowly, somehow sat up, leaned back against a wall, and tried to see, but the light hurt too much. Not knowing where he was seemed more painful than the light, so he tried again and looked around as best he could.

The room was like a large shed, with various sized sheets of corrugated tin making up a patchwork roof, and the floor was entirely bare ground with small patches of weeds poking out. There was a single door and window, and a cast iron stove in the middle of the room. The beds along the wall were boards, no mattress, no straw... just plain, rough boards. A man saw that Jerzy was awake now, so he came over and sat next to him, handing the boy a small rag. "For your nose," he said.

Jerzy touched it to his upper lip and winced, then put it back more gently to dab a little blood away.

"I thought I would never see you again," the man said. He had a familiar accent. Jerzy looked again through his squinting eyes.

"Benvenuto?" he said.

"The Germans must run short of meat... looks like they try to turn you into grounda beef."

Jerzy smiled, but even smiling hurt. He stuck a finger in his mouth to see if any teeth were broken or lost. "What is this place?" he said.

"It is called a punishment camp, my young friend. People without papers are sent here to work... at least for a while."

"Then what?" the boy asked.

"Then they are sent to a concentration camp, and that, I believe, is a end of the line. Finito."

"Holy crap," Jerzy said. "We have to get out of here."

"What you need is to get better, my young friend. Heal, and then we talk of escape."

Jerzy merely closed his eyes again and nodded.

* * *

At five o'clock the next morning, a shrill whistle awakened them, followed by the voice of a German guard yelling, "ROUST, ROUST." They all ran to the latrines, where they were given five minutes to clean themselves in a trough they shared. Jerzy still had the double-edged razor blade that he hid in his jacket, but nothing to hold it with. Looking around, he saw a small stick on the ground, which he fashioned into a handle of sorts. Unfortunately, it cut his face as much as it shaved him. Maybe more.

No sooner had he finished when another loud whistle blasted into the silence of the camp. This one meant they were to run outside and stand at attention in the yard. It was raining lightly, and cold, but that did not matter. No talking was allowed, nor was any movement, so each prisoner became a living statue.

"Unauthorized movement carries strict penalties," said the camp commandant. "You will stand here at attention until you are told to go back inside. Is that understood?"

While they endured this pain and humiliation, they could see through the windows the German soldiers casually drinking coffee indoors. Nevertheless, Jerzy and the others could do nothing, except stand without movement and wait. Apparently, this was going to be the daily routine, no matter what the weather. Eventually, they were released to return indoors.

For breakfast, the whistle blew once more, and they had to go outside again, even during the rain, where they formed a line that moved toward the commandant, who personally gave each of them a single slice of bread. This was their entire breakfast, which they brought back into the barracks to eat while standing around the stove, because there was no furniture to sit on.

At lunchtime, the routine remained almost the same: they would grab a bowl, a spoon, and a knife and run outside to see a man with a kettle who served them soup, only it was mostly water. Sometimes they might get a tiny piece of potato or a cabbage leaf. To get both was like winning a lottery.

The next day there was no rain, so people from the outside came to get free laborers. Every prisoner who was not chosen returned back inside the barracks to await instructions.

Punishment camp... Jerzy wondered what he was being punished for.

Benvenuto had escaped easily from the chemical factory weeks ago, and like Jerzy, was beaten when caught. But that did not matter. He resisted the German orders repeatedly, calling them bad names, the worst names he could think of, in his beloved Italian language. He repeatedly refused to follow orders, and was beaten again and again.

Eventually, he learned to obey, but he did not forget, nor did he forgive.

He had been using his time in the weeks of his mock obeisance watching, waiting, learning. He saw where all the guards were posted, noting their schedules and when they changed shifts. The exact times could not be determined because those Nazi bastards stole his watch, but he saw when the guards relaxed and became casual. If he planned it right, his idea just might work. It had to work—he could not take any more of this treatment.

That night there was just the smallest sliver of a moon. He had been waiting for this... it had to be now. He knew he would never get another chance like this. In this darkness, Benvenuto went outside the shack, which was connected to several others. The tower guard was almost asleep. Earlier, Benvenuto had seen a nearby rain barrel. Luckily, it was empty. Now, rolling it quietly, he moved it to the side of the building away from the guard, turned it upside down, and quickly, but as quietly as possible used it as a stepping stone to climb to the roof. From there, all he had to do was carefully travel the length of the roofs to the last shack, which was close enough to the fence for him to jump over to his freedom.

Crawling on the corrugated metal roof, he was about a quarter of the way when one of the sheets of metal slid out of place, making a scraping sound that alerted the guards.

"Oh shit," he said.

Whistles blew, searchlights came on, and he heard a crashing sound at the end of the building. When he turned to see what was happening, a large German Shepherd bounded onto the roof from a plank that had been put nearby for just such an occasion. He sprinted toward the fence, but running fiercely behind him, the dog was closing in, barking as though he wanted to awaken the dead. He was followed by two other dogs, also barking in anticipation of the chase. There was no way Benvenuto could outrun them, but he had to try.

The other captives in the shacks below were awakened by the pounding of feet on the rooftop, followed by the crashing sound of Benvenuto as he fell, the loud crash filling the shack below with the noise of his defeat, followed by his screams of agony mixed with the growling of the dogs as they had their way with him in their primeval frenzy. All the dogs' training had come down to this moment: a euphoric sliding away of the veil of canine civilization, returning to those earliest memories of their kind, long forgotten, but now coming to the surface again, a time when strength and cunning were all, and when taking down their prey with pure savagery was its own reward.

When they were done with him, what was left of Ben rolled off the roof, thumping to the ground, where it was now the soldiers' turn to kick and beat what was left of him still further.

Later, everybody was called outside where the Nazis dragged the torn and bloody body, feet first, through the camp, to show everybody what happens to those who try to escape. Jerzy knew it was Ben, and his stomach tightened. He wanted to kill them all.

An unknown man just a little older than Jerzy stood next to him. "You friend?" he said.

The boy nodded, tears threatening to make their way out.

"Those svoloch's will pay for what they do to us," he said softly.

"Svoloch's?" asked Jerzy.

"Bastards," explained the man. Turning to the Germans, he said, "Shtob tai debe deti nosrali v sup," which he then translated to Jerzy. "I say to them, 'I wish for your children to crap in your soup.'"

The boy smiled a little.

"I am called Yuri Vladimirovich Mikhailov," the man said, offering his hand. "I am Ruski."

"Jerzy Czaplicki... Polski." He shook Yuri's hand, taking an immediate liking to this stranger.

"So, what bring you here, Polski?"

Again, the boy smiled a little, wiping his eye. "The Nazis brought me to work in a chemical factory in Germany, but I escaped after a bombing, then they caught me again. You?"

"I am captured in Leningrad and they make me to work like slave on German farm, and I get away, but those bastards finding me again like you, and send me here. I come here yesterday night, but I going to escape again."

"Maybe we will go together," said the boy.

Yuri looked at him, but said nothing.

* * *

Two days later, they were standing in formation outside as usual when an important Colonel arrived in the camp. They all saw that he was a man to be feared, a man with power, because all the officials, including the commandant scraped their noses to the ground in an attempt to bow lower than the others. Jawohl... jawohl was all they said to this man.

He stood before the prisoners. "Can anybody here fix things?" he said.

Moving only his eyes, Jerzy slowly looked to his left, then to his right. Nobody volunteered.

The colonel repeated the question, but still there were no volunteers. What the heck, Jerzy thought, and he slowly raised his hand.

"Are you a repairman?"

"Ja," Jerzy lied, sensing that this might be his ticket out of this place.

"Can you fix a washing machine?"

Jerzy did not even know how washing machines worked. He had heard of them, but had never seen one. "Ja," he said.

Everybody else was dismissed and went back to their shacks.

"What is your name?" the colonel said.

"Niklas," he lied.

"Ah, Niklas. Good, good. Come with me."

The day was sunny... a good omen. Together, Jerzy and the important colonel left the camp on foot, boarded a trolley and rode for a while with neither of them speaking, then they walked some more, finally arriving at a large brick building where he rang the doorbell. A manservant opened the door, saying nothing, but standing at stiff attention while holding the door wide open. Inside, the colonel then brought Jerzy to the kitchen, where the colonel introduced him to his eighteen-year-old housekeeper. The girl had been brought over from France, apparently one of the spoils of war.

"Margarete, get something for Niklas to eat and drink." She was beautiful, and obeyed the colonel without hesitation.

She curtsied. "Oui monsieur," she said softly, and turned to do as she was told.

The boy did not dare to look at her, so he sat silently with his head down while she prepared a meal for him. He could feel the pity she felt as she served him, but Jerzy did not care as long as he had some real food.

The colonel stared hard at him.

"What tools will you need?" he asked.

Jerzy was wondering how to answer when the colonel realized that his question was foolish, as the boy had not yet seen the machine, so there was no way he could know what he would need. The boy could not have answered anyway — he was shoveling the food into his mouth so fast he barely had time to breathe.

"Never mind. I will bring you all of my tools and this way you will be ready for every possibility," he said, hoping to cover his foolish question.

When Jerzy finished eating, the colonel brought him down to the musty basement to see the broken machine. It was dark in there, despite the single bulb trying hard to illuminate everything.

As his eyes adjusted, the boy saw what looked like a basic round tub with some sort of mechanism beneath it, sitting alone in a corner. He also saw grooves dug into the cellar floor. They are probably for the water, Jerzy thought. I wonder how this thing works.

"This is it," the officer said proudly. "Can you fix it?"

"Oh ja, I can fix it, Jerzy lied, hoping he could figure out how it worked."

The colonel smiled. "Good. I will be back later to check on your progress," he said, leaving the boy with his tools and a package of cigarettes.

Jerzy sat down on the cellar floor, leaned back against the cool cement wall, and tapped out a cigarette for himself. He lit it with one of the matchsticks the colonel left for him and inhaled sharply. It was the first cigarette he had had since he and his gang had smoked together as boys, and it made him lightheaded. When the room stopped spinning, he inhaled again, watching the tendrils of smoke weave themselves into beautiful patterns, and he wondered why life could not always be like this.

While smoking, he was also looking at and thinking about the machine standing next to him. "Well, at least it does not use electricity," he observed. "Maybe my training as an automobile mechanic will come in handy now."

Looking the machine over, nothing seemed obvious, so he slowly took it apart, carefully noting where each piece went, what it was connected to, and the sequence of disassembly. After a while, the boy saw some patterns and thought he now understood how it all worked. Unlike an automobile, where the cylinders were forced to move by the power of gasoline explosions from the spark plugs being fired, this thing was forced into action from water pressure, which pushed a lone cylinder back and forth. There was slime and rust everywhere, so hoping that it was just frozen from all the sludge, Jerzy continued tearing the machine apart, scraping and cleaning each piece as he went along.

He took his time, had another smoke, and wondered if this would be a good time to make his escape, but, he realized, he had no money and did not know this city. He even looked suspicious. No, this was not right the time, he decided... not the right time at all.

So, Jerzy celebrated his brilliant decision with yet another cigarette, watching the smoke gather about his head in fascinating patterns, and he realized that he was much like the smoke, just sitting there with nowhere more important to go. What a life, he thought, as he put the parts back together again, hoping that he reassembled it correctly.

The boy heard heavy footsteps coming down the basement stairs. As the footsteps grew closer, however, he saw the uniform, and stood up to greet the colonel.

"Well, is the machine fixed?" he asked.

"Jawohl," Jerzy said sharply, even though he had not had a chance to test it. He just looked straight ahead. And prayed that the God of Mechanics was watching over him.

The colonel opened a water valve to turn the machine on, looking at the boy with a blank expression all the while. Jerzy held his breath and crossed his fingers as he watched the mechanism, hoping against hope that it would work. If anybody asked him to speak at this moment, he would be unable... the stupid machine would either save his life or end it, right here, right now.

The water poured in, but nothing was happening, and the colonel just stared at Jerzy with that blank look on his face. The boy trembled from somewhere deep inside, and he began to wonder what it would feel like to die.

Then the machine slowly began to groan, shaking him out of his thoughts, followed by loud creaks like the noise a castle door might make when being opened for the first time in a thousand years. Sounds crawled out that Jerzy had never heard before, metal scraping against metal, sounds that ran down his spine, and then finally, a faint trickle of water, and slowly, oh so slowly, the machine began to show signs of life, until it ran at last just as it did so long ago, when it was new. The colonel beamed at the boy as though he was a genius.

"Ah, you are a good mechanic," he said, shutting off the water and inviting Jerzy upstairs again for a sandwich and a cigarette.

When the boy finished his cigarette, the Colonel gave him a half a mark — exactly the money he would need to get back to the camp, no further.

When he returned to the camp gate, Jerzy rang the bell. The commandant himself was there to open the gate, and Jerzy could tell by his hanging jaw and wide-open eyes that he was surprised to see him. Apparently, he thought that the boy would see this as an opportunity to escape, giving the Germans a good reason to shoot him, but instead of trying to get out, he was trying to get in, so the colonel just stared at Jerzy in silent amazement.

"Did you fix the machine?" he said.

"Jawohl," the boy answered proudly.

"Good. Go on inside."

Finally, Jerzy thought... I have trust.

Twenty-Two

Sugar Cubes

A few days later, the same high-ranking colonel came to the camp again, handpicking five men for a special work detail. Because of the work Jerzy did earlier, he was the first one chosen. Three of the group were Italians who deserted their posts at the Russian front, but they were young and strong, and strength was needed for this job. The Italians spoke very little German and no Polish, but Jerzy had picked up some German along with a little Italian, so the colonel made him the translator. The officer left and three German soldiers escorted them into town, where they were shown the rubble from a bombed out building and told to dig an entrance through the debris.

The first command for Jerzy to relay was to start digging. Not knowing how to say this in Italian, he told them in German, but they just looked at him as though he was an interesting bug, so he said it again, only this time in Polish. The results were no better. Out of frustration, he now just pointed to them, then to the rubble, and demonstrated a digging motion with his hands.

"Aaaaaaahhhhhh," they said, nodding their heads in understanding. They smiled and copied his motions. Jerzy walked over to the rubble and signaled to the Italians to join him. Using their bare hands, they were able to successfully remove the larger fragments, and they used their shovels for the smaller ones. Within a few hours, they made an impressive opening.

"Czaplicki, come here," said the sergeant in charge. He was just a few years older than the boy, and not so cruel like so many of the other German soldiers. "This building was once a butcher shop. I want you to get these men in there to help you retrieve a heavy safe that is in there somewhere."

Jerzy nodded, gesturing for the Italians to enter, but they shook their heads no. What was left of the building looked as though it would collapse, and they were no braver now than they were at the Russian front.

Jerzy shook his head and decided to go in alone. He stooped down to his hands and knees, then lower, to fit through the small hole the men had made, slowly crawling on his belly with only a flashlight to guide him. The dust flew up his nose and made him sneeze repeatedly. He moved slowly, partly because it was so dark in there, but more so because he was afraid of the debris coming down on him and crushing his unworthy head. Then the flashlight uncovered something of a much higher value than a safe.

The light fell upon packages of sugar cubes... hundreds of them. With a need born of extreme deprivation, Jerzy grabbed as many cubes as he could, shoveling them into his mouth where they each found a new home, handful after handful of sweet salvation. His pulse shot up as he continued to gorge himself until finally feeling a little full. He could not help but smile while he chewed.

Moving on, he next came upon an open field of crackers and sausages. "Oh my God, real food." Now, he wished he had waited before eating the sugar, but he ate some of this new find anyway because even though his stomach was full, he still felt hungry somewhere deep inside... it was a hunger that would not go away easily.

A voice from outside the rubble disturbed the beautiful silence. A German voice. "How are you doing in there?" The sound reverberated throughout the chamber.

"Oh, it is very difficult in here... very dangerous. There is room for only one person," he said, listening to the echoes of his own voice while stuffing his face. He knew that nobody else was brave enough to go in there, and he was scared too, but he was so hungry that he just did not care. Besides, the food was his find, and he did not want others ruining it for him.

Finally, Jerzy could eat no more, his stomach stretched to capacity. He moved on again, but this time he crawled slowly, because he was stuffed, not afraid. He felt like a snake that just ate a goat. Moving the flashlight carefully, he saw a half-collapsed brick wall leaning on a barrel, so he moved to investigate. It was cracked open from the weight of the wall, and when he peered inside, he saw that the barrel was filled with sticks of butter... beautiful golden butter, which had become a luxury everywhere because of all the shortages.

He also saw many ration cards on the floor, some of which he grabbed and hid inside his jacket.

Then he turned, retracing his path from the outside, where the guard was waiting for him. He crawled out through the small opening, squinting at the bright sun, and stood up, brushing the dirt off his body, and paying particular attention to the crumbs around his mouth.

"Herr Sergeant, I looked very hard for the safe but I just could not find it. I am sorry." To soften this news, he added, "But I did find a whole barrel full of butter." He did not mention the ration cards.

The soldier looked at him thoughtfully, then without a word, took off, leaving the other two soldiers to guard the workers, but that was okay because it gave Jerzy a chance to rest. Since the Italians did not help him, Jerzy saw no reason to share anything with them.

When the sergeant returned, he was dragging a small bathtub behind him, with a long heavy cord attached.

The soldier told him, "Czaplicki, since we cannot find the safe, we must go back with something to show for our efforts, so send the Italians back in there with this tub, and have them scoop the butter into it."

Turning to the Italians, Jerzy asked for volunteers, but they were still scared, which he should have known. If they were brave, they would never have been on this detail in the first place, so again, Jerzy went back in there alone, eating as he went along. When he came back out again, he went over to the guard.

"Sir, I have worked very hard for you in there. I found some food remnants... crackers and so on, but much of what I have found is getting old. This is not food that Germans would eat. With your permission, can I take some of it back to the camp? It will just rot completely otherwise."

The guard looked at Jerzy, noting his half-starved body, and thinking about how bravely the boy worked for him. "Okay, Czaplicki, but do not be obvious about it."

Jerzy almost ran back inside. Tucking his pants into his socks, the boy dropped countless sticks of butter down his pants legs, then stuffed as many crackers and sausages into his pockets as he could. The butter was cool in the beginning, but in a short time it was warming up from the heat of his legs and becoming soft. It felt weird.

Coming back outside for the last time, he found that walking normal had now become a challenge. In fact, it was almost impossible.

When they returned back to the camp, the soldier chatted with the guard, distracting him so Jerzy could get in without creating a problem. The guard, who was hungry for someone to talk to just glanced at Jerzy and quickly waved the boy on in, then turned his attention back to the other soldier.

Jerzy did not understand why that soldier helped him, but he did understand that he would never again try to walk with butter in his pants.

At lunch the next day, when they were in their shack, Jerzy cut a slice of butter for each guy there, dropping it into their soup, but there were no thanks; the deprivation was so severe that the men had become like mindless automatons. He did not share the sausage or crackers with anyone but his new Russian friend, Yuri.

"You are good comrade, Czaplicki," he said. "Your stomach think like mine."

"Yuri, can you keep a secret?"

The Russian nodded his head. "Of course... I honorable Comrade Ruski."

Looking around to make sure nobody was watching, Jerzy reached into one of the inside pockets in his jacket and pulled out the ration cards, not all the way, but enough so that Yuri could see what he had, then quickly put them back.

Yuri whistled softly. Then his eyes got big. "Listen my Polski friend... is new man in camp. Maybe you know him... maybe not. He is Frenchman... short, fat man. He goes out to city any time he wants. Czaplicki, maybe this man can use ration cards you find and buy us more food when he goes to town. What you say?"

"I do not know, Yuri. How do you know we can trust him?"

"My comrade, where he can hide?"

The two looked at each other, smiled, and decided to meet with the Frenchman who slept in a different shack. They would meet with him right after the morning recruitment.

The next morning, they inquired of several men, and finally were directed to the shack which housed the Frenchman. His name was Jean Mercier, and he was a stark contrast to the rest of them... he was a hefty porker, definitely not a candidate for immediate starvation. Jerzy was immediately suspicious.

"Jean, why are you not skinny like the rest of us?" he asked.

"Give me time young Pole... I just arrived here last week, but listen, they are not feeding me any better than the rest of you. In fact, I think I feel the hunger even more than anybody else because I am so used to eating well."

"Look," said Yuri. "I hear you allowed to leave camp whenever you wish. Why that is?"

Leaning in closer between them, Jean spoke in a hushed tone: "I have the confidence of these German fools. A little lie here, a little lie there... they trust me completely."

Jerzy and Yuri looked at each other and Yuri nodded. Turning back to their new friend, Jerzy sighed, reached into his coat pocket and showed Jean the cards.

"Would you buy some bread for us the next time you go into town?"

Jean's eyes grow large, and he nodded his head as Jerzy handed him all of the ration cards.

Two days later, Jean brought them the bread he promised. He also bought some for himself without even asking, but Jerzy did not care. He and Yuri now had both bread and butter. This was a true feast, so they shared with the others.

That night they laid down, but even though their stomachs were full, it was difficult to sleep, partly because their bones were now close to the surface of their skin and they hurt against the bare boards they laid on, and partly because they slept in the same clothes each day, and lice were everywhere.

* * *

Eventually Jerzy had finally fallen asleep, but not for long, when he was awakened by a flashlight in his eyes and a German Shepherd growling in his face. He woke up fast.

"Where did you get the ration cards, Czaplicki?" He knew that voice.

"Colonel Heisinveld ..."

Two other soldiers flanked him. "I asked you a question, Czaplicki." The soldiers drew their rifles and aimed them at the boy.

Jerzy knew immediately why he was in this spot now, so he decided to tell the truth.

"Sir, I was working hard, very hard to find the safe and these cards were just lying there on the floor and I was so very hungry, but it was dangerous in there and I thought I would probably be killed but I kept working anyway, even though everybody else was too scared, but I stayed with it, Herr Colonel... I did... I worked very hard for you."

Jerzy spoke more out of desperation than conviction, all the while images of concentration camps dancing in his head. The dog continued to growl. He heard the rifles click and he squeezed his eyes closed.

But then, just as quickly as they appeared, they lowered their weapons, turned and left, leaving Jerzy to puzzle over the workings of the German mind.

Damned Frenchman. And damned Heisinveld. Was that man everywhere?

Twenty-Three

The Wilderness

The next day, the weather was cold and wet, but again, everybody was forced to stand outside until they were soaked to the bones. When the commandant finally dismissed them, they almost ran back indoors just to stand around the stove in search of warmth. Nobody spoke, and Jerzy found himself reliving the events of the previous night. One man clenched an empty pipe between what was left of his teeth, the others shared a single cigarette. By mutual agreement, only one puff was allowed per person. Yuri stood nearby, eating leftover bread. He looked over and saw Jerzy shivering and broke the bread, offering him half. No words were spoken, but the gratitude was understood.

"We need escape, Czaplicki, but I want you, me, go together," said Yuri.

"That is good, Yuri, but I cannot find a way to escape from this camp. You saw what happened to my Italian friend. So I think first we must leave the camp officially... maybe find work details with the best opportunity, then escape. What do you think, my Ruskie friend?"

Yuri thought for a moment. "If we do such, must be outdoor job.

Maybe tomorrow we volunteer, if you feeling ready. I have some small money, Czaplicki, but I give you half. This way if we cannot travel together, each of us maybe can take bus or trolley alone. We be friends, no?"

"We are best friends, Yuri."

That night, as he lay in bed, Jerzy watched the sky through their tattered roof, and he saw the German searchlights roaming through the clouds, trying to grab on to the American bombers flying overhead. And he thought about his promise to Ekaterina, wondering what she was doing now.

In the morning, Jerzy brought his light trench coat to wear outside for their morning ritual, but he was told to go back and remove it. He returned to the shack, but instead of removing the coat, he tucked it into his trousers, tightened the belt, then bloused the coat a little so it would look more like a shirt. Knowing that the Germans did not like to be fooled, he tried to be extra careful about how it looked. The boy returned to the formation, but thankfully, none of the guards noticed.

A group that was forming for a new work detail still needed two more workers, so Jerzy and Yuri joined them. They were going to repair a three-story brick schoolhouse where the roof was partly burned away. It was not far from the camp, so they walked there. When they arrived, Jerzy noted that some of the rafters could be seen through the charred remnants of the burned-out roof, like the exposed bones of an overcooked beast. That reminded him of the chemical factory, which reminded him of Ekaterina, and he became even more determined to find a way out. He looked around, trying to figure out the best way to escape. A nine-foot brick fence with a raised cement top surrounded the school. And shards of broken glass were embedded in the cement.

This must have been some school, Jerzy thought.

Since he was assigned to help fix the roof, he grabbed a few small rolls of tarpaper along with a bucket of hot tar and struggled upstairs, slowly, inching his way to the attic. He was careful not to spill any of the tar... the Germans got angry when you wasted anything of theirs. A short fat guard was waiting for him up on the third floor.

"You," he said. "Take that stuff up to the roof." Jerzy looked at him and could not help but think that if that guard tried to carry this stuff himself, he would have a heart attack. The image made him smile.

At least the weather is not hot, he thought. He looked around for Yuri, but could not see him. They must have him working downstairs. After two hours straight of laboring, Jerzy started to feel tired, and he slowed down. The lack of nutrition was taking its toll, but Jerzy no longer thought about that. He merely existed from day to day, like a plant that everybody stepped on, and he just did what he was told. The guard in charge saw the boy slow down from his location down below.

"Hey, get moving, pig," he said loudly. "Schnell... SCHNELL."

When Jerzy looked down at him, he also spotted one of life's opportunities offering itself, like a beautiful present, and his heart beat to a new tune. On his next trip downstairs, he checked it out closer, and saw his chance to escape. Freedom, perhaps only twenty feet away. He wanted to get Yuri, but he knew that this chance might disappear quickly if any of the guards saw it, so he had to take advantage while he could.

"Yuri will understand," he said.

Without even thinking about it, Jerzy looked around quickly and saw no one, so he ran without hesitation to an unhung door that was leaning against the brick wall. Bracing one foot against the doorknob, he pulled his long sleeves over his hands to protest them from the broken glass embedded there, and grabbing the top of the outside wall, he leaped over. His heart was racing, and he expected to feel a bullet going through his body at any second, but he could not stop now. Once outside the fence, he pulled his trench coat out of his pants, straightened out his hair, and slowly walked away, trying to blend in with the German civilians. A gentle ding-ding sounded as a trolley appeared right by his side. Every noise, no matter how innocent, made him jump, but he saw this trolley as a gift from the gods, so the boy boarded it, not caring where it was going, and allowed it to carry him away.

After four stops, Jerzy got off and boarded a different trolley, just in case anyone was following. This time, he rode for six stops, and changed trolley cars yet again. Having only a few marks left, he boarded one last trolley. Fortunately, this one was going toward the outskirts of the city, where there were uninhabited areas, some of them still wild.

After disembarking, Jerzy looked to make sure nobody was watching, and pulling his overcoat more tightly about him, went into the woods. It was late October and the wind had a chill, but he had spent much time outdoors on his uncle's farm and learned about surviving on what he could find growing wild.

As he traveled into the forest, the wind became almost unnoticeable as it was now buffered by the trees, so the chill became more tolerable, and Jerzy began looking in earnest for food. The first thing he found was a field of wild mushrooms. He smiled at the memory of his uncle teaching him which ones were safe to eat, wondering if he was still okay and living on the farm.

Walking deeper into the woods, Jerzy saw some leaves that looked familiar. Going closer, he stooped down and was delighted to find that they were potato leaves. All he had to do was dig a bit, and he would have some good eating. He tried using his bare hands, but the ground here was too hard. Then he had an idea. He found a fairly good-sized rock, but it was too rounded for digging, but if he could split it in half... maybe. He put the stone atop a larger one, then, using a third, heavier stone, he brought it down like a hammer and hit his intended shovel hard... and watched it crumble into small, useless pieces.

With practice, however, Jerzy got better at it, eventually making a fairly usable digging tool, and with it, unearthing a few wild potatoes, along with whatever other edible roots he could identify. Nevertheless, hunger was still a constant problem. The boy's stomach was constantly rumbling, noisier than any other time that he could remember.

He had been in the woods for five days when he spotted a rabbit, and the rabbit saw him at the same time. They both froze, staring at each other.

If only I can catch that thing, I can eat him, he thought. But Jerzy had slowed down from the weakness that extreme hunger leaves within. And as he studied the hare, he thought, Rabbit, I am in the same situation as you. Both of us are wanted, preferably dead. He looked at the animal some more... he looked in the eyes of this other living creature, a being that merely wanted to continue living, could feel the rabbit's heart beating faster with fear, and then the boy lost his appetite for meat. The rabbit also lost interest, turned his head, sniffed the air a few times and hopped away in his own search for food.

* * *

Time progressed, and the boy lost track of what day it was, nor did he have a destination in mind, yet he stayed on the move constantly, trying to stay one step ahead of the Germans, but as winter was rolling in, this became more difficult. He was waiting for the Americans to come, but he knew he could not just wander forever or he would end up in Russia. On occasion he saw others, but he kept away from them because groups, even groups of two, could be spotted easier than a lone man.

After two weeks of living in the woods, Jerzy stumbled on an isolated farm area, far away from the city. He watched from behind a tree to see who lived there. Maybe there was a German soldier hiding there, just waiting to fill the boy's stomach with lead, so he could not be too careful.

But the only person he saw was an old woman who came out from her little house behind the barn with a bucket of old potatoes and carrots and some leafy green vegetables that she was dumping out to feed the chickens and ducks that she called. The birds squawked and pecked at each other, but she ignored them and walked back to house. As soon as she disappeared, the boy ran to gather as many vegetables as he could carry back to the woods. The whole time he was trembling fiercely, partly with lust over having these vegetables to eat, and partly from the incessant fear that he would be caught by the Nazis just waiting to beat him to within an inch of his life for thinking he was good enough to eat this excellent German food. He was emotionally bankrupt and kept looking over his shoulder even as he ate, constantly moving while he chewed because he did not dare to sit down and get caught. He wanted to scream, LEAVE ME ALONE, DAMN IT.

But he said nothing. The quiet was safer.

And so, he continued wandering. Alone... always alone. He remembered Ekaterina, and then he looked down at his dirty, tattered clothing and laughed aloud. Oh, she would really want me now, he thought. I am a big catch. And in his utter despair for himself, he sat down under an old birch tree and cried, the tears making clear tracks down his dirty cheeks.

He wondered anew why he had ever been born. He was but a poor, skinny fugitive with no education, no money or status, and no hope for the future. It all made no sense, and Jerzy found himself living only in order to stay alive. "But for what?" he asked. Why was he still living on this side of the dirt? "My life has no joy, no meaning." Many times, he wanted to just lay down on the bare ground and give up, yet he persisted without knowing why.

Forty days of aimless wandering changed nothing but the weather, which began to get seriously cold. Jerzy was thinking about his girl all the time now, and he remembered anew the promise he made to her. He needed to save her, even if it meant his life.

That day at dusk he saw a silhouette at the edge of the woods. It was a barn, offering protection and possibly food. He crept up to some nearby bushes, crouching there like a scared rabbit to see if it was safe. The thick blanket of pine needles on the forest floor offered some protection from the cold ground, and up above, the treetops bent in the breeze. It was quiet, but just to be sure, he waited for over an hour. Hearing and seeing nothing, Jerzy slowly approached the barn, opened the door an inch at a time, and peered into the darkness. When the door was open enough, he walked slowly and quietly inside, feeling his way around, and discovered a haystack. He was tired, and dug a hole in the straw just big enough to crawl into, making a bed for himself and fell asleep.

In the morning, he awakened to all kinds of noises and trembled with the thought of getting caught. Staying inside his little straw cocoon, Jerzy listened and heard the voices of many different people speaking many different languages, but German was not one of them.

They must all be refugees, like him. It sounded like the voices were outside the barn.

Jerzy slowly came out of hiding, brushing the straw off of himself and wandered outside where he saw people cooking and talking to each other in small groups. He heard Italians, Poles, and then... Russian. He approached them, listening in particular to the one whose back was facing him.

"Privyet," said Jerzy to the speaker.

The Russian spun around quickly. "Czaplicki," he said, wearing his biggest grin, and jumped down from the huge rock he was sitting on. They clasped each other in a strong hug, each patting the other hard on the back.

"Yuri, I thought I would never see you again."

The Russian held Jerzy at arm's length to look at him. "You look not so good," said Yuri, shaking his head.

The boy laughed. "Spaciba," he said. He could smell the food cooking, and his stomach roared like a lion in response.

"Come, my friend. I hear you stomach talking, and is not speaking like good friend. We have food to quiet such noise," he said, patting the boy's shoulder. He looked at Jerzy more carefully now and saw how skinny he had become. He felt bad for the boy.

"I happy you get away, but what you do now? Perhaps you stay with us," he said.

"I cannot," Jerzy replied between bites. He wiped his mouth on his sleeve. "I must go back to Leverkusen to get my girlfriend. She is all I have to look forward to."

"Use head, boy," he said, pointing to his own temple. "We all hunted. That all we have to look forward to. To be hunted, and some day to die, no more Jerzy, no more Yuri."

"But not now, Yuri. The Americans are coming. I hear their planes every day dropping bombs on this hellhole. And if I stay here, waiting, what will become of my Ekaterina? Answer me that... will the Nazis let her live? No, Yuri, I must try to save her."

"Czaplicki, if those German bastards catch you again, it will be finish for you. I think maybe this girlfriend she soften your heart, and maybe your head, too." He looked in the sky and saw hundreds of smoke trails from the American bombers. "But..." and a smile crept onto his face, "she is Russkieya, so she must be much woman, and I understand such deep passion." He looked at Jerzy and grinned. "So, I go with you, keep you out of trouble, hey?" and he whacked the boy hard on the back, laughing at the promise of new adventure.

Saying goodbye to their Russian friends, Yuri and Jerzy set out to find their way back to where Jerzy's German captivity began, back to the chemical factory in Leverkusen. They had only a few marks left between them, so they had to be careful of how they spent it. As they walked away from the farmland and toward the town, Jerzy saw Nazi troop movements, and he wondered for the first time if he was doing the right thing, but then he looked at the confident face of his Russian friend, and his doubts were comforted.

Leaving the woods, the sounds of combat rumbled in the background. Yuri saw a trolley and he began running to catch it, yelling behind him, "Run, Comrade." The trolley was just starting to leave when they caught up, waving their arms and yelling, "Stop... stop."

As they boarded, the first person they saw was a police officer. "Why are you in such a hurry?" he said.

They looked at each other, and Yuri nodded to Jerzy, as though saying, this was your idea, so you come up with a good excuse. Jerzy licked his lips, and said, "Sir, we just came back from a funeral and need to get back to work at the Farbenfabriken factory in Leverkusen."

Yuri nodded his head as if to affirm the truth of his friend's story.

"I see," the policeman said. "Papers?" He held out his hand for them.

"We were so anxious to get back, we forgot them," said Jerzy.

"Both of you?" He signaled the driver to stop at the end of next block. "You two need to come with me," he said.

As they walked along, a soldier was walking toward them, at rifle point, guarded by two Nazi soldiers. Jerzy recognized the uniform from pictures he had seen. The prisoner was an American pilot, and as they passed each other, he looked right at Jerzy and Yuri and then he did the damnedest thing... he smiled at them. SMILED.

The end of this war was just a matter of time now, and everybody knew it. Everybody except the Germans.

The police officer took them to a building with a large swastika over the door, and inside, to a guard who brought them to another room where they were told to wait. Jerzy could feel his friend glare at him as the door closed. They could hear the lock closing. A German officer walked in from another door, staring at them silently. While he was looking, they heard distant artillery, like thunder, as the Americans were advancing from France. Jerzy smiled at the thought of a German defeat. The officer caught his expression, and brought his face so close that Jerzy thought he was going to kiss him.

"So, perhaps you think Germany is going to lose this war?" he said.

Trying to answer fast, but without thinking, Jerzy answered, "Ja."

Yuri cringed.

Jerzy saw the officer turn red and reach for his sidearm. He shut his eyes tightly, waiting for the bullet to end it all, no wife, no little Czaplickis running around. He saw a flash of light, but it was behind his eyes as the butt of the pistol crashed down on the top of his head. He dropped to the floor, and all the lights went out.

Twenty-Four

Shhh...

Three months after Jerzy's escape from the factory, Ekaterina was awaked in the middle of the night by the harsh banging of a large, empty metal trashcan against one of the posts in her barracks.

"WAKE UP... ROUST. EVERYBODY UP. WE ARE GOING ON A LITTLE MARCH TODAY..."

Amid the moaning and groaning, all the ladies climbed out of bed to comply with the new orders. No matter how tired they were, they were conditioned; to disobey any order from the Germans was certain death. Everybody was running in every direction. Ekaterina was scared about this. They were never awakened in the night for any reason. Something was not right.

She covered her head with the burlap blanket, and slowly allowed herself to slide off the bed, using the wall behind her to slow her fall. She lay hidden on the floor beneath her bed, partially wrapped in the burlap, and hoping nobody would see her.

The others gathered together in formation between the rows of beds in the center of the barracks, not speaking, but wondering where they were going. The last few women were joining the others, when one woman did not see her friend. "Hey, where is Ekaterina?" she said as they were leaving.

"STOP." The German officer looked around. "Ekaterina, show yourself now. ROUST," he said.

She trembled with a fear conceived in the womb of insecurity, and whimpered quietly.

"Where is her bed?"

Four women pointed to it.

The officer motioned with his head for two of his soldiers to go over there and check. They lifted the blanket and saw nothing. Then one of the soldiers bent over to look under the bed and saw her, trembling, eyes bugging out like a scared puppy. He grinned, and then motioned with his curled forefinger to come to him. "She is here," he yelled to the officer in charge. He lifted his side of the bed, and grabbed her tiny wrist pulling her out.

"Stand up, SHNELL."

She rose, still trembling.

"Do you fall out of bed every night?" he said, laughing. The other soldiers laughed as well. Then with his rifle, he motioned for her to join the other women. "I believe they are all waiting for you." She grabbed a small folded handkerchief off her bed. It had what little money she had saved folded within, and she put it into the pocket of the jacket she had worn to bed. The soldier did not care. These women were all going to die anyway, and whatever she had in there would soon be his.

They began marching out as Ekaterina joined the column. She knew that they were going to be killed... she could feel it.

The women were marched away from the factory and across the railroad tracks, right next to the woods. Ekaterina looked at the trees, careful the guards did not see where she was looking, imagining herself running into the cover of the woods, but she continued to tremble. There were so many guards. If she looked at them too much, surely they would see her and would know what she was thinking. Her heart pounded.

She looked at the woman next to her, who also looked at the

woods and nodded, quickly putting her forefinger in front of her lips to be quiet. They continued on, some of them fearing that each step they took brought them that much closer to their end. Nevertheless, the march continued.

One of the women asked a guard, "Where are we being moved to?" But the guard did not answer, so they walked on in silence, but the further they went, the more scared the women became. They had already marched about three kilometers, and the Germans had not said a word.

In the silence, they heard one of the women fall. She could not rise again, having gone beyond her endurance. A soldier told her to get up. In response, she merely looked down at the ground. So, he unshouldered his rifle, cocked back the bolt, aimed at her head, and told her one more time to get up. She did not move, so he shot her without hesitation and rejoined the group.

Suddenly, all hell broke loose as a woman near the front of the column panicked after hearing the gunfire and ran to the trees. Soldiers from near Ekaterina ran to the front. They fired at the woman.

Then the woman next to Ekaterina elbowed her and whispered, "Now." So, she and the other woman also ran to the woods. Several others decided to take a chance and they ran also. Guards also fired at them. The woman next to Ekaterina was hit, and from the corner of her eye, she saw her fall, but instead of stopping, she ran even faster... faster than she ever ran before in a desperate attempt to elude the certain death that staying would bring.

She ran on and on, changing direction every now and then, running on and on until she was out of breath, when she finally stopped to crouch, leaning back against a tree. She had no choice. When her breathing was back under control again, she listened for the sound of soldiers following, but all she heard was quiet. She wandered on again, but slower now, listening, always listening... just in case.

As the sky lightened with the promise of daybreak, the woods ended, as all woods do, and Ekaterina found herself in a suburban neighborhood. She looked around in the back yards, and soon found what she was looking for. Quickly running to the clothesline, she removed what she thought might fit her and ran back to the safety of the woods again, where she could change. Fortunately, she still had her jacket, but immediately cut off the patch with a hidden razor blade, as Jerzy had showed her, and threw it away. "He was right," she said quietly... "...I should have gone with him when he wanted."

She wished she had a hairbrush so she could look nicer and blend in better.

She resumed her travel in a direction away from this neighborhood where the owner of the clothes she stole might recognize her own stuff, and hoped she could again emerge and find a trolley that would take her away from here. Far, far away.

Ekaterina thought about Jerzy, wondering where he might be, never giving up hope completely, but miserable that she missed her opportunity with him. The tears in her heart quickly found her eyes.

Twenty-Five

The Front Lines

When Jerzy awakened, he was lying in the back of a transport truck. He blinked a few times, but everything was a blur. The truck hit a bump and his head bounced on the wooden bench. "Ow," he said.

"Serve you right, idiot," said Yuri, who was sitting across from him with his arms folded. "Why you say that about Germans losing? I was right... girlfriend melting you brain."

Jerzy looked at the guard and saw that he was just ignoring them.

"I know, Yuri... I was not thinking. I am sorry, but when the Nazis ask a question, they want an answer immediately... and I answered with my heart instead of my head." He raised himself up on one elbow, moaned, then sat up slowly, feeling his head. "Do you know where they are taking us?"

"All soldier said was, 'I hope you know how to use shovel,' then they take us out to truck," Yuri answered, shaking his head.

The sounds of combat were getting closer as they drove. Allied fighter planes were shooting up the roads, and their truck was forced to stop. Jerzy and Yuri just looked at each other, their thoughts tumbling in a whirlwind of imaginings.

The guard jumped out, but another appeared at the rear of the vehicle and pulled open the curtain. "You stay in here," he said, and then he ran into the adjacent woods for protection, leaving the passengers as sitting ducks. Their only cover was under the truck's benches, so they scrambled under there quickly, curling into a fetal position and covering their heads from the thundering death that surrounded them. One explosion rocked the truck, almost knocking it over, but in the end, it merely bounced the prisoners inside a bit. Jerzy bumped his head again and moaned.

When the attack was over, one of the guards returned.

"Welcome. You are now on the front line of the war. We fight grabenkrieg here, and you will be digging trenches for us." He then handed them small shovels.

Yuri looked at Jerzy with amusement. "Nazi bastard who hit you on head must think you want see Amerikanski soldier very close."

Digging was becoming impossible. It was snowing hard, the ground was frozen, and the harsh wind kept them from seeing what was right in front of their faces, which was good because the trenches were getting filled up faster than they were dug out, so one of the guards took them into a building in the town with an auditorium where the others were gathered. Maybe a dozen Polish prisoners were there and what looked like a hundred and fifty Italians.

After the Germans left the room, a few of the Italians came over to check out Jerzy and Yuri, and soon the room was filled with laughter.

"Hey, new companions, you just inna time. We cook a big feast with all kinda sugar beets, red beets, cabbage, carrots, and a few cut up potatoes we find, and we mix everything inna huge bowl where we spice everything... vinegar... a little sugar. Oh boy. Then we cook inna big pot. Mmmmmm... mwah." He opened his fingertips with a big smack of the lips, to emphasize just how good this meal would be. "... Magnifico."

The Italians were wonderful hosts. Jerzy saw a giant kettle in a far corner of a small adjacent room, it was sitting between two sinks, and a fire was burning on a stone floor beneath it. One Italian went over to it and lifted the lid, removing two wires with sugar beets that were cooking and handed them to the newcomers.

So many people were cooking that they had to eat in shifts. They knew that their time was short and soon they would have to go outside to dig the trenches again, snowing or not, so they hurried, sometimes accidentally knocking someone else's beets off the wires and into the water, which caused tempers to flare. Fists soon began flying, and while some of them were fighting, a few others grabbed shovels in an effort to find the beets that fell into the water. Others who were anxious to eat forced the lid back on, which knocked the shovels into the water, causing more fists to fly. It was a three-ring circus with five rings, and Jerzy and Yuri watched in awe as the drama unfolded before them.

When the eating and fighting finally simmered down, a few of the Italians began to sing. The others listened quietly, a few of them joining in, and soon they were all laughing and telling jokes as though no fighting ever happened.

A German guard appeared at the front doorway, yelling at them to go outside to dig. "SCHNELL," he yelled.

As they were marched to their work in the open fields surrounding the town, American fighter planes spotted the Italians, who were wearing their uniforms and carrying their shovels like rifles on their shoulders. One plane circled around to get a closer look.

When he banked, a German soldier yelled to the prisoners, "Stand there, and do not run." Then the German soldiers hid among them as the plane went whooshing over them, neither soldiers nor planes firing.

"Pilot not shoot... he must know," said Yuri softly

The Allies were pressuring the Nazis with ever-increasing attacks, Americans and British from the air and Russians on the ground. It was cold now, bitterly cold, and everything was white, including the trails in the sky from all the allied aircraft that flew over daily. The prisoners were brought out at five A.M., long before the sun rose, to start their digging, and they dug fast, making a ditch for themselves first. Jerzy stared at the trails in the sky, amazed at the complexity from so many planes, and thrilled with the prospect of freedom from his long-time oppressors. Then he felt a rifle barrel poke him.

"Get to work, dog." The soldier pointed to where he wanted the trenches dug. It was all snow and ice.

Jerzy knew that the guards did not care if he lived or died. There were always others who could replace him, but for now he was still alive, and that was all that mattered. He would do as they ordered, but they could not stop him from dreaming about the inevitable Nazi defeat, and dream he did, all night long.

* * *

He had been doing this for a month now, but was losing track of the days. At about seven or eight o'clock one morning, his digging was interrupted by the thunder of American B-17 bombers unleashing their bombs to soften up the target area behind the front lines, then was quickly followed by fighters which flew in low and fast, looking for targets of any kind. The alarms in town blared as the few antiaircraft guns they had opened fire.

Jerzy was digging in an open field outside the town, the woods about a quarter-mile away, so targets in this large white landscape were not hard to find. He worked feverishly, and when the first bombs fell within running distance, he dove into his own foxhole.

After the bombers had passed for the day, American fighters dropped down from the skies to strafe the area with machine gun fire. One of the bullets landed in Jerzy's trench, just inches from his face, and that was when he snapped. The boy quickly glanced over at the German machine-gunner for whom he had been digging and saw that half his head was missing, and that was all Jerzy could take.

"DAMN IT," he said, throwing his rucksack out of the trench. Following right behind it, he leaped out and heard himself growling a deep guttural sound from somewhere deep within. "Aaaaaaaaaarrrgh," he said loudly from between his tightly gritted teeth as he took off, running with every fiber of strength he could command, straining his muscles to help him make it to the woods. He picked up the rucksack on the run, listening for sounds of the planes. As he heard one of them approaching from the rear, he zigzagged to make himself a more elusive target, throwing himself on the ground every few steps, then getting up again quickly and running some more, along with uttering a few choice words, but always fine-tuning his peripheral vision. The Germans were too busy shooting at the fighters to worry about him, so it was just the pilots he had to worry about. "I AM ONE OF THE GOOD GUYS," he screamed at the sky.

Suddenly, one of the straps on the backpack broke, so he had to hold on tighter to the other strap, the entire pack bouncing and slapping against his back with every step. He began to feel cocky, but that stopped when the belt on his pants also broke, forcing him to use his other hand to hold up his britches.

He heard the plane coming at him again from behind. He also saw a road, just before the woods, and as he crossed it he saw a big square hole in the ground, made originally for an antiaircraft gun. He dove in headfirst, still holding onto his pants and rucksack just as the plane passed overhead, shooting right at him. He went in headfirst, and his back hit the wall, which bounced him onto the floor, hard.

The hole was occupied by at least a dozen others. They looked at each other, but then they heard the approach of another plane from a different direction. Everybody ran to the side closest to where the plane was coming from so the bullets found only empty space on the far wall. Jerzy followed. As the plane banked, everyone ran to the opposite side, alternating back and forth until the pilot tired of this game and flew away.

Before the all clear sounded, Jerzy climbed out of the shelter and headed into the woods, glad to be on the move again. He did not know where he was, so until conditions were better, he gave up his dream of returning to Leverkusen. "I have not forgotten you, Ekaterina," he vowed.

But every time he thought of her, his faith in their ever seeing each other again dissolved just a bit. And even if they somehow did reconnect, what did he have to offer? He was a fugitive now, always on the run. He loved her with all his heart, and he wanted more than anything to be with her again, but the more he thought about it, the more hopeless it seemed.

Jerzy continued wandering with no idea of where he was going, but knowing that his first priority was to get as far away from the Germans as possible, and his second was to find food. The woods went on and on, and Jerzy was thankful. There was safety in solitude. Unfortunately, it was also the dead of winter and food was not to be found easily, even with his knowledge of mushrooms and potatoes, which were plentiful during any other season. The snow was just too deep and the cold had a biting grip on him.

The next day, he neared the edge of the woods again and came across a street. His stomach cramped, and out of sheer hunger, he decided to take a chance in the town.

"Why not?" he said. If I do not eat soon, I will die anyway, so what difference does it make?

He was looking down at the ground when he heard a sound in the distance... the sound of chains rattling against a metal surface. He looked up, and there, maybe two blocks away, he thought he could make out someone in a German uniform, riding a bicycle towards him.

Jerzy slowed down, not that he was walking fast anyway, but he had learned the wisdom of caution, and he was definitely not in a hurry to be shot. He also knew that he could quickly run back into the woods again if need be.

He squinted, trying to make out the uniform coming toward him, but he was still having trouble seeing past his hunger. As they approached each other, Jerzy could see that the bicycle rider was young, like him, and he was only an enlisted man, so he was no longer scared.

When they finally met, they both stopped and faced each other. The soldier rubbed his bare hands together and blew on them to stave off the cold, but he was eyeballing Jerzy's gloves the whole time. In similar fashion, Jerzy was eyeballing the loaf of bread in the basket on the front of the bike.

"Those look like really warm gloves," the soldier said.

Jerzy's stomach began rumbling. "I will tell you what," he said. "I will give you these gloves in exchange for your bread."

The soldier grinned and handed over the bread, and as he did so,

Jerzy took off his gloves and gave them in exchange. They were still warm when the other boy put them on. Both boys were happy, and nodding to each other, they went their separate ways, with Jerzy going back into the woods again. He wanted to eat his bread alone, with no chance of it being taken away.

As he tore into it, he knew that he could always keep his hands warm in his pockets, so he smiled at the shrewdness of his deal, knowing in his heart that he got the better part of the bargain.

Two days later, he was alone in the freezing woods, eating whatever he could find to stay alive when he spotted a small farmhouse with a stack of wood outside needing to be split. It was getting dark, so he walked faster, his legs fueled by the thought of warm food.

He reached the farmhouse exhausted and knocked at the door. The farmer's wife, an elderly woman, opened it.

"Yes?" she said.

Jerzy's stomach rumbled as he spoke. "I see that you have some wood that needs splitting. I would be glad to do this, or any other work you need done in exchange for a warm meal and perhaps a place to sleep tonight." He was too exhausted to be suave today.

"Hold on," she said. "I will ask my husband."

She came back quickly, and Jerzy looked at her with much hope in his eyes. "I am sorry," she said. "We do not need any help. Perhaps the next farm can use you."

"Oh... well thank you anyway," he said, then turned and walked dejectedly down the steps. There was a small boulder in the front yard, and he sat there, trying to figure out his next move. He was just so tired, and his stomach would not stop rumbling.

The old lady watched him through the window... he was just sitting there. He sat for about ten minutes when she opened the door again. She stared at him for a minute, then motioned for him to come inside. "Maybe you can stay after all," she said in a kindly voice.

His hopes shot up again. Oh man, he thought. Inside, Jerzy saw a small, but solid elderly man, maybe five feet tall, smiling at him. His teeth were huge, like a horse's, but they were all straight and even.

"What kind of farm work can you do?" he said.

"Well, I worked on my uncle's farm for a year or so, and I learned how to plow and plant many kinds of food, then harvest it when ready, I can care for livestock, like chickens, cows, and horses, I can mend fences, chop wood, fetch water... just about anything that needs to be done. Also, I worked in a garage for a while, so if you have a car, I can also do most automobile repair. I do not have any tools, though."

"A man cannot do much without tools."

"No sir, that is very true. But if you have any tools, I know how to use them."

"Maybe I can use you here after all," the old man said, nodding thoughtfully. What are you called?

"I am Hans," he lied... he suspected that he was on many wanted lists now, and he knew he had to be constantly cautious.

It was late afternoon, but the old woman saw Jerzy looking in the kitchen.

"Are you hungry?" she asked.

"Oh Ja," he said, so she brought out some stew that was left over from lunch, along with a large bowl of potato salad.

"And what would you like to drink, Hans?"

He looked at her, almost pleadingly. "If you have any, I have not had a drop of milk in three years," he said.

She poured him a tall glass of goat milk, which Jerzy drank down quickly, then he ate all of the leftover stew, and most of the potato salad. He sat back, but the old man was anxious to show him the farm.

The barn was larger than the house. They walked inside, and Jerzy saw three cows, a pig and a goat all at one end of the building. At the other end was a huge pile of squash. They walked outside again, but there was no rush, and no fear of capture. Looking around reminded him of his uncle's farm, and Jerzy closed his eyes, lifting his face to the sky. He could smell the freshly cut hay, and at that moment the world was good.

He looked at the farmer, who was wrinkled with the years, but energetic. The old man grinned at Jerzy, displaying his huge teeth again. The sun gleamed on them.

"Do you work this farm all alone?"

"No, my old wife helps me," the farmer said. "Also, my youngest son's wife lives with us, and she does much to help while her husband is away, fighting in this war."

As they walked back into the little house, the old woman appeared at the door. It was almost time for supper, and even though Jerzy had just eaten, she did not want to appear rude, so she asked him if he would like to eat with them.

"Ja," he said, "Ja, I would like that." She saw how much he had eaten just a short while earlier so she did not expect him to join them. But she said nothing.

The old couple ate a hearty meal, and when they finished, they were amazed that Jerzy was still eating. They left the table, and Jerzy continued until the food was gone. When he got up from the table, he looked pregnant, yet he still felt hungry.

The old lady looked at the boy strangely, then took him upstairs and showed him the bath.

"I am boiling some water and you should bathe," she said.

She brought up some hot water and went back downstairs for more.

"Please let me help you," Jerzy said.

"No Hans. I am used to this. You go in there," she said, pointing, "… get undressed, and leave your clothes on the floor just outside the door."

He went upstairs, and after the last bucket of hot water was poured, he finished undressing, then closed the door and slid into the tub, moaning with the pleasure of the moment. He tried to remember the last time he was allowed to bathe and he could not recall when that was.

"And I think she is even going to wash my clothes," he said.

After he had soaped his body and washed his hair, he just lay back in the tub and stayed there until he wrinkled. When he finally emerged, he looked out the window and saw a fire in the yard, but this was no ordinary fire. The old woman was not washing his clothes after all… she was burning them.

"Crap… she must have seen the lice on me." They were so thick before his bath that he could scoop them out of his armpits by the handful, but it had become so normal to him that he had given it no thought. "Now what am I going to wear?"

As he was pondering this, there was a gentle knock on the door. "Hans, I am leaving some clothes outside the door for you to wear. They are my son's, but he is about your size."

When he heard her footsteps returning downstairs, he opened the door slowly, saw the nicely folded clothing, and brought them inside to put on. New clothes and no bugs... he was feeling almost human again.

* * *

A few days later, they were all eating supper, and as usual, Jerzy had a second helping, eating until his stomach stretched out. The farmer noticed that after they finished, Jerzy always went outside and disappeared. Curiosity finally got the best of him and he decided to investigate. The old man waited a few minutes, and then quietly followed him to the barn. Opening the door just a crack, he saw his young farmhand sitting with his back against the pile of squash, peeling and eating them. Jerzy caught a glimpse of him watching, but realized that it was no use lying, so he pretended not to see him. The farmer's eyes were opened wide with the disbelief that the boy was still hungry.

In awe, the old man slowly entered. "Hans, why did you not tell us that you were still hungry after eating? We would have given you more food."

His hands, along with the half-eaten squash he held, fell to his lap. "I was too embarrassed," he said. His eyes began to tear up. "I have been without food for so long that I always feel hungry, and no matter how much I eat... it feels like it is never enough."

"I will tell the old woman," he said. "She will give you more."

"No... no, it is okay," he said. "I will be fine."

But they gave him more food anyway, and finally, after another eight weeks, Jerzy was able to leave the table and feel that he had enough to eat.

Twenty-Six

First Drink

As spring began, there were many rumors all over Germany that the war might soon be over. One day the farm Jerzy had adopted heard much commotion outside. The old woman began yelling, "Hans... Hans, Amerikaner coming." Jerzy ran out to the porch to see for himself, but when he got there, he beheld Nazi uniforms and Nazi vehicles. It was a Panzer division that was being pushed back by the Americans.

Jerzy trembled. Without asking permission, the soldiers confiscated the farmhouse for their own use, as they did all the other houses in the village. They were all busy tending to their individual wants and needs... washing up, smoking, some of the men drinking steins of alcohol from a few kegs they brought along, laughing and telling jokes. They were getting hammered.

Since they were so happy, Jerzy decided to take a chance and ask one of the soldiers for a cigarette. Another soldier was nearby, leaning against the barn.

"I will give you a whole pack of cigarettes if you will have a drink with us," he said, smiling.

Everybody was looking at Jerzy. He was twenty-one and a half years old now, and he had never had a single drink of alcohol. But, he figured, surely one small drink would not hurt him, so he nodded his head.

"Ja," he said. "I will do that."

Cheers went up from the Nazis gathering around to watch this show. They handed him a large stein and filled it with straight whiskey while shoving a pack of cigarettes into his shirt pocket. He looked at the size of the stein, and tried to say no, he could not do this.

He shook he head as the glass was being filled.

"Oh, you have to now," they said. "You gave us your word. You are not a liar, are you? Because we do not like liars. When we find one, we shoot him dead right on the spot, do we not?" he asked his friends. "Oh ja, ja," they said. "Boom, dead."

Jerzy was terrified, but they called him comrade, patting him on the back and laughing. He knew that he was being forced to do this, but there seemed to be no way out.

Well, if I drink all this slowly, he thought, ...I will be much drunk for sure, but maybe if I just drink it down fast, all at once, I will be okay. Lifting his glass to the soldiers as though toasting them, he brought it to his lips, and as he drank, the soldiers began urging him on, cheering and clapping and laughing and there was no escape, so he continued to chug the liquid down his throat, swallowing and wondering when he would ever find the bottom. He still had a third of a glass to go when the effect of this drink hit him, and he had to breathe, so he brought the glass down, gasping for breath.

Seeing much fun here, the soldiers urged him on. "Come on, finish your drink. You cannot stop now."

So not knowing any better, he put the stein to his lips again, and as he tilted his head back, he saw the farmhouse floating way up into the sky... and then the ground came up to meet him. Why is the world spinning around me? he thought. He got up, just barely, and staggered over to the big tree near the house, and he hugged it just before collapsing again.

When he opened his eyes, it was dark, the soldiers were gone, and the old couple was in the cellar. Why will they not they help me into the cellar, too, he thought. I cannot even move a finger. Then the lights went out again.

* * *

In the morning, Jerzy was awakened by many pats on the back as the German army was packing to move out. "Goodbye, comrade," they said. "You are a good drinking partner. Take care of yourself." They picked up everything they brought, leaving no trace that they were ever there.

It was light out now, but Jerzy did not care. His world was still spinning, so he went back to sleep by the tree. A huge BOOM filled the air, and he lifted his eyelids a little with much effort, then dropped them again. More booms followed, but he just listened without looking... easier that way. It was artillery fire. One shell hit part of the chicken coop, squawking chickens and chicken parts flying everywhere, along with pieces of the cage. Then it was quiet again, so Jerzy resumed his sleep.

* * *

At daybreak he arose again, feeling thirsty... parched. He also had a monster headache and every muscle in his body announced itself with pain. Even his eyelashes hurt. Staggering over to the well, he pumped water into his stein, and chugged it all down. This made him drunk all over again, so now he staggered over to a haystack between the barn and the house, where he collapsed and fell asleep once again.

* * *

It was around noon when the old woman shook him.

"Hans," she said shaking him again. "Hans, Americana coming. Wake up... Americana."

He moaned, then got up and staggered over to the porch, but stopped before reaching the front. She was right this time. He leaned against the corner of the house, watching through his red, swollen eyes as the American GIs cut through the barbed wire and swarmed all over the field. He just stood there in awe, even as they approached. One of the soldiers, the first black man Jerzy had ever seen, took his rifle, and poked the bayonet towards Jerzy's stomach. "Nazi?" he asked. "Nazi?"

"No," said Jerzy, slowly shaking his head. "Polski."

"The soldier smiled, patting him on the shoulder and went into the house. In no time, the entire squadron was on the property, doing exactly as the Nazis had done, unpacking their gear, washing up, cooking, and just making themselves at home. One GI gave Jerzy a helmet and army jacket, so he put them on and smiled, remembering the Nazi officer who beat him for thinking that the allies would win the war. He wished that bastard could see him now.

As Jerzy walked among the soldiers, a few of them told him that he was free now. He heard this news, but did not know what he should say. He had dreamed about this moment for years.

But where does a free person go? he thought... What does he do? It was exciting, but so confusing at the same time.

A soldier approached him. "Come with me," he said, bringing Jerzy over to see a young officer.

"Dzień dobry," the lieutenant said in perfect Polish. "Jak masz na imię?"

"Good morning, sir. I am called Jerzy Czaplicki."

"Skąd jesteś?"

"Lublin, born and raised there," he answered.

The officer had many questions, asking all about Lublin, who the president of Poland was, about different streets, even what movies he saw. Satisfied with the answers, he then gave Jerzy some chocolate and cigarettes. The soldiers then rounded up the local German farmers and put all of them in one farmhouse, but Jerzy was free to roam about.

Czaplicki had read much about Americans, but had never seen one before. They were different. Europeans were always stiff and formal. Everything they did was an act. Even eating. But the Americans exuded an independent spirit... everything about them was easy and relaxed. And they were so natural. He watched a jeep go by with five GIs inside, helmets tilted, legs hanging outside, the driver with one hand on the wheel, and another soldier standing on the running board while talking by walkie-talkie to a spotter plane above.

Jerzy was in awe. It was like a giant circus.... the whole place was pandemonium, cats and dogs and chickens running around, soldiers tending to their individual whims, everybody happy. It was as though Americans were on a permanent picnic—he had never seen such freedom. Never even knew it existed.

He turned just in time to see a soldier with his pistol slung low, the holster tied to his leg just like Tom Mix and the other American cowboys he had seen whenever he snuck into the movies as a boy. The soldier gazed ahead intently, but Jerzy had no idea what was happening. Suddenly the gunslinger drew the pistol out of his holster quickly and POW, he shot a chicken, which squawked as it went flying up in the air, feathers all over, then it fell, dead. And nobody bothered to pick up the chicken to eat. Then the gunman brought the pistol pointing straight up in front of his face, blew the smoke away from the end of the barrel, then brought it back down again by his side, spun it around backwards a few times by the trigger guard, and spun it right into his holster. That soldier had to be a real cowboy.

At the noise, another guy came running over to see what the excitement was all about.

"Jerzy?"

He turned. "YURI," he said loudly. The two jumped toward each other, grasping one another in a tight bear hug, then pulling apart again and holding each other by the upper arms. Where have you been, my Russian friend? I thought you were gone for all times."

"Comrade Polski, you should know better. Can not get rid of strong Ruskie bear so easy," he said, laughing.

"I should have known," said Jerzy, wearing the biggest smile possible. It is so good to see you again. Where you were all this time?"

"I work to removing tree stumps for farmers."

"That is very hard work, Yuri. You could not find easier jobs?"

"Nyet... work easy, Polski..." He leaned in closer... "I use dynamite and blow tree roots all to hell. Nothing left but little pieces," he said, showing Jerzy the small size with a tiny space between his thumb and forefinger, and he smiled the smile known only by those who have found true satisfaction. "Big happiness making things to go boom. Much fun. Last job was at farm there," he said, pointing towards some trees. "Is on other side of woods."

"Crap, I never knew that a farm was over there, Yuri."

"You want I show you?"

"Ja, but not yet, Yuri. I have waited many years for this day. I cannot tell you how happy I feel," he said, patting Yuri on the shoulder, his eyes filled with water. "The war is almost over, my friend, and right now all I want to do is enjoy it with the Americans all around me."

And then he could no longer stop the tears from coming. He cried for the loss of his father, and for his long slavery, for the loss of so many good friends, for all the times he was beaten and threatened... and he cried for his loss of the one woman who brought him happiness in the midst of all his suffering... he cried for his Ekaterina. He knew he would never see her again.

Amid all the commotion, Jerzy saw some soldiers unfold a small wire contraption, put it on a large rock, light a small tablet beneath it, and then open an envelope of powder that they poured into a small pan of water on top of the device. The odor drifted to where he was watching, and then he understood. "Oh my God, they are making soup," he realized. "What a technology."

But not everybody was doing this. Some of them had meals in a can. And nearby, the army cook was making a large kettle of soup with gallon-sized cans that he was pouring in. He saw Jerzy watching and asked if he want to help. "Ja," he said. "I like to do that."

The cook pointed to several large cans. "Here," he said, handing him an opener. "Get those open for me."

The cans were filled with some kind of pink liquid, and as fast as Jerzy opened them, the cook poured them into the kettle, stirring them with a large paddle. Then he took out some loaves of bread and trimmed them. They were white and fluffy. The only bread Jerzy had seen before this was dark and heavy. When the cook finished, a ding-ding-ding rang from a large iron triangle that he was banging on to announce dinner, but surprisingly, very few soldiers appeared, so he just fed them and then dumped all the rest into a big hole in the ground. Jerzy watched this and his eyes grew large. So many times, I was starving, he thought. So many times, I had to fight to survive my hunger, and now I see much food that the soldiers just throw away like it has no meaning... no value. How can this be?

One of the cooks saw Jerzy watching with his mouth hanging open, so he gave the boy a tray and a metal dish. Then he signaled Jerzy over to where some other foods had been prepared. Before he knew what was happening, the cook put two big pieces of toast on his dish, then he watched as a magnificent slab of beef was placed on top. The meat alone was like six years of whatever meat he might have gotten from the Nazis, but all in one piece. Tears began to form in his eyes again as he could only stare at this unbelievable treat. But the cook then broke his reverie to signal Jerzy to the next place in line where a scoop of mashed potatoes was thrown on top, and on top of that, a beautiful ladle of gravy was added... and then, as if that was not enough, a delectable pile of peas and carrots was placed on top of that.

But the best part, the absolutely best part was yet to come at the end of this line, where Jerzy watched in amazement as a huge glob of chocolate syrup was added to the peak of his mountain.

After just a few bites, he quickly decided that nothing in the universe was better than chocolate covered roast beef. Nothing.

After finishing, he went into the house, where he saw shoes and jackets and helmets all over the floor, on the furniture, and empty bottles of wine from the cellar were lying wherever they were when emptied. Everybody was doing whatever he wanted, and Jerzy watched it all unfold in amazement.

* * *

Two days later, when he awakened, not a soldier was in sight. He looked around, and saw overcoats, a few shoes, sweaters and other stuff lying around. No, they did not leave," he said. Then he walked outside, where he saw their entrenched positions no longer covered with branches, but the wires they laid out were still on the ground.

The old farmer then appeared. "Where are the soldiers?" he asked.

"I do not know, but I do not think they left. Their stuff is still here... even the food and cigarettes."

Then Jerzy looked up and saw his Russian friend coming over. "Yuri... do you understand what is going on?"

"You do not know?" he said. "Big news. Russia in Berlin... Hitler dead and war finished... we all free. Can go home now."

Jerzy just stared at him, his jaw hanging.

"Is true, Polski," he said, laughing. Then he whacked Jerzy on the shoulder. "But first, I show you big secret, then we celebrate. Come, I show you now."

Twenty-Seven

In the Forest

They walked through the field that Yuri just appeared in, and Jerzy realized that the soldiers really were gone. When the Germans left, they packed up everything, even unrolled their telegraph wire. You knew they were gone. But the Americans left everything. They must be unbelievably rich to do such a thing.

Going into the woods brought back memories of his time in hiding there, but now it was safe. Nobody was hunting for him, and he did not have to always be on the lookout for food. This newfound freedom made Jerzy's heart race. He had no idea of what to do next, but he did have the companionship of a good friend who was leading him to something he found, something special, he said, and that was enough for now.

"Is just beyond these trees." Yuri said.

When Jerzy saw the big surprise, Yuri beamed. The woods were polluted with American riches... food, cigarettes, weapons, ammunition, pots and pans... it was like a dream. As an added bonus, it was right next to an apple orchard, and the trees there were exploding with ripeness.

"Yuri, when did you find all this?"

"Yesterday night," Yuri said proudly, with his chin held high.

Excited now, Jerzy ran back to the farmhouse to get something to carry all that he wanted. He had gone from poverty to extreme wealth in a heartbeat, and he could not think straight.

"What is it, Hans?" said the old woman.

"The woods... filled..." he said, out of breath "...American treasure, everything, but we need something big... something to carry it in. A large box, maybe?"

The old woman thought for a moment, then realized that they had many burlap bags for the potato crops. She grabbed some and told Jerzy to get the wheelbarrow from the barn, and together they went back to harvest this new crop.

It was Christmas in late April. Word was spreading fast, and other farmers were already there to share in the bounty. Jerzy and Yuri filled their sacks with clothes and food and whatever else they could carry. Yuri made sure he filled a large sack full of explosives.

Then, while they were still looking around to make sure they did not miss anything of high value, a neighbor came over and greeted the old woman. "This is not all that the woods are holding," he said, pointing to the east. "There is even more treasure a short way from here... but it belongs to the Nazis who came through a few days ago." Jerzy and Yuri looked at each other, and ran to find it.

When they got there, they discovered typewriters, sugar, flour, even automobiles. Jerzy was just staring in awe when Yuri poked him in the ribs. He was looking up in the air. Jerzy followed his gaze and saw a cow hanging from a tree. He slowly shook his head. There was enough treasure here for two entire villages.

Then Jerzy spotted the ultimate prize. He recognized it from his work as a mechanic... it was a 1937 Mercedes-Benz 320, and a convertible at that. It had a straight six engine and could do about 75 miles per hour. "What a find, Yuri," he said. "This must have been the staff car for some Nazi big-shot. We must have this, but there is no key in here, and I do not want to lose it if the owner comes back. I need to disable it somehow."

"You have tools?"

"No... at least not here, but I have an idea." He opened up the hood and stared at the ignition wires in order to memorize their location to attain the proper firing sequence. Then he switched the second, fourth and sixth wires, hoping nobody would notice. He closed the hood again, walking slowly to the rear then back to the front again, touching the hood ornament and looking over the entire car with deep admiration. "Jeez, what a beautiful car," he said, looking at his friend.

"Yes, it is, Czaplicki," said a voice coming from behind him. They turned and saw Colonel Heisinveld, who was aiming a pistol at them. "And it is MY car, so please move away from it." He stepped inside the vehicle, throwing his duffel bag in the rear.

"You have been one pain in the ass, Czaplicki, and have caused me no end of embarrassment with my superiors. Did you know that? Every time you escaped, I had to explain how you did that. But no more, eh? The war is officially over, and now, so is your life. And yours," he said, pointing the gun at Yuri. He put the key in the ignition and turned it, but the engine would not catch when he pressed the starter button.

"WHAT DID YOU DO TO IT?" he shouted at Jerzy.

"Colonel, I was hoping to take the car for myself. It is beautiful — why would I do anything to it?"

"Fix it, Czaplicki. You were a mechanic... fix it now."

Jerzy's eyes were large. "With what, Colonel. I have no tools."

The colonel stepped out, walked to the back of the car, and opened up the small trunk, all the while keeping an eye on the two young men, and keeping his pistol aimed at them. He pulled out a toolbox and brought it over to them. "Now you have tools. If you do not fix it, I will fix you; I will kill you right here, right now. Is that understood, my young Polack?"

Jerzy merely nodded. But he also knew that once he fixed it, he and Yuri would both be killed anyway. Damned if you do, damned if you don't.

The colonel looked around. There were other supplies he needed to take, and they were all here.

Then Jerzy had an idea. "Colonel, is it okay if my friend helps me?" Jerzy said.

"I do not care... just get it done."

When the colonel looked at the supplies again, Jerzy looked at Yuri and moved his eyes over to the burlap sack he had filled earlier with explosives. He nodded his head ever so slightly, motioning for his buddy to bring it over to the car. Yuri understood, but when he grabbed the sack, the colonel saw and said, "Stop." He had seen the way they were acting. What is in that bag?"

"Sir?"

"Open it right now... SCHNELL!"

The friends looked at each other. Jerzy closed his eyes, his hands trembling, and Yuri slowly opened the sack. Not hearing anything from the Colonel, Jerzy opened one eye and looked himself, but instead of explosives, all that was visible were apples. Yuri must have put the fruit on top earlier. Thinking quickly, all Jerzy could think of to say was, "I like to eat while I work. For a very long time, I had such little food... I was always so hungry, and even now, I need to eat much, just to remind myself that I will not starve. It gives me comfort," he said, shrugging.

The officer nodded in understanding, then turned back to his task. "I will be watching both of you, so do not do anything to my automobile. I would not hesitate to shoot you both right in the head. Or maybe I would shoot you in the legs first, just so you could not run. Then a few other bullets elsewhere, not enough to kill you—just enough so you could feel some pain before I finally snuff out your pathetic little lives." He stared hard at them. "Now get to work," he said.

"Yuri, you get under the car, beneath the engine and I will tell you what to do," said Jerzy loudly enough to be heard by the colonel. "And hand me an apple."

Fifteen minutes later, the officer brought all his supplies over and loaded them into the car, just as Jerzy closed the hood, holding a half-eaten apple between his teeth.

"Are you finished?" the Colonel said.

Jerzy took the apple from his mouth. "Yes sir, but I have not had a chance to test it yet."

"Move back," the colonel ordered, stepping into the driver's seat. He aimed his Luger at them. "I will test this, Czaplicki... I am not giving you a chance to sit inside and drive my car away. In the event that you were successful in fixing it, do you have any last words?"

"Sir, may I at least hear the sound of this beautiful machine before I die? Please?"

The colonel laughed. "Even at the end, you always find ways to delay the inevitable." He inserted the key and turned it. "But it does not matter. Since you are the only mechanic around, I will let you live until the motor starts, Czap—"and as he looked down to press the starter button, he caught a barely perceptible glimpse of Jerzy and Yuri turning quickly and diving downward at the same time, away from the car just as it exploded into a thundering fireball.

Jerzy had unwittingly leaped into a bush filled with heavy thorns while pieces of debris flew out in all directions, some of it just missing them as they huddled on their sides into fetal positions on the ground, covering their heads for protection from the pieces of metal and other debris that rained down on them from the sky.

His hands, along with the top of his head bled profusely from his impact with the thorns, but otherwise, he was alright. Peering through the mist from the explosion, Jerzy and Yuri started to get up when a thump hit the ground right next to them, which made them both jump backwards. Looking back, they saw it was the hood ornament, all that was left of the once beautiful car. A moment later, something small and shiny fell slowly from the sky. It landed with a light tinkling sound right in front of both their faces, spinning on its edge, then it slowed down and wobbled, until finally falling over. It was the colonel's monocle.

Looking over at his buddy lying next to him on the ground, Yuri blinked with both eyes. "NOW Nazi war over," he said.

Crawling away from the debris, Jerzy looked up to make sure no more parts were coming down, then he just stared at what was left of the vehicle, remembering all that they had been through. He had just killed a person and did not feel happy, but he was not sad, either, for it was self-defense. He did not know what to feel, other than bruised and worn, as though he had been carrying a supremely heavy load for years, and he was just now noticing.

They decided to go back to the farmhouse and celebrate a new beginning. The wheelbarrow was heavy, and it took both of them, one on each handle, to move it there.

That night, Jerzy was restless as he laid in bed, wondering why we always fought so hard to live, sometimes doing terrible, unforgivable things, when ultimately, we were all going to die anyway? We eat every day, just to keep living. We work hard to keep living. We even kill other life so we can continue living. And for what? Why bother finding a happy life? What difference did it make to fall in love and have babies? If life was so damned precious, why did it always end in death anyway? The thoughts would not go away, and kept him awake for most of the night.

Twenty-Eight

Displaced Persons

The next day, Yuri found an unexploded artillery shell and banged it repeatedly against a tree to open it up while Jerzy hid behind a different tree, yelling at him to knock it off.

"Are you crazy?" said Jerzy.

"Oh, much gunpowder here, Polski comrade. Will make big bang." Then he laughed and pounded it against the tree again. The shell opened up at last, like a walnut, giving up its inner prize to the persistent Yuri. With it, he made many hand-made fireworks and set them off all over the field. Sometimes he also set off hand grenades and other explosives for his own amusement, but Jerzy always stayed well away. He had survived up until now, and he wanted to continue that trend.

The old man just watched and shook his head. "Stupid kids," he said. "Hey you two, come here."

They walked over to the old man. "You called us?" Jerzy said.

"Do you know, in the whole war there was not as half much noise as you two made since you arrived? You want to do something useful?" He wagged his finger at them. "Why do you not remove my tree stumps? That is hard work, and it will do you both good." He showed them his big teeth.

They looked at each other and smiled, liking that idea very much.

With the help of all the explosives they had accumulated, they blew up one tree stump after another. Sometimes the stumps would just turn into sawdust, and one would never know a tree had ever been there, and sometimes the stump would remain almost intact as it went flying like a rocket halfway across the field.

When they ran out of long fuses, the crazy Russian tried a short fuse. He lit it, ran about ten steps, but tripped and fell flat on his face. The dynamite exploded with a big bang. After the debris had fallen, he got up, his large white eyes peering out through a dark mask of dirt, and just stared at his friend. Jerzy laughed.

Early that evening, just as they were finishing supper, an Army jeep pulled into the yard. The two young men heard it and stepped outside to see what was up.

"Jerzy, I was just coming to see you," said the sergeant behind the wheel. He was one of the American friends the boy had made among the occupying army a few days ago.

"Why were you coming to see me? I am a nobody," Jerzy said.

"Listen, American and British forces have taken over this area, and new orders have just come in. Effective immediately, all foreigners in the area are being ordered to report to a displaced persons camp that has been set up in town for refugees. You can no longer live among the Germans, my friend. That applies to you, too," he said to Yuri."

"Okay comrade Sergeant," Yuri said. We do this."

"Maybe we can get you back to your own countries," the sergeant said. The boys looked at each other. "In the meantime, get your butts over to the refugee camp, along with whatever you can carry... by tomorrow."

Watching the jeep turn around and drive away, Jerzy turned to his Russian friend and grinned. "Yuri," he said... "Let us go to the refugee camp in style."

"I no understand what you thinking, but I like you words," said Yuri.

The next morning, they went back into the woods and found a brand-new Volkswagen. Both men dressed in new clothes they had found... even shiny new shoes, and it took Jerzy only a few moments to get the covering off the steering column and determine the wires he needed so he could hot-wire the automobile.

"Do you know how to drive a car, Yuri?" asked Jerzy.

"Comrade, I know only how to make car go boom," he said. "I never drive before. You can drive car?"

"I drove a few, but only from the front of the garage to the back," he said. "I hope I can remember how."

They both hopped inside, Jerzy connected the battery wires, then touched that connection to the ignition wire, and the automobile started right up. They grinned at each other, then Jerzy put the car into first gear, and released the clutch. After a single lurch they stalled out. He tried again, and even though he drove it in jerks, and Yuri was flopping all over, Jerzy soon remembered and got the hang of it as they made their way into town.

As they entered the city, two American MPs stopped them. "Why do two kids have a car?" one of them said. "And a new one at that," said the other.

"We not kids... we two refugees," Yuri said, sticking out his chest, chin raised high.

The guards looked at each other and smiled.

"Okay," one of them said, calmly. "Just pull this over to the side of the road and leave it there," he said, nodding to the spot. "The refugee camp is over there," he added, pointing to a building on the corner.

Jerzy turned the car around, pulled it to the curb, and disconnected the wires again to shut the car off.

"The guards let us go, Yuri, so I think maybe they want the car for themselves." They grinned at each other and got out, but instead of walking into the refugee camp, they turned and went back to the woods.

An hour later, they pulled up to the same guards in a different car. When the guards saw who it was, they burst out laughing. "I am sorry, my young friends, but you cannot just take any car and call it your own." Without saying another word, he merely pointed to the same spot as before.

After Jerzy parked this car in back of the first one, the guards called both of the young men over and patted them on the back, then checked to make sure they understood exactly where the camp was.

Yuri smiled the whole way. "At least we dressed good, Polski," he said. "We still have class, yes?"

"All the way, Yuri. All the way."

Walking inside, they were awed by the large number of people. The building was loud with music and talking, and there was dancing and drinking here. They looked around, but the din was overwhelming to Jerzy. "Crap, this is too much. I think I would rather be back on the farm," he said.

"Not me. This like good Ruskie party. I want to sing, dance... much fun here," said Yuri, with a huge smile plastered on his face.

Jerzy was making plans to sneak out and was eyeballing the door when he heard a voice behind him that stopped him in mid-thought.

"Jerzy?" It was a girl's voice, soft and pretty.

He turned around slowly, not believing what he saw.

"Ekaterina?" he said softly, just staring at her.

She squealed and ran to him, and they clasped each other with a firmness that promised to never let go again, his heart thumping erratically.

"How...?" he said, trying to understand how she got here.

"Last week, the Germans in charge of the factory must have known that the war was ending soon and I found out that we were going to be marched to another place, and I was so scared, Jerzy, I heard many horrible stories and I thought maybe they were bringing us somewhere to be killed, and one of the other women was shot because she could not go on, and another one was being shot at for trying to go into the woods, and I knew I could not just stand there, so in all the confusion, I ran out into the woods too, then I stole some clothes and did like you showed me, by cutting the emblem off my coat, and then later, with some money I had saved up, I hopped on one trolley after another, not knowing where to go, but I just kept on riding anyway until I ran out of marks, then I ended up in this city and found a job helping in a hospital, but it paid so little and I had no money when I found out the war was over, but I had not had anything to eat in four days and I must have collapsed... I do not remember, and the American soldiers found me and brought me here, and some people came in, they said they were from a Red Cross, whatever that is, and —"

"Whoa... take a breath my beautiful pateechka." Despite his best efforts, he could not stop smiling.

"Oh Jerzy, I did not care where I went, as long as it was far away from that awful place. I missed you so much, and I am so, so sorry that I did not go with you. I looked for you everywhere, and all I had left was hope."

He watched her as she spoke, feeling his love for her rise to the surface of his heart, and this time he vowed that nothing would ever separate them again.

* * *

They strolled outside together and just walked on and on without going anywhere in particular. For the first time, Jerzy seriously looked at his surroundings in this now-battered city, taking in the devastation from the bombings, and thinking about all that had happened since that first day of the war when his own city was attacked. Neither of them noticed the stranger approaching them from behind.

"Such a waste," the man said, staring at the ruins.

They looked at him. He had only one leg and was in a wheelchair.

Jerzy merely nodded.

"Where are you from?" the man said.

"Why do you ask?" said Jerzy.

"Just curious... everybody seems to be from somewhere else." He paused. "Forgive my poor manners. My name is Klaus... Klaus Boellman," he said, extending his hand.

"Jerzy Czaplicki," he replied in turn, taking the stranger's hand in his. "And this is my girlfriend, Ekaterina Ivanovich Tikhonova."

The man nodded, then tried to light a cigarette, but his hands were shaking too much and the breeze blew out the flame.

"Please, allow me," said Jerzy, taking out a wooden match of his own and lighting Klaus's cigarette.

"Thank you," said the man. He blew out the match with a puff of smoke, and turned to Ekaterina. "Your name is Russian?"

"Yes... I come from the city of Minsk," she said.

"And you?" asked Boellman, pointing to Jerzy.

"I am from Lublin, in Poland."

Klaus laughed aloud. "I cannot believe this," he said.

"What is so funny?" said Jerzy.

"I am sorry. Lublin, in Poland, you say? This is truly inconceivable. I was one of the German pilots who flew with the initial attack on Lublin. I will never forget... it was on the first week of the war, September 6, 1939. We had much success, but just as I was heading back to my base, a small Polish fighter unexpectedly closed in on me from behind. By then I was almost totally out of ammunition anyway, but that bastard's attack caught me by complete surprise. I had no idea what my tail gunner was doing or why he did not see this enemy plane coming, but when I yelled for him to shoot back after the first bullets hit us, but he was already dead. The worst part is that I was on my way to becoming not just a pilot, but an ace pilot. Instead, I was blasted out of the sky forever by a stupid Polish dog."

He stared at Jerzy, seeing in him all that was wrong with the world. "Unfortunately, I was too low to bail out, and as you can see, my landing was not the best, so that day was both the beginning and the end of my golden aviation career." And he laughed yet again. "And today, here you are, one of the hunted, lighting a cigarette for the hunter. Who would have guessed?"

Saying nothing, Jerzy looked at the wheelchair and the leg stump of the man who sat there, the man who brought the war to his home city, and he thought about that day. He thought about his brother's death and all the violence this man had inflicted on those unarmed civilians who wanted only to escape, and he shook his head with disbelief. He remembered his father, and how he had to die alone because his only living son was working as a slave for the Nazis while slowly being starved to death. And then he looked again at the spot where the man's leg should have been.

Ekaterina, not knowing any of this, hugged her boyfriend from the side, nestling her head on his shoulder, looking up at him. He looked in her eyes... and he could no longer hate. Jerzy put his arm around her, and with his own eyes closed, lifted his head up to the sky, breathing deeply, thinking of all the waste, and tears formed in his heart. I cannot believe it is finally over, he thought. Despite all the carnage, the death and heartache, he had finally escaped, no longer having to serve the monsters who destroyed his world, yet he felt a longing for forgiveness in his heart. "No more violence," he said.

He wanted only to put the past behind him, to love, and to be loved, thanking God for having survived it all, and for being given the chance to have children, and maybe even grandchildren with the most wonderful woman in the world. He had paid dearly for this promise.

Eyes still closed, he embraced his future, smiling at the amazing wonder of life... and then an unexpected insight to all his questions about the cruelty of life slammed into him like a massive wave, slow but powerful. Everything was coming together now, and he trembled with a sudden knowing...

Despite all that had happened, the many changes, he saw that it was all connected... and as the wave moved over him, Jerzy felt his life to be a magnificent tapestry that united everything and everybody with everything else, a web made up of all the individual lives which composed the universal whole. He saw each person, friends and enemies alike, as strands of the infinite, weaving everyone together, even in suffering.

This growing awareness came to him in neither words nor images... it was more rhythmic... a dance to the music of life's impulses... a reliving of all that had happened to him... the Nazi terror, his friends and family, Ekaterina... everything now expressing itself through this present moment, that razor's edge of time without beginning or end. Jerzy just was, yet each now-moment of life was an eternal now that never ended.

And at last he began to understand... metal rusts, people age, flowers come and go... and nothing stays the same... ever. He saw everything, everybody as never-ending changes, from moment to moment, swirling like a visible current in a constantly churning ocean, and he realized that change is all that really exists. We have names for all those things that change so slowly we don't see it, but we do not name those things that change rapidly. We speak of babies and houses and even mountains as though they will be around forever, but things and people are actions, not the names we call them. And then he knew... creation is not a one-shot deal... it bursts forth endlessly, lording it over both past and future... death has no meaning. And Jerzy was awed by the immensity of it all. He found himself flowing in a new universe, one that rewrites itself with each thrust of life, and he saw every moment as a resurrection.

Klaus quietly pulled a Luger from his coat pocket, and aimed it straight at Jerzy. The young refugee slowly opened his eyes and saw what Klaus was holding. They stared at each other, and Jerzy gently put both hands on Ekaterina's shoulders, pushing her away. She did not understand, until she looked at what Jerzy was staring at and saw the gun. Her hands flew over her mouth and she shook her head. "No... no... oh please God, no..." She was no longer breathing, keeping all her screams on the inside so they would not, could not betray her.

"NOOOOOOOOOOOooooooooo..." she cried, the tears flowing freely down her face, squeezed from tortured eyes that could bear no more pain.

But Jerzy did not flinch. Without saying a word, he calmly raised his arms straight out to the sides, palms facing Klaus, and while inhaling deeply, raised his chin up, so his face was aimed at the infinite sky. It was as though he was freely offering his life so that Klaus might find the peace that had eluded him for these many years. Jerzy slowly closed his eyes and focused on the faint sound of his brother's voice, calling to him. He had not thought about Ruslin in a very long time. Then he heard his father, and he knew at that moment he would soon be joining them.

And Klaus, the pilot who brought this world of death and hatred right to Jerzy's front door, saw this and raised his pistol, for it was a game after all and this would be the last point scored... but his hand began to tremble. He wanted to avenge his father at last... and he resolved to commit this final act of retribution... but when he looked at this ultimate act of love that was Jerzy, he no longer saw him as a symbol for the loss of his father's arm... Jerzy was now something larger, a beacon, not of racial inferiority, but of a divine tranquility in the face of certain death, and Klaus could not understand. His hands continued to shake, eyes beginning to tear up, and he could no longer see his target clearly. Instead, he saw for the first time man's inhumanity to man, and he began crying for what he had become, for the loss of his own humanity. He choked on his tears, his grip on the Luger weakening, and he sobbed until finally his head and his gun-hand dropped from the futility of it all. He sobbed from somewhere deep within, chest heaving with guilt and despair until finally he could sob no longer. He could not bear to look at Jerzy. But his father had sacrificed his arm for him... and so, in a final act of desperation, he blindly raised his gun again and at last squeezed the trigger.

The bullet's impact sent Jerzy spinning halfway around until his body landed face-down, arms still stretched out like an airplane.

Ekaterina's scream filled the quiet night air as the German pilot turned his wheelchair around and slowly left, crying over what he had done.

Part Two

Twenty-Nine

Not Here - Not There

He never felt the bullet. One moment, Jerzy Czaplicki was standing with the woman who owned his heart, facing a stranger in a wheel-chair, a man pointing a gun at him, and the next moment, he was five feet away. How had he moved? The world had not tilted, yet he was no longer where he had been.

Then he saw it. The body on the ground, twisted, lifeless. The blood spreading like spilled ink, dark and final. And kneeling beside it, Ekaterina—his Ekaterina—clutching the broken form, her wails carving through the night, raw like an open wound. The sirens screamed in the distance, but even they were no match for her anguish.

He reached for her, his fingers desperate to wipe away her tears. *Pateechka, I am over here*, he whispered. *Do not cry, my love. Look—I am fine. See? I am right here.*

But she did not hear him.

She did not see him.

She wept, not for him, but for the body she held.

The realization came slow, like ice creeping across a frozen lake. He turned back to the broken form on the ground, to the vacant eyes staring into eternity, and the truth struck him like a hammer to the soul.

That is ME.

That... corpse, that shell, that discarded thing. It is me.

But how? How can I be here... and there?

His memory surged—the man with the gun, his wheelchair, the bitter accusations of vengeance. A war fought and lost, a leg taken in the fire of battle, the price exacted by the Polish pilot who downed his plane. And now, after all these years, the price had grown heavier.

Jerzy had pushed Ekaterina aside, shielding her from the shot, but he had felt nothing—no pain, no impact. Only the shift.

And now—now he was neither here nor there, floating between the worlds. A ghost. A whisper caught on the wind.

Panic clawed at him. He reached for Ekaterina again, but his hand passed through her like mist. He turned, searching, seeking, but the world had forgotten him. No one looked. No one saw.

Alone. Totally alone.

The weight of it crushed him. He was dead. But the billions who had died before—his father, his friends, the legions of the lost—where were they? Where were the hosts of the dead, the spirits who should have come to guide him?

Unless—

No—No, no, no...

This was not Hell. It could not be Hell... could it? A torment of silence, of solitude unending? A cruel eternity where he was nothing but a shadow cast upon a world that would never see him again?

He fell to his knees—not physically, for he had no body to kneel—but his soul bowed under the weight of terror.

God... oh dear God... please. Please help me.

The prayer was raw, ripped from that deepest part of him. And as the words were formed in his mind, the world began to shift again. But this was different. He was not moving now. He was... unraveling. Expanding.

The trees shrank beneath him. The buildings, the streets, the city

—all fell away as he swelled beyond them. Germany became a speck. Then the world. The moon. The sun. He stretched, his essence growing vast, unfathomable, merging with the fabric of creation itself.

Yet there was no fear. Only awe.

The colors—God, the colors! Hues unknown to mortal sight, shades beyond the scope of human language. He was no longer flesh, no longer bound by the weight of bone and sinew. He was mere thought. No—more than thought. Even without eyes, he could still see. In fact, he could see in every direction at once. He felt like pure energy, an apotheosis of life, woven into the very texture of existence itself.

And then—

A voice... Familiar. Resonant.

His father's voice.

And in that instant, all of creation stood still.

Jerzy, it is alright. You are not being punished.

He did not hear his father so much as sense him, feel him with an understanding, of which there was no doubt. It was as though they were now a part of each other, and each could feel what the other felt, but it was not a mere memory, or trick of the imagination... it was more of a knowing. A certainty. He had always been empathic, but this brought those feelings to a whole new level.

Papa, said Jerzy. *Oh my God, Papa! — I have missed you so much. More than I can even say. I am so, so very sorry for ever leaving you. Please, please forgive me, Papa.*

His father's presence swelled around him. *Oh, my son, you did nothing wrong. Those who tore us apart had to use great force to do so. It was never your fault.* There was such love in his voice, vast and unwavering. *You are cherished so much more than you can ever imagine, and not just by me. Stretch out your heart, Jerzy and feel it with all your being,* he said.

Jerzi hesitated. He wasn't sure how to do this, but he mentally closed the eyes he no longer had and reached out with his feelings, stretching beyond himself, searching.

And then—

Light.

Brighter than the sun, yet soft. It rushed toward him, or he toward it, and as he and the light converged, he was overwhelmed by an infinite love such as he had never known, could not even have imagined, and he wanted to stay there always, for as it embraced him, it made him feel held and loved and safe in ways he never experienced, never even dreamed of.

And then a voice older and wiser than forever spoke to him the same way his father had, and asked:

Jerzy, would you like to come with me?

And the answer was immediate. *Yes,* for he could not even imagine anything more wondrous and he yearned to be a part of it.

Instantly, he stood before a great temple, its pillars reaching toward a sky that was not a sky. He did not know how he knew, but this place had been here forever. It called to him—not with words, but with a pull that was undeniable.

He stepped inside.

The hall stretched impossibly far, lined with towering shelves filled with books beyond counting. This was no library. It was something far greater.

Where are we? he asked.

The Hall of Records, came the answer.

Before him, a book opened, massive, endless. As he gazed upon it, he fell... but not downward. Not outward. But inward. And suddenly, he found himself living his life all over again.

Not as a memory. Not as a dream, or even a movie. But as a reality, unfolding all at once, yet with perfect clarity. He saw his birth, felt arms lifting him for the first time. He relived every conversation, every choice, every moment. But this time, there was something more.

Now, he experienced not only his own emotions and thoughts—but those of everyone he had ever touched. It was as though he was himself and everyone he had known all at the same time.

His small, thoughtless words burned the most. The times he had shrugged off his little stepbrother, too caught up in his own world to see the hurt in the boy's eyes. The pain in his stepmother's silence. The sharp words he had spoken without thinking, leaving unseen scars behind. Even what he had said to Boguslaw about being held back in school so many times.

Shame curled around him. He had not meant to hurt anyone. But he had.

The voice from the light returned, steady, kind. *Jerzy, do not punish yourself. This was learning, nothing more. Look.*

The pages turned...

And... Jerzy now saw and experienced all the good deeds he had done. He saw the way he had treated Nik and his uncle and had honored his father's wishes by caring for his stepmother after the German attack on Lublin, and bringing her safely to his Uncle's home, and all the Nazi slaves he shared his butter with, and he relived so many other loving acts of kindness he gave to others, all the way up to his last days with Ekaterina. And by watching all this, he again experienced his own feelings as they occurred, along with those of the people he treated nicely, now knowing the effect of those words and acts which helped others to feel better about themselves. And as he watched, he felt their relief, their gratitude, their quiet joy.

It was all there—the hurt and the healing. The failures and the love. His life had not been perfect, nor without fault. But it had been passionate, and it had been meaningful.

And the light embraced him, steady and unwavering.

Yet despite everything he had seen and felt, a knowing settled deep within him—he would not be allowed to stay.

Jerzy, the light spoke at last, *I showed you all this because you now have to make a difficult choice. You may remain here, within the benevolence of this existence, or... you may return to the life you left behind.*

The answer came instantly. *No way I am going back there,* Jerzy said. *I finally feel like I belong. I am home, and I want to stay.*

I understand, the voice said gently. *But consider this carefully. Ekaterina's life is inexorably linked with your own, and if you choose to remain here, she soon will follow, never fulfilling her own destiny.*

Jerzy stilled, his mind racing. He wanted nothing more than to escape the brutality of his old life. The war was over, yes, but the world was still full of dangers. And who would help her? Protect her?

But if she joined him soon, would that be so terrible? They could be here forever, in the light, free from suffering.

No... that is so selfish.

He didn't even know what destiny she was meant to fulfill. Would she have children—his children? Would she change the course of another life, perhaps something even greater?

Damn it.

He loved Ekaterina way too much to just abandon her. She had given him her heart, her trust, her love was unconditional — how could he repay her with loss? It wasn't fair. She didn't deserve that.

A heavy sigh filled his being.

Alright... I will go back.

You have chosen wisely, Jerzy, the voice said, for you listened to your heart. *Just know that your physical body will heal quickly, and if you continue to listen carefully, you will hear us as we will try to help guide you on your path.*

Jerzy hesitated. *Will I be allowed to remember this?*

A warmth surrounded him. *A little bit, my son. But not everything.*

Before he could respond, the light was gone and Jerzy felt himself falling, as though zooming down an endless tunnel with no control...

getting smaller...

smaller...

Then —

Nothing.

* * *

He woke up slowly, feeling very small, extremely dense, and in great pain. Gradually, he began to stir. His eyelids were closed, yet the light seeping through them hurt, and he responded with a low moan, rocking his head slightly and slowly back and forth. Then, somewhere in the dark recesses of his mind, he heard a voice... a woman's voice.

"JERZY! Oh My God. NURSE... NURSE... COME QUICK-LY," shouted Ekaterina, who had been glued to his side since he came out of surgery. Nobody could persuade her to go home, and when they saw the determination in her eyes to stay, nobody dared to challenge her.

Not knowing where he was, Jerzy tried opening his eyelids, but the blinding light forced him to slam them shut again. A nurse came bursting into the room and seeing him struggle, quickly closed the blinds for him, then moved to his bedside. It had been three days since he had been shot. He tried sitting up, but before the nurse could stop him, the searing pain forced him to give up that idea on his own.

Jerzy then tried again to open his eyes, but more cautiously this time. Everything was blurry at first, and he was confused by his surroundings. "Am I still dead?" he asked.

Ekaterina laughed, holding his hand in hers and kissing his face all over.

"If you are, then I am dead with you and we are both in Heaven," she said, tears streaming from her eyes. "Oh my God, Jerzy, I was never so scared in all my life. I thought I had lost you forever."

The nurse took his other wrist, feeling for his pulse and smiled at him.

"A nice, strong pulse, young man," she said. She was just about to take his blood pressure when she was interrupted by the strong baritone voice of Jerzy's surgeon behind her.

"Well Jerzy," the doctor began. "You have been awake for only a few moments and already you have more beautiful women fawning over you than I ever had." He smiled, not at his joke, but because he was supremely happy to see Jerzy was going to make it after all. The world was a little bit lighter today.

Jerzy just looked at him.

"What happened?" he asked.

"What do you remember?" said the doctor.

"I remember the war," and turning to face Ekaterina, continued, "...and I remember this beautiful woman holding my hand... but the rest is all fuzzy."

The doctor stared hard at his young patient.

"You were shot, Jerzy, high, in the center of your chest. You should be dead, you know, but somehow the bullet hit right between your lungs and barely nicked the aorta, although not seriously, and it continued all the way through you without hitting any other bones or organs," he said. "Everybody who gets shot in the chest has at least a rib or two shattered, maybe even the spine, and often a major organ like a lung or the heart... but not you. I have never seen anything like it. We brought you into surgery and after your x-rays came in, we figured this would be easy because all we had to do was sew up the entrance and exit wounds and replace the blood you lost, but instead, you went into shock. And then your heart stopped.

"Jerzy, I will be honest... I was so angry and frustrated because of your heart stopping for no reason that made sense, none, and I lost it, shouting at your young, lifeless body, and pounding you on the chest, until the other doctors pulled me away... but then, somehow, your heart began beating again. When we heard it on the monitor, we all just looked at each other in disbelief. It was a miracle. But then, instead of waking up after the anesthesia wore off, you became comatose, so once again, we were not sure you would make it. The only thing we could do at that point was cross our fingers. Well, that roller coaster ride was three days ago, but your young lady here would not leave your side, and I think that somehow she did more than we ever could to bring you back."

Jerzy lightly squeezed her hand, and Ekaterina squeezed back, bringing his hand to her lips. He grinned and with the forefinger from that same hand, gently wiped a tear from her cheek.

* * *

Ekaterina used the time before Jerzy's release from the hospital to apply for a site within the Polish section of the camp where they could live close to each other, but she could not find any places for both Polish and Russian refugees in the same area. For the time being, the British had put her in a barracks for unattached Russian women and children, which was her present home, but that was on the other side of the camp from the Polish refugees. All she could do now was go back to the hospital with her bad news.

"Jerzy, I tried so hard but everything is impossible. We could go to Poland, but you said no."

"Sweetie, Poland is occupied now by Russia, and I heard that many Poles who go back there are shot on arrival by the communist authorities. I have already been shot once, thank you. No, Poland is out. But I do have another idea..."

Jerzy knew how she would react, but he had to at least try. "Look, I love you with all my heart, and you said you love me, right?"

She nodded.

"And I hate being away from you," he continued, "especially after all we have been through. Soooo... maybe... you and I could find a small place somewhere for just the two of us and we could have our own little Ruskie-Polack community. At least we would be together." He gave her his best puppy-dog look.

"Jerzy! You know how I feel about that. No, only if we are married. It might be okay for you because you're a man, and apparently, it's okay for guys, but what would people say about me? Huh? I would be afraid to show my face in public, and do you know what kind of horrible names people would call me? All the guys would see me as a loose woman, and you know how they would treat me. Is that what you want? Do you really want me to live like that? No Jerzy. No, no, no. I'm sorry, but even as much as I love you, no. It's just—"

"Okay, okay, okay... you win, my pateechka." Jerzy rolled his eyes upward. He looked deeply into her eyes, but all he saw was a stubborn, but resolute determination. He sighed. "And do you know what?" he continued. "I'm disappointed, yes, but... you are so damned honorable, and adorable, and I love you all the more for it."

"Watch your language," she chided. But then she hugged him, and reminded him of her utter love and devotion to him.

He smiled. "Alright, let me see what I can do when they release me, okay? I really do love you."

* * *

A week later, Jerzy left the hospital with Ekaterina, found a bus, and went back to the British Occupied Zone in Hamburg, which housed their separate living quarters within the Displaced Persons Camp. After seeing Ekaterina home, all he could think of was the way they were separated back when they first met, while forcibly working for the Nazis in their chemical factory. How is this any better? he thought.

He then took another bus back the center of town and stood on the sidewalk, just looking around and thinking. A few stray dogs wandered the streets, looking for food. It was almost lunchtime, and Jerzy could hear his stomach talking to him. The hunger spoke of memories, back when he was enslaved. He trembled.

Turning a corner, he noticed a small building with a big sign out front. "Hmmm... Bürgermeister. I wonder what a Bürgermeister is," he said to no one in particular. "Sounds important."

Knocking on the door, a gruff voice called to him to enter.

The Bürgermeister was just finishing a phone call and slammed the receiver into the cradle of the candlestick speaker he was holding with his other hand. He saw Jerzy and bellowed, "What do YOU want?"

Jerzi just stared at him. That is one hell of a greeting, he thought. "Nothing sir," he said, shaking his head. "Sorry to... never mind," and he turned to leave the way he had come.

"Get over here!" The Bürgermeister yelled, while screwing up his face, staring hard at Jerzy. "If you came in here, you wanted something, so what is it? Talk, and talk like a man, huh? ... not like some chicken-shit kid who cannot even wipe his own ass."

"Yes sir," said Jerzy. He took a deep breath. "My name is Jerzy Czaplicki. I am new in the local refugee camp, and I am trying to find somebody who can marry my girlfriend and I."

The Bürgermeister stroked his chin while staring at the young man before him. Finally, he leaned in, looking Jerzy up and down. "You do not look like you have a whole lot of money," he said. "Just how were you planning to pay for this service?"

Jerzy looked him straight in the eye, and figuring this man could perform the wedding ceremony, said, "You are right, sir—I have no money... yet. But I am young and strong, and I can do any kind of work you might need done around here."

"Do you know what a Bürgermeister is, young man?" He slipped his thumbs under his suspenders at the front of his chest, stretching them out as though demonstrating his importance. Not waiting for a reply, he answered his own question, "I am the town mayor," he said, his chin held high. "As such, I already have all the help I need. Tell you what, though..." he leaned in closer and said, almost in a whisper... "Cigarettes here are really hard to come by. You get me a couple of cartons and maybe we can make a deal."

Jerzy broke out in a big grin. "Yes sir, I will do just that sir, I promise." And he ran out the door, anxious to tell Ekaterina that they were going to be married.

But for now, he had a different problem... where to get the cigarettes he promised the Bürgermeister.

Looking at the different buildings in town, Jerzy's first thought was his memory of the farm where he had worked just before the liberation. He knew there were lots of cigarettes, along with many other riches that were just abandoned in the nearby woods by both the Nazis and the Americans, but he had no way to get back there now. Nobody he knew here had a car, and it was too far to walk. Besides, the place was probably picked clean by now and he needed a job, and he needed it immediately, otherwise what would they eat? During the war, all he had to take care of was himself, but he would be married soon, he thought, and he would need to take care of his wife as well. He thought about this all day, and for most of that night, until sleep finally descended upon him.

* * *

Jerzy realized he would never find work by just thinking about it, so that very next morning, he began looking, starting right in the camp. His first thought was to do what he did best, which was to fix cars, but hardly anybody here had an automobile, and there was no garage here anyway, not to mention tools, so that was a useless idea. Then he thought of the time he had spent working on his uncle's farm, plus the additional time working for the German farmer, but there were no farms within the refugee community. He was merely a displaced person now, apparently of no use to anyone.

When he finally arrived back in camp, he spotted a building with many well-dressed British soldiers coming and going. He approached one of the Brits staggering out and asked what this place was.

"Oh, THAAAAT... ish the finest building... hic... in thish whoooole country, lad" he said, putting a wobbly arm on the young man's shoulder, and pointing with the other arm. That there," he sputtered, pointing a rather unsteady arm toward the building, "ish the British Ooooofficers' ... hic, Club, hic!" He then nodded his head, as though in agreement with himself, and wobbled off in search of more adventure.

Jerzy remembered when the Nazi soldiers made him drink with them until he passed out, and decided that maybe working in the Officers' Club might just be a fun place to earn some cash.

Thirty

The Club

He walked in and easily found the manager. He was the guy yelling on the phone. Jerzy smiled. "Hi," he said when the man hung up. My name is Jerzy, and I am a Polish refugee. I am new here and looking for a job. I am a very hard worker and can do many things. And if you hire me, I promise I will be the best worker here." Then he shut up and waited to see what this man would do.

"Oh barmy," the older man said. "What makes you think you can work harder than anyone else works here?"

"Easy. I will watch the others while I work, and if anyone else is working harder than me, I will just double my efforts until I am doing more."

He looked long and hard at the boy, sizing him up. "Hmmm... Jerzy, you say? You are either totally barmy, or you have some serious bollocks. Either way, I like you."

Jerzy smiled.

"Tell you what," the man continued. "...be here tomorrow

morning at 7:30 A.M. But if you are even ten seconds late, you will be made redundant... understand?"

"Yes sir." And even though he did not understand all the words, Jerzy caught the gist and ran out with much good news to tell his beloved after work tomorrow.

* * *

His job was going well, and Jerzy was making friends along the way. He was also making enemies. He started out by bussing tables, but when he found out that the waiters earned tips on top of their salary, he applied for that job. He had done so well at his first position that his superiors felt it would not hurt to give him a chance at the same salary. Tips consisted largely of cigarettes, usually two at a time. And you had to ask for them, otherwise, no tip. Fortunately, this was exactly what he needed in order to pay the Bürgermeister for the wedding ceremony. Unfortunately, Jerzy was doing so well that some of the other workers started complaining about him to the manager because they felt he was getting their tips.

After a few weeks of this, the boss, Captain Fairchild, called Jerzy over one day, and told him that he needed him to go on a special errand for him.

"I need a counter stretcher," he said, ...and I want you to go to the Quartermaster's Store to get one. "They carry exactly what I need," he said, and I am trusting you to bring it back without breaking it."

Jerzy had no idea what a counter stretcher was, but he promised to be extra careful when bringing it back.

"And when he tells you how much it is, tell him to just put it on my tab," he said.

Jerzy nodded, and left.

As soon as Jerzy went out the door, the Captain looked out the window to make sure he was gone, then he got on the phone and called the Quartermaster, explaining about his sending Jerzy over there for a counter stretcher, and asked them to go along with the gag.

"Just tell him you handed out the last one you had this morning, and say that he can probably find one at Engineering, then when Jerzy leaves there, call them and repeat the story, asking them to send him to the Transport Section, and afterward, those chaps can send him to the Kitchen stores, and finally, to the Infirmary. Maybe the medics there can even give Jerzy a medical stretcher, which I'll have returned tomorrow." That provoked a good laugh from both of them.

That should deflate that pompous Polack, he thought, and maybe now he'll think about the other workers.

When Jerzy finally arrived back at the club, he felt like such a failure, explaining what he had been through, and finally showing them the stretcher they gave him.

"The Infirmary said they were out of counter stretchers, but they said that maybe you could use this instead," he said, showing the medical stretcher to the captain.

Nobody could hold it in any longer, and they exploded in laughter.

Jerzy did not understand, and his face was beet red. He just stared at all of them.

Finally, the Captain Fairchild could see Jerzy's embarrassment, so he put his hand on Jerzy's shoulder.

"Don't feel bad, chap. The blokes you work with complained to me, saying you were getting all their tips, and they didn't feel it was fair. Today was just a message to tone it down a bit."

"Captain, let me make sure I understand you right. You are saying that it is wrong to try to please the officers who come in here by working hard to serve them? And that it is better for me to be as lazy as many of the other waiters?

"Wait a min—"

"So that means," Jerzy continued, "...that lazy workers get rewarded, but hard workers get punished?"

"Jerzy, I—" he said, then paused. "Bollocks, you're right, young man. I have been blinded by how long those others have been with me. But you know what? You are absolutely right—I don't owe any of them one bloody thing. I have been so bloody stupid. I am sorry, Jerzy."

Jerzy listened in silence.

"And you know what else? The next time one of them complains about you getting all the tips, I am going to tell him to work harder then, and maybe that will help him earn some damned tips!"

Jerzy finally smiled a small, but sincere smile. "Thank you, sir."

* * *

Once in a while, American officers came into the club. The British hated them, but Jerzy loved them. He could not help but make comparisons. While the Brits were stiff and formal, the Americans were laid back and natural. The British ate in a straight-back position, no slouching, and would quietly bring the soup spoon in a slow and dignified manner up to their lips. Alternately, the Americans would have their elbows on the table, slurping their soup, sometimes drinking directly from the bowl, and laughing uproariously with their buddies while eating. The Brits drank tea. The Americans said that tea tasted like piss, and they preferred coffee. If you asked a Brit for a cigarette, he might gingerly take out a pack from his shirt pocket, tap out a cigarette, two if feeling generous, and hold the tip in his hand for you to come and get it, as though he was doing you a royal favor. The American soldiers, on the other hand, always tipped you, always, and instead of handing you a cigarette, they would take out an entire pack and throw it to you, even from across the room, then wink. Jerzi decided right then and there that he wanted some day to immigrate to the United States. He had even heard that the streets there were literally paved with gold.

But first, he thought, he needed to once again woo the woman he loved. He was so totally wrapped up in work that it became almost obsessive. He was the provider, after all, and in his circumstances, this was the only way. But something was wrong; he could sense a difference in her, as though she thought he was ignoring her, or not caring. She didn't say anything—but she didn't have to. Women are so damned good at this.

So, beginning the very next day, and every day after, Jerzy plucked a handful of wildflowers from the edge of the refugee camp on his way home after work, brushing dirt from their roots before making his way toward the Russian women's barracks. The flowers were simple and always the same—daisies, a few scraggly violets, and something that might have been a weed—but to Ekaterina, they were treasures.

As he approached the barracks, a familiar chorus of whispers and jealous muttering reached his ears. He smiled, knowing full well what was coming.

"Again?" one of the women, Anya, huffed, crossing her arms. "Every day, Jerzy?"

Ekaterina stood in the doorway, her arms extended expectantly, eyes alight. "Every day," she said with a teasing grin, taking the flowers and brushing them against her cheek.

Another women sighed. "Why doesn't my Nikolai bring me flowers?"

"Because he is lazy," Anya shot back. Then, narrowing her eyes at Jerzy, she asked, "Where do you find them all?"

Jerzy chuckled, then he twisted his fingers across the front of his lips, as though he was buttoning them shut.

The next morning, just before dawn, Jerzy slipped through the quiet camp on his way to work, moving past rows of makeshift shacks and barbed wire fences. The air smelled of damp earth and lingering smoke from the night's fires. He walked quickly, glancing over his shoulder out of habit. Trust was a dangerous thing, and he had learned long ago that loose lips could be deadly.

He reached the grove where the wildflowers grew—untouched, hidden beyond a collapsed section of fencing that no one else seemed to notice. The sight of the tiny blooms, fragile, but stubbornly alive, made his chest expand with pride; Ekaterina's expression never grew old. The flowers were beautiful, but if he picked them now, they would be wilted by the end of the day, so he turned and continued on to his job.

Walking home after the workday ended, Jerzy daydreamed most of the way, all happy thoughts. As he was approaching his most secret stash, he knew Ekaterina would be waiting at her home, so he had to pluck a handful quickly.

But he wasn't alone.

Turning his head slightly, he caught a flicker of movement behind a broken cart. Someone was watching.

Jerzy didn't react... he didn't give anything away. He continued walking, acting as if nothing were wrong. But his pulse quickened. And then he saw.

The flowers were all gone. Every. Single. One.

Damn.

Jerzy clenched his jaw as he walked to the Russian barracks. Ekaterina met him at the door, confusion in her dark eyes.

"Jerzy?"

He shook his head, "There are no more. I am sorry."

The other women overheard. Anya snorted, arms crossed. "Because those idiots stripped them bare."

Across the room, a group of men stood together, grinning. One of them, Grigory, a burly Russian with too much pride and too little sense—caught Jerzy's eye.

"Too bad about the flowers," Grigory called. "But don't worry. We made sure everyone had some."

Laughter followed. Jerzy said nothing. He simply turned and walked away. But in his mind, another thought was forming. If he couldn't give Ekaterina flowers, maybe he could give her something even more valuable...

Thirty-One

New Deals

The next day, Ekaterina saw how low he was feeling, not knowing that he was depressed because he truly loved her and could find no way to show her how much she meant to him.

So, wanting to do something to cheer him up, she decided to make a special meal for him the next day, but she could not afford the ingredients she would need, nor could he.

She told Jerzy what she wanted to do, hoping he could find a way to get the necessary elements, and that was when inspiration struck. His face lit up like a Roman candle, and he looked at her with eyes as big as saucers. "That's it!" he said.

Back in his school days in Poland, the science class had to learn all about how fruits and vegetables grew, plus each student needed to actually grow them for a grade. Later, after Poland was attacked, he learned even more by working at his uncle's farm. And after his escape from captivity, there were endless days of working on a German farm. He knew he could do it.

"Listen," he said to Ekaterina. "Tell all the ladies here that if they can afford anything to help me get a few roots and vegetables to plant, I will solve much of their food problems by building the biggest garden I can for all of you right here, in the back of this building. Katya, I have big farming experience and I can do this. All I ask is that nobody else touch it; just let me take care of it, and that includes rotating the crops and digging them up at the right time. After that, everyone can share. I can plant potatoes and cucumbers, tomatoes, cabbage, beets, berries, even some spices... so many things. And once they have grown, Katya, none of us will need to buy anything anymore except meat and bread," he said, "and we should be able to afford that with the money we save. And maybe we will even have enough to buy a few canning jars and preserve some of the food." Then he gave her a quick kiss and ran out the door. Her heart surged.

Because Jerzy had picked so many flowers for his love, all the women in Ekaterina's barracks were already seeing him as larger than life, so giving whatever they could to help him was no problem. Unfortunately, though, he had no tools, nor did they. Remembering what he had learned from working in the garage, however, when they had to hand-make all the parts they needed to fix the cars, Jerzy started by gathering scraps of wood and bent metal from the officers' garbage. The tools he made were crude, but they could do the job.

The patch of land behind the Russian barracks was worthless to most—rocky, uneven, filled with debris. But to Jerzy, it was an opportunity.

With careful planning, he cleared it, working only at night when no one would see. And with the Russian women's help, he collected many tiny contributions—salt, flour, coins—enough to bribe a guard for seeds. Slowly, the garden took shape.

Carrots. Peas. Radishes. Cucumbers. Basil. Tomatoes. Things that can be planted next to each other. Just a few things at first. But there would be more when the crops were rotated. Much more.

It was their secret. And it was a wonder to behold.

For weeks, the women helped him tend to it, pulling weeds, watering the plants with tin cups. Slowly, the crops grew. It wasn't much, but it was theirs.

Then, one morning, everything was gone.

The garden had been destroyed. Stalks ripped from the ground. Leaves crushed under heavy boots. The soil, once rich and dark, was torn apart, as if something had been searching beneath it. But this was no animal. Ekaterina let out a small gasp.

Jerzy's hands curled into fists.

Someone had found out.

Jerzy spent the day watching as he went about his daily activities. He knew the camp well — who bartered, who stole, who whispered in corners. And when he saw Grigory and his men near the warehouse, munching on raw carrots, his suspicions hardened into certainty.

But Jerzy didn't confront Grigory immediately. That would be foolish. Instead, he observed. Listened. The men who had torn apart the garden had no long-term plan—just hunger, frustration, and a need to prove themselves. And that gave him an idea.

That evening, Jerzy approached Grigory while the man was repairing a broken fence near the officer's barracks. The others were nearby, listening but pretending not to.

"Grigory," Jerzy said calmly, squatting beside him. "You were right."

Grigory looked up, suspicious. "About what?"

"The garden," Jerzy said. "It wasn't fair that only a few had food. That's not how we survive."

Grigory narrowed his eyes. "You change your mind so quickly?"

Jerzy shook his head. "No. And I haven't forgotten about the flowers, either. But I change my approach when I need to." He picked up a rock and ran his thumb over its rough edge. "We can't undo what's been done. But we *can* make something better."

Grigory snorted. "And what would that be?"

Jerzy leaned in slightly. "You and your men took the food because you needed it. I get that. I almost starved to death under those damned Nazis, so I know what hunger does to a man. But tearing up that garden means there's nothing left—for you or anyone else. That wasn't smart.

"But... if we work together, instead of against each other, we can grow enough for everyone—not just a handful of women in the barracks. Only we do it right this time. Bigger. Hidden better. We get the old men, the women, even the children involved. If we do this right, no one has to go hungry."

Grigory looked uncertain, glancing at his men. They were watching now, interest flickering behind their usual bravado.

"And what do you get out of this?" Grigory asked.

Jerzy smiled. "Less trouble. More allies. And a full stomach. So what do you say?" He held out his hand.

Grigory hesitated, then grunted and shook it slowly. "Fine. But if you cheat us—"

Jerzy chuckled. "If I cheat you, I go hungry, too."

The deal was made. By the end of the week, the garden was reborn —bigger, stronger, and guarded by the very men who had once destroyed it.

And Jerzy? He had turned thieves into farmers, and enemies into allies.

Just in time for his wedding.

* * *

As Jerzy made new friends in the camp, he shared his excitement about his upcoming wedding. It did not take long before some of the other young men, equally smitten with their sweethearts, admitted they wanted to marry as well. But there was a problem—they were all as broke as he was, and the Bürgermeister had made it clear that his services did not come free. That gave Jerzy an idea. He told the other groom hopefuls his plan, and they all agreed.

One crisp afternoon a few months later, with the scent of burning wood drifting through the air, Jerzy made his way to the Bürgermeister's office. He remembered where the old man worked, and since this was official business, he figured he could drop in unannounced. Formalities were not exactly the most pressing concern in a refugee camp.

Reaching the heavy wooden door, he grasped the large brass knocker and gave it three solid thumps. The sound echoed through the narrow hallway beyond. Without waiting for an invitation, Jerzy turned the knob and stepped inside.

Behind a broad, well-worn desk sat the Bürgermeister, just as stout as ever, with a face that always looked slightly irritated, as though the weight of the world rested on his shoulders. He was poring over a stack of papers when Jerzy entered, and he looked up with a scowl.

"What is this?" he barked. "Do people not wait for an invitation any more?"

Jerzy, unfazed, flashed his most disarming grin. "Herr Bürgermeister, I've come with a business proposition that might just brighten your day."

The old man squinted then, remembering he was still on the phone, and yelled at the person on the other end, "I'll call you back," slamming the mouthpiece down.

"I remember you," he grumbled. "You are the young whipper-snapper who wanted to get married without a pfennig to his name." He leaned back in his chair. "What now? Come to beg for charity?"

Jerzy chuckled. "No, sir. Quite the opposite. I have come to offer you a deal that is—how can I say—mutually beneficial."

The Bürgermeister folded his arms. "Go on, then. Let us hear about your big deal."

Jerzy stepped closer, lowering his voice just slightly. "You told me you would officiate my wedding for two cartons of cigarettes."

The old man's bushy eyebrows lifted. "Ah, so you have them already?"

Jerzy's grin widened. "Even better." He let the silence hang for a moment, drawing out the suspense. "How about SIX cartons?"

The Bürgermeister narrowed his eyes. "Six? What's the catch?"

Jerzy leaned on the desk, his confidence growing. "Well, sir, you said yourself that cigarettes are scarce these days. And as it turns out, I have five friends who also want to get married. Now, none of us has two cartons to spare, but, if we each contribute one, that makes six. So, here's my proposal: You marry all six couples in just one single ceremony... the same amount of work, but you walk away with three times what you originally asked for. One ceremony, six cartons. What do you think?"

The Bürgermeister tapped his fingers on the desk, considering.

"Hmph. If I were to marry six couples individually, that would be twelve cartons."

Jerzy shrugged. "That would be true—if we had the cigarettes. And it would also be six times the work for you. On the other hand, if you do not take advantage of this deal, it would mean no cigarettes at all for you. And even though you would not marry us, I am certain we could find someone else willing to do it for the same price."

The Bürgermeister's lips twitched, and then, without warning, he burst into laughter. His whole body shook, and he slapped Jerzy on the back so hard the young man nearly stumbled.

"Jerzy, I don't know where you learned to negotiate like this, but damned if you don't have me over a barrel." He wiped a tear from his eye. "Six cartons for just one ceremony. Why not? You have a deal, young man."

Jerzy extended his hand, and the Bürgermeister shook it, his grip firm and warm. "Thank you, sir," Jerzy said, still grinning. "Now everybody wins."

* * *

At last the big day arrived, with all six couples arriving at the Bürgermeister's office, all dressed in the best outfits they could manage. All were European by birth, and had seen countless traditional celebrations in the countries they grew up in, but war and misfortune had rendered such memories mere dust of the past. Some of the men had managed to find jackets, though most were mismatched. One groom wore an oversized British officer's coat with brass buttons, another had repurposed an old German uniform stripped of its insignia. The brides, too, wore whatever they could piece together—Ekaterina, always the practical one, had fashioned a simple white scarf over her shoulders, and another woman had borrowed a lace curtain to use as a veil. Despite it all, however, they stood proud, hands clasped, hearts full.

The Bürgermeister, dressed in his usual neck tie, suspenders and rolled-up sleeves, smoothed his red mustache and cleared his throat. He had written special vows, specifically for this group, for he had never before officiated for a wedding of more than one couple at a time.

"We are gathered here today... and for quite a lot of you, it seems..." A chuckle rippled through the room. Because the couples and languages and customs were so mixed, the ceremony was void of any one religious or even civil leaning. He ran through the vows quickly, unavoidably mispronouncing a few names, but nobody minded. When he asked if anyone objected to the marriages, one of the grooms elbowed his contrary friend and muttered, "You say one word and I will be going home with those big teeth of yours in my pocket."

Jerzy was beaming with pride. When everybody gave the mayor their cigarettes, he proceeded to get everybody's names and addresses. Because the war had just ended, most of the people before him were displaced without paperwork from their countries of origin, so the mayor bypassed proof of identity and allowed everybody there to simply vouch for each other.

It was a hell of a ceremony, and much crying took place—even the Bürgermeister shed a tear or two. By the time the ceremony ended, there were tears in every eye.

"I have been saving this for a special occasion, and I cannot think of anything more special than this." He pulled out an old bottle of champagne from his desk drawer, and blew the dust off of it, careful not to get it on any of the blushing brides. He had only a few glasses, but nobody minded sharing.

When Jerzy and his new bride got their drinks, the young groom raised his glass, and he grinned at the Bürgermeister, saying, "I would like to propose a toast—to the best Bürgermeister in all of Germany." Everyone cheered, and the mayor stuck his thumbs under his suspenders, pulling them forward a bit, then shook hands with all the husbands, congratulating them, and gratefully accepting a kiss on the cheeks from each blushing bride, along with a grateful thank you from all.

Afterward, all the newlyweds shared a bus ride back to the camp, spilling into the streets, their friends and neighbors rushing to congratulate them. Some threw flower petals, others clapped and whistled. Someone started playing a harmonica, and before long, a spontaneous celebration broke out.

Jerzy wrapped his arms around Ekaterina and pulled her close. "Well, Mrs. Jerzy," he whispered, grinning.

She looked up at him, her eyes bright with happiness. "Well, Mr. Ekaterina," she teased back.

He laughed, then dipped her into a loving kiss as the music played on.

Thirty-Two

Paradise

After the wedding ceremony, most of the newlyweds were moved into open-bay barracks, their placements determined by nationality. It was a matter of practicality, not decency. Privacy was more a dream than a reality, with couples stringing up sheets between bunks to create makeshift walls between the families, and nobody would admit to hearing the intimate moments shared by their neighbors. It was what it was... a survival mechanism, a denial of the intrusion upon each other's dignity.

Jerzy and Ekaterina, however, were among the lucky ones. As the barracks were completely full, they were assigned a one-room wooden shack near the outer edge of the compound. It was small, battered, drafty, away from everyone else, and had large cracks in the walls, but it was theirs. Theirs alone. And they did not care because they were together again, at long last.

Their new home was shown to them by Zofia Kowalska, the camp's self-appointed tour guide and gossip. She was the wife of a former blacksmith, but like so many others, her husband was now just another man scraping by, another shadow in the camp's weary existence. To compensate for their loss of status, Zofia took great pleasure in showing all newlyweds to their new domiciles, offering unsolicited history lessons about their predecessors. It made her feel important.

"The couple who lived here before you," Zofia began, open palm gesturing to sweep in the tiny interior through the shack's sagging door, "were all set to immigrate to England. They had their papers and everything. But then—one week before their departure—her husband, Witek, got caught with another man's wife, "...if you know what I mean," she whispered. She raised her eyebrows meaningfully and lowered her voice to a more dramatic whisper: "The woman's husband, Mieczysław, found them together and... let's just say he took his revenge. With a rusty knife... if you know what I mean."

Jerzy frowned. "What do you mean?"

Zofia sighed impatiently, as if she shouldn't have to explain such things. "Witek became a... eunuch," she whispered, "that's what I mean! And of course, the wound got infected. He was... dead... in days." She clicked her tongue. "A real shame. So close to a better life."

Ekaterina clutched Jerzy's arm, her eyes wide. "And Witek's wife?"

"Oh, she had to move out, of course. This beautiful cabin is for married couples only. Rules are rules. She stayed with some other women for a while, but, well..." Zofia leaned in conspiratorially. "Some say she died of a broken heart," she nodded, as if confirming it to herself. "Tragic, really."

Jerzy and Ekaterina exchanged uneasy glances.

"Anyway," Zofia said briskly, her cheerful tone returning, "it's all yours now! Home sweet home." She clapped her hands together, then turned to leave, humming to herself as she went.

Alone at last, Jerzy pushed the door closed, and the rusty hinges groaned in protest. Inside, the air was stale, thick with dust and the lingering scent of damp wood. The walls, rough and riddled with cracks, barely seemed capable of holding back the wind. A rickety table and two mismatched chairs stood in the corner, left behind by the previous occupants. The bed, complete with a thin mattress lay in the far corner, covered in a scratchy wool blanket.

Ekaterina wrinkled her nose. "It smells... like mice."

Jerzy grinned. "Then we'll have to make friends with them. Maybe they'll keep us warm."

She elbowed him, laughing, but it was half-hearted. She traced a finger along the wall, following a deep crack. "If we speak too loudly, the whole camp will hear us."

Jerzy exhaled, surveying the damage. "It needs repairs. If I had tools, I could fix this place up."

"But we don't have tools," Ekaterina reminded him gently. "Or wood. Or nails."

"Details." He winked. "I'll figure something out."

She smiled, but her expression was weary. For all their excitement, the reality of their situation was sinking in. They had no privacy, no security, no real certainty about the future.

But still, they had each other.

Jerzy took her hands in his and squeezed them gently. "We made it this far, Katya." he said. "Together. That's what matters."

A slow smile spread across her face, her worries momentarily forgotten. "Together," she echoed.

And for that moment, despite everything, it was enough.

* * *

Jerzy continued to work in the British Officers' Club, however, it was still difficult to make ends meet, such was the post war economy. Depression had become a way of life for many. But his mind was always looking for inspiration, and one fine spring day, after Ekaterina had returned from her meager grocery shopping, Jerzy had an idea. The large garden Jerzy built to replace the first one outside the Russian barracks had failed, but this one was not killed deliberately— this one fell only because it was large and frail, which required many people to be custodians, and they constantly fought among themselves.

But what if now Jerzy planted a smaller, humbler plot in back of their new home? For just two of them?

The soil he was eyeballing for the garden was hard, packed tight by years of neglect and trampled under by too many desperate feet. And just beyond the back yard was a patch of woods at the outer edge of the camp where Jerzy could savage dead branches for the stove, and dead leaves for compost.

A few days later, Jerzy was ready. A crow flew over him, cawing, as though telling him this was crow territory. Jerzy looked at him as he flew away, then pressed his boot against the handmade spade, driving it in with slow, steady force. The earth resisted, but he had known worse battles. He worked in silence, the rhythmic scrape of metal against dirt filling the air. It was like music to his ears, and each thrust of the spade sent a dull ache through his arms, yet he welcomed it. Pain meant progress.

Ekaterina sat nearby, legs tucked beneath her, sorting through a small pile of scavenged seeds—half-rotted potatoes, a handful of beans, a few tomato seeds saved from a borrowed meal. She rubbed a seed between her fingers, rolling it absently against her palm.

"You think they will grow?" she asked.

Jerzy didn't answer immediately. He knelt, scooping up a handful of dirt and rubbing it between his fingers. Dry. Weak. He had no compost yet, no manure—only what he had been able to gather: ashes from their small stove, crushed eggshells, vegetable peels fished from the officers' refuse. He sifted the mix into the earth, working it in with his hands. It wasn't much, but it was something.

"They'll grow," he said finally. Because they had to.

The sun inched lower, shadows stretching long behind their shack. Jerzy's shoulders burned with exhaustion, but he didn't stop. The land had to be ready. Each row was laid out with careful precision, measured by a length of twine tied between two stakes. It wasn't a field, not even a true garden yet, but it would be.

With what scraps of wood he could find—broken crates, splintered planks—he fashioned a small barrier around the patch of earth. Not much of a fence, but enough to keep out the worst of the scavengers. He eyed it critically, then wiped the sweat from his brow with the back of his hand.

Ekaterina had gone inside, but she returned with a battered tin cup of water. She handed it to him, her fingers brushing his as he took it. "You can't do everything in a single day," she said.

Jerzy drank, letting the warm water wash the dust from his throat. "If I don't, who will?"

She didn't argue, only settled beside him in the dirt, reaching for the small pile of seeds. Together, they pressed them into the soil, their fingers brushing in the darkness. He marked their resting places with precision, etching lines into the earth as though carving his intentions into fate itself. No insecticides, no unnatural hands—only the daily ritual of nurture, each frail seedling cradled with reverence, for in Jerzy's eyes, they were not mere plants; they were a promise.

* * *

That night, the rain came without warning. A sharp wind rose, rattling the loose boards of their shack. Then the downpour struck, hammering the roof like fists. Jerzy woke to the sound and was on his feet in an instant.

His garden.

He ran outside, barefoot, the ground already turning to mud beneath him. Cold water soaked through his thin shirt, but he barely felt it. His eyes searched frantically through the darkness. The seedlings—too delicate to withstand such a beating—were drowning.

Dropping to his knees, he dug with his bare hands, carving trenches, trying to push the water away. Straw and cloth—whatever he could find—became shields, small barriers against the flood. His hands bled, nails caked with dirt, but he didn't stop.

A figure appeared beside him. Ekaterina. She was holding something—an old pot, bent at the rim. Without a word, she knelt and began scooping water away, throwing it aside. Together, they worked in the rain, breathless, desperate.

The storm passed before dawn. The sky remained heavy with clouds, but the worst had moved on. Jerzy sat in the mud, breath coming in sharp bursts. His arms trembled with exhaustion.

Ekaterina dropped the pot and lowered herself beside him. She touched his shoulder, her fingers gentle against his damp shirt. "You'll break yourself over this little patch of earth," she murmured.

He gave a tired smile. "It's worth breaking for."

She didn't argue.

The first sprouts came days later. Tiny, fragile things, but alive. Jerzy crouched, running his fingers over the tender leaves, whispering, Grow strong.

Ekaterina stood behind him, arms crossed against the morning chill. "You talk to plants now?"

He grinned, brushing dirt from his hands. "They listen better than most people."

She smiled, but there was a lighthearted acknowledgement behind it.

By the time the first tomato ripened, they had enough to eat. Not much, but enough. They sat by the garden one evening, sharing a simple meal, the last warmth of summer fading into autumn's chill.

Beyond the last row of plants, a patch of wildflowers swayed in the breeze, untouched, unplanned. He had left it by accident, a forgotten corner of earth. He didn't know, not yet, what it would become. But one day, he would kneel there again, pressing his hands into the soil, feeling its warmth, and its terrible weight.

Thirty-Three

Sunny Side Up

And so it was that the days turned into weeks, and weeks became months, and the garden grew, but not much else changed. At least not until that fateful day in September when Ekaterina came home anxious to tell Jerzy

the good news, but also fearful that he might be angry. He was, after all a man, held captive to cold facts and logic rather than the warmth of a woman's emotions.

"Katya," he said when she walked in the door. "Where were you? It is not like you to be away when I return from work and I was worried."

"I am sorry, my love. I was at the doctor's office, and did not wish to say anything until I knew for sure."

He stared, not sure how to react or what to say, but his protective instincts came to the forefront as he recalled the tales he had heard of the ravenous illness that stole his mother away when he was but a small child. "Are you alright?" he asked, grabbing her upper arms. "What is wrong?" They had been married for only a few months, and he could not stand to lose her. Especially not after all they had endured.

"No-no-no, it is not like that," she said, shaking her head. "I am okay. In fact, I am better than okay." She lowered her eyes in that beautifully alluring way she had about herself, then continued, saying softly, "I have something important to tell you though."

He continued to stare at her, still not knowing what to say because he had no idea what she was talking about.

"Oh Jerzy," she began, almost laughing... "you are going to make such a wonderful father," her beautiful eyes twinkling with love and happiness.

It took a few moments before the meaning of her words finally registered, and when it did, his eyes looked as though they would pop out of his head.

"You mean..." he sputtered.

She merely smiled a smile big enough for the two of them, and slowly nodded her head.

Without even thinking, Jerzy grabbed his wife, hugging her tightly, then thinking he might hurt the baby, he backed off and apologized. But Katya just laughed and told him she was fine and that she loved him more than he could ever know. But he did know, because he was sure he felt the same way about her.

Apparently, he had planted more than one garden here, he thought, and seeds were ripening everywhere. But his past life experience was only with fruits and vegetables, so he left the planning and tending of this most sacred garden to his wife, for surely she knew what needed to be done. She had to, for he felt himself to be a total idiot in such affairs.

Together, they owned so little, yet despite their extreme poverty, they were rich beyond comparison with love and tender feelings for each other.

And now, Jerzy decided, it was even more imperative for him to find a way to immigrate to America, where he could surely flourish, and at last provide properly for his family.

* * *

The days, though long, quickly rolled on with an urgency of their own, until finally it happened. At almost 3:00 AM one cool April morning, he was awakened with the utmost urgency.

"Jerzy, JERZY... go get Nadia," she said. He merely grunted and rolled over. "NOW! The baby is coming." Nadia was the midwife that Ekaterina had told her husband about months ago.

"Who?" Jerzy asked, half asleep.

"Aaaaarrrrgggghhhh! Nadia," she yelled. "NOW!"

Jerzy jumped out of bed, afraid for his life to anger the goddess who slept beside him. It was early in the month, and jumping quickly into his now chilly clothing from yesterday, he scampered as quickly as possible to get out of there and get to the midwife before his wife exploded. Fortunately, Nadia lived in the Russian sector of the same compound, which was a reasonable distance for a young man at this dark hour outside in the early morning air.

When he arrived at the barracks where she lived, the front door was locked shut and all the lights were out. "Dammit," said Jerzy, and he began pounding on the door. Finally, a rumpled old Russian woman the size of a linebacker opened the door, but just a little bit.

"Do you know what time it is," she yelled? She started to slam the door shut, but Jerzy's frantic need was accelerating his reflexes, and his foot shot out quickly between the door and the jamb.

"Please," he begged. "My wife is pregnant and ready to pop like a tick! She told me that Nadia is the only midwife she wants, and is living here. If I do not return with her, my wife will rip my head off and I will never get to see our child."

The woman at the door hesitated, considering Jerzy's fear and desperation.

"Okay, she said begrudgingly. Wait here." Then she kicked his foot out from where it was wedged and slammed the door in his face. Jerzy frantically paced in small circles before the door as he waited, the seconds seeming like hours. He hoped the baby could wait until at least he returned with help to escort him into this new life.

It felt like forever before the door finally opened again and a tiny and quite young Russian woman emerged carrying a large black bag. Quickly, Jerzy grabbed her bag without even greeting her, and they ran back to his home in the blackness, and the drama within. They couldn't get there fast enough, thought Jerzy.

Finally, they arrived, having sprinted the entire way. Running inside, Nadia wiped the sweat from her forehead with the back of her wrist, still huffing and puffing, her hands trembled slightly. This was it —her first solo delivery. She had assisted before, but never had the full responsibility of bringing life into the world all by herself. And now, in the dim glow of a sputtering oil lantern in a drafty refugee shack, she could hear the early morning quiet outside as if still mourning all the lives lost in the war.

Ekaterina was relieved to see Nadia, but the pain and uncertainty about everything initially kept her from speaking.

"Please help me," Ekaterina finally moaned.

Realizing that she was no longer a mere apprentice, but now the one in charge, was a heavy responsibility, yet Nadia composed herself and reassured her that everything would be alright, then showed her how to control her breathing. She sent Jerzy to get some hot water, and also some cold water. He put some wood he had been saving for this day into the stove and ran to the community well, returning as quickly as possible. Putting one pot on the stove, he paced as though it would make the water boil quicker, then brought it in as quickly as he could, anxious to see how his wife was doing.

Ekaterina let out a sharp cry, gripping Jerzy's arm tightly. His knuckles turned white.

Hours elapsed, yet each moment was forever.

The baby should have come by now, thought Nadia. But something was wrong. Too much time had passed.

The midwife swallowed hard. She had been trained for this, hadn't she? Think, Nadia! She felt the mother's stomach, and finally realized that the baby was face-up—which meant a more painful, difficult delivery. If she didn't act quickly, the mother could tear badly, or worse, the baby could get stuck.

She took a deep breath, steadying herself. Then she saw Jerzy staring at her; she didn't like being watched.

I need to get this man out of here, she thought. "Jerzy, more hot water."

He hesitated.

"Now!" Her voice was firm, though her heart pounded.

Jerzy hesitated. "More? I just—"

"Now, I said!"

As he rushed back to the fire, Nadia reached into her worn leather satchel, pulling out a small tin of lard. It wasn't much, but it would have to do. She scooped a bit with her fingers and rubbed it over her hands to warm it before gently applying it to the mother.

Then came the real test. She would have to reach inside and try to turn the baby. She had seen it done before, but never with her own hands.

"Nadia," Ekaterina gasped, sweat dripping from her forehead, "is something wrong?

Nadia forced a smile. "No, my dear. Your baby is just playing games with us."

She took a deep breath, steeled her nerves, and slid her fingers inside. The baby was indeed stubbornly facing up. Nadia pressed gently, attempting to coax the little one to turn.

For a moment, she thought all was right with the world again.

But then—as if defying her, the baby turned right back again, settling once more in the face-up position.

Nadia blinked in disbelief. What kind of child is this, so determined to enter the world on its own terms?

Ekaterina let out another strangled cry. Nadia had to act now.

She reached for her boiled scissors, waiting on the cloth nearby, making sure they were within arm's reach for when the time came. Then she cupped Ekaterina's belly gently, whispering, "Your baby is coming its own way... sunny-side up. You must help it."

Ekaterina barely nodded, exhausted but trusting.

"Okay, ready? Push now... hard!"

Ekaterina screamed, and screamed again... pushing and grunting, and at long last—the baby emerged, still face-up, eyes shut tight to keep out what must have seemed like intensely bright lights from the dim lanterns, compared to the amniotic cavern from which it just emerged. Hearing her scream, Jerzy wanted desperately to burst into the room, but he also did not want to cause her more pain by distracting the midwife. Besides, he knew that fathers, by long tradition, were not allowed in during these sacred moments.

For a second, the room was silent. The baby was not breathing. Nadia held the newborn by the ankles as she had been taught and spanked its little bottom, but nothing. Quickly cradling it face-down on her lap, she then patted it on the back, but still nothing. Desperately now, the midwife took a cloth to clear the baby's throat. Again, nothing. Then, out of sheer desperation, she quickly laid the baby down face-up on the bed, bent down and sucked out what mucus she could, spitting it onto the floor.

Then, finally... a wail. Loud, strong, defiant, like his father's. And like a little lamb. It was then that they saw... it was a boy. Finally, Jerzy was called in, and without taking a breath, he ran, not knowing what to expect.

When he saw Ekaterina, she was propped up, holding their baby for the first time, so proudly, and her eyes were watering with a profound love for this most stubborn and loud, but beautiful little boy.

Jerzy exhaled sharply, his hands trembling. Ekaterina sobbed in relief.

And Nadia? She stared at the newborn in awe, tears stinging her own eyes.

Her first delivery. And already, she had met a fighter. And a stubborn one at that.

She reached for her scissors and cut the cord, her hands no longer shaking.

"Hot damn," she thought, wearing her biggest, smuggest grin... "I did it."

Thirty-Four

Rules are Rules

They named the baby Kaspar, after Jerzy's father. Without a crib, they arranged two kitchen chairs beside the bed, facing each other, and swaddled him in a quilt, securing rolled towels along the sides with twine to create a makeshift cradle.

Kaspar was ten months old when his first great snowstorm arrived. As was their custom, they kept a bucket of water from the well beside the bed, but this morning, it was frozen solid. Each night, Jerzy fired up the stove, but its warmth never lasted, quickly swallowed by the drafts that crept through the cracks in the walls. He had stuffed them with rags, paper, even mud, but still, the cold found its way in.

Kaspar awakened in his usual jovial mood, and today was supposed to be an especially joyous day—his baptism. Jerzy and Ekaterina had planned everything carefully, wanting to mark the occasion despite the hardships of camp life. The only thing they never counted on was the snowstorm. Jerzy adjusted Kaspar's tiny white cap, his hands trembling slightly. The baby squirmed in Ekaterina's arms, fussing against the chill in the air in their shack. The single oil lamp flickered in their cramped quarters, casting nervous shadows. Outside, the gray drizzle had turned the refugee camp's dirt paths to mud.

A sharp knock at the door startled them. Ekaterina exchanged a look with Jerzy before he opened it. A small girl stood there, shivering, her braids damp from the mist.

"The priest wants to see you," she said, shifting nervously from foot to foot. "Now."

Jerzy's heart sank. He turned to Ekaterina, saw the worry in her eyes, then back to their bundled son. Swallowing hard, he nodded and grabbed his coat.

* * *

The Polish priest's quarters were sparse, lined with old books and the faint scent of wax. Father Wojciech sat behind a battered wooden desk, fingers steepled.

"What do you mean, you cannot baptize my son?" Jerzy's voice was tight, his Polish accent sharpening under strain.

The priest sighed. "I did not realize your wife is Orthodox."

Jerzy stiffened. "What difference does that make? She is Christian. We are family."

Father Wojciech folded his hands. "The Church has its rules. Baptism is sacred. There must be unity in faith."

Jerzy's fists clenched. "After everything we have endured—war, starvation, death—you deny my son his baptism because his mother prays a different way? Is this what God wants?"

The priest's expression did not change. "I am sorry."

Jerzy trembled with rage, his breath coming in sharp bursts. He turned on his heel and strode out into the sleet.

* * *

Back at their barrack, Ekaterina saw his face and gasped. "No..."

"He refuses. Because you are Orthodox."

She clutched Kaspar tighter. "But... what do we do?"

Jerzy's jaw tightened. "There is a Protestant church in the village. We go there. Now."

Their friends, Stefan and Helena, were already dressed for the ceremony and ready to witness. Without hesitation, they agreed to go with them.

The taxi ride was silent except for the baby's soft coos. The village church was small, its steeple disappearing into the mist. Inside, warm golden light flickered through the stained glass. But the service was still going, and the doors were shut.

Huddled outside, the cold seeped into their bones. Ekaterina pulled Kaspar's blanket tighter around him, her lips pressed to his forehead.

At last, the minister emerged. He was tall, with graying hair and gentle eyes. "Can I help you?"

Jerzy stepped forward, his voice unsteady but firm. "We wish to baptize our son. The Polish priest refused. My wife is Orthodox."

The minister sighed, looking down at the baby. "I understand. But I cannot do this unless the Catholic priest confirms his refusal. The church must have order."

Ekaterina let out a choked sob. Jerzy felt his nails bite into his palms. "You mean, we must go back? In this weather?"

The minister nodded. "If he states in front of witnesses that he will not perform the baptism, return to me. Then I will do it."

Back they went, the cold now biting through their coats. Jerzy stormed into the priest's quarters, dragging Stefan and Helena behind him.

"Father," Jerzy's voice was steel. "Say it now, before these witnesses. Will you baptize my son or not?"

The priest hesitated only a moment. "No. I will not."

Stefan's face darkened. "You shame the cloth you wear."

Jerzy said nothing, just turned and left.

The second journey to the Protestant church felt even longer. Kaspar, restless from the cold, whimpered against Ekaterina's chest.

When they arrived, the minister was waiting. He gestured them inside, where candlelight and warmth wrapped around them.

"Babies are innocent," he said, his voice calm and kind. "God does not care which hands pour the water, only that it is done with love."

Tears filled Ekaterina's eyes as the minister took Kaspar in his arms. "What name do you give this child?"

Jerzy cleared his throat. "Kaspar."

"Then, Kaspar," the minister said, dipping his fingers into the water, "I baptize you in the name of the Father, and of the Son, and of the Holy Spirit."

The water dripped down Kaspar's forehead. For a moment, silence held the room, thick with something holy.

Ekaterina let out a shaky breath. Stefan placed a hand on Jerzy's shoulder. Helena wiped her eyes. Jerzy looked down at his son—finally baptized, finally blessed.

But as they stepped back into the night, the new father noticed the baby's shallow breaths, the rattling in his tiny chest. Jerzy gritted his teeth against the burning in his eyes.

* * *

At first, it was a small thing, a hitch in the baby's breathing that made Ekaterina's heart quicken. She pressed a gentle hand to his forehead, but he was not feverish. Still, the sound unsettled her. When the cough deepened, rattling in his tiny chest, they did what they could with what little they had.

Ekaterina had once heard older mothers speak of burnt sugar water to ease a cough. Honey, she knew, was too dangerous for a baby so young, but sugar—perhaps that would help. Jerzy held Kaspar while she melted the sugar in their dented pan, mixing it with warm water.

She lifted the spoon to Kaspar's lips, but just as she tipped it, he coughed violently, spilling the precious mixture. Again, she tried, but his frail body shuddered, his small hand flailing, knocking the spoon away.

"This is all we have left," she whispered, staring at the last spoonful. Jerzy rubbed the baby's back, humming softly. "Shh, little one. Just a taste now." Ekaterina brought the spoon to his mouth, but

Kaspar, his body shaking with another fit, coughed so forcefully that the liquid sprayed onto his mother's wrist.

Handing the baby to Ekaterina, Jerzy exhaled sharply and moved to the stove. "I'll make more."

His fingers, rough from labor, fumbled with the sugar, but Ekaterina was grateful for his determination. She pressed the baby to her chest, feeling his warmth seep into her as she rocked him. His coughs were nearly constant now, his tiny body struggling.

"Jerzy, his cough is getting worse. I am scared."

Her husband did not hesitate. "Katya, we need to get him to the clinic. Now. Even in this cold air."

She looked toward the door. Snow had piled up overnight, and the wind still howled outside. The thought of taking their fragile son into the storm made her stomach clench. "Is he going to be okay?"

Jerzy did not answer. Instead, he kissed her forehead, then reached for a thick woolen shawl. They bundled Kaspar as best they could, tucking him beneath Ekaterina's coat, letting him share her body's warmth. Then, bracing themselves, they stepped out into the night, into the biting wind and swirling snow.

* * *

The clinic was a long walk through the drifts, their boots crunching through ice. The baby whimpered against his mother's chest, his cough muffled by her coat. When they finally arrived, the dimly lit room held only a single patient—a refugee with a bleeding hand being tended to by the on-call doctor.

Kaspar coughed again, a horrible rasping sound, and the doctor's head jerked up. His eyes, dark with exhaustion, widened. He abandoned the wounded man without a word and strode to them.

"Hey!" the patient protested. "What about my hand?"

"Wrap it yourself," the doctor snapped. "This is an emergency."

Ekaterina tightened her hold on Kaspar. The doctor had not even examined him, yet he already knew how dire the situation was.

"This clinic is not equipped for this," he said, pressing a hand to the baby's back. His brow furrowed. "He needs a hospital. Immediately."

The doctor barked orders to his aide. "Warm up the jeep."

The aide ran out, but moments later, he was back, breathless. "Flat tire, sir. It'll take time to change it in this weather."

The British doctor cursed under his breath. "Call the Redcaps. Tell them we need an urgent transport."

The MPs arrived within ten minutes, but the journey was treacherous. The roads were slick, snow piling high. The baby coughed and cried the entire way, his tiny body shivering despite Ekaterina's best attempts to warm him.

After a harrowing fifty-five minutes, they slid to a stop in front of the hospital. Jerzy leapt out, helping his wife carefully navigate the icy ground. The moment they stepped inside, medical staff rushed to them.

Ekaterina flinched at the acrid scent of bleach, but there was no time to dwell on it. Before she could react, the baby was taken from her arms.

"No," she gasped, reaching forward.

A nurse intercepted her. "We need to run tests immediately, and you need to stay here. The room is sterile—we can't allow outside germs."

Ekaterina's breath hitched, but she nodded. They watched as the doors swung shut, their child vanishing behind them.

As the minutes dragged on and became hours, Jerzy and Ekaterina took turns sitting and pacing, jumping up each time anyone wearing white came anywhere near them. Finally, they were told there was nothing they could do, and that they really should go home.

"No, Kaspar is only a baby and I am his mother," said Ekaterina, crossing her arms. Jerzy knew that stance and he wisely said nothing. The nurse looked at her for a long moment, and as a mother herself, she relented. "We don't have any spare rooms for you to sleep in, but I will try to find a cart for you, and you can sleep in the hallway. The father, however, will have to go home."

Copying his wife, Jerzy folded his arms and said, "This is my wife and I am the baby's father, so I am not going anywhere either." At that, the nurse merely shook her head and left in the hope of finding two carts. But neither of them could sleep.

More hours passed in an endless loop of pacing, sitting, standing, waiting. Every time a white-clad figure approached, they jumped to their feet, only to be met with silence or hurried words that gave no answers.

Then, finally, in the early morning hours, a nurse approached. Her face was too carefully neutral.

"I'm so sorry," she whispered. "The baby had pneumonia... and we did everything we could."

Ekaterina swayed. Jerzy caught her before she fell, his own body stiff, locked, as though not moving, not even breathing, would somehow make all of this not real.

"No," Ekaterina choked out. "No. He's just a baby. He's my baby."

The nurse's eyes glistened. "Would you like to see him?" she asked softly.

"Yes, of course I do. Where is he?"

Numbly, they followed her down the hall. The room was cold, too bright, too clean. Kaspar lay still, wrapped in a white blanket, impossibly small. Ekaterina collapsed beside him, sobbing, pressing kisses to his cooling forehead. Jerzy stood frozen. His hands trembled as he reached out, tracing his son's tiny fingers, his soft cheek. He wondered why the baby's hair had been shaved off.

And then, his eyes caught something.

Faint, almost imperceptible—small marks on Kaspar's skull, as if from a needle. Small. Precise. Too many to be from routine injections. Besides, why would anyone inject a baby in the skull?

A slow, terrible understanding curled in his gut. He had heard the stories, the whispers from the war—Nazi doctors, experiments on the weak, the helpless, the unwanted... in the name of science.

His breath shuddered. His hands clenched into fists, but what could he say? Who would listen? What proof did he have? He was not a doctor—he was a nobody.

So, he said nothing.

Instead, he bent over his son, resting his forehead against the baby's. And as his wife wept, he wept with her, swallowing his rage, his fear, his terrible, gnawing suspicion.

His stomach twisted.

Had they done something to him?

His eyes darted to the doctor, who looked at him with professional detachment.

He wanted to demand answers, to scream.

But what proof did he have?

None.

And so Jerzy clenched his jaw but still said nothing.

Ekaterina had already lost too much. If he spoke of his suspicions aloud, it would only break her further.

He swallowed his fury and buried his questions.

Because no matter what had happened here, no matter what had been done—Kaspar was gone.

And he carried his son home.

Then he found that neither church would provide a burial plot for a family that was not already a regular member of their parish.

Ekaterina wrapped him in a blanket and Jerzy laid him to rest in an outer corner of the small garden he had so carefully cultivated—the place where hope had once grown, now frantically digging and chopping at the frozen ground. And they wept the tears of a love stripped from their hearts.

As a new snow settled over the camp, Jerzy stood over the fresh mound of frozen earth, fists buried in his coat pockets, whispering a promise to his son...

He would get the boy's mother out of this place.

No matter what it took.

Thirty-Five

The Boar

Food was available, but with little money, variety was sparse. While his small garden provided for them during the warmer months, and Ekaterina was able to can a few foods, the winter supply was scarce. Jerzy, who, as a German captive during the war, was no stranger to food deprivation, and again now stared at the thin potato broth in his bowl while his stomach rumbled. The other faces around him at the camp were echoes of the same quiet desperation, so when news came that a wild boar had been spotted in the nearby woods, excitement flared among the men. The possibility of fresh meat was too tantalizing to ignore.

Talk of a hunting party spread quickly. Despite the war stripping civilians of their guns, they were not deterred, for bravery always asserted itself wherever men gathered as men, for they were the providers after all, and the protectors of their families. It was in their very spirit, something that could not be taken away, no matter the circumstances.

Jerzy found himself among the group of seven who gathered at his home before dawn, their breath curling in the cool air, boots scuffing against the hard ground. Inside, the cramped room smelled of damp wool and boiled potatoes, the last meal scraped from near-empty pots. They stood in silence, some adjusting their coats, others gripping the makeshift weapons they had scraped together.

Patryk Zawadski, the youngest at sixteen, stood beside him, quiet but eager. Jerzy saw the way the boy looked at the older men with a mix of admiration and longing, having learned at a young age about the value of listening to his elders, and so had heard many of the really old stories, when the men talked the high talk of those dangerous times in the woods, times when it was just man against beast, and about how men relied on the ancient ways of developing an acute sense of hearing and smell, along with that primal sixth sense which helped them feel and locate the game they sought, and he yearned to be a part of it, to prove himself as had his own father, and his father's father before him, for who knows how many generations. Jerzy understood. He, too, had once been that boy, yearning to be seen as a man.

"When his Papa was killed in the war, Patryk became the head of the household, even though he was only fourteen... it is tradition, you know," his mother told them, but at his young age, he still felt a need to prove himself, and so he volunteered to join this band of providers to demonstrate his worthiness as a man in a world of men, for his bravery had not yet been tested. As a boy-man, he had one prized possession: a hand-carved cedar walking stick his father had made. Besides bringing him closer to his dad when he used it, the stick somehow made him feel like a man, so he walked with it everywhere.

The oldest man in the group was Sulisław Ropeleski. They called him Sully. He was forty-seven and an alcoholic, but he was always good to the women and children in the camp, so the others decided he could join them as long as he pulled his weight, which he gratefully promised to do. Besides, he was an experienced hunter, and his tracking skills would be invaluable.

Jerzy was twenty-four now and had no trouble getting accepted into the group, for he had already proven himself among the men in the refugee camp with his creative ways of adapting since his arrival. That he had no experience with hunting was a secret which he kept faithfully, but he did have experience with catching farm animals that had no wish to be caught.

Then there was Alf Levenberg, a farmer who did not know how to hunt, but he raised pigs before the war and knew how to butcher them. If they had a successful hunt, surely his skills would be necessary.

All the rest of the hunting party came because jobs were scarce and they could not afford to buy any meat, but they had small children, and this was the only way they could provide meat for their families.

From the doorway, an older man spat into the dirt. "This boar's not just an animal. It's a devil. Too smart. Knows the land better than we do."

"Nobody is forcing you to go," said Jerzy.

"Oh Hell," said the old man, smiling... "...always wanted to kill me a devil."

Jerzy slung a sack of provisions over his shoulder. "Then we learn. We move together, no wandering off. We set up camp before nightfall."

The men grumbled but nodded. They filed out into the cool morning air, their shapes swallowed by the dawn mist as they left behind the brittle warmth of the house. The ground crunched beneath them as they walked, breath fogging, shoulders hunched against the wind. The forest loomed ahead, black and endless.

As the sun began to set, the men walked to the edge of the woods. Since guns were not allowed, they brought whatever sounded like it might be useful: shovels, a small axe, carving knives, some rope, and a healthy supply of moonshine, to keep them warm, and in good spirits.

"Before we go any further," said Jerzy, we need to have a plan. Up ahead is a clearing in the woods which can be our base of operations." In agreement, they built a fire upon their arrival and hunkered down around the crackling flames, holding their crude weapons drawn and ready in the rapidly cooling night air, looking and feeling as their earliest ancestors had with their bone tools at the ready, squatting in preparation before their common fire. The night was still, and the wilderness beckoned them. It was an occasion that called for that homemade brew which makes all ceremonies somber. This was a male tradition after all, not a woman's, not a child's, a paramount convention necessitated by the gravity of their collective purpose, the likes of which was hundreds, perhaps even thousands of years old, passed down from one generation to the next, as was the drink that preceded it. The stars were watching, twinkling in agreement over the solemnity of this immortal moment, for each of these men was to earn his place in the pantheon of virtue where heart and courage bear fruit in the natural order of things.

Sully pulled a jar from his knapsack and took a swig before handing it to Jerzy. "First sip's for courage. Second's for luck. Third's just for fools."

When Sully lifted the jar, Jerzy noticed something he hadn't seen before. Sully had a tattoo on his inner forearm, but it wasn't of an animal or flowers; it was just a series of numbers. He had seen this same tattoo before, on the arms of others, who had been prisoners in the notorious Nazi death camps.

Jerzy thought about his son, mourning him still. He took the jar, inhaled the sharp bite of moonshine, and drank. "Then let's not get to there. Which camp were you in?" asked Jerzy quietly, nodding towards the tattoo as he handed back the jar. Without answering, Sully then took the first of what would become many swigs, and passed it around. "How hard could it be to bring down a wild pig?" he said, looking at their primitive weapons. "Even if it is two hundred pounds, there are five of us and only one of him."

Jerzy did not pursue the question, as he now understood the pain behind Sully's drinking.

Two of the hunters then spoke of rumors they had heard that this was no ordinary boar. "I heard that this is a malevolent beast," and that "it is eight or maybe even nine feet long, with tusks that could rip apart a man with ease," and that "it probably weighed anywhere from twelve to fifteen hundred pounds, filled with an indomitable rage towards anything human. No, this was not just a boar," they said... "it is a monster, born in the depths of Hell itself."

Patryk exhaled hard, shifting his grip on his weapon. "It's just a pig. Bleeds the same as anything else."

Sully gave him a sidelong look, voice low. "You sure about that?"

In the quiet of this solemn evening, the great boar was becoming a modern legend, upping the importance of this mission for each man. Their odyssey was no longer a hunt for meat alone, but a quest to assure the safety of their loved ones, a promise of continuity, and even the chance of becoming part of a heroic legend.

Nobody spoke for a while, preferring instead to just stare at the flames while soaking in the enormous import of what they were about to do. Jerzy added more wood to the fire.

In the quiet, the men cautiously looked around at their surroundings. The jars of moonshine were almost empty now, strewn about the ground like a display of the men's eagerness to open each new jar. "Well, this is where the Devil says goodnight," mumbled Sully, as the last of the jars was emptied. They agreed that hunting in the dark was too dangerous against such a formidable foe, plus, they were all pretty hammered, so they decided instead to sleep by the fire and start afresh in the light of dawn. They spoke this way until the moonshine was completely gone and their words grew fewer in the silence of this eternal night. Then they slept the sleep of the Gods.

The next morning, they slowly arose as the rising sun pricked at their eyelids. Patryk, who normally slept until almost mid-day, had no alcohol, and went to bed early, so he was up before the roosters, and just raring to go.

"I am going to get me some goooood pork today," he said to nobody in particular. "Cannot wait to chomp on one of those fat juicy legs."

"Do not divide the skin while it is still on the bear," said Alf.

"You are just jealous because I am still young and full of energy."

"You are definitely full of something," Alf answered. The others laughed. Alf was speaking light-heartedly, as a father would to his son, but the boy was embarrassed.

Patryk said nothing, instead just glaring at Alf before grabbing his walking stick and stomping off into the woods while mumbling something incoherently to himself. Jerzy started to go after him, but Alf grabbed him by the arm.

"Let him go, Jerzy. He is just a boy trying to be a man. He will come around after he stews awhile and calms down."

Jerzi looked at the others, then back at Alf. "I am just worried about him out there in the woods by himself. We have no idea where that boar is and I do not want him getting hurt."

"None of us want that, either, Jerzy, but he will just be embarrassed if we bring him back in tow like a little kid," said Alf. No, he wants us to see him as a man, so let's just give him a little space so he can keep his dignity."

Nobody else said anything, so Jerzy nodded, but he worried anyway. He remembered the forty days and nights he spent alone in the woods, hiding from the Nazis. It was not cold today, but still, he shivered.

Thirty-Six

Looking for Patryk

The men spread out through the thinning woods, eyes scanning for trees with long, straight branches. The spears had to be sturdy enough to hold against the weight of a thrashing beast, yet light enough to throw if it came to that.

Sully ran his hands along a thick branch, nodding. "This one'll do." He brought his hatchet down in measured strokes, working the wood with the practiced patience of a man who had done this before.

Jerzy hefted a branch of his own, testing its weight.

"Make sure they're smooth," said Sully. "Last thing we need is splinters tearing open our hands when it matters most."

They worked in near silence, save for the rhythmic chop of blades and the occasional crackle of the fire they'd built to temper the spear tips. One by one, they held the points over the flames, careful not to scorch them brittle. Sully turned his spear slowly, watching the wood darken.

"Too much heat, and it snaps on impact," he muttered, half to himself. "Learned that the hard way in the war."

Alf arched a brow. "That before or after you learned how to steal rations?"

Sully grinned, showing yellowed teeth. "Same time, more or less."

The sun slipped lower, dragging the shadows long across the ground. Jerzy straightened, stretching his stiff back. "Patryk still hasn't come back."

Alf exhaled, staring toward the trees. "He left this morning. Been that long already?"

Silence settled over them, heavy and uneasy. The fire popped, sending a shower of sparks into the dimming sky.

"We should look for him," Alf said.

No one moved. The forest had already turned black at the edges, the deep kind of dark that swallowed a man whole.

Jerzy shook his head. "We go in now, we'll only get lost too. At first light, we find the boy." He let the words settle, then added, "And the boar."

The others nodded, some hesitant, some grim.

They sat by the fire, sharpening their weapons, but sleep was slow to come. Without alcohol to dull their nerves, the silence stretched, thick with unspoken thoughts.

* * *

The sun was just barely peeking over the horizon that next morning when they were awakened by the sound of pure terror. It was a blood-curdling scream, a raw, primal screeching straight from the bowels of Hell, echoing in the silent air, and it could have come only from Patryk. Jumping up, they grabbed their spears, axes, even shovels and ran into the woods in search of that God-awful din.

Sulisław led the way, trying to pick up Patryk's trail from where they saw him exit the campsite. The boy was a babe in the woods, so his travel was fairly easy to follow, which allowed the hunters to move at a good pace. Then there was blood, and they stopped.

Another scream, even louder than before. And then, quiet.

Such sudden silence created even more urgency, so they briefly glanced at each other, and with an intuitive understanding, they ran. They were close now, but the woods were dense, limiting visibility.

Finally, a small area where the woods thinned enough to peer through the foliage, and what they saw stopped them in their tracks. Peering through breaks in the dense foliage, they saw Patryk on the ground, with his back against a tree, eyes wide open, as though staring at something. The men followed his gaze and they saw it at last... a beast from the depths of the underworld, the boar, lying motionless with the metal tip of the boy's walking stick embedded in its chest as he lay panting, and staring back at Patryk's motionless eyes.

Jerzy ran to the boy, who was also panting, checking him all over for wounds, and finding a deep gash in one of his calves, with a broken branch poking out of it. He grabbed the boy's shoulders, shaking him. "You scared us to death, Patryk," he said. "What in the hell happened?"

Before he could answer, Sully grabbed his shovel, and raising it as high as he could, and brought it down hard on the mighty boar's skull, cracking it at last, and ending the horror.

Jerzy shook him again, calling his name, when the boy finally snapped out of it, shaking his head, then realizing he was no longer alone. He grabbed Jerzy's sleeves in desperation.

"Oh God, I was so scared, Jerzy," said Patryk. "I thought I was dead!" He was silent, trying to collect his thoughts, then continued. "I was lost and couldn't sleep because I was afraid that boar might find me, so I was just wandering, hoping to find my way back to the camp. And then I heard this monster, snorting like a bull. He was close. And I think he heard me, too, because next thing I knew, he was coming my way, fast, so I did the only thing I could think of and climbed this here tree," he said, patting the one he was leaning against, "because I knew pigs can't climb trees. But this monster was angry—I don't know why, and he decided to knock me out of the tree by charging at it, again and again. And finally, I lost my balance and fell. Then I looked up and saw the beast reared back and was charging at me again, but when I ducked my head down, waiting for him to kill me, I saw my staff on the ground right next to me, and without thinking, I raised the tip of it up like a spear with my end on the ground just when the boar leaped at me, and he impaled himself on the stick, and when he finally dropped down, he just laid there, staring at me. Then, while I was waiting for him to get up again and finish me off, you guys showed up."

Alf saw the tears began to well up in the boy's eyes, and he patted the boy hard on his shoulder. "Wow," he said. "Patryk, please let me be the first to congratulate you."

The boy looked puzzled, shaking his head in confusion.

"There is no question, son. You are now officially a man," said Alf. "NO, you are among the best of men, for you did what none of us did, you brought down this ferocious beast, and you did it all by yourself."

The rest of the men nodded in agreement, and they all joined in on congratulating the newly-minted man, watching his chest puff with pride as they helped him up, pulling the branch out of his leg and binding it, which was the most painful thing Patryk ever felt, but he was a man now, so he merely grunted, despite the tears in his eyes. Later they would bring him to the clinic.

Finally, Patryk had earned his place among the pantheon of courageous men, and it was good.

Thirty-Seven

A Dance to Remember

Winter in the camp had been bleak, but it was now June, early summer, and the British officers, weary of empty nights and the monotony of rationed whiskey, longed for a distraction. It was Lieutenant Barker who first proposed it — an evening of music and dance in the canteen, a way to lift spirits.

And so it was that a dance was scheduled, a grand affair with music and drinks, but there was one glaring issue— too few women to balance the eager ranks of young men itching to spin a lady across the floor.

"I say, Barker, this is a bloody disaster," grumbled Captain Whitmore, drumming his fingers against the bar. "What's a dance without partners? We can't have the lads waltzing with each other."

Barker, the youngest among them, leaned back with a sigh. "We need someone who knows the camp inside and out. Someone who can... procure things."

At that, Lieutenant Dawson, a man who had spent enough time

among the refugees to learn their ways, smirked and took a sip of his whisky. "You need Jerzy."

"Who the devil is Jerzy?" Barker asked, raising an eyebrow.

Dawson chuckled. "A Polish fellow. Smart as a whip. Minimal formal education, but somehow, he just knows how to get things done." He swirled the whisky in his glass. "If anyone can round up some respectable ladies for this soiree, I'm sure it's him."

"You had better be right, Dawson." The captain gave a silent nod to Barker.

And so, the mission was set. Jerzy was summoned with great formality, an invitation sent by courier, though the officer delivering it could barely keep a straight face. When Jerzy arrived at the officers' quarters, Barker leaned in conspiratorially.

"Mr. Czaplicki, I have heard some good things about you... that you seem to have a way of... solving problems."

Jerzy, suspicious already, folded his arms and looked straight into Barker's eyes. "A man does what he can, Lieutenant."

"Well, here is the situation... we need some women for an upcoming officer's dance. Respectable ones, of course. Ladies, not... well, you understand. Can you arrange it?"

Jerzy considered for a moment, rubbing his chin. "How many?"

"As many as you can manage."

Jerzy considered the future ramifications of such a happening.

* * *

That night, by the light of a single candle, Jerzy broached the subject with Ekaterina. She sat by the stove, darning a sock with the precision of a surgeon.

"Katya, my love," he began in that honeyed tone he used when asking for something unreasonable.

She did not look up. "What do you want, Jerzy?"

"There is to be a dance. The officers need women."

Now she looked up, one brow arched. "And you volunteered me?"

Jerzy placed a hand over his heart as if wounded. "Never! But I thought, perhaps, you might know some ladies who would enjoy an evening of warmth, music, and free food."

Ekaterina sighed, setting the sock aside. "How many do you need?"

"As many as you can find."

Her eyes narrowed. "Not for you, I hope."

He laughed and kissed her forehead. "For the British! Though I will not object to the occasional dance."

The next morning, Ekaterina set to work. She spoke to the women at the bakery, the laundress, the widows who gathered to knit in the communal hall. Word spread, and by afternoon, a small army of eager women had assembled, giggling like schoolgirls at the prospect of dancing with uniformed men. No, not just men—real officers.

Jerzy, ever the showman, arranged two military trucks with canvas covered backs for their chariot. As they rolled toward the canteen, packed with chattering women dressed in their finest, he stood at the front, grinning like a king surveying his domain. When they arrived, the officers gawked in disbelief, then ran to help the ladies out.

"Good God," Barker breathed. "How on earth—?"

Jerzy merely tapped the temple of his head. "I used my kidneys."

The dance was beautifully chaotic. The band played, boots stomped on the wooden floor, and for a few hours, the isolation and the loneliness were forgotten. The British, grateful beyond measure, were so happy they refused to let Jerzy's glass go empty. He protested at first, then accepted his fate with a magnanimous shrug. Duty is duty, after all. By the end of the night, Jerzy was being toasted by officers who would normally never even share a table with a refugee.

When he finally stumbled home, he was, as Ekaterina would later describe, 'lit up like a cathedral at Christmas.' He tried—valiantly—to appear sober, but the effect was somewhat ruined when he missed the door handle three times before finally grasping it.

Ekaterina, waiting in bed, watched him with mild amusement. "You're drunk."

Jerzy swayed slightly, then placed a hand over his chest as if affronted. "Celebrated."

She reached up, pulling him down beside her. "And did you dance with all the ladies?"

He nuzzled into her shoulder, his breath warm against her skin. "Only the ones who asked nicely."

She smiled, tracing a finger along his jaw. "Well, hero of the dance, it seems we have something to celebrate ourselves."

He lifted his head and blinked, slow and bleary-eyed. "We do?"

She took his hand and placed it gently on her stomach. Her eyes met his, full of something unreadable. Then, softly, she said, "I think I am with child. And I pray that it is a boy... for you."

For a moment, the world held still. Then, despite his drunken haze, Jerzy's expression softened into something rare and unguarded. He pressed his forehead to hers, whispering against her lips.

"Oh, my beautiful pateechka. Boy... girl... it does not matter. The child is ours, and we will love either just the same."

Then he closed his eyes, and giggled the laugh of true happiness and love. And as sleep claimed him, a foolish grin still lingered on his face, the echo of music still drifting somewhere behind his eyelids.

Thirty-Eight

The Artificial Police

Jerzy was still working at the British Officer's Club when the opportunity came, as these things always came, not like a gift wrapped in ribbons but like something half-buried in the earth, something a man had to dig out with his own hands and then decide whether it was worth keeping. He was polishing glasses behind the bar, watching the officers talk in the easy way of men who had never gone hungry for more than a day, when Captain Alistair Graves sat down across from him and folded his hands on the counter, his fingers long and pale, the nails neatly trimmed, the hands of a man who had never dug ditches, who had never built anything from the ground up, but whose voice carried the weight of decisions that could change the course of a life.

"Mr. Czaplicki," the captain said, his tone casual, like they were discussing the weather or the price of a bottle of whiskey. "I have been watching you."

Jerzy said nothing.

"I must say, I'm impressed. The group wedding, the garden you somehow coaxed from the rock and dust of this place, the hunt for that wild boar, the dance you arranged with all those women... it is all as if you were running some kind of grand estate rather than a camp for displaced souls. And you did all of it while working here, full-time, without missing a shift."

Jerzy wiped down the counter, took a glass, held it up to the light. Still, he said nothing.

The captain leaned in slightly. "The camp police chief has quit. Gone. Vanished. And we need a new one."

Jerzy set the glass down, met the man's eyes. "Why did he quit?"

The captain laughed, shaking his head. "Now, that is a story. There was a widow in the camp, lonely, determined, the sort of woman who decides on a thing and will not be moved. Anyway, she fell in love with the police chief and became obsessed with marrying him. She proposed to him daily, every morning like clockwork, bringing him gifts—a stale loaf of bread one day, a pair of socks with holes in the heels the next. He refused, but that did not matter to her. She declared herself his wife anyway. Sewed a wedding suit out of stolen blankets, announced the ceremony to the entire camp. The next morning, he was gone. Vanished into the night. We have not heard from him since."

Jerzy laughed, shaking his head.

"Well," the captain said, "I think you would do well in the position. You know how to read people, how to handle them. You think for yourself, and that's something most men struggle with, especially when power is involved. So, what do you say? Would you like the job?"

"What does it pay?"

The captain exhaled, gave a small, knowing smile. "Not much. But there are... other benefits."

Jerzy waited.

"We can get you and your wife out of that shack," the captain said. "Give you something better. Much better."

And that was when Jerzy felt it, that small shift inside him, the part of him that had learned how to survive in the war, that had carried him through the forced labor, through the punishment camp, hunger and cold and loss, the solitude in the woods, the fear that he had lost Ekaterina forever... the part of him that knew a man could endure anything for a while, but that the weight of suffering became heavier with each year, each day, each moment, until it was something no man could carry.

Still, he said nothing.

"And," the captain continued, watching him carefully now, like a man setting a hook, "I hear you want to emigrate."

Jerzy's hands stilled. "Keep talking."

"Well," the captain said, leaning back, as if he knew he had already won, "as police chief, you will make a great many new contacts. Some of them will be influential. Some of them may be able to help you with that dream."

Jerzy thought about Ekaterina in that shack, her thin hands red from the cold, the way she pulled the blanket around her shoulders at night, tucking it in as if she could make the walls hold warmth that was not there. He thought about the men in the camp, the ones who carried themselves like they were still soldiers and the ones who had long since given up the pretense of being men at all, who had surrendered to whatever it was that time and war and displacement had done to them.

"That is all good," Jerzy said finally, "but I still need to eat." He let the words settle, let the captain feel the weight of them. Then, after a moment: "I tell you what—I'll take the job. BUT... I want at least the same pay I have now. I want the better home, as you said. And I choose my own men."

The captain smiled, nodded. "You drive a hard bargain, Jerzy. But I'll see what I can do."

And just like that, it was done.

* * *

Jerzy walked home in the fading light, the dust of the road kicking up in pale ghosts around his boots, the distant sound of a child crying mingling with the harmonica wheeze of some tired song in a shack three doors down from his own, and he thought about the things a man must do, the things he must become, to shape the world to his liking instead of letting it shape him. The club was now in his past, and the entire camp ahead, a place where men without nations still tried to carve out small dominions, where women without husbands still cooked whatever scraps they could scavenge into something resembling a meal, where children born in transit still clung to words from languages they barely understood. He thought about the promise of a real home, a roof that would not weep when the rains came, a door that would hold against the wind, a place where Ekaterina would not have to huddle against him for warmth, where maybe, just maybe, she could feel secure again.

She was waiting for him in the dim glow of an oil lamp, her hands folded over her lap like something precious she had long ago learned to guard, her face unreadable in the flickering light. He sat beside her, let the moment stretch out between them like a thread pulled too tight.

"They want me to be the police chief," he said finally, and the words tasted strange in his mouth, like something he had borrowed from another man's life.

Ekaterina did not answer right away. She studied him the way she always did, as if she could see past the words to the thing that lay beneath them. "And what did you say?"

"I told them I would do it," he said, "on my terms."

A slow nod. Approval, perhaps, or just the quiet acknowledgment that Jerzy had never been the kind of man to accept a thing without shaping it to his liking. "And what are your terms?"

"A better home. A decent wage. And I choose my own men."

Now she smiled, just a little. "Then you have already begun."

The next Monday, Jerzy stood outside the station, watching the men move past him, men with nothing but the weight of their pasts and the hunger for something more, men with too much violence in their bones or too much sorrow in their eyes, men who had learned that to survive was to endure but who had never quite mastered the art of living.

He did not want soldiers. Soldiers had orders in their blood, the need to follow and be followed, the expectation of combat. He did not want men who dreamed of power, who saw in a badge the chance to be something more by making others feel less.

No, what Jerzy wanted—what he needed—was something different.

He picked Josef, because Josef had been a thief once, and a good one, plus, he was a man who had lived on both sides of the law could understand the minds of the desperate.

Next, he picked Sulisław, because old men saw things young men did not, and because he had seen Sully talk a would-be murderer down with nothing but a slow smile and a well-placed joke.

He picked Patryk, because the boy was still too young to be cruel, and sometimes all a man needed to do the right thing was someone beside him who still believed it was possible.

And when the others asked him what he was doing, why he chose these men and not the ones with strong fists and straight backs and unquestioning loyalty, Jerzy only smiled and said, "Because I do not need men who know how to fight. I need men who know how to think."

And then he walked away, because there was work to be done, and he had always been the kind of man to do it.

* * *

Jerzy's first task as Chief of Police came at the hands of a small man with a sharp voice, the kind of man who spent his days watching and waiting for others to make mistakes so he could seize upon them, the kind of man who had survived the war not by strength, but by knowing when to grovel, when to run, when to whisper in the right ear and place blame in the right direction. He came in breathless, his coat unbuttoned, his hat askew, and pounded his fist once on Jerzy's desk, as if the urgency of his mission demanded that kind of punctuation.

"There is a criminal in this camp," the man said, his voice tight with righteousness. "A lawbreaker. A man who thinks he is above the rules we all must live by."

Jerzy looked up, unimpressed.

"My neighbor," the man went on, "is making moonshine. I have seen him. I have smelled it. It is illegal. You are the Chief of Police, are you not?"

Jerzy said nothing for a long moment, only let the weight of the words settle in the air between them, watched how the man's fingers twitched against the wood of the desk, how his eyes were too bright, too eager, the eyes of a man who wanted something more than justice.

Finally, Jerzy stood, nodded for two of his men to follow him.

The apartment was small, the kind of place where every sound carried through the walls, where every breath was shared like a secret between unwilling conspirators. Jerzy sent the complainer back to his own apartment.

"I will handle this," he said, then stepped inside, looked around. The air was thick, but not with the sharp burn of distilled liquor. No hidden barrels, no suspicious bottles. There was no place to hide them. The husband stood stiffly near the door, his jaw clenched, his wife at the stove, stirring something with a spoon that trembled ever so slightly in her hand.

On a hunch, Jerzy turned to her. "What are you cooking?"

The woman flinched, just slightly, but enough.

Jerzy stepped forward, peered into the pot. And there it was, the trick of it, the deception—moonshine bubbling thick and slow beneath the steam, cooked not in some hidden chamber but out in the open, disguised as something else.

He turned to his men. "Dump it."

The wife gasped, but she said nothing as the men took the pot, carried it outside, let it spill into the dirt where it darkened the ground like something already buried.

Jerzy turned to the man who had been caught. "Do you know the penalty?"

The man swallowed, slowly shaking his head no.

"Automatic twenty years," Jerzy said. "Twenty years for this."

The man paled, his knees nearly buckling beneath him, his wife clutching his sleeve like a lifeline. But Jerzy only shook his head, exhaled slowly, let the moment stretch before him.

"This time, you walk free," he said. "Next time, you will not."

The man's relief came like a flood, gratitude tumbling from his lips as he clasped Jerzy's hand, thanked him again and again, voice breaking over the words.

But it was not over.

Later, the first man, the one with the sharp voice and the eager fists, returned to the police station, striding in with a smile too smug for a man who had done nothing but talk.

"You should have thrown him in prison," he said. "The law is the law, and he broke it. You were too soft."

Jerzy said nothing at first, only studied him, watched how the satisfaction curled at the corners of his mouth, how his fingers drummed against the desk like a man waiting for his reward.

And then Jerzy saw it—saw the small stain on the man's sleeve, saw the faintest trace of something acrid clinging to his coat, saw the way he had spoken the law so quickly, so easily, as if he had already thought of what he would say if ever he found himself accused.

And Jerzy understood.

"How much do you make in a week?" Jerzy asked suddenly.

The man blinked. "What?"

Jerzy leaned forward slightly. "How much moonshine do you sell?"

The man's breath hitched. His fingers stopped drumming. His shoulders stiffened just slightly, just enough.

Jerzy tilted his head. "Would you like to go to prison with your neighbor?"

The man's face went pale. His mouth opened, then shut, then opened again, but no words came, nothing but the sound of air leaving his lungs like something escaping before he could hold it in.

Jerzy waited.

And finally, the man looked down, his shoulders sagging, his shame swallowing him whole.

Jerzy said nothing more. He did not need to.

Thirty-Nine

Sugar & Spice

During the relentless months of his wife's pregnancy, Jerzy had been wrestling with the past, caught between the weight of memory and the pull of the unknown, haunted by the memories of his firstborn, by the ice in his lungs when he saw his son blue and still, by the futility of his own heart pressing against the unrelenting silence. And now, this new life, this second chance, yet it carried with it the specter of the first. He did not know how to hold both joy and fear in the same breath, how to shape his heart around hope without crushing it beneath the heavy pain of doubt.

It was in this state of unrest that Ekaterina came to him, the small amulet cradled in her hands like something fragile and sacred. She told him of the Russian gypsy woman, of her dark, knowing eyes, of the way her fingers, thin as twigs, had pressed the charm into her palm and whispered words that clung to the air like incense.

"All life begins in the stars," she had said to Ekaterina, her voice a wind through bare branches. "And to the stars it will return. Your baby will carry this light in its heart. Protect it well, and the child will shine."

Jerzy took the charm, turning it between his fingers, the dim light catching flecks of something inside—quartz, mica, perhaps even something rarer, something not of this earth. Like stardust. The sight of it stirred something deep, a memory that was not memory, a vision that had burned into his mind years ago, in the space between life and death. His own death, when he was shot. He saw again the endless expanse, the stars swirling and colliding in the vast tide of the universe, and he remembered the voice—not a voice, not exactly, but a knowing —that had told him Ekaterina's path was inexorably bound to his own, their destinies entwined, inseparable.

And now, our child. Was this the link? The reason he had returned to the land of the living? He walked outside, looking up at the starry sky, and let the thought take shape in the quiet, let it unfurl like a vine climbing toward the light. He imagined, as all incipient fathers do, the boundless potential of this unborn child. He imagined it growing, stepping out beyond the ruins of war and exile, stepping into something larger than all of them. Could this be the one, in some small, imperceptible way, to shift the world toward a kinder way? To make it better, even by a fraction? And was that not enough—to set a ripple moving through time, even if they would never live to see where it reached?

He closed his fist around the charm, inhaled deeply, let the weight of it settle in his palm, in his heart. Then, for the first time, he let himself believe—not in fate, not in superstition, but in the wild, fragile hope that life itself was a force beyond understanding, and that perhaps, just perhaps, this child was really meant to be.

He met Ekaterina's eyes, who had silently joined him, saw the same unspoken questions, the same quiet yearning, and he nodded. "We will keep it," he said, his voice steady now, as if the words were an anchor in shifting sands. "For the child."

And somewhere beyond the shanties and the barbed wire, beyond the sorrow and the hunger, the sky stretched on, infinite and waiting, a sea of stars turning in the dark.

* * *

December 17, 1947, was a day Jerzy would never forget. He stirred before dawn. The shack held the night's cold, but the air had changed —thicker, charged. He sat up. Ekaterina lay still beside him, one hand resting on her stomach, the other curled near her face. Her breath was even, her expression calm. Unlike last time. Unlike the fear, the terror that had stolen into their bones when their son fought his way into the world.

The time was getting close. He swung his legs over the bed, pressing his feet to the cold floor. Reaching for the small wooden crate beside him, he counted again. Cloths, folded in tight squares. A tin cup, half-full of water to be boiled. The knife, sharpened. The string. The honey, bartered for last week—someone had told him it might be useful.

Ekaterina shifted. "Jerzy."

He turned. Her eyes were open now, steady upon him, filled with something he did not understand.

She smiled softly. "It is time."

His heart knocked once, hard, but he nodded. "Then we are ready."

She reached for his hand, squeezed it. "Yes."

He rose quickly, moving with purpose. Fire, to heat the water. A cloth, to lay over the bed. Then, he pulled on his coat and stepped outside, his breath curling in the frigid air. His boots crunched over the frozen ground as he hurried to the Russian barracks for single women.

A sharp rap on the door.

Nadia answered this time, bleary-eyed but alert. "It begins?"

He nodded. "She says it is time."

The woman grunted. "Of course. She would know."

She stepped back inside without waiting, gathering her things. Jerzy turned to leave, but she caught his arm. "And you? "Do you remember what to do?"

He hesitated. "I have prepared everything."

Nadia nodded silently.

By the time they returned, the shack had come alive. Word had traveled swiftly, passed from woman to woman in the silent language of shared experience. Neighbors had seen Jerzy rush out unusually early and sensed it was that time, and unseen messengers had summoned the others. Women from the camp gathered to care for Ekaterina, speaking in hushed tones. One heated more water. Another placed a cool cloth to Ekaterina's brow. When he arrived back home with the midwife, an older Polish woman, her face lined with years, patted Jerzy's cheek. "Are you the one having the baby?"

The women chuckled. Jerzy's head was spinning.

Nadia stepped in, waving them all aside. "Out, out—only the husband stays." She turned to Jerzy. "And you. Is the water hot yet?"

He checked. "Yes."

He brought it in, then gently brought the back of his hand to his wife's cheek.

"Jerzy, please wait in the kitchen."

Ekaterina's voice, soft yet firm. "No. He can stay."

The midwife studied him, then nodded once. "Then stay. But stay out of my way."

Jerzy forced himself still. He counted the seconds between Ekaterina's breaths, the moments between each wave of pain. The fire flickered. The midwife moved with precision, hands sure, voice low and steady.

This delivery somehow seemed easier than the last...quicker... almost as though the baby knew to make it so.

Eventually, the time came.

"Push." Then, a growl, followed by the sharp cry of intense exertion. After three of these, Ekaterina gasped, and in an instant, the baby came out with such force that it flew through the air, past the midwife's hands and slid into her upper arms. Nadia's arms curled, instinctively catching it in mid-flight, stunned by what just happened, and silently holding the child in her arms as though scared it would get up and fly some more.

"Yokarny babay!" exclaimed Nadia.

Jerzy said nothing, but his eyes grew huge.

A moment of silence.

Then, a wail, sudden and piercing.

The midwife laughed, not able to take her eyes off the baby. "This one could not wait to get here."

Ekaterina's breath hitched, then broke into relieved sobs. She reached weakly, and Jerzy moved first, lifting the swaddled child into her arms.

A daughter.

He stared down. Dark lashes. Tiny fists. Eyes open, beautiful eyes, like her mother's, steady, as if she had always been here, always known her purpose in life.

Ekaterina whispered, voice thick, "She is love."

Jerzy's throat tightened. Recalling his near-death experience after being shot, he barely heard himself speak. "She has always known she is special."

That night, long after the voices had hushed, after the camp had settled into sleep, Jerzy sat in a chair by the window. The stars stretched endless above him, crisp against the dark. He cradled his daughter, feeling the weight of her, the warmth.

He thought back yet again to his time on the other side. Of the light. The voice that had called him back.... he had not understood then.

But he did now.

He whispered, so only his daughter could hear, "You are stardust... and you will shine."

* * *

They named the baby Dorota, meaning Gift of God, a traditional and well-known Polish name. That was the least they could do for her.

The loss of their son still lingered, shaping their every instinct. Jerzy and Ekaterina watched over little Dorota with unwavering care, wary of every cough, every cry, every tiny disturbance. They bundled her in extra layers, checked her breathing throughout the night, and hesitated to let anyone else hold her for too long, and on cold nights, nights when the bucket on their floor turned to ice by morning,

Dorota slept in their bed, between them so she could be protected all night by their warmth and love.

Jerzy worked long hours, but when he came home, no matter how tired, he would always try to hold her. He loved making her laugh, a rapid, high pitched giggling sound that filled the small shack with warmth and happiness. It was a ritual that probably went all the way back to the cave, but no matter how much he delighted in her happy response, she always had one predictable response—spitting up on him.

One evening, determined to avoid another accident, Jerzy sat at the kitchen chair while Ekaterina held Dorota on her lap on the other side of the table. He made silly faces, wiggled his fingers, and cooed at his daughter who ultimately rewarded him with her usual bubbling laughter.

And then, with perfect timing, she spit up yet again, and almost as though it were deliberate, arched it all the way across the table to land squarely on his chest.

Ekaterina burst into laughter, pressing a hand to her mouth. Jerzy wiped his shirt with an air of resignation. "She is precise."

"She is her father's daughter," Ekaterina teased, eyes twinkling.

But beyond the laughter, there was an underlying cross-current of truth Jerzy had not anticipated. Though he loved his daughter fiercely, she clung to her mother in a way he could not bridge. If Ekaterina ever stepped out, even for a moment, Dorota would wail, inconsolable, her tiny face scrunched in distress.

One afternoon, Ekaterina had to leave, totally entrusting Jerzy with their child for the first time. At first, the baby merely fussed, but within the first ten or fifteen minutes of her mother's departure, her cries rang sharp and desperate. Jerzy checked to see if maybe she had some gas and needed to be burped. Nope. Dirty diaper? Again, nope. He then thought maybe she was hungry, but she was breast fed, so she was out of luck there. Checked her diapers again. Still dry as a bone. So he walked her, sang to her, and promised her the moon if only she would stop her crying. Nothing worked. She was like his uncle's cow who would not be milked by him.

An hour later, Ekaterina finally returned and the moment she stepped through the door, Dorota heard her and began waving her arms in excitement, gurgling coos of delight. And all her tears vanished immediately.

Jerzy blinked. "When you left, Dorota went crazy and started screaming — not crying— screaming, and then the minute you returned home she changed into a real human again. She torments me."

Ekaterina chuckled. "Jerzy, she is just a baby. You are being dramatic."

She did not quite believe him.

Until a few weeks later, when she left again but once at the side-walk, realized she forgot her handbag. As she turned back, just a few moments later, she heard the screaming for herself before even walking through the door. Then, as soon as she stepped inside, the crying totally ceased, replaced by joyous laughter.

She met Jerzy's knowing look. He turned so the baby now faced her mother. "Now do you believe me?"

Ekaterina shook her head, laughing. "Dorota, why do you do this to your father? He loves you." But as soon as Ekaterina got close, the baby reached out her arms, leaning, wanting her mother to take her.

Jerzy exhaled and kissed the top of his daughter's head. "She has already chosen her favorite," handing her over gratefully.

Ekaterina smiled softly. "She loves you, Jerzy. Look at how she laughs each time you come home from work."

"And then throws up on me."

"That is because you always make her laugh so hard. She will grow out of that."

Jerzy nodded, though he was not quite sure. But as he gazed at the tiny bundle in her mother's arms, he thought—hopefully her love, like yeast, simply needed time to rise to the occasion.

Forty

The Immigration Game

Hamburg, Germany: The United States Consulate

The first form asked for his name.

Jerzy stared at it, pen in hand, the paper white and waiting, his mind blank, as if the sum of his life, his existence, had never been more than air, a shadow moving through time, now called upon to prove that he had ever been. He had filled out dozens of documents, more than he could count, yet each time, the same paralysis, the same question hammering at the edges of his mind, whispering to him that a man without a country is a man without a name, and still, he wrote it, as if ink on paper could hold together the pieces of himself that war and exile had scattered.

Jerzy Czaplicki.

Beside him, Ekaterina shifted their daughter from one tired arm to the other, the child's breath warm against her neck, small fingers curled into the folds of her coat, and he knew without looking that she was watching him, that she was reading the tension in his hand, the stiffness in his shoulders, her silence a question she would not ask.

Her own fingers, red and raw from cold, clutched the bundle of papers that held the fragile thread of their identity—what little proof remained that they were real, that they belonged together, that they were more than refugees moving through a world that had no place for them.

More questions.

Date of birth. Place of birth. Current residence.

He hesitated, feeling the weight of the lie he would not tell, the truth he did not wish to write. Displaced Persons Camp, Hamburg.

Ekaterina's voice, low, a breath barely spoken: "Do you think they will separate us?"

His fingers clenched around the pen. A question neither of them dared to voice too often, because once spoken aloud, it became a thing with teeth, something that could take hold, could burrow deep, could become real. Families were separated every day, divided by quotas and forms and the blind, indifferent machinery of bureaucracy that had no time for love, for promises, for the fierce, unrelenting need to stay whole.

"No," he said, though his chest was tight with the knowing that his words meant nothing, that it was not his choice to make. "We stay together."

More forms. More questions.

Employment history.

What was a life measured in work? He wrote what little there was —Chief of Police in the camp, the officer's club, the jobs he had taken, the ones that had kept them fed, the ones that had meant nothing except another day survived.

Ekaterina, her voice softer this time, steady: "Write down my work too."

A seamstress. A mender of cloth, of torn hems and unraveling seams, of the small, invisible labors that kept the world from falling apart. But would that be enough? Women with children were burdens, not assets. They were not looking for mothers—they were looking for men, for workers, for the ones who could build with their hands, who could lift and carry and sweat for America's future.

More questions.

Political affiliations? No.

Communist Party membership? No.

Then the one that made his stomach twist—Sponsorship.

A name. A person to vouch for them. Someone to stand between them and the void, to promise that they would not be a burden, that they would not fail, that they would not ask for more than what was given.

He had no such name.

No family waiting, no letters from America, no hands reaching out across the ocean with the promise of work and shelter.

Still, he wrote: Seeking sponsorship through the Church.

Ekaterina's grip on Dorota tightened, and for a moment, they did not look at each other, because they both knew what that meant, knew the weight of the silence between them, knew that this, too, was a gamble. But that worry would come later.

For now, there were the papers. The documents. The proof.

Jerzy gathered what he had, what remained, what little scraps of history had survived along with him—old worn records from before the war, British work permits, ration cards from the camp, the yellowing marriage certificate that had followed them from one home to the next.

But in the end, there was nothing here that could prove that he was still the man he had been before.

And so he wrote, as if the act of writing could make it true.

* * *

The train was overcrowded, packed with bodies pressed too close, the air thick with the weight of breath and sweat and the sour exhaustion of too many people who had waited too long, who had spent too many nights on hard cots in rooms that were never theirs, who had learned that space was a luxury and silence an impossible dream. The seats were worn, splintered, the rough wood pressing into Jerzy's back as he sat stiffly, his arm around Ekaterina, holding her close, though the cold still crept in through the gaps between them, through the cracks in the carriage where coal smoke seeped in, curling into their clothes, settling into their skin, mixing with the stale air, the smell of hunger and damp wool and the restless shifting of strangers who had nowhere else to be.

Dorota lay curled in Ekaterina's lap, her small chest rising and falling, her lips parted in the heavy sleep of a child too young to understand waiting, too young to know that they were moving but not yet free.

It had taken two weeks.

Two weeks to receive word that Frankfurt, not Hamburg, would be the place where their case would be processed. Two weeks of standing in offices where no one looked them in the eye, of filling out more forms with the same answers, names and dates and places that no longer existed, of pleading with the camp officials for permission to leave, of scraping together enough ration coupons to make the journey, weighing each meal against the miles still ahead, hunger measured in paper and ink.

Ekaterina shifted, her head resting against his shoulder, her voice low, a whisper that barely reached him over the rattle of the train.

"What if they turn us away?"

Jerzy swallowed hard.

"Then we find another way."

She did not answer, because there was no other way, and they both knew it.

Frankfurt.

A city they did not know, another consulate, another line, the cold wind cutting through the thin fabric of his coat, through his sleeves, through the soles of his shoes where the leather had thinned, where the damp had settled in. They stood for hours, moving forward in slow, shuffling steps, Dorota shifting against Ekaterina's hip, her small hands curled into her mother's scarf, her face turned inward, seeking warmth.

Then, at last, the door opened.

Inside, warmth, though it was the kind that did not comfort, only suffocated, the air heavy with the presence of men in suits, papers stacked on desks, the scratch of pens, the shuffle of documents passed from one hand to another, the sharp click of a stamp sealing fates in ink.

A voice, dispassionate, precise.

"How did you come to be displaced?"

His throat felt dry. The words sat heavy inside him, too large, too tangled, too full of nights without sleep and miles walked in hunger and the sound of trains that had taken him from one country to another without ever bringing him home.

"I was taken by the Nazis as a forced laborer."

The American across from him barely looked up. "Do you have proof?"

Proof.

Who carried proof of their suffering?

He had scars. He had memories that came in flashes of sound, in the weight of toxic fumes without masks, in the hollow ache of days spent beneath a sky that had belonged to no one. But he had no papers, no signatures, no stamps on yellowed pages declaring: This man was taken. This man lost everything.

He reached into his coat, fingers brushing over the few worn documents he carried, and placed the only thing he had on the desk.

"My work permit. From the officer's club."

The American glanced at it, barely a pause, a flicker of disinterest before it was set aside, another paper, another number, another life reduced to something too small to matter.

Then came the medical exams.

They stood in line, silent, stripped of coats and sweaters, waiting their turn beneath the harsh white light, surrounded by the sharp smell of antiseptic, of metal and cold air and the quiet murmurs of others trying not to shiver. The doctors moved quickly, their hands impersonal, pressing, prodding, measuring, searching for weakness, for sickness, for anything that could end it all before it even began.

Breathe in. Hold. Breathe out.

They obeyed, because there was nothing else to do, because failure was not an option, because their bodies were no longer their own but something to be examined, judged, deemed worthy or unworthy of a future.

After the medical checks, the final interview.

And Jerzy, sitting across from another stranger with another stack of papers, knew that everything—everything—came down to this.

* * *

The hall smelled of damp wood and sweat, of too many bodies pressed too close for too long, of waiting and whispering and the kind of desperate hope that made men stare down at the papers in their hands as if sheer will alone could make the ink change, make the names rearrange themselves into something more acceptable, more worthy.

Jerzy sat stiffly, Ekaterina beside him on the hard bench, her body wound tight with the tension that never left her now, not in the cold mornings when they woke to another day of waiting, not in the nights when she curled herself around Dorota as if she could shield their daughter from hunger, from uncertainty, from the world itself. The baby shifted in her sleep, a tiny hand curled into the worn fabric of her mother's dress, her breath warm against Ekaterina's arm.

Around them, the others murmured in low voices, heads bowed, hands gripping papers, clinging to them like talismans against the unknown.

At the front of the room, the priest lifted a hand, dismissing another man, another case, another life with a simple flick of his wrist.

"When was the last time you were in church?"

The man hesitated. "I... I do not remember, Father."

The priest sighed, heavy with judgment, with disappointment, as if the man's very existence had been a waste of his time.

"Next."

Ekaterina's fingers tightened around the edge of the bench.

"What does church attendance have to do with a sponsor?" she whispered.

Jerzy shook his head, slow, deliberate.

"Nothing," he murmured. "But it has everything to do with him."

The same priest.

The one who had turned them away when their son lay fevered

and gasping, when Jerzy had stood in this man's doorway, pleading, hands shaking, voice cracking, begging for baptism, for a blessing, for something—anything—that could sanctify the life slipping away in their arms.

The one who had refused.

Refused to bless. Refused to bury.

Refused to look Jerzy in the eye when he said, Please, Father, he is only a child.

And now, here he sat, behind a desk, arms crossed, deciding—again—who was worthy.

The line moved.

Jerzy's name was called.

He rose, helping Ekaterina to her feet, feeling the weight of her exhaustion, the weight of Dorota shifting against her shoulder, the small whimper of a child jostled from sleep, rubbing tiny fists against her eyes.

The priest barely looked at them, flipping through their papers with a practiced air of indifference, his fingers moving in the same rhythm they had moved for the man before them, and the man before him, and the one before that—turning pages, scanning names, making decisions in the time it took a breath to leave the lungs.

"You have no trade," he said, flat, uninterested.

"I can work," Jerzy said quickly, the words coming fast, spilling over themselves. "I was an auto mechanic. A farmer. I have built things, repaired things—" He gestured toward Ekaterina, desperate now, desperate for him to see, to understand. "My wife has worked, too. Sewing, mending—"

The priest raised a hand.

Enough.

"And your sponsor?"

Jerzy hesitated.

"We were hoping the Church could help."

For the first time, the priest looked up.

"The Church helps the faithful."

Jerzy felt Ekaterina stiffen beside him, felt her breath catch.

Something inside him cracked, splintered like wood under the weight of too much pressure, too much grief, too many nights spent staring at the ceiling, wondering how much more a man was meant to endure before he broke apart entirely.

"Faithful?" he repeated, his voice soft, but honed like a blade.

He saw the priest's lips press thin, watched the flicker of something—annoyance, recognition, memory—pass behind his eyes.

"When my son was dying, I came to you," Jerzy said. His voice did not shake, not yet, but it was raw, worn from years of swallowing down words that had never been answered. "I begged for his baptism. You turned me away."

The priest was silent.

"I buried him myself." The words were a whisper now, barely more than breath, but they filled the space between them, filled the cracks in the wooden floor, pressed into the walls like something alive. "No blessing. No sacrament."

Ekaterina clutched Dorota closer, her arms a barrier between the world and her child. But she did not interrupt.

Jerzy inhaled, slow, steady.

"And now you sit here," he said. "Judging me."

The priest said nothing. Then, without looking at him again, he picked up the papers, stacked them neatly, slid them back across the table.

"I cannot help you."

The words fell heavy, final, like a gavel striking wood.

Jerzy took the papers with numb fingers, turned, stepped past the rows of anxious faces, past the quiet murmurs of others waiting their turn, past the hope still lingering in the room like something fragile, something foolish.

Dorota, still drowsy, reached out her tiny hand, touched his cheek. "Tata?"

He stopped, exhaled, pulled her close.

Ekaterina's eyes shimmered, but she did not cry.

Not here.

They had failed.

Again.

And there was no one left to save them but themselves.

Forty-One

Quotas

A few days after the attempt to immigrate, Jerzy was approached by a man he had never seen before. The man was thin, with a sharp nose and deep-set eyes, his clothing as ragged as anyone else's in the camp. He stopped Jerzy near the mess hall, glancing around before speaking in a hushed voice.

"Do you want to go to America?"

Jerzy squinted at him, confused. "What?"

The man's lips curled into a faint smile. "I have an application if you want to go. You just need to fill it out."

Jerzy let out a dry chuckle. "You're joking."

The man shook his head. "No, this is for real." He reached into his coat and pulled out a folded piece of paper. "The World Council of Churches in America is helping people emigrate. It's a Protestant organization."

Jerzy frowned. "Protestant?" The word meant little to him. He had been raised Catholic, but faith had become a distant thing, lost in the war's brutality. But what did it matter now? If this could bring him, Ekaterina, and their daughter to America, he would sign anything. "Where did you get this?"

"I told you—it's legitimate. If you want, come with me. I'll help you fill it out."

Jerzy hesitated only a moment before nodding. He followed the man to his barracks, where they sat at a crude wooden table under the dim glow of a lantern. Together, they worked through the form, the man guiding Jerzy's hand over the unfamiliar words. When they were done, the man took the paper and folded it carefully.

"I'll turn it in for you," he said. "Now, you wait."

Jerzy left the barracks, shoving the thought from his mind. He had learned not to believe in hope. Hope was dangerous.

* * *

A month passed. The camp remained the same—its rows of barracks and crude wooden shacks, the smell of damp earth and boiled potatoes, the distant cries of hungry children. Jerzy had long forgotten the application when the same man found him again.

"Jerzy—You've been accepted; congratulations."

Jerzy just stared, shaking his head. "You must be joking."

"I told you before—I don't joke."

* * *

Two weeks later, the Czaplicki family found themselves on a train bound for the transit camp. The journey was cramped, the carriage filled with other hopeful families from other camps, clutching their meager possessions. Jerzy, Ekaterina and Dorota had only a single half-empty suitcase between them. Around them, others had wooden crates, even Red Cross packages tied with twine. Jerzy watched them with quiet envy, but he said nothing. They were all leaving, weren't they? That was what mattered.

The transit camp was a vast, sprawling place, filled with people from all over Europe. The air buzzed with languages Jerzy barely recognized. They were processed like cattle—forms, signatures, questions repeated again and again. The wait was endless. Background checks, medical exams.

Jerzy's stomach and intestines gnawed at him constantly, not just from hunger but from the ailments he had carried silently since the war. He felt it twisting inside him, a quiet enemy. He did not tell Ekaterina. What would be the point? If he failed the physical, it would be over. He kept his head down and prayed no one would notice. When the exam was finally given, Jerzy lied about any past medical problems.

More waiting. They stood in a long line, shuffling forward inch by inch. At the front of the line was a door, and behind it, the final man who would decide their fate. Jerzy held Ekaterina's hand tightly, their daughter sleeping in her arms. The wait felt like eternity, but he was too close to quit.

Then the door opened, and a man stepped out. His face was tight with exhaustion, his expression unreadable.

"Sorry, folks," he said. "The quota has been filled."

Silence fell over the crowd. Jerzy felt his body go numb.

"The people in front of you," the man continued, looking at Jerzy and Ekaterina, "were the last ones approved."

The world seemed to tilt. Jerzy stared at the closed door, the weight of crushed hope pressing down on his chest.

Ekaterina's grip on his hand tightened. He swallowed hard, but there were no words to say. Nothing to do.

They had been denied...

Again.

Part Three

Forty-Two

The Letter

The news came so suddenly that Jerzy barely believed it at first. Three weeks. That was all it took. Three weeks after they had been turned away, President Truman had signed a new quota allowing another two hundred thousand European refugees to enter the United States. And this time, Jerzy and his family were among the first in line. The last rejection had placed them at the front of this new opportunity. But could it be real? Could it truly happen this time? He dared not believe it. Neither of them did.

When the letter from the American consulate arrived, summoning them for another interview, Jerzy and Ekaterina exchanged an uncertain glance. Their daughter clutched her mother, sensing the weight in the air.

"It is happening again," Ekaterina murmured. Her voice was tight, her fingers gripping the thin envelope as if it might crumble. "They will call us in, ask their questions, and then send us away once more."

Jerzy exhaled slowly, rubbing his jaw. "Maybe," he admitted. "But we have no choice. We must try."

The walk to the consulate's office felt impossibly long, each step heavier than the last. The waiting room was filled with hopeful, weary faces, people clutching documents as if holding onto a lifeline. The Czaplickis had seen it all before—the hushed prayers, the restless shifting, the quiet sobs when another hopeful refugee was turned away. The process was always long, the questioning exhaustive. But they had no other path forward.

At last, their name was called. They stepped forward cautiously, almost timidly, expecting another cruel twist of fate. The American consulate officer, a middle-aged man with thinning hair and kind but tired eyes, gestured for them to sit.

"Mr. and Mrs. Czaplicki," he said, his voice even, measured. He opened their documents and began reading silently. The room was still, save for the occasional scratch of his pen against paper.

Jerzy sat rigidly, his hands folded in his lap, but his eyes never left the man's face. He had watched this consulate officer for days, seen him question other immigrants for what seemed like hours, dissecting every aspect of their lives. But this time, something was different. The man's brow furrowed, his lips pressed together, but there was no interrogation, no barrage of questions. Just silence, careful study. Was this good or bad?

And then, something shifted. The officer's expression softened. His gaze lifted from the papers, resting on them—not as a bureaucrat inspecting a case file, but as a man seeing another human being. He saw them. Their suffering, their desperation, their endurance. And in that moment, Jerzy knew. He could see it in the man's face—compassion, deep and unshaken.

The officer inhaled, setting down his pen. Then, without a word, he leaned forward, extending his hand. Jerzy hesitated for only a fraction of a second before grasping it, and when he did, the man clasped his hand with both of his own. It was not a handshake of formality, but of profound understanding.

"Good luck in America," the officer said, his voice thick with sincerity.

Jerzy felt the breath leave his body. He couldn't stop it—the sting in his eyes, the sudden wetness blurring his vision. His grip tightened around the man's hands, his other trembling as he reached for Ekaterina, his fingers brushing her arm. She gasped softly beside him, pressing her free hand to her mouth, their daughter cradled tightly in the other arm. For so long, they had known only struggle, only rejection, only the weight of a door closing in their faces. And now, finally, the door to a new life was open.

Jerzy swallowed hard, blinking rapidly as a single tear slipped down his cheek. He was still holding the consulate officer's hand when he whispered, "Thank you."

And for the first time in years, he felt hope settle in his chest, warm and steady, like the promise of a new beginning.

* * *

June 1948

The sun glinted off the waves as the SS Liberty Star rocked gently in the harbor. A sea of weary yet hopeful passengers lined the gangway, waiting to board. Among them stood Jerzy carrying their lone ragged suitcase, and Ekaterina carrying Dorota, as they took in the sight of the massive steamship that would carry them to their future.

It was hard to believe this moment had finally come. After years of struggle, of waiting, of cruel disappointments, they were finally on the manifest. This time, there would be no rejection, no bitter return to the refugee camp. This time, they were actually leaving.

As they stepped onto the deck, a deep voice boomed through a loudspeaker.

"Welcome aboard the SS Liberty Star!" The captain stood on a raised platform near the ship's bridge, his uniform crisp, his bearing strong. "You are all bound for the United States of America, and we will do everything in our power to get you there safely. However, to accommodate as many of you as possible, we are sailing with a smaller crew than usual. That means we will need volunteers among the passengers. If you have skills, step forward. We will find a place for you."

Murmurs spread among the crowd, and a few men hesitantly

stepped forward—carpenters, cooks, even a former fisherman offering to help in the galley.

Jerzy hesitated. Then, squaring his shoulders, he moved toward the front.

"What's your profession, sir?" the captain asked when it was Jerzy's turn.

"I was... chief of police in the Displaced Persons Camp," Jerzy said. He wasn't sure how that would translate to life at sea.

The captain considered this, then nodded. "Good. You'll be in charge of ship security. We don't expect much trouble, but we do expect confusion. Your biggest job will be making sure no one gets lost."

He handed Jerzy a folded map of the ship. Jerzy opened it and studied the maze of decks, stairwells, and passageways.

"I will not let you down, Captain," he said, slipping the map into his coat.

The captain clapped him on the shoulder. "See to it, then."

Hours later, the ship was well out to sea. Jerzy walked the decks, keeping an eye out for trouble, though thus far, there had been little more than children playing underfoot and a few nervous passengers clutching the railing as they adjusted to the rolling waves.

That was when he saw her...

An elderly woman sat on a bench near the railing, her shoulders trembling. Even from a distance, he could see her wiping at her eyes with a lace-trimmed handkerchief.

Jerzy approached gently. "Madam, are you all right?" He tried Polish first, then Russian, then German. He even tried a few words of the little Italian he remembered.

Each time, she only shook her head, sniffling, clearly not understanding.

Frowning, Jerzy looked around. A young man stood near the railing, watching the waves with a relaxed air. Jerzy had overheard him speaking several languages earlier.

"Excuse me," Jerzy said, waving him over. "Do you speak...?" He gestured toward the woman.

The young man studied her for a moment before his face lit up in recognition. "Yes! She's speaking Yiddish. I can help."

He knelt beside her, speaking softly, and immediately, the woman launched into an impassioned flurry of words.

After a moment, the young man grinned. "She's not lost. She's looking for her chicken."

Jerzy blinked. "Her what?"

"Her chicken. The captain allowed a few passengers to bring small animals for food or comfort—she brought a hen named Peshke. But when she tried to feed it some crumbs, it got loose, and now she can't find it."

Jerzy exhaled sharply. Of all the emergencies he had prepared for, a runaway hen had not been one of them.

"All right," he said, rubbing his temple. "Let's find the bird."

The search began discreetly—at first. Jerzy quietly asked a few nearby passengers if they had seen a stray chicken. They had not. Then word spread, and soon half the ship was involved.

Children peered under benches, sailors checked behind barrels, and a cook swore he had heard suspicious clucking near the galley. A group of passengers made wild gestures to describe what they imagined the fugitive hen looked like. Some even mimicked its probable movements, much to the amusement of onlookers.

Finally, from the lower deck, a triumphant shout rang out.

"I've got it!" A crewman emerged, holding a very plump, very indignant-looking hen under one arm.

The elderly woman gasped. "Peshke!"

The crewman handed over the rogue chicken, and the woman clutched it to her chest like a long-lost child. The passengers erupted into laughter and applause, and the young translator gave Jerzy a knowing grin.

"Well," Jerzy said, shaking his head, "if this is my biggest security issue, I think we'll have a smooth voyage." "Thank you, young man," Jerzy said. "You made an old woman very happy today, and I cannot think of anything finer." The young translator walked away feeling happy... even proud to have been part of such a grand event.

For the first time in years, Jerzy allowed himself to believe that perhaps—just perhaps—things were finally going right.

* * *

The first sign of trouble came at dinner, when the soup sloshed over the rim of the bowls and the silverware trembled on linen. A woman in a navy dress pressed her napkin against a spreading stain, lips tight, while across the room a steward hurriedly set down a tray before the ship lurched again and sent it skidding, porcelain shattering against the floor. Someone laughed, quick and brittle. A few others crossed themselves.

Jerzy swallowed the last bite of bread, heavy and dry, no taste to it but salt. The hunger of the past never truly left him; even now, his body, remembering, told him to eat while he could. How many nights had he lain curled in the woods, stomach wrung out and empty, the air too cold to sleep, waiting for daylight so he could dig for half-rotten potatoes in a field already stripped bare by men more desperate than him? He had thought himself dead more than once. The body endured, somehow. It just endured.

The ship rolled and a glass tipped, spilling wine like blood across the table.

The woman to his left put a hand to her chest. "It's only rough water," she said, though no one had asked. Her voice was too loud.

Jerzy said nothing. It had been years since he had feared anything the world could throw at him. He had stood at gunpoint in the front line of a war that had already been lost, shovel in hand, digging the trenches where the dead would lie before the living even had a chance to fire their last shots. He had pressed his belly to the frozen earth, listening for movement beyond the trees and in the skies, the gnawing of hunger louder than the artillery. He had watched men die beside him with no space left in him to feel, only to keep moving, keep digging, keep breathing. A storm at sea was nothing.

By nightfall, the real waves came. The ones that lifted the ship too high before slamming it back down, metal groaning, the floor pitching beneath their feet. Dishes slid from tables in the dining hall. A woman sobbed into her hands. The corridors filled with the sick. Jerzy walked among them, careful where he placed his feet. The smell of bile hung thick in the air. A man lay stretched across a bench, arm flung over his eyes, his body rising and falling with each heave of the sea. A boy sat beside him, his small fingers clenched into the fabric of his father's coat, knuckles pale in the dim light. His lips were pressed shut, tight, trembling. Dark curls, olive skin, the sharp bones of his face too angular for his age—Italian, most likely.

Jerzy sat.

The boy did not look at him. His fingers twisted in the wool of the coat, as if he could anchor himself there, as if the storm would pass if only he held on hard enough.

"You've made it this far," Jerzy said.

The boy swallowed, throat tight. His voice, when it came, was strained and small. "I don't like the sea."

Jerzy leaned back against the bench, closed his eyes, felt the motion of the ship in his bones. There had been a night, once, long ago, when he had crouched in the dark beside a factory wall, lungs raw from the acid that clung to the air, listening for the sound of boots. The storm inside his chest had been worse than this one. He had run that night. He had made it out. He had been caught, and he had run again. And again.

The sea would end. The storm would end. There was always an after.

Jerzy opened his eyes. "It's just another test," he said.

The boy looked at him then.

Somewhere beyond the walls, the ship climbed another crest, tilted, plummeted down. Another plate shattered. Another voice prayed. Another hour passed.

And the storm raged on.

* * *

The ocean stretched out forever, gray and restless under a low, brooding sky, the ship's wake churning behind them in a thin white line that unraveled and dissolved into the vastness. Jerzy stood at the rail, hands curled over the cold metal, the salt wind threading through his hair and stinging his eyes. It was quiet except for the steady throb of the engines beneath his feet, the sound of waves slapping against the hull, the occasional creak of the ship's bones as it cut through the dark Atlantic. He should have felt excitement, maybe relief, but all he felt was the weight in his chest—that and the cold biting through his thin coat.

Then he saw it. A man in a stained apron emerged from the ship's galley, dragging a heavy metal bucket across the deck. The man's face was bored, almost annoyed as he heaved the bucket up and over the rail, throwing its contents into the sea. Jerzy heard the splash before he saw what it was. He leaned over and watched as the water bloomed with pale shapes—bread, meat, vegetables—whole loaves bobbing for a moment before the waves swallowed them. Another bucket followed, then another, chunks of food scattering across the surface like refuse, drifting and sinking, gone.

Jerzy's breath caught. His stomach twisted painfully, a deep, hollow ache he thought he'd buried years ago. His hands tightened on the rail as his mind pulled him backward, to nights of his imprisonment by the Nazis when he lay awake, his ribs pressing against his skin, his mouth so dry it hurt to swallow. The emptiness in his gut had been worse than the cold, worse than the sound of men dying in the night beside him. He remembered the feel of the water pretending to be soup, ladled into the tin bowl, the hunger that made him dream of bread. And here—here they were throwing real food into the sea, like it was worthless. Enough to feed a dozen men. A hundred.

He felt his chest shake. His eyes blurred, and his throat tightened with something sharp and burning. He drew in a shaky breath, forced himself to straighten, but the tears were already forming. He pressed his fist to his mouth and turned away from the rail, blinking hard at the gray horizon. He could feel the sting of salt on his cheeks.

A man passing by—a fellow passenger—nodded to him and smiled faintly. Jerzy swallowed, nodded back, his mouth twisting. He stood there a long time, feeling the weight of the ocean below him, the weight of hunger still inside him, knowing that even though he was heading toward a new life, some part of him would always carry the ghosts of those empty days.

* * *

On the seventh day, the S.S. Liberty Star rocked gently on the waves as it drew closer to the harbor, the early morning sun casting golden light over the water. The scent of salt and oil filled the air, mingling with the murmur of passengers crowding the deck. Some whispered prayers, others stood in silence, their gazes fixed on the horizon where a great lady in green awaited them.

Jerzy gripped the rail, his knuckles white. His breath hitched as the ship rounded the final bend, revealing the towering figure of the Statue of Liberty. The moment he had dreamed of, the moment he had dared hope for through years of war and uncertainty, was now here.

His eyes traced the folds of her robes, the crown upon her head, the torch raised high in defiance of darkness. He had read about her in borrowed books, had seen sketches passed from hand to hand among refugees like sacred relics. But nothing—nothing—compared to this. He could not read or speak English, but in his mind, he recited the words he knew by heart: *Give me your tired, your poor, your huddled masses yearning to breathe free...*

His lips trembled. *Hey, that's us,* he thought.

Beside Jerzy, Ekaterina held their already six-month-old daughter close, rocking her gently as the baby whimpered at the noise and movement of the crowd. She looked up at him, her blue eyes mirroring the same awe and disbelief he felt. He reached out and placed his arm around her, offering silent reassurance. They had made it.

Jerzy placed his other hand over his heart and whispered, "Thank you, America." His voice was thick with emotion, the weight of his journey pressing against his ribs. Tears welled in his eyes, but he did not wipe them away. There was no shame in gratitude.

The ship's horn bellowed, signaling their final approach. In the distance, Ellis Island loomed, a grand red-brick station where their fate would be decided. Lines would form, papers would be examined, names recorded. Some would be detained; some would be sent back. But in this moment, none of that mattered. For the first time in a long time, Jerzy felt hope—not the fragile, desperate hope of survival, but something stronger. A hope that spoke of new beginnings, of a future he could shape with his own hands.

A soft hand touched his arm. He turned to see Marta, a young girl they had met on the journey, her wide brown eyes filled with the same awe he felt. "It is beautiful, no?" she whispered in her native Polish.

He nodded, unable to speak.

Behind them, a murmur spread through the passengers as the ship slowed, the crew shouting orders. Ropes were thrown, gangways prepared. The moment had come.

Jerzy straightened his spine, smoothing his threadbare coat. He was no longer just a refugee. He was something more now—a man standing at the threshold of a dream. The journey had been long, the sea unkind, but this—this was the beginning of everything.

He took one last look at Lady Liberty and stepped forward, ready to meet his new life.

Forty-Three

Holding in the Tears

Time on the boat had seemed endless, the slow churning of the sea, a metronome marking time not in minutes or hours but in an unbroken, aching stretch of waiting, of existing, of holding on to hope as though it was a lifeline cast overboard in a storm, and now, standing on solid ground, they found the earth beneath their feet to be more illusion than certainty, as if the water still carried them, as if they had not yet been delivered from its endless hunger. But then, there was the voice, the man from the church, clean-shaven, proper, speaking with an accent they did not understand but whose tone was kind, welcoming, shepherding them from the gray harbor, the great island of ghosts and names and numbers stamped in ink upon paper and flesh alike, and after the ritual of customs, toward a quick ferry ride first, then the long road, the road that would take them from New York to a place called Pawtucket, Rhode Island, a name they repeated in their minds like a talisman against the unknown, the syllables strange and thick upon their tongues, yet carrying the weight of promise. And though the drive was long, it was not the kind of long that stretched into the soul, that hollowed a man out like the belly of a ship, no, this was the long of anticipation, of movement toward something rather than away from it, the long of waiting for a door to open rather than the long of watching one close.

"It is far," Ekaterina murmured, her arms wrapped around the baby, pressing her close as if to shield her from the vastness of this new land, as if she could still be small enough to be held in the familiar world she had known, though that world was now as distant as the shore they had left behind, and the child, only six months old, slept against her breast, unaware of the miles, of the road, of the great machine that carried them toward what her parents had come to call a future.

"But not as far as on the ship," Jerzy said, his hands resting on his knees, his back straight despite the ache that had settled into his bones, not the ache of labor but the ache of endurance, of having held on long enough to see this moment, and now the moment was here, and it was a strange thing, to arrive, to have reached the other side of suffering and find that the body still carried the memory of the journey.

"You are lucky," the man from the church, Mr. Radoslaw, said in his broken Polish, turning slightly in his seat, his words slow and careful, as if choosing each one with great effort. "A home, already, and with furniture. You will like it."

A home. The word sat between them, heavy, full, waiting to be lifted, examined, tested against the raw places in their hearts where the idea of home had been torn away time and time again.

And then the car finally came to a stop, and the man stepped out, beckoning them forward, up the narrow stairs to the second-floor apartment, to their home, their first home, their castle, their miracle. Ekaterina, eyes wide, pressed her hand against the exterior wall, as if expecting it to dissolve beneath her fingers, as if this could not be real. "It is solid," she whispered. Her voice trembled—not with fear, but with wonder. "We are safe." Climbing the stairs, there was a moment in which none of them spoke, none of them breathed, for here, inside the house, there was actual light from electric lamps, no candles, no oil, no darkness creeping in at the edges, and there was plumbing, water actually flowing indoors, clean and clear, no bucket, no well, no bedroom ice to be broken in winter, no outhouse... and there was a stove, a stove that did not require coal or wood, that did not demand the labor of breaking and carrying and stacking, of feeding the fire like a beast always hungry, and the walls... there were no drafts, no wind slipping through cracked boards, no cold gnawing at their skin as it had in the camp, as it had in every place before this, and there was furniture, chairs, a table, a bed. A real bed, not something stuffed with straw. Jerzy stepped forward, touching the stove, the smooth enamel surface, the metal unscarred by firewood, unmarked by the soot of burning coal. "No smoke," he said, almost to himself, almost as though he could not believe the truth of it. "No smoke, no ash, no splinters in my hands."

Then Mr. Radoslaw showed them something that they never even heard of—a refrigerator, and it was cold inside, and filled with food donated by members of the church that sponsored their trip, as though some unseen hand had prepared it all just for them, as though providence itself had stepped forward to say here, here is where you will begin again.

And that was when Ekaterina could not hold her tears in any longer. Still holding their baby, she turned into the arms of her husband and cried, tears of gratitude, tears of wonder, of awe... and not knowing what she did to deserve any of this.

The man from the church chuckled. "America," he said simply, as though the word itself explained everything.

They were strangers in a strange land, had no money, no job, no friends, did not even speak the language, yet they felt like the richest people on Earth.

Ekaterina adjusted the baby in her arms, feeling her small weight, her steady breath, the warmth of her tiny body against hers, and she thought of the nights in the camp, the cold that had crept through the walls, the wind that had howled through the slats of their shelter, and how she had curled around her, wrapping her in her own thin coat, whispering to her in the darkness, telling her stories of places she had never seen, places where the walls held warmth, where the water ran clear, where the air smelled not of smoke and damp and hunger but of something clean, something safe, and now here they stood, inside the story she had told her, and she wondered if she would ever know, if she would ever understand the journey that had carried them here, if one day she would take for granted the light, the heat, the solid walls that did not bend to the wind.

Jerzy turned, taking Ekaterina's free hand in his, his grip firm, steady, and she met his gaze, seeing in it the same question, the same quiet, trembling wonder, and he smiled, the first real smile in what felt like years, and she smiled back, because here they were, and the second floor did not matter, not at all, for they had been lifted, carried, raised from the low places, from the damp and the dirt, and now they stood in warmth, in comfort, in something so close to what they had once called impossible that they did not yet know how to touch it, how to let it settle within them, and perhaps they never would, for to be here, to be in America, to be in a home that was safe and whole and warm, was nothing less than manna from Heaven, nothing less than the breath of angels stirring in their lungs.

Forty-Four

Hello Jesse

A few days later, Jerzy was picked up early by Mr. Radoslaw to begin his new job with a local jewelry manufacturer, arranged by his sponsors. There were many such companies in Pawtucket, and he was anxious to begin.

The factory had a quiet hum to it, the kind that felt almost like a breathing thing, its rhythm and pulse settled somewhere in the air between the workers and the machines. It was tiny, compared with the vast behemoth chemical factory he worked at in Germany, and the workers were here because they wanted to be, not because they were enslaved, so it was soothing. There was no heat, no smoke, just the sharp, metallic scent of brass, polished and smooth, the quiet clink of tools, and the whir of equipment at work. Jerzy, still unfamiliar with the place, still clutching the edges of the new reality that wrapped itself around him, stood at the threshold, feeling the weight of it, feeling the stares of the men who passed him by without a word.

Beside him, Mr. Radoslaw muttered something to the foreman, but Jerzy's attention wasn't on the words. It was on the machinery that seemed so far beyond him, the tools in the workers' hands that were foreign but instinctively fascinating. He couldn't have even imagined tools like this back when he was helping to make parts of automobiles as a mechanic. There was a calm here, a far cry from the frenzy of his memories. He wondered, briefly, if this might be the world that would change him, if this could be the life that would offer something he had not yet dared to dream.

The foreman looked him over, then raised an eyebrow. "What's his name again?"

"Jerzy," Radoslaw replied, enunciating each syllable slowly as though the name was a string of foreign notes on a piano. "YEH-zhee."

The foreman frowned. "Say that again?"

"Jerzy," Radoslaw repeated. "YEH-zhee. It's... Polish."

"Polish, huh?" The foreman squinted as though trying to catch a glimpse of something hidden. He tried it again, this time more deliberately. "Yeh-zee?"

"No, no. *Yeh-zhee*," Radoslaw insisted.

Finally, the foreman just nodded as though he got it, which was fine with Radoslaw, who had other pressing business to take care of.

"Hey, kid," one of the workers said, stepping forward. He was thickset, with a cigarette tucked behind his ear. "What's your name?"

Jerzy's eyes flicked toward him, but he didn't respond. He understood the tone of a question, but the words were a blur.

The man glanced at the others. "He get that?"

A wiry, balding worker frowned and scratched his chin. "Maybe he don't speak English."

"No kidding."

They stood there for a moment, shifting awkwardly. Then the first man's face lit up with an idea. He slapped a hand to his chest. "Jimmy," he said slowly. "Ji-mee." He separated the syllables, exaggerating each one as though speaking to a toddler.

Jerzy's brow tightened.

The balding man caught on. He pressed a hand to his chest. "Anthony." Then he slowed it down, splitting it apart like he was giving instructions. "An-tho-nee. You calla me To-ny... 'ay?"

A third man, taller, with oil-streaked hands, grinned and slapped his chest. "George." He repeated it, slower this time. "George."

Jerzy's brow furrowed deeper. He understood now—they were naming themselves. Trying to help him understand.

Then George pointed at Jerzy's chest. "You?"

Jerzy's mouth opened slightly. He hesitated, then pressed a hand to his chest. "YEH-zhee."

The men exchanged looks.

"Jerry?"

Jerzy shook his head. "YEH-zhee."

"Jersey?"

"No..." Jerzy's face tightened.

"Jesse?" Jameson asked.

Jerzy hesitated. Jesse... it wasn't his name—he knew that—but it wasn't so far from Jerzy, was it? He gave a small nod.

"Jesse it is!" George said, clapping him on the back, everyone shaking his hand in welcome.

A ripple of laughter passed through the group, rough and easy. Jerzy smiled. Jesse would do.

* * *

Jesse. The name landed in Jerzy's chest with an unfamiliar warmth. It was simpler, cleaner, like the air in the factory. It wasn't his name, not the one that had been etched into his soul through years of hardship, but it felt like a choice. It felt like it belonged to him. He felt the weight of it settling in his mouth, testing it—*Jesse.*

The older man with the crooked nose clapped him on the back, a thick, calloused hand heavy on his shoulder. "Welcome to America, Jesse."

Jerzy—*Jesse*—felt something inside him shift, like a lock clicking open. He had been nobody for so long. Nobody but a number. Nobody but a shadow. Now, here, in this moment, in this reality, he was something new. Reborn, with a name that could be his. His hands went to his chest and breathed it in deeply, as though making sure it was real, as though he could feel the name settling into his bones.

The rest of the morning passed in a blur, a muted cacophony of movement and sounds that Jerzy could barely track. His thoughts were still with the name—*Jesse*—and what it might mean for him, for his future. And gradually, his surroundings began to make more sense. The workers moved like clockwork, shifting, bending, guiding sheets of brass through presses and molds, each one performing a role that seemed as natural as breathing.

Jerzy was shown how to handle the brass sheets, how to feed them into the hydraulic presses. The metal was cool to the touch, its surface smooth and unmarred, but under the force of the machine, it would emerge shaped, ready to become something beautiful.

He was guided—first by one man, then another—how to set the sheets of metal into the press, how to position them with precision, then step back, waiting for the heavy die to come down with a mechanical groan, stamping the shape into the metal with a sharp, decisive sound. A bang. There was a rhythm to it, a certain flow that made the work feel almost like a dance, but one that didn't need to be learned. Jerzy—*Jesse*—felt it in his bones, the way the tool guided the metal with delicate force, the way the press responded to the pull of human hands. It was instinct, something that hadn't been taught, but something his fingers knew how to do.

His hands, awkward at first, grew surer. He began to understand how to manipulate the press—how much force, how much pressure, when to step in and when to step back. It wasn't something he needed to be told. He just *knew*.

There was a quiet sort of bonding that happened between him and the other men. No words, just shared experience, and shared space. They did their work without much need for conversation, their movements speaking louder than any words could. One man—big, with a thick beard—reached over to correct Jerzy's hand placement, a gentle but firm movement. Another showed him how to adjust the pressure on the hydraulics, a small, simple gesture that was as much about connecting as it was about teaching.

The work was slow at first, clumsy, and Jerzy wasn't sure if he was doing it right. But the others didn't mind. They just kept on with their tasks, including him, not in a way that felt forced or patronizing, but as if he was simply part of the whole, moving in sync with them. The factory's pulse wrapped itself around him, and for the first time in a long while, Jerzy felt that pulse match his own. He was no longer the outsider, the stranger, the nobody. He was part of something now.

Later, as the day wore on, and the bell marking the end of the day sounded, Jerzy realized he had no idea how he would get home. The factory was a maze of half-finished jewelry and scattered tools, a labyrinth of progress and noise, and when the bell rang signaling the end of the day, the workers began to file out, their faces blank, their postures tired but satisfied. Jerzy stood there, rooted to the floor, unsure of the next step.

He looked at the men around him, but there were no words to ask how he was to return to his apartment, to the place where this incredible new life had started. He knew only *home*—the word he had learned at the officer's club. He made a small, questioning gesture with his index and middle fingers walking, miming the action of travel, of departure, then raising both hands upward in a questioning movement.

One of the men noticed. The big, bearded man from earlier gave a short, gruff laugh. "Where's home for you, Jesse?"

Jerzy, remembering the word, *home*, pointed vaguely in the direction he thought might be right, but his expression betrayed his confusion. Then Jerzy—Jesse—remembered... he had been given a piece of paper with his address printed on it. He reached into his shirt pocket.

The man took a few steps toward him, giving him a pat on the back. "Don't worry. I'll get you there. You're good, Jesse. You're one of us now."

And Jerzy—*Jesse*—felt something inside him warm at the words. It was a small thing, this moment, this kindness, but it was enough. Enough to let him believe, just for a moment, that this new life might not be so foreign after all.

* * *

The days had bled into weeks, and those weeks had bled into months, each one indistinguishable from the last in its passing, until Jesse—no, *he*—began to feel the warmth of his new name as something more than just sound, as something deeper, something that belonged to him, not only as a mask but as a choice he had fully embraced. He learned things. Yes, things about the manufacturing of jewelry, about the delicate precision of die-cutting, the soft malleable wax molding that would become a shape, a thing of beauty, if only the right hands would touch it with the right skill. It was a form of creation, not unlike the automobile parts he had to craft as a mechanic, yet far more precise. And then there was plating, and polishing, even hand-engraving, and something about it all—the process, the burnished metal, the gleam of the polished edges—spoke to him in a language he almost understood. He learned some of that language, too, the rough tang of English, enough to know the words but not the melody, not enough to bridge the gap between what he wanted to say and what he was capable of saying, not enough to hear the thoughts of others as something more than just sounds. He wanted so much to speak, to share a laugh, an idea, a piece of his soul with the men around him, but the words hung in the air like smoke, too thick to touch, and so he remained silent, feeling more and more like a shadow among men who had names, and lives, and stories to tell.

And then, in the quiet dark of the evening, in that place where thoughts gather like flies around a lantern, he realized that what had seemed like his solitude was nothing in comparison to what Ekaterina must endure. She was alone, all day, every day. *Her* silence, her isolation, her quiet suffering—it had to be worse, so much worse. He had a job and human connections, but she had nothing, no one but him, and the weight of it hit him like a hammer on stone. He felt small, ashamed, his thoughts too selfish, too narrow. She never complained, but he knew. He could not fix her loneliness, could not fill the hollow of her silence, but in that moment, something turned in him, a spark, a sudden heat, a burst of clarity that was almost painful.

He would do it. He would do what no one expected, what would give them both something, a chance, a path, a road to the future. He would get a car, learn to drive, not for himself but for her, for them both. He would take her, take her to other places, away from the humdrum of the daily grind, away from the words they both struggled to speak. They would explore, wander together, as they should have done from the very beginning, in the vastness of this new land, a place still strange, still distant, but somehow more theirs than it had been before. And maybe, just maybe, in that vastness, they would find the connection in this new life that had eluded them for so long.

Forty-Five

The Nash

It began with the sound. That deep, resonant clamor of steel and air, the rhythmic pounding of the hydraulic presses, the hiss of hot metal cooling, the sharp edge of a hammer strike swallowed whole by the endless hum beneath it all. The factory was a living thing, breathing, exhaling steam and heat and smoke, alive with the scent of oil and lacquer and metal shavings, the glow of polished brass catching the low light like fire caught in glass. Jerzy stood at the edge of it, feeling the pulse of the place in his bones, the same pulse he had felt in the machines themselves when he first laid hands on them, that sense that they were more than metal and pressure and heat, that there was some quiet understanding in the way gears met and turned, how a die cut into brass or steel left a mark like memory.

Then came the near-miss. It was Jameson who had nearly lost a hand. Or maybe it was Anthony. Jerzy couldn't remember anymore, only that there had been the sharp sound of the machine misfiring, the abrupt halt of motion followed by a long silence, followed by the foreman swearing under his breath as he pulled the man to his feet and shook him hard by the shoulder. "You're not gonna get paid if you lose a damn hand," the foreman had growled. Afterward, the other men had laughed about it—nervous, short bursts of sound—because that was how men handled fear in a place like this, when their livelihood depended on how fast they could work and how close they could edge to disaster without tipping over into it.

"You got a head for machines," the foreman had said, calling Jerzy into the small office at the back of the factory floor, the walls scarred with oil and rust and sweat. "You learn quicker than the others. You think maybe you can help me with this?"

Jerzy stood there, hands in his pockets, feeling the hum of the factory floor beneath his feet, the thrum of it in his chest.

"They're paid by the piece," the foreman said, rubbing the back of his neck. "You know how it is. Faster means better pay. But they're cutting corners. Feeding the press with one hand, hitting the release with the other. You know what happens if the one hand moves faster than the other." He didn't need to say it. Jerzy had seen the scars on the older men's hands, the missing fingertips. "Company policy says both hands on the machine. But I can't be everywhere at once."

The hum beneath Jerzy's feet seemed louder now, pressing against the soles of his boots. The foreman was looking at him hard. "You got any ideas?"

Jerzy frowned, the factory's rhythm playing in his head. The presses, the dies, the way metal bent under pressure. His mind moved through the machinery, through the sequence of action and release, action and release. He nodded once. "Saturday."

The foreman blinked. "What?"

"I need Saturdays...," Jerzy said. "...to work on this."

The foreman hesitated. "You figure it out, there's a bonus. A big one."

Jerzy shrugged. "How much?"

"Jesse, if you are half as good as I think, I will make it worth your time."

* * *

Time. It had a way of folding in on itself in the factory, the days stacking up like sheets of metal waiting for the press, the hours collapsing into the hum of machines and the hiss of steam, until a month became a season and a season a year. Jerzy had learned some English at the British Officer's Club, the same way he had learned not only other languages, but the sound of metal under pressure, the cadence of words fitting into his ear like the click of a latch, the bite of a cutting die. He knew how to listen—he had always known how to listen—and language had come to him through the hands as much as the mouth, through the way the men spoke with their bodies, the way a shrug or a glance or the hard line of a jaw could tell you more than any string of words.

The foreman had been watching him—he had been watching from the start, really—but now there was something else in his eyes when he looked at Jerzy, something edged with relief, with quiet calculation. Because Jerzy could see how the machines worked, how they wanted to work, how they needed to work. He had that rare kind of sight, the kind that could look at a problem and see the shape of the solution already forming in the machine. And the foreman, who had spent too many nights trying to figure out how to stop the men from risking their hands, risking their lives, now saw in Jesse the thin glimmer of an answer.

It took three Saturdays. Three long afternoons in the quiet of the factory when the machines were still and the air felt heavier without the noise to fill it. Jerzy took apart the press, studied the mechanics, traced the lines of tension and release through the steel and hydraulics. It was a matter of control, of making sure the machine couldn't fire unless both hands were clear, both hands on the machine, but he just didn't see that at first. He tried foot pedals. Failed. Tried levers. Failed. The hum beneath his feet felt sharper each time, the weight of the need, pressing down on him.

It was on the third Saturday, with the light slipping low through the factory windows and the sound of his own breathing loud in the emptiness, that it came to him. Two buttons. Of course. One on each side of the machine. A dead circuit unless both were pressed at the same time. Both hands engaged. No chance for the press to fire unless the hands were clear.

He wired it up, double-checked it, stood in front of it and tested it himself. The press held still beneath his hands, the buttons waiting beneath his palms. He took a breath, pressed both buttons. The machine slammed down clean and fast, the force of it vibrating up through his arms. He let go. Pressed one button alone. Nothing. Then the other. Stillness. He smiled, the faintest curl at the corner of his mouth.

On Monday, the foreman stood beside him, arms crossed as the men lined up to try the modified machine. Jerzy stood with his hands in his pockets, listening to the soft sound of metal cutting clean through brass. The men grinned at each other when they realized it worked. Safer. Just as fast. Jameson slapped Jerzy on the back hard enough to nearly knock the wind out of him. Georgie laughed and said, "Guess we got ourselves a real engineer."

Jerzy smiled. He could feel it in his chest—the hum of the factory, the weight of the work in his hands, the quiet understanding that this place, this noise, these men—they were beginning to feel like home.

And so it was that Jerzy took his bonus money and bought himself his first car, a 1939 Nash, which needed some work, but Jerzy figured, if he could get a few tools, maybe he could figure out the worst of this car's problems and fix it himself. It wouldn't be the first time.

* * *

The hood creaked open beneath his hands, the stale tang of old oil hitting his nose. His fingers traced the contours of the engine like a map, searching for the fault line. He remembered his old friend Nik's hands—broad and rough, the skin always stained with grease—showing him how to coax life from metal. But Nik's hands were gone now, the memory of them lingering only in the calluses on Jerzy's own palms. He tightened a bolt, felt the engine shift beneath him, something unlocking. The sound of it—soft, sharp—settled in his chest like breath after a hard climb.

"You sure you know what you're doing?"

Jerzy looked up from beneath the hood. Eddie, from work, stood there, thumbs hooked in his belt, cigarette bobbing as he talked.

"I think so," Jerzy said. He turned the wrench, the bolt giving way with a sharp metallic snap.

"That sounded promising," George said, coming around the front of the car with a grin. "If you get it running, first round's on me."

Jerzy smiled. "You pay if it runs. I pay if it does not?"

George's grin widened. "Deal."

It took two hours to get the carburetor apart, and another three to realize he'd put it back together wrong. His hands were raw by the time he sat back on his heels, sweat running down his neck. He closed his eyes, listened to the distant clink of someone hammering in the garage next door. He breathed. Then he leaned forward and tried again. It was dark when the engine finally coughed to life, the low growl of it filling the air like breath after silence. Jerzy smiled, grease staining his teeth. He reached out and ran his hand along the fender. "Good girl," he murmured. "We will get there."

He stood back, wiped the grease on his jeans, and smiled. It wasn't perfect, but it would get them where they needed to go. Then he thought of Yuri, and wondered where he was and what he was doing. Probably still blowing things up.

The next day, he took what was left of his bonus and told Ekaterina they were going shopping.

"I do not need anything," she said, folding her arms across her chest.

"You do not," Jerzy agreed. "But you will want something nice to wear. Church is expecting us this Sunday."

She frowned. "Since when do you care about church?"

"Katya, they paid for our immigration here, and they have been asking," he said. "Every time they asked before, I told them we did not have a car. Now we do, so I think we need to show our gratitude."

Ekaterina sighed. "Do you know where it is?"

"Maybe," Jerzy said, laughing. "Don't worry, Pateechka... I will find it."

* * *

At the department store, Ekaterina's hands lingered over the smooth fabrics, soft pastels and crisp whites. She fingered the hem of a blue cotton dress and glanced toward Jerzy.

He saw the longing on her face. "You like it?" he asked.

She hesitated. "It is too much."

"It is not," Jerzy said. "Try it on."

She did. And when she came out of the fitting room, Jerzy's breath caught. The blue settled over her like sunlight over water.

"So beautiful," he said. "Now, maybe we can give God something nice to look at on Sunday."

Ekaterina blushed, but she felt her heart swell nevertheless.

* * *

Sunday morning came, and so did the hill. The car handled fine on the flat streets, but that steep climb to the church at the top of the hill was another matter. Jerzy would get halfway up when another car would slip out of a side street, forcing him to brake and lose momentum. He'd have to back all the way down to the bottom again, back up even more to get a little momentum, clutch burning under his feet, and gun it.

Ekaterina sighed from the passenger seat. "We are going to be late."

"Probably." Jerzy ground the gearshift into place and tried again.

It became a pattern.

Sometimes it took three or four tries because of slow traffic. The hill had a way of reminding him where he'd come from, how much farther he had to go. But eventually, the engine would catch and they'd roll into the parking lot, Jerzy pulling his tie straight while Ekaterina adjusted her dress. Dorota, sitting between them, kicked her feet in excitement, her little hand clutching the hem of her mother's skirt.

They were always late. And every time, when Jerzy pushed open the large squeaky door at the church's entrance, the minister would pause in his sermon, smile, and say, "Well, that must be Jesse—finally made it up the hill, and it looks like he's brought some help," eliciting more than a few goodhearted smiles and chuckles from the congregation.

On this first Sunday, however, Dorota stood on the pew between her father and mother, her little legs wobbly but determined. The bald man in the pew in front of them leaned back in his seat to listen to the sermon, the bright light from the stained glass catching the smooth dome of his head. Dorota's eyes widened. She raised her hand, her tiny fingers curling toward the tempting shine. She was about to slap it.

Jerzy saw it just in time. He caught her hand mid-swing and pulled it gently to her chest.

Dorota looked up at him with big eyes. Jerzy shook his head, stifling a smile. Ekaterina pressed her lips together, holding back a laugh.

Jerzy's hand settled on Dorota's back as she leaned against his chest. He smiled then, as he saw the collection plate heading their way. "We have indoor plumbing, heating, and a warm home, even a refrigerator and now an automobile... we are rich beyond measure," he whispered, as he slipped a dollar bill into the plate of coins. Maybe he could aid the church in helping others to immigrate here.

Forty-Six

Birth of a New Future

Jerzy had heard about it from one of the die-cutters—over lunch, through the hum of the factory floor, the occasional chatter of men who'd been there longer than him. An art department. Upstairs. He didn't even know what an art department looked like, but he was curious. He pictured men in clean shirts, maybe wearing ties, sitting at large desks with long pencils, drawing things too delicate to be touched by hands like his, hands shaped by wrenches and grease and the hard weight of steel.

But still... he loved drawing as a kid. And he was good at it.

On his lunch break, he wiped his hands on the rag in his pocket and climbed the stairs. His steps sounded too loud against the tile, his breath too sharp. At the top of the stairs, he hesitated. Through the open door, he could see them—three men, maybe four—seated at desks with wooden drawing boards on top, beneath the soft white glow of lamps with shades shaped like bells. Their sleeves rolled up to the elbow, the soft pssst of some tool he had never heard of, on paper filling the room like whispers.

The art director glanced up. "You lost?"

"No," Jerzy said, stepping inside. He was suddenly aware of the grease under his fingernails, the callouses along his knuckles. He tucked his hands into his pockets. "I... I work downstairs. I wanted to see what you do here."

The man leaned back on his chair. He had a thin face, with sharp cheekbones and a long, fine nose. "What do you do?"

"Machining."

"Machining?" The man's eyebrow lifted. "And you're interested in... design?"

Jerzy's gaze slid over the table—a sheet of paper pinned beneath a metal arm, delicate lines curling into the shape of a school graduation ring, intricate and precise, looking better than real, and bright, and shiny. "It is... beautiful," he said.

"Airbrush art and design," the man said. He smiled a little, amused. "Not really the same thing as physically shaping metal."

"But it is... where everything begins," Jerzy said. He stepped closer, tracing the line of the design with his eyes. "Shapes that tease the eye. Machines work because the parts are designed right. Airbrush art and design... you create from nothing... the shapes all mean something." And this was the birthplace of all he manufactured downstairs... the soul behind the product. He could not stop staring.

The man studied him for a moment, then slid off the stool. "You think you can do this?"

"I do not know." Jerzy hesitated. "But I would love to learn."

The man's mouth pulled to the side, skeptical. He gestured toward a clean sheet of Bristol Board at the end of the table. "Draw something, then. In pencil."

Jerzy stood frozen.

"Not now," the man said, amused. "Take it home. Try."

Jerzy took the paper carefully between his fingers, feeling the weight of it. Much more delicate than steel, but no less real. "And then what?"

"Bring it back," the man said. "We'll see."

* * *

Jerzy sat at the kitchen table that night with the stiff paper spread out before him, a single pencil resting beside it. Ekaterina put Dorota to bed and stood behind him, watching as he sat there, not moving.

"You do not have to do this," she said.

"I want to."

She touched his shoulder. "Then draw."

But it was harder than he thought it would be. His mind, so quick with blueprints and machine parts, stumbled against the softness of the task. He could picture it—something simple, maybe a medallion, two sides with one message—but when he put pencil to paper, the line wobbled, curved too sharply. He frowned, erased, tried again.

Hours passed. Ekaterina went to bed, and the house settled into quiet. Jerzy sat at the table, pencil scratching over paper. He closed his eyes, thought of the feel of metal beneath his hands, the sound of machinery moving, the delicate click of parts fitting into place. His hand moved.

When he opened his eyes, the shape had come together—one side, an eagle, modern, slick, curling into an intricate design that spiraled around a single gemstone. Simple. Perfect.

He sat back, the pencil slipping from his fingers. A deep breath filled his chest. It wasn't like building an engine—but it was close. The same precision. The same clarity of mind.

When he finally went to bed, Jerzy lay awake, staring at the ceiling. Ekaterina stirred beside him, the soft breath of Dorota from the crib at the foot of the bed. His hands lay open on his chest, calloused and rough. But now he could see them differently. These hands, they had built machines and fixed engines. But they could make other things too—things not just to look at, but to wear, to hold.

Images that added beauty to the world.

"We will see," he whispered to the dark.

Sleep proved impossible, so he got up again and stayed up verylate that night, hunched over the kitchen table beneath the yellow light of the single bulb, the paper thin beneath his hands. His daughter asleep in the next room, his wife's soft breathing rising and falling with the quiet of the house. He sharpened the stub of a pencil with his pocket knife, the shavings curling onto the table. He thought of the machines

—how they worked because they had to, because every piece depended on the others. He sketched a curve, then another. A lion's head, the mane radiating out like rays of the sun. Symbolic images, fitting inside non-symmetrical shapes. He erased. Tried again. It wasn't art yet, not really, but it was something close.

The next day, when the lunch bell rang and the factory settled into its restless quiet, Jerzy slipped away. Up the stairs. Down the long hall. He stopped at the edge of the door, the murmur of voices inside, the soft scratch of pencil on paper.

Jerzy hesitated, then stepped inside. He didn't touch anything. Just watched. The curve of the designs, the sweep of lines over paper, delicate but deliberate. Like a blueprint but softer. Like machinery, but not.

"You brought some samples of your art?" one of them asked. It was the same man he spoke with the day before, the man who asked him for samples of his art.

Jerzy nodded his head tentatively.

"Let's see." The man took Jerzy's artwork and studied it. Then he looked at Jerzy and gestured to him to have a seat.

Jerzy sat down. The man then introduced himself as the art director, and asked Jerzy if he was interested in learning how to make such incredibly realistic art. Jerzy nodded. So the man took Jerzy's art and praised him first for his creativity, then explained to him why it would not work structurally, explained about die breakage that happened when metal with thin indentations is struck by a force like a sledgehammer. Jerzy asked if he could try to fix it.

He stayed long after the lunch bell had rung. When he stood, the paper lay beneath his hand—simple, but whole. A design that worked.

* * *

Downstairs, it didn't take long for the foreman to notice Jerzy's lunchtime absences. A few days later, the foreman called him into his office. The room smelled of smoke and old paper, the window half-open to the clang and rattle of the factory floor below. The foreman sat behind the desk, rubbing his temple with thick fingers.

"You've been upstairs," the foreman said.

Jerzy nodded.

The foreman sighed. "They say you've got something. Some kind of eye for it. Design."

Jerzy said nothing.

The foreman leaned back, the chair creaking beneath his weight. "Problem is, Jesse, I need you down here. Production's already tight. Can't have you running off to chase some... art thing."

Jerzy's gaze lowered.

"But," the foreman said, the word landing hard, "...they seem to think you could help. They want to train you—some airbrush work, some fine detail work. Said your understanding of the production process might make a difference."

Jerzy's head lifted.

"If you want it," the foreman said, "you'll have to make it work. No special treatment. You hit your production numbers first—every day. And if you fall behind, you make up for it on your own time. Saturdays, Sundays. Whatever it takes."

Jerzy nodded.

"And it's not permanent," the foreman added. "You screw it up, Jesse, you're back on the floor."

Jerzy smiled—just a little. "I will not screw it up."

* * *

The next day, Jerzy found himself between two worlds. Morning hours were spent on the factory floor, sleeves rolled to his elbows, hands raw from working all day with raw metal. The old rhythm was still there—the hum of machines, the weight of the press, the measured alignment of gears fitting into place. But the afternoons were different. Upstairs, at the desks beneath the bell-shaped lamps, he held a different kind of tool— a sharpened mechanical pencil. Once the pencil sketch was ready, it was the knife. The X-Acto knife, slim and silver and sharp, the blade catching the light as the art director handed it to him. "Careful," he said, his voice low and even. Jerzy held it the way he held his tools in the factory, steady and sure, the weight of it light but balanced. The art director placed a sheet of frisket in front of him, pale and thin beneath his hands. "You're cutting the mask," the art director said. "Clean edges. Not too deep. It has to be perfect."

Jerzy bent over the table, the light spilling down from the angled lamp above, and began to cut. The blade slipped at first, digging rather than gliding. He adjusted his grip. His breath slowed. His focus sharpened. Soon the blade moved cleanly, following the curve of the line he'd drawn. His fingers learned the angle, the pressure. A mechanical skill, but with the precision of art, lifting the parts where he would be spraying first.

And then came the airbrush. The paint mixed just right, not too watery, not too dry. He handed Jerzy some finished art to use as a reference. The piece was to be like gold, with the polished surfaces to look shiny, reflective.

The art director stood behind him, took Jerzy's hand in his, and guided the small metal cylinder into his palm. "Feel the weight," he said. Jerzy nodded. From behind, the art director's hand closed over his, his fingers adjusting Jerzy's grip. "Now watch." He guided Jerzy's finger to the trigger, and a soft hiss of air as he pulled back the trigger, and paint bloomed from the tip.

"Not too much pressure. Let it flow gently."

Jerzy's hand trembled. The art director's grip tightened slightly. "It's not just the machine. It's the motion." He moved Jerzy's arm in a smooth arc, the fine mist of paint trailing across the surface. "Like a dancer," the art director said. "Not brute force. Grace."

Jerzy's eyes narrowed. His hand steadied. His body remembered the machines on the factory floor, the smooth rhythm of metal and motion. But this was different. This was the machine serving the hand, the mind shaping the work. He exhaled slowly and followed the motion, the arc, the weightless glide of the brush across paper.

A ballerina, gliding through air.

It was hard at first. His hand, so used to force and weight, stumbled over the delicate curves of the design. But in time, muscle memory crept in, adapting. The same precision he used to shape metal now shaped graphite and paint. The same patience that let him coax a reluctant engine into life now let him trace the line of a flat design as he shaped it with paint, adjusting all with the delicate balance of an airbrush's trigger. And he learned to make highlights and shadows afterwards with a small paintbrush.

The men in the art department were curious at first. A machinist among artists. But Jerzy's hands were steady, his focus complete. Slowly, the skepticism gave way to quiet approval.

And in the evenings, after the factory had gone quiet, Jerzy would stay late—first at the machines, catching up on production, his arms aching from the press of metal beneath his hands. Then upstairs, beneath the soft glow of the lamps, his hands hardened by manual labor, now learning the art of fine design.

One part feeding the other. A perfect fit.

And then the unthinkable happened. The orders piled in, faster than they could keep up with, the factory floor a restless, grinding thing—machines pounding, metal clanging, the sharp smell of oil and electroplating thick in the air. The foreman's eyes dark with the pressure of it, the demand to fill orders faster, faster, until the men in the factory were working through their lunch breaks, until the lights burned late into the night. Jerzy's hands raw from the weight of the metal, the cold bite of the press handle.

The pressure grew to be insurmountable. And so the foreman did exactly what he had said he would do. He pulled Jerzy from the art department.

"You're needed down here," the foreman said, his voice heavy with finality. "We don't have the luxury for this art stuff right now."

Jerzy stood there for a moment, the cold truth of it settling into his chest. He didn't argue. He couldn't. Not with the factory drowning in work, not when the others were breaking their backs just to keep up. He nodded. Put his head down. Went back to the factory floor.

But it was too late.

Because the machine was no longer enough. He had seen too much. He had felt it—the airbrush in his hand, the fine line of paint stretching across the paper, the curve of a setting drawn in delicate shadow. He had stood beneath the high ceilings of the art department

347

and breathed in the quiet hum of creation, the sound of pencil on paper, of minds reaching toward beauty instead of just production. He had known what it was to make something not because it was needed, but because it was imagined.

And sometimes, late at night, he would take out the portfolio he was creating and turn through the pages. The curves of the designs catching the lamplight. His fingers brushing over the paper. Remembering the weight of the airbrush in his hand. The sound of the art director's voice at his ear. The press of his hand on Jerzy's wrist as he guided him through that first stroke.

And now at work, the machines felt so much heavier. The press handles harder to lift. The noise of the factory sharper, cutting through his skull. He still worked fast—he always worked fast—but the work no longer filled him the same way. He would go home at night and sit at the kitchen table with a stub of pencil and a sheet of paper, his fingers tracing shapes in the low lamplight. A curve, a clasp, a hinge. Pieces of a future that didn't yet exist.

The art director didn't say much when Jerzy stopped showing up upstairs. Just gave him a brief nod when their paths crossed in the hall. But a few weeks later, Jerzy found a small package in his locker: a new X-Acto knife, the handle cool and smooth in his hand. No note. Just the knife.

And Jerzy smiled. Because deep inside, he knew.

Forty-Seven

Ideas

It started small. A quiet urge beneath his skin, a pull he couldn't quite name at first, just that feeling, that restless hum in his fingers even when he wasn't holding the airbrush. He needed more time, more space—more of *something*—so he took what little money he could spare and bought himself a drawing board, a second-hand airbrush, a small compressor that whispered instead of roared. Some paints, bristle board, frisket—the right tools, finally, all his own. He cleared a corner of the living room, shifting the worn armchair to the side and nudging the table against the wall until he had enough room to work. Ekaterina frowned at the clutter, but said nothing when she saw the way his hands moved over the paper, how quiet he became, how steady.

And so he practiced. Night after night, long after Dorota was asleep, long after Ekaterina had turned off the light in the bedroom, he sat beneath the dim cone of the floor lamp, the quiet hiss of the compressor filling the room. At first, the strokes were uncertain—his hand too quick, the paint too thick—but then his muscles began to remember how the good strokes felt. The curve of the airbrush between his fingers, the tilt of his wrist, the breathless lift of his arm—it all started to settle, to feel natural. Then learning to accentuate the highlights and shadows with a small hand brush to make the art pop.

Eventually, it became like driving, like shifting gears in the Nash, the clutch moving beneath his foot without thought, the hand reaching instinctively for the shifter, the feel of the road beneath the tires speaking to him without sound. His hand began to glide across the paper in the same way, effortless, the motion no longer separate from his thoughts but part of them, bone and tendon and muscle aligning into something whole. He was no longer trying to control the paint—it was flowing through him, his hand and the airbrush and the paper caught in the same current.

And that's when it started to happen—the initial designs began to change. Shapes he hadn't intended, lines curving where they hadn't before, a depth and texture that hadn't been there in the beginning. New styles never before seen in this industry, modern, sleek, and purposeful with no unnecessary fluff, medallions etched with sleek details in sharp relief, light and shadow working together in a quiet kind of harmony. Things he hadn't seen before, things nobody else was doing.

And sometimes, as his hand moved across the paper, his mind would wander. Back to the war, the smoke and the hunger and the cold, the faces of men who didn't make it. Back to the Displaced Persons Camp, the way Ekaterina's hand felt curled into his in the dark, the sound of Dorota's soft breathing against his chest in the middle of the night. And sometimes, even back to Poland, the sharp scent of machine oil in the garage, the clang of hammers on steel, the quiet pride in Nik's face when Jerzy's hands first found their way around the worn edge of a wrench.

He had come so far. More than he'd ever imagined back in those early years. But he wasn't done yet.

Not even close.

It happened almost without thought, the way big things sometimes do, the way a door swings closed behind you before you realize you've gone through it. It wasn't planned. Not exactly. But it had been there, underneath, for a while now—a quiet itch under his skin, the weight of the machines pulling at his arms, the cold iron of the press leeching the warmth from his fingers. So, about a month after the foreman barked at him that morning, snapped that he couldn't spend another hour upstairs, that they had orders coming in faster than the machines could stamp them out, that he needed him down here on the floor—well, Jerzy just... stopped. Stopped and walked over to the foreman, apologized and told him, calmly, that he was done. And then he turned and walked out the door.

It wasn't until he got home that the weight of it settled on his chest. He stood in the quiet of the apartment, listening to the clock tick. Sat down at the table, stared at his hands. Poured himself a drink —not because he wanted it, but because his hands needed something to do. His stomach had gone tight. His mouth was dry. *What did I just do?*

The front door creaked open, and he heard Ekaterina's footsteps, light and sure, the sound of paper bags rustling in her arms as she stepped inside. Dorota's soft babbling floated behind her. Jerzy stayed seated, glass in hand, as Ekaterina set the bags on the counter. He didn't look up when she crossed the room, the warm scent of the bakery lingering on her clothes.

She stood still for a moment, looking at him. Then, softly, "Why are you home?"

Jerzy's eyes flicked to her face. He opened his mouth to answer, but nothing came. She set her hands on the back of a chair and leaned forward slightly, brow tightening.

"Jerzy?"

He took a breath, forced a smile. "I quit."

She blinked, mouth parting. Then: "You quit?"

He nodded. His pulse was hammering now, his hands tightening around the glass. "I could not..." He shook his head. "The machines. The noise. I could not do it anymore."

She sat down across from him, her eyes softening but still wary. "But—what will you do?"

And that's when it struck him, clear and sharp. He sat up straighter. "I will show you."

He stood, crossed the room to the cabinet where he kept his portfolio, pulled it out, and flipped it open. Ekaterina's eyes followed him, a line forming between her brows. Jerzy spread the pages across the table—designs of medals and medallions, graduation rings and service awards.

"They need this," he said. "Someone needs this."

She was quiet, fingertips grazing one of the sketches, her lips parting slightly.

"This area is the jewelry capital of the world, Katya. I will go to them," Jerzy said, voice sharpening with resolve. "I will take these to every manufacturer in this city if I have to. In all the cities around here...someone will see."

Ekaterina's eyes lifted to his, searching. And then, slowly, she smiled. It was small, cautious—but it was there.

"And if they do not?"

Jerzy smiled back. "They will."

He was already grabbing the phone book, flipping through the yellow pages, pencil in hand. Ekaterina watched him for a moment longer before standing, brushing her hand across his shoulder as she moved toward Dorota's crib.

Outside, the city thrummed, a low and steady pulse beneath the window glass. Jerzy barely heard it as he traced his finger down the list of names. He had something now. A direction. A chance.

And he wasn't going to waste it.

And then he was moving. Tucking the portfolio under his arm, shrugging into his coat. Out the door. Into the car. Engine coughing awake beneath his hand. Driving through the streets, cold wind slipping through the window seam, stinging his face.

The first place was a factory in a narrow brick building. He walked through the door, was greeted by the bored-looking secretary behind the front desk.

"I am here to see the company president."

"Do you have an appointment?"

Jerzy shook his head. "No."

She sighed, looked him over with a thin-lipped frown. "Wait here."

A few minutes later, Mr. Garvey stepped into the reception area, his suit a little too tight across the chest, his glasses sliding down his nose. Jerzy opened the portfolio.

"Hi, he said. My name is Jesse Czaplicki, and I am a freelance designer," he said. And I just wanted to introduce myself and show you my work."

Mr. Garvey's eyes narrowed behind the glasses. His mouth opened to send Jerzy packing— And then he saw the designs.

Slowly, Mr. Garvey's expression changed. His mouth closed. His eyes widened just slightly. He picked up one of the sketches. Turned it toward the light. The delicate airbrushing, the subtle beauty of the designs, the colors designed to catch the eye in even the smallest details.

"You created these?"

"Yes."

"Jesus," Garvey whispered. "We don't make work like this."

Jerzy smiled. "You could."

Three more stops that day. Three more company presidents. And three more times, the same reaction: first doubt, then curiosity, then wide-eyed disbelief as they turned the pages of his portfolio. And suddenly it was happening.

Contracts. Orders. Designs. His phone ringing at night. The art department at Garvey's factory sending over specifications. Awards. Rings. Trophies. Regalia. Medallions. Orders from factories he never even heard of. And suddenly Jerzy was a freelance designer. Suddenly there was money. Not a fortune—but more than ever before. Way more. Enough to pay for new shoes for Dorota, for a new dress for Ekaterina. Enough to breathe.

And it was his. His designs. His work. His future.

It was only the beginning, but it was beginning.

* * *

It had been two years since Jerzy had walked away from the factory floor, two years of waking when he chose, of setting his own hours, of sitting before his drawing board with the sun streaming through the wide windows, the compressor's steady thrum across the floorboards, the delicate hiss of the airbrush a constant accompaniment to his thoughts. Two years of freelancing, and more money than he had ever made in the factory, more money than he could have imagined back when his hands were rough from machine oil and lacquer, when the sound of the hydraulic presses filled his ears even in his sleep. Now it was different. Now it was his hand that birthed the work, his designs that filled the glossy sheets of bristle board. His clients—factory owners whose names he had once heard only in rarely, if at all on the factory floor—were calling him now, asking him to create designs for them: medals, service awards, and regalia that seemed to hold more weight in the sweep of his line and the softness of his shading than in the gold and silver themselves.

* * *

Dorota was getting big. She had long ago abandoned the unsteady wobble of a toddler's steps and was now running across the house, climbing furniture, her laughter echoing through the rooms as if the walls themselves were learning joy for the first time. Next year she would start school, and that got Jerzy thinking—not just about school, but about where. He had spoken with some of his clients, the factory owners in Massachusetts, the ones with their empires of gold and silver, and they had spoken highly of the schools there. It made sense, after all. Massachusetts—the world capital of the jewelry industry, where the factories lined the narrow streets like cathedrals to craftsmanship and wealth. A place where the sound of hammers on metal and the soft burr of polishing wheels were as constant as the ringing of church bells. If his designs were already there in their showrooms and catalogs, why shouldn't he be there too? Why shouldn't Dorota walk to school past those same streets, grow up in a town where art and industry lived side by side?

So, he began looking. His business was steady now—better than steady—and there was enough money to buy a house. A small one, nothing too extravagant, but brand new, and with a living room large enough for a real full-sized drawing board and compressor, for the paints and brushes and rolls of frisket. Eventually, he found such a home, brand new, in a quiet neighborhood, with a yard just big enough for Dorota to play in, and a street where the houses leaned comfortably into each other as though they had been resting there for a century. It had good light—that was important—and a fireplace, which Ekaterina had always dreamed of having. And Jerzy, practical, yet a dreamer as always, had the house fitted with a fancy doorbell, one that played eight clear notes in a chime that echoed through the house like the opening of a song. When Dorota first heard it, she laughed and clapped her hands, and Jerzy smiled, thinking how far they had come from that broken shack in Germany. Thinking how much further they could still go.

He sat down before his drawing board the night they moved in, the odors of a fresh home still lingering beneath the scent of Ekaterina's cooking, and he had an idea. He recently learned about them—a large company that dealt in religious pieces, the same tired catalog of saints and sacred hearts and crosses that all looked like they'd been pulled from the same cookie-cutter mold that was ancient, tired and lifeless. He knew he could do better. Not just better—different. Modern. Streamlined. Nothing extraneous, no shapes for the sake of just filling empty space. He sat down at his board, the hum of the compressor low in the background, and worked on it for almost two hours, the ideas emerging like popcorn, twelve designs taking shape beneath his hand—Saint Michael with the barest suggestion of wings, Saint Christopher with a single sweeping line of strength, Mary not crowded with stars and robes but distilled to the quiet tilt of her head. This was a subject Jerzy knew intimately from his childhood. He sketched out his ideas in pencil and cut the frisket. The compressor hummed softly at his feet. He picked up the airbrush, pressed the trigger, and let the thin mist of paint bloom across the board, his hand steady, the motion effortless now, like waves flowing effortlessly across the ocean, only this was a tsunami. His mind drifted as his hand worked—back to the factory floor, the press of heat and noise, the clang of metal, the voices in languages he barely understood then. Back to Poland. Back to the DP camp. The ache of hunger in his stomach and the cold, and the sound of Dorota's laughter now in the next room seemed almost impossible, almost like a dream. But here he was. And here she was. And tomorrow, and the next day, and the day after that—he would sit before his board, and he would work, and Dorota would grow, and they would build a life together.

The next morning, he took the designs to them, laid them out on the table one by one. The men frowned at first, uncertain, until one of them leaned in, then the others followed, the room growing quieter as they studied the clean lines, the simplicity that somehow carried more weight than ornament ever could. Jerzy studied their reactions carefully, remembering what he had learned so many years ago from his uncle about negotiating. "How much?" one of them finally asked. He knew then. "One hundred dollars each," Jerzy said without blinking. They exchanged glances, some raising their brows, but none of them argued. They simply nodded. He left lighter, not just because of the money but because he knew his real worth now—they saw it too.

* * *

When Dorota was ready for her first day of first grade, Ekaterina had spent the entire last week getting her ready, explaining the idea of school to her, all the other children her age who would be there, and then on that exciting morning, carefully choosing a cute little dress, pinning up her hair just so, and even slipping on a pair of shiny little shoes that made a soft clinking sound with each step. When Dorota stood before them, she was the very picture of a beautiful little girl off to school. Jerzy watched her with a smile that couldn't quite hide the pride, but also the uncertainty of a father watching his daughter embark on a world beyond his reach.

Her first day went by in a blur of excitement and confusion. When she came home that afternoon, her face was glowing, her eyes bright as she tried to tell them about it, her words tumbling out in a mix of broken English, Russian, and Polish. "We—uh, we go outside, and the lady—Miss, I think? — she... she says, 'Sit down, sit down!' And then, I make... we make like... uh, 'art.' I draw... house! I draw house!" She smiled proudly, but the frustration bubbled under her words. She could barely follow everything happening there, and when

356

she had questions, it felt like nobody could answer them the way she wanted.

Jerzy nodded along, smiling warmly at her attempt to recount the day. But Ekaterina frowned slightly. "Is that all, Dorota?" she asked. The question was more for herself than for the little girl who only knew how to say what she could. But she smiled again, brushing a strand of hair from Dorota's face, her mind already swimming with thoughts of how to bridge the gap between her daughter's excitement and her confusion.

The next morning came too soon, as mornings often do when one is young. Dorota was still bleary-eyed when her parents roused her from sleep. She groggily tried to pull the covers over her head and ignore the world, but Ekaterina was having none of it. "Dorota, you must get up, or you'll be late for school," she said, her voice firm but loving.

The little girl squinted at her mother. "What, again?" she asked, rubbing her eyes in disbelief.

Ekaterina exchanged a knowing glance with Jerzy, who chuckled softly. "Yes, Dorota," he said, "again."

As the sleepy girl reluctantly got out of bed, Jerzy watched the scene with a fondness in his heart, yet a vague unease brewing in his chest. She would grow up, of course—she would have to—but as long as she was still small, Jerzy would want her to stay just a little bit longer in that world of innocence, a world that was as fleeting as the morning light.

Forty-Eight

What Next?

Just before that, however, in August, when Dorota was still on summer vacation, getting ready to enter the first grade, still teaching her parents the English she had been learning, another lesson was preparing itself. The wind had been rising since the morning, slow at first, creeping under the doors, rattling the windowpanes with a low, insistent moan that built itself into something fierce by midday. Jerzy had not heard any warnings, yet he had listened to the radio crackle with the voices of men forecasting a big storm, their words clipped and efficient, their tone resigned. He had taken the usual precautions —brought in the tools from the yard, checked the roof for loose shingles, made sure the basement was dry. But there was no preparing for this, not really. It was taking on a life of its own.

By afternoon, the sky had turned the color of slate, thick and swollen with the weight of the storm, the trees bending like old men in prayer. The rain came in sheets, then sideways, sometimes in sudden bursts that made the walls shudder. The wind howled, peeling down the street like an unseen force ripping at the world, stripping

358

branches, lifting shingles, wrenching power lines from their poles. Ekaterina sat in the living room with Dorota pressed against her side, their hands knotted together, watching out the window, where the world had become a smear of water and motion.

Jerzy stood by the doorway, staring out into the chaos, listening to the house creak and settle, feeling the air shift with the violent gusts. Remembering that day when Poland was attacked by Nazi Germany, he ushered the family into the basement, just as a precaution. He had known storms before—man-made storms that left towns shattered, left people wandering through the ruins of what had once been their homes, their lives. But this was different. This was not war, not the bombs that fell like fire from the sky. This was something older, something indifferent. They learned later that it even had a name; they called it Hurricane Carole.

But now came the crash.

A sound like the world itself splitting open, the violent snap of wood giving way, the heavy thud of something immense meeting resistance. And a crash inside the house, like dishes breaking.

Ekaterina screamed. Dorota screamed with her. The animals ran for cover, eyes opened wide, their feet straining for traction.

Jerzy was already moving before he registered what had happened. He ran upstairs, across the house, throwing open the back door, the wind slamming into him, the rain stinging his skin like needles. He saw it then—the large oak tree, the one that had stood just beyond the fence line, its roots torn from the earth, its limbs reaching like fingers pointing to the sky. It had fallen against the house, its long branches splintered and twisted, the bulk of its trunk pressed against the roof at an angle, like some great beast that had collapsed against their home to die.

He turned back inside, shaking the water from his hair, his clothes already soaked through.

"Everyone all right?" His voice was sharp, urgent.

Ekaterina nodded, one hand pressed against her chest, her face pale. Dorota was clutching her mother's dress, eyes wide, the small rise and fall of her shoulders the only sign that she was breathing.

When the wind slowed, they cautiously went back upstairs.

Then Jerzy saw it. The cuckoo clock.

It lay in ruin on the floor, the delicate ceramic shattered, the tiny painted bird lost among the fragments of what had once been whole. He stared at it for a moment, the memory of the day he had bought it flickering in his mind—the way Ekaterina had paused in front of the shop window, how she had tilted her head just slightly, her lips parted in that quiet way of hers when something caught her heart before she even realized it. He had gone back for it that evening, had watched her eyes light up when she unwrapped it, had felt something settle in his chest knowing he had given her a piece of something beautiful, something small and good.

Now it was broken. Just like that. It took just a second, a storm, and it was gone.

He knelt, gathering the pieces with careful hands, the sharp edges pressing into his fingers, the fine dust of shattered ceramic clinging to his skin.

Ekaterina said nothing, just watched him, the lines in her face deepening.

"Maybe it can be fixed," he murmured, more to himself than anyone else.

"One thing I need to do first, though." Grabbing some dry clothes, he checked to make sure there were no leaks from the tree against the roof. Fortunately, it seemed okay.

For hours he worked, bent over the kitchen table, the glue drying too quickly or not quickly enough, the pieces refusing to fit the way they once had. The hands of the clock were missing. The tiny bird was in three separate pieces. The minute details of the painted flowers on the base were chipped beyond recognition. The more he tried, the worse it seemed to get, his fingers shaking, his vision blurring, the strain of it building until, finally, finally, he set the last fragment down and exhaled, the sound almost a laugh, almost a sigh.

"It's no use," he said, wiping a hand across his forehead.

Ekaterina touched his shoulder, her fingers cool against his skin. "It was just a clock, Jerzy."

He looked at her, then at the mess of broken pieces before him. He knew she was right. It was just a clock. But it wasn't.

Outside, the wind was dying, the storm already moving on, leaving behind what it always left—silence, ruin, the slow, steady work of rebuilding. He looked at Dorota, now asleep against her mother's side, her small fingers curled into a fist, the faint remnants of dried tears on her cheeks. He reached out, brushed a lock of hair from her face.

A tree had fallen, but the house was still standing. The walls were still intact. His wife and daughter were here, breathing, whole. That was what mattered. Not the storm. Not the clock. Not the pieces of what had been, but what remained.

Still, he let the broken shards sit on the table for the rest of the night before he finally swept them away.

* * *

It had been a few months now since Dorota had started school, and her parents, in their own way, had begun to learn more about the world than they had ever expected to. It wasn't anything they could have planned for, or even really understood at first, but their little girl, their baby, had started coming home with words and phrases they didn't know, words that sounded strange and sweet, words that made Ekaterina look at Jerzy with a mixture of confusion and a kind of quiet awe. They had begun to realize, without knowing it, that Dorota was teaching them, the same way children always do when they pick up language from the other kids.

At first, it was simple things. "School big," she'd say, her voice a soft lilt as if she were tasting each word before it left her mouth. "Big like... uh... uh... house!" Her gestures would widen, arms flung out as if she could somehow fill the room with her words. Jerzy and Ekaterina would nod, trying to understand, trying to catch up to the sounds that were now so familiar to their daughter.

But then slowly, it began to change. It wasn't just the words; it was the way she said them. It was easier for Jerzy than Ekaterina, because he was out in the real world every day. A slight lilt creeping into Dorota's voice, a quicker rhythm to her speech, the cadence of someone who spent her days in the company of other children, learning the language they used to talk about the amazing world around them with that burst of frenzied activity so common children of that age.

One morning, however, she didn't get up when called, and Ekaterina, used to the bounce of her daughter's energy at that hour, felt a tightness in her chest. She ran upstairs into the bedroom, and found her daughter still in bed. The warmth of the blankets against Dorota's body felt wrong. Ekaterina's hand, reaching for the soft curve of her daughter's head, pulled back sharply. Heat. Way too much of it.

"Jerzy!" she cried, her voice an edge of panic. "Jerzy, something's wrong!"

Jerzy, sitting at the kitchen table, half-absorbed in a cup of coffee, stood up so quickly the chair scraped back, the sound sharp in the quiet morning air. His pulse quickened before his mind could catch up, and then Ekaterina's voice brought him to his feet, sharp as a knife. "She is burning up."

He reached for the phone automatically, dialing the doctor's number with practiced urgency, his hands shaking slightly, more from a fear of not understanding, and of having no control over whatever was happening.

The doctor arrived, barely a half-hour after the call, his face tight with the knowledge that something was gravely amiss. "Temperature's way too high," he muttered, bending over Dorota's form. He placed the back of his hand to her forehead, as if to double check the thermometer, then stood straight, looking at Ekaterina, his voice low and grim. "We need to get her to the hospital. Now." Then the doctor called the hospital so they could be prepared. Jerzy, silent, nodded, the world narrowing down to this single, urgent moment. The doctor moved fast, barking orders, his hands sure as he helped lift the sick girl from the bed and into the car.

The hospital was a blur of white, too bright and too sterile, and the air felt colder than it should have. They had barely arrived when the word came, a shock so sudden it left them breathless: Poliomyelitis. The doctor's words were a fog in their minds, but they knew what he meant. Jerzy had heard about when it first hit the news, and explained it then to Ekaterina. Their daughter, their precious

Dorota, was ill in a way that could not be fixed with anything less than time and all the strength they had... along with a lot of luck. No visitors, they said, no one, not even the parents. Not yet.

It was then that the memories, long buried, came flooding back in waves. Ekaterina saw her son, his face so small and full of life, the spark in his eyes so much like Dorota's. She remembered how the baby had clung to her side, how she had held him as the pneumonia had taken him, in just a few days. And now polio threatened their daughter.

"NO!" Ekaterina's voice broke the silence, raw, desperate. "Not again," she wailed. Her knees buckled beneath her, and she sank to her knees, her body shaking with sobs that tore through her as though she were being ripped apart from the inside.

Jerzy was there in an instant, lifting her, his arms around her, pulling her close as if holding her could hold back the flood of memories, the flood of dread that threatened to consume them both. He could feel her trembling against him, her body wracked with the sobs of a grief she had not yet allowed herself to face, not fully. He knew exactly what she was thinking, what was running through her mind, because it was the same thought that had twisted itself into his own heart, a darkness he had tried to push away but could not.

He held her tighter, pressing his cheek to her hair as she cried, his own heart breaking for himself and the woman who had already lost so much. His mind traced the path that led to a memory so painful, so sharp that he could scarcely breathe. Their son, gone, the small body that had once been his world now reduced to a memory that haunted them both.

Ekaterina clung to him as though she could not hold on long enough to keep the past from swallowing them whole. "Not again, Jerzy," she whispered through the sobs, as if saying the words would make them true, would make them stop. "Not again, please."

Jerzy's arms tightened around her, and for the first time, he allowed himself to feel the weight of the fear that had been creeping up on him since the doctor's words. The doctor's grim face. "The iron lung," he said.

It was a return to a nightmare Jerzy thought he had left behind.

He could feel Ekaterina's pain as though it were his own, and for a moment, he couldn't tell where she ended and he began. He wanted to tell her it would be okay, that it would pass, that Dorota would be fine. But even as the words formed in his mind, he knew the truth—they couldn't know yet. Not until the fight was over.

"I'm here," he whispered, his voice a rasp, a plea for some kind of strength he didn't have. "I'm here, Katya. We're together, and we'll get through this."

But even as the words left his mouth, they felt like empty promises. The silence that followed was heavy, like the weight of all the things they could not say, all the fears they couldn't face. And so they held each other, both of them lost in the memories of what they had already lost, praying for a miracle they feared would never come.

Forty-Nine

The Zoo

Four days later, the hospital called. They could visit their daughter for emotional support—she had been crying for them every day—but only they could visit. No friends, no siblings. Just parents. And they would need to wear protective clothing and face masks, all provided by the hospital.

When they arrived, a nurse led them down a hushed corridor to a small, white-walled examination room. The doctor met them at the door with a calm smile.

"She's doing well," he said. "She was having difficulty breathing, so we placed her in the iron lung, but only as a precaution—and today, there's no paralysis, no more trouble breathing, and no more fever. If all continues to go well tonight, we'll take her out tomorrow. After that, we'd like to keep her here another day or two, just for observation, and then, if all stays well... she should be ready to go home."

Ekaterina's breath caught. Tears filled her eyes as she hugged the doctor, then the nurse, her words tumbling out in breathless thanks.

Jerzy stood beside her, his hands clasped in front of his mouth, his head bowed. Silent tears ran down his face. He couldn't speak. He could only watch as he and his wife found the answer to their prayers.

"Also, we'd recommend keeping her home from school for another week," the doctor added gently. "Just to be safe."

Ekaterina nodded, still clutching the nurse's hand. Jerzy wiped his face with his sleeve. Relief and gratitude settled in his chest like a weight lifted after too long. Their little girl was coming home.

The doctor smiled softly. "Would you like to see her now?"

Ekaterina's eyes widened. "Yes, of course!"

The doctor nodded to the attending nurse, who gestured toward a side hallway. "Follow me."

They were led to a small, brightly lit area where the nurse helped them into pale yellow gowns, stiff plastic masks, and crinkling shoe covers. Jerzy adjusted the mask over his nose and tried to see Ekaterina's face through the thin plastic shield, but all he could make out were her wide, worried eyes. The nurse led them down a hushed corridor to a room at the end of the hall.

Before they even reached the door, they heard her crying.

Jerzy felt Ekaterina's hand tighten around his arm. The sound sharpened into soft, hiccuping sobs. Then a nurse pushed open the door, and they stepped inside.

Dorota lay inside the massive iron lung, the machine's polished steel surface cold and impersonal against the smallness of her body. Only her head was visible, framed by white pillows. Her eyes were squeezed shut, tears running down her cheeks. When the door opened, she turned her head toward the sound, blinking in fright at the two masked figures standing at the foot of the machine.

Her face twisted in fresh panic. She cried even louder.

Ekaterina's hand flew to her mouth. "Dorota, it's us," she said through the mask, her voice cracking.

"Mama?" she whimpered. "Papa?"

Jerzy crouched down beside the machine, his gloved hand reaching to brush the tears from her small cheeks. "We're here, little one. It's okay."

Dorota's eyes widened, her breath hitching. Then she let out a fresh wail, but this time, the cause was overwhelming happiness. "Mama! Papa!"

The nurse stepped forward to adjust a strap on the machine, but Dorota was already crying harder, her free hand straining toward them, but she could not reach the openings used by the doctors and nurses to tend to her needs. Ekaterina dropped to her knees and pressed her gloved hand against Dorota's cheek. Jerzy bent his head, resting his masked forehead against the side of the machine.

It was chaos—the doctor appeared at the door, the nurse was saying something about calming her down, the iron lung let out a soft hiss as it cycled, and Dorota was sobbing so loudly it seemed to echo off the walls.

Jerzy turned toward the nurse. "Has anyone told her the good news?"

The nurse hesitated. "No. The doctor wanted to speak with you both first."

Jerzy looked at Ekaterina. Her eyes were already shining with tears.

"Dorota," Ekaterina whispered, stroking her daughter's damp cheek. "Listen to me. You are going to be okay. The doctor says you are going to get out of this machine tomorrow. No more fever. No trouble breathing. You are going to be fine."

Dorota's crying slowed, her mouth trembling. "Really?"

"Really," Jerzy said. He kissed her forehead. "You will come home soon."

Dorota let out a watery laugh and then started crying again— softer this time—while Ekaterina kissed her forehead and Jerzy brushed her hair with his hand. Relief settled into the room like a quiet breath. Their little girl was coming home.

The next day, the doctor said it as though he was commenting on the weather, like it was just another piece of business to attend to— "She's out of the iron lung now, breathing totally on her own, and doing remarkably well. We'll keep her another day just to be sure."

And then, just like he promised, they were driving home two days later. Jerzy glanced at Dorota in between him and Ekaterina, her small face still pale, the bruises of exhaustion still under her eyes, but her mouth tugging upward at the corners in a way he hadn't seen in almost a week. Ekaterina's hand rested lightly on Dorota's knee, the thumb running small circles against the fabric of her dress as though reassuring herself that she was really there, that this was really happening, that their daughter had been pulled back from that thin, sharp edge where they had stood before and watched helplessly as her life was in question.

Dorota's eyes were half-lidded when she spoke, soft and sleepy. "Papa?"

"Yes, my little pateechka?" Jerzy kept his eyes on the road, though he could feel Ekaterina shift in her seat beside him, her hand going still.

"Can I have a puppy?"

Jerzy's eyebrows lifted. "A puppy?"

Dorota nodded, eyes brightening. "There was a girl in the hospital. She had a puppy. She told me all about him. How he waits for her at the door when she comes home from school. How he sleeps next to her bed. And when she feels sad, he always knows and licks her face." Dorota paused, frowning a little as she considered this. "She said puppies know everything about you, even the things you don't tell anyone."

Ekaterina, remembering her own childhood dog, smiled faintly. "That sounds like a very smart puppy."

Dorota nodded solemnly. "She said he makes her feel better, even when she's sick. He just knows."

Jerzy and Ekaterina exchanged a glance—one of those quiet, wordless conversations they had gotten good at over the years. And then Jerzy's hand tightened on the wheel, and without saying a word, he pulled the car over to the side of the road, and when traffic was clear, made a quick U-turn.

"Jerzy?" Ekaterina asked, her hand gripping the edge of the seat as the car jerked back onto the road.

"There was a sign," Jerzy said, already accelerating, the determination in his voice making it clear that his mind was made up. "A few days ago. A house near the town center. Free puppies to good homes."

"Papa!" Dorota's eyes widened.

Jerzy smiled. "If you want a puppy, my little Stardust, then we're getting you a puppy."

It took less than fifteen minutes to get there. A small blue house with white shutters and a sagging porch, the hand-painted sign still staked in the lawn but bent sideways now, the letters faded. FREE PUPPIES TO GOOD HOMES. Jerzy pulled up, shut off the engine. Ekaterina was already getting out of the car, helping Dorota out of the seat. The house door opened, and a woman with a tired smile stepped out, wiping her hands on her apron.

"Come for a puppy?"

Dorota nodded shyly.

"Well," the woman said, glancing toward the side yard, "you're just in time. Only one left."

They followed her around the side of the house, where a little dog sat beneath the shade of a tree, ears perked up, tail thumping lazily in the grass. He was small, honey-brown with a white patch on his chest, and his left front paw curled inward awkwardly as he stood. He took a few uncertain steps toward them, the lame leg dragging slightly behind.

Dorota's face lit up. "Oh!"

"He's a sweet one," the woman said. "But no one wanted him on account of the leg."

Dorota was already crouching down, her hands reaching out. The puppy waddled toward her, tail wagging so hard his whole back end wobbled. He sniffed her hands, then pressed his wet nose to her wrist and licked it. Dorota laughed.

"What's wrong with his leg?" Jerzy asked.

"Vet says he was born that way," the woman said. "Nothing to be done about it. He gets around fine, though."

Dorota gathered the puppy into her arms, and he let her, curling into her lap without hesitation, licking at her face with small, eager kisses. "I love him," Dorota said.

"You sure?" Jerzy asked gently.

Dorota's face was serious now. "He is special." She kissed the puppy's head, resting her cheek against the warm fur. "He is like me."

Jerzy's throat tightened. He cleared it and looked away. Ekaterina touched his arm.

"I think he found his home," Ekaterina said softly.

Jerzy knelt down, running his hand over the puppy's head. "What will you call him?"

Dorota frowned, considering. Then her face brightened. "Tippy!!"

Ekaterina raised an eyebrow. "Tippy?"

Dorota nodded. "Cause he has a bad leg. And maybe he will tip over, but I will love him anyway."

Jerzy laughed, then glanced at Ekaterina, who was smiling too despite herself.

"Well," Jerzy said, rubbing the puppy's ear, "Tippy it is."

The woman smiled. "You've got yourself a good one," she said.

Jerzy stood, scooping Dorota and the puppy into his arms. "Yes, we do," he said, as he carried them back to the car.

* * *

In time, Tippy was joined by a cat, a rabbit, and even a hamster, whom Jerzy called Hamsterdam without knowing why, only that it seemed right, the sound of it rolling around pleasantly in his head like the echo of a half-remembered joke. Because he loved to chew on paper, they kept Hamsterdam in a cage; the other animals were free to roam the house. And once in a while, as Jerzy sat hunched over his drawing board, the airbrush balanced precariously between his fingers and the faint ache of concentration pressing at his temples, he would catch the blur of a little racetrack out of the corner of his eye—the rabbit tearing past first, all frantic feet and flying ears, the cat right behind with that low predatory coil in its spine, and then Tippy lumbering after them both, his lame leg giving his chase an odd, lopsided rhythm, the whole thing like some small, ridiculous carnival peeling through the room.

And then a few minutes later, as if the natural order had inverted itself, the rabbit would be chasing the cat, who in turn was chasing the dog, the whole parade folding back in on itself while Jerzy sat frozen, eyebrows raised, airbrush in hand, and Ekaterina, perched on the edge of the worn sofa with her knitting resting in her lap, would glance up from the tangle of yarn and needles, her mouth just barely curved into that quiet, knowing smile.

"They'll sort it out," she'd say, and Jerzy would shake his head, wondering how anything so ridiculous could be happening under his roof, under his name, and yet feeling—without quite understanding why—that it somehow belonged, that the chaos was its own kind of order.

* * *

Dorota loved all of her animals with a rare, unwavering devotion, the kind of love that didn't soften with time or habit but only seemed to grow more determined with each passing day. When she found out where meat came from, she cried—big, wracking sobs that left her pale and trembling and clutching Tippy so tightly to her chest that the little dog squirmed and licked at her chin until the tears slowed. Her parents tried to explain—it was good for her, it would make her strong, give her healthy bones—but Dorota would never argue. Instead, she would simply sit at the table with her back straight, her face pale and composed, and obediently lift a bite of meat to her mouth, chewing slowly. Then another bite, and another, until her cheeks were so full that she couldn't close her jaw, her face turning pink with the effort. And Jerzy and Ekaterina would exchange a weary glance, and finally Jerzy would say, "Okay, go spit it out." And she would, quickly and quietly, and by the time she got back to the table, Ekaterina would have rearranged her plate so neatly that there was no trace the meat had ever been there, just the clean order of vegetables and bread and the small glint of relief in Dorota's eyes as she picked up her fork and finished the rest of her meal without a word.

Every morning, she dressed the cat in doll clothes—a blue dress with lace trim on Tuesdays, a striped bonnet on Fridays—and somehow the cat allowed it, sitting perfectly still as Dorota adjusted a ruffled sleeve or retied a bow. The rabbit got a carrot each day, peeled and trimmed to just the right size. Tippy ate from his bowl while

Dorota hummed to him softly. And she helped her mother clean out the litter box, which was shared by both the cat and the rabbit—a fact that seemed to strike everyone as vaguely unseemly except for Dorota, who accepted it as perfectly natural. She spoke to her animals with the same calm authority that her parents used with her, explaining patiently why Tippy could not sleep on the sofa, why the cat had to keep the dress clean, and why the rabbit should really learn to stop nibbling on her daddy's shoelaces. And she seemed so sure they understood her that after a while Jerzy stopped wondering if maybe they did.

And then one day, the rabbit died. No sickness, no anything. He just died. Dorota sat curled on the floor, her arms wrapped around her knees, her face blotchy and wet, and nothing Jerzy or Ekaterina said could reach her. Finally, Ekaterina whispered something to Jerzy, and they gathered up the rabbit's small body and walked with Dorota into the woods behind the house. Jerzy dug the hole while Ekaterina wrapped the rabbit in a piece of linen, and Dorota stood stiff and silent, her hands trembling at her sides. Ekaterina murmured a prayer in Russian. Dorota laid a single carrot on top of the linen, and Jerzy filled the hole. And as they walked back toward the house, Dorota slipped her hand into Jerzy's, her small fingers wrapping tightly around his, and he squeezed her hand in return and he thought, not for the first time, how delicate and fierce love could be.

Fifty

Brother?

Spring 1959

Jerzy sat across from Mr. Whitmore, a factory owner and client who had become a friend. He paid well and spoke plainly, the kind of man who ordered a whiskey without looking at the menu. They were at a small bar off Tremont Street, a late lunch stretching into an early dinner, Jerzy half-listening as Whitmore talked about the recent trouble with union negotiations and the rising cost of gold. Then Whitmore's tone shifted, softened.

"You know," he said, swirling his glass, "I've been looking into my family tree lately. Hired one of those genealogy researchers. A real professional. Turns out I've got a great-great-great grandfather who was a drummer in the British Army. They called him Drummer-Boy Whitmore. And a distant cousin who was a fish-monger in colonial Boston." He chuckled. "My wife says I'm obsessed, but it's funny, isn't it? To learn where you came from after all these years."

Jerzy smiled politely, not wanting to dig up his own broken past, the pain in particular, but in truth, he was fascinated, and couldn't let go of the possibilities. He drained his glass. "Interesting," he said, though his mind was already wondering.

It started as a small itch beneath his skin, a quiet stirring of something buried. He had always avoided thinking too deeply about the past—what good could come from dragging it back up? But that night, lying awake, he could see the faces of his parents, blurred at the edges, the memories thinning like old paper. He had come so far. But from where, exactly? And from whom?

By April, the itch had grown unbearable. He booked a flight to Warsaw, rented a car, and drove south to Lublin, his hometown. But the city had become a stranger. The house where he had grown up— gone. The school where he had learned to read—gone. The café where his father had taken him on Sundays—gone. His friends—scattered or dead or vanished into the cracks of history. He stood on a street corner, the cold wind pressing against his coat, and it was as if someone had reached into his chest and hollowed him out. This was not the Lublin he remembered.

It wasn't until he drove east to Urszulin that he found something intact. The farm was smaller than he remembered, but there was Uncle Frydryk, sitting on the porch with a cigarette hanging from his mouth, his eyes pale and watery beneath the sag of his cap. Frydryk squinted at him for a long moment before recognition settled.

"You're back," Frydryk finally said.

Jerzy grinned.

They sat at the table in the kitchen, the wood worn thin from decades of elbows and spilled soup. Here, nothing had changed. Jerzy brought his uncle up-to-date on his life since they last saw each other, then asked about the family, about names and dates, about records lost in the war. Frydryk listened, his fingers wrapped around a chipped mug, and said nothing for a long time. Finally, he sighed.

"There's something you should know," Frydryk said. His voice was thin as old paper. "I was never going to tell you, but... I'm old now. And I suppose you ought to know."

Jerzy waited.

"The man you knew as your father... he wasn't. At least not by blood."

Jerzy's mouth went dry.

"Your mother... before she met him, there was another man. He was married, but they... well, it was love, but it couldn't last. When your mother met the man you called Papa, she was already carrying you." Frydryk's eyes narrowed."

"Did Papa know?"

"He knew, Jerzy, but he loved your mother so very much, it did not matter to him. He was proud to raise you as his own."

Jerzy leaned in. "Do you remember his name?"

He hesitated. "I know the man's name." And then Frydryk told him.

"Any idea where he's from?"

"Last I heard, he was living in Lublin."

Jerzy asked around. Two days later, he stood outside a narrow apartment building in Lublin, hands in his pockets. An older woman answered the door, her face hard with the wear of postwar Poland. When he asked about the man, she shook her head. "Killed in the war," she said flatly.

But at least Jerzy hadn't come up empty. "Any kids?"

"He had a son," the woman added. "But he's in prison."

It took only $300 American dollars to secure his newfound brother's release—an obscene sum to a communist bureaucrat, a bargain to Jerzy. They sat in a smoky bar afterward, the man's hands shaking as he lifted his glass. His name was Marek. He had dark, curly hair like Jerzy's and the same quiet set to his mouth.

"It's so weird, Jerzy... I never knew I had a brother, and now, looking at you, there is no doubt. You look more like my dad... OUR dad, than I do."

They didn't talk much about the war or the years in between, but they drank together, and for a moment, Jerzy thought he might have found a piece of himself that had been missing.

They promised to write to each other, and at first they did. But with time, the letters grew fewer and fewer in between. Two years later, Marek died of an overdose in a filthy tenement in Lublin. Jerzy received a telegram about it. He folded it in half and tucked it into the bottom drawer of his desk. Some things were better left buried. Besides, Jerzy still remembered, after being shot, meeting his father, the man who raised and cared for him, on the other side, and feeling his love. He knew that that man would always be his real father, biological or not.

Fifty-One

Recital

The house was never silent any more. From the moment Dorota first plucked the strings of her very own guitar, something in the air had changed. They would give her lessons at school, but she had to provide her own instrument. It had started with simple chords, hesitant fingers finding their way over the frets, the sound thin and searching. But as the years passed, the music had grown with her, weaving itself into the rhythm of their days. It was there in the mornings before school, when she played softly by the window, sunlight catching in her hair. It was there in the evenings, filling the space between homework and dinner, between the clatter of dishes and the quiet hum of the world settling down for the night.

Jerzy had been skeptical at first—he had tried to talk her into the piano, something structured, something dignified. But Dorota had insisted. The guitar felt right in her hands, she had said. It was closer to her heart. And so, he and Ekaterina had bought her one, a modest instrument with a rich, warm tone, and they had found her a teacher outside the school. They had watched her practice, watched her fingers grow calloused, watched as her music became more than notes, more than sound. It became expression, emotion, a language all its own.

Now, in the junior high school auditorium, Jerzy sat in the second row, his hands clasped together as he waited. The stage was set with a single stool, a microphone angled just so, the backdrop a heavy curtain of deep red. Around him, parents murmured, shifting in their seats, craning to catch glimpses of their own children backstage. He felt Ekaterina's hand on his arm, a gentle squeeze, reassurance or shared anticipation, he wasn't sure. He looked at her, and she smiled.

Then Dorota stepped onto the stage.

She was taller now, her limbs leaner, her features more defined, but in his eyes, she was still the same little girl who had once clutched a broken-winged bird in her hands, tears streaming down her face because she could not bare to see it suffer. She had always been like this—tender-hearted, open, carrying the weight of the world in ways she did not yet understand. And now, she carried it in her music.

She sat on the stool, adjusting the strap of her guitar, her fingers brushing lightly over the strings. The room quieted. She leaned toward the microphone.

"I wrote this song myself," she said, her voice steady, clear. "For everyone who's ever needed a little love."

Jerzy felt his throat tighten.

Then she played.

The first notes were soft, almost hesitant, like a whisper in the dark. Then the melody took shape, rising and falling, a gentle ebb and flow, like waves against the shore. Her voice, when it came, was light as breath, carrying lyrics that spoke of kindness, of longing, of love that endured. And as she played, the room seemed to fade, the walls dissolving, the ceiling opening to the vast expanse of sky. There was only the music, and the girl who created it, and the man who listened with his heart wide open.

Jerzy did not realize he was crying until he felt the dampness on his cheeks. He let the tears fall, unashamed, his hands gripping each other in his lap. He thought of all the roads that had led him here, all the storms he had weathered, all the moments of loss and pain. And yet, here she was. His daughter. His Dorota. Pouring her soul into the world with six strings and a voice like the stardust he always knew she was.

When the final note lingered and faded into silence, there was a moment—just a moment—where the world stood still. Then the applause rose, loud and insistent, filling every corner of the room. Dorota smiled, ducking her head slightly as if to hide the flush in her cheeks. Jerzy stood, clapping until his palms ached, until Ekaterina stood beside him, until the entire auditorium was on its feet.

Dorota looked for him then, past the rows of people, past the bright stage lights, her eyes seeking his. And when she finally found him, and so close, he saw the question there—Did I make you proud?

He could not answer with words, so he only nodded, his vision blurring again.

Yes, my love. A thousand times yes.

And the standing ovation echoed in his heart.

* * *

The years passed in a way that felt both swift and slow, time moving like the tide—sometimes gentle, sometimes with an unforgiving pull, but always forward. Dorota grew, her childhood slipping into adolescence, her limbs lengthening, her features maturing, her mind expanding with new ideas, new dreams. She continued to play her guitar in the evenings, filling the house with music that spoke of something larger than words, something that came from deep within her, something that neither of her parents had quite expected but both recognized as hers alone.

Then, in high school, came the invitation. A father-daughter dance.

She asked him if he would be her date, her voice light, almost teasing, but Jerzy heard the sincerity beneath it, felt his heart clench in a way that was both joyous and aching. He had watched her grow, had witnessed her first steps, her first words, the first time she had played her own song in front of an audience. And now, she was asking him to share this fleeting moment, a dance before time pulled her further into the world.

The night of the dance, he stood in the hallway, adjusting the cuffs of his suit, waiting as Dorota descended the stairs in a pale blue dress that shimmered in the light. She was radiant, her hair carefully curled, her smile nervous but bright.

"You look so beautiful," he said, his voice thick with emotion.

She grinned. "You look pretty cool yourself, Daddy."

She was sixteen now. The same age he was when the Poland was attacked by the Germans in 1939. The same age he was when his brother was killed and his world ended forever. But she knew none of that, and he was glad.

At the dance, surrounded by fathers and daughters swaying under the warm glow of string lights, Jerzy felt something deep and unshakable swell within him. When the band struck up "Daddy's Little Girl," Dorota turned to him, her eyes shining, and took his hand. They danced, her small fingers laced through his, her head resting against his chest.

That night, when they returned home, Ekaterina met them at the door. She saw the quiet pride in Jerzy's eyes, the love that had no words, only presence. And she loved him more than ever.

Fifty-Two

The Telling

The years had slowed him, but they had not stopped him. Jerzy moved with a deliberateness now, a measured pace that spoke of experience rather than age. His hands, still strong though marked by time, worked the earth with patience, coaxing life from the soil in the neat rows of his garden which had grown huge. He had always found comfort in growing things, in the quiet persistence of seeds becoming sprouts, then leaves, then fruit. It was work that did not rush, that followed the rhythm of the seasons rather than the whims of men. And now, more than ever, he understood the value of patience, of tending to what could be tended, of letting go of what could not.

Beyond the garden, in the small wooden shed he had built himself, his homing pigeons cooed softly in their lofts. He remembered his neighbor, Mr. Ruszkowski, who had kept them when Jerzy was young, and Jerzy had marveled at their grace, their loyalty to home. Now, such birds were his again—his companions in the early morning, his solace in the stillness of dusk. Dorota had taken an interest in them too, standing beside him as he fed them, watching as they strutted and fluffed their feathers, as they took flight in great, sweeping arcs against the sky.

"They always come back," she had said once, eyes following the birds as they circled above them.

Jerzy had smiled, watching the way the light caught in her hair. "If they know where home is, yes."

One afternoon, Dorota was with him when he opened the coop, lifting his arm to release one of his favorites, a sleek gray high-flyer with white-tipped wings. The pigeon hesitated for only a moment before bursting into the sky, climbing in easy spirals, stretching its wings in the warmth of the day.

Then, Jerzy saw it—a shadow slicing through the air, a movement too swift to be mistaken. A hawk.

His stomach tightened, but he said nothing. Instead, he touched Dorota's shoulder and pointed upwards.

"Watch," he said, his voice calm.

Dorota followed his gaze, her brow furrowing. "What's wrong?"

"Nothing is wrong," Jerzy murmured. "Just watch."

The hawk was climbing, drawing closer to the pigeon, its movements calculated, deliberate. The pigeon, unaware or perhaps simply obeying instinct, continued its ascent. Higher and higher the hawk led it, forcing it into thinner air, into open space where there was no cover, no escape.

Dorota gasped. "It's just like what you told me. From when you were a boy."

Jerzy nodded. "Yes."

And then, as before, the moment of violence—the hawk reared back, turned, and struck, a blur of talons and feathers, a sudden explosion of motion. The pigeon never had a chance. Dorota flinched, her breath catching in her throat as the loose feathers floated down, soft and weightless, as though they did not belong to what had just happened.

She turned to Jerzy, her eyes wide, full of sorrow. "It's gone," she whispered sadly.

Jerzy placed a steadying hand on her back, looking up at the sky where the hawk now circled, where the pigeon had been only moments before. "No," he said softly. "Not in the way we expect."

Dorota blinked up at him, searching his face for understanding. He smiled, the lines around his eyes deepening, but there was no sadness there, only a quiet acceptance.

"It was never lost," he continued. "Not really. That pigeon was meant to fly. And it did. It flew higher than it ever had before. And now, it is part of something greater."

Dorota's eyes shimmered, her lips pressed together as she tried to reconcile what she had seen with what she wanted to believe. "But it's gone."

Jerzy shook his head. "Its spirit is forever, Dorota. Just like everything else. Just like us. Nothing truly ends."

She turned her gaze back to the sky, watching the hawk disappear into the horizon. The wind rustled the trees, the garden swayed, the pigeons in the shed cooed softly, unbothered, untouched by what had just happened.

Dorota exhaled slowly, and Jerzy knew that she understood, even if it would take time for her to put it into words. She was growing, stretching beyond what she had been, learning how to hold both sorrow and wonder in the same breath.

Jerzy reached for a handful of feed and poured it into her waiting palm. "Come," he said gently. "The others are waiting."

And together, they returned to the coop, to the pigeons still fluttering and bobbing in their wooden home, to the ones who would fly again.

It had happened so fast that she had doubted it at first, even as she stood there, the courtyard tilting under her feet, the warmth of the afternoon turned suddenly cold. A rush of wings, the blur of something darker moving through the light, and then nothing—nothing but silence and the slow, drifting fall of gray feathers that caught in her hair, clung to her sleeve, swirled weightless against the stones.

No corpse. No proof. Only absence.

Now, hours later, the feather was still between her fingers. She turned it over in the lamplight, the barbs catching, pulling apart slightly before falling back into place. It had been alive. And then it hadn't. And it had happened so quickly that she could almost believe she had imagined it.

Almost.

"It was its time," her father had said.

She had not answered. Had only frowned, rubbing her thumb over the spine of the feather, feeling its fragility, its near-nothingness. She believed him. And yet—

They were just stories.

All his words, all his truths, the things he said about life, about death, about meaning, about how nothing was ever truly lost—she believed he believed them. But they were stories, just like the ones in the books she used to beg him to read when she was small, stories that made the world make sense back then, that softened its edges, that turned sharp things into lessons.

And yet the pigeon had been here. And now it wasn't.

She sat at the far end of the table, watching the lamplight flicker against the walls, her arms drawn close over her ribs, not from cold, but from something else, something unspoken. Ekaterina sat next to her, her hands still, her expression quiet. She knew this weight, this silence, the way something hovered, waiting to be said.

And then her father exhaled.

"You know," he said, his voice steady but distant, "I died once."

Dorota's head lifted.

She studied his face, expecting a smile, the flicker of humor that sometimes came before a story—but there was none. Only the slow shift of his fingers along the tabletop, tracing an invisible shape.

She had heard stories of him being shot, of the hospital, of how he had survived when he shouldn't have. But not like this. Never like this.

"I did not feel it," he said. "One moment I was there. And then—everything shifted."

Something moved behind his eyes, something deeper than memory.

"I was watching," he said. "From outside myself. From—somewhere else. I saw the street, the people, the sky, as if I stood above it all.

I saw your mother holding me, screaming for me to wake up. And I tried. I really tried to touch her. But I could not."

Dorota swallowed, the feather still tight between her fingers.

"I was not alone," he said.

Ekaterina's breath caught. She had known there was something more. She had waited years for him to say it.

"My father was there," he continued. "The one who raised me. My real father. Dorota frowned, not understanding what he was talking about.

"He told me it was not my time," Jerzy said. "That I had a choice."

For a long moment, the room was silent.

Dorota exhaled. "But you came back."

"Yes." He looked at her now, his gaze steady. "For her, nodding to her mother. And for you."

She didn't speak. Didn't look away.

The feather bent under the pressure of her fingers, its barbs breaking apart.

Something settled in her chest—not belief, not understanding, but something quieter.

She pushed her chair back and stood.

At the window, the coop stretched empty beneath the moonlight, the stones at its base still and bare. No proof. Only absence.

"It was time for the pigeon," she said softly.

"Yes," he said.

She nodded once, as if deciding something, then turned away from the window. "I think I'll go to bed now."

She hesitated, just for a breath, then crossed the room and brushed her fingers lightly over his shoulder before disappearing down the hall.

Ekaterina let out a slow breath, shaking her head with the smallest of smiles.

"She is just like you."

Jerzy huffed a quiet laugh. "God help her."

He ran a hand over his face, feeling, impossibly, lighter.

Fifty-Three

July, 1969

The television flickered, the grainy image twisting and stretching, the antenna adjusted and readjusted, a ghostly figure moving within a sea of blackness, the sound crackling, voices overlapping, the distant hum of something greater than himself, something so vast, so incomprehensible, it made his hands tremble as he reached for the glass, the cognac warm on his tongue, his pulse heavy in his throat.

Four days. He had watched, listened, waited. The news reports, the diagrams on the screen, the men in suits explaining trajectories, velocities, burn rates, every number, every calculation mapped out like scripture, like fate written not in the stars but in fuel, metal, and mathematics. America, reaching beyond the weight of earth, beyond war and worry, beyond the aching grind of daily life, sending three men into the abyss, into the black, into the forever. Jerzy had come to this land with nothing but his hands, his mind, his hunger, and now he sat in his chair, his knuckles white around the armrests, watching as a man stepped onto the surface of the moon.

His breath caught. The world held still.

"One small step for man..."

It was a whisper, an echo distorted by space, by time, by the limits of radio waves stretching between one world and another, and yet it struck him, burrowed into his ribs, settled deep in his chest where it would remain forever.

His America.

He had come on a ship, with only a wife and a baby, a young man with nothing but the weight of a war that had left his country broken, his childhood buried beneath rubble and ash. He had stepped off onto a soil that was not his, learned the language that twisted and turned, its consonants difficult, its vowels strange, had found work, built a life, taken an oath to a flag that was not his by birth but had become his by choice. And now—now—he watched his adopted country land two men on the moon.

Dorota had called earlier, breathless, excited, her voice a rush of wonder. "Are you watching, Daddy? Can you believe it?" She was almost twenty-two now, nearly finished with college, her future stretching before her like the vastness of the sky, limitless, boundless, full of music and promise. He had wanted this for her. A life where she could dream without fear. A world where the only thing that separated humanity from the impossible was time, patience, and will.

The image wavered, the white suit stark against the blackness, the dust rising, settling. He exhaled, long and slow, his chest expanding, something tightening behind his ribs. He set down his glass, his fingers steady now, his head clearing with each moment that passed.

He remembered the nights in Lublin, when the city had been dark, when the sky had been open and endless, the stars stretching out like scattered pearls, unreachable, untouchable. He remembered lying on his back in the fields beyond the town, listening to his Uncle Frydryk speak of things greater than war, greater than hunger, greater than even the weight of suffering. "There is always more," his uncle had said. "More than this. More than what we can see. More than what they tell us is possible."

He had not believed it then. He had been young. He had seen only the ruined streets, the hollow faces, the walls that held in sorrow and held out hope. But here, now, in this moment, he understood.

America had taken the impossible and made it real.

The voice in the television carried on, narrating, explaining, filling the space with words, but Jerzy barely heard them. He saw only the man moving across the gray expanse, the footprints left behind in dust that had never before known the weight of a human step.

A deep breath, a long exhale. His chest swelled.

He was American. And for the first time in his life, he felt it like fire in his blood, like something written into his bones.

Outside, the summer night was thick with humidity, the crickets singing their endless song, the moon hanging high above, no longer distant, no longer an untouchable thing. He stepped out onto the porch, looked up, stared hard, as though he might see them there, tiny figures moving across the silver face of the sky, and he laughed—soft, breathless, full of something he had no words for.

Dorota was watching, too. She would remember this night. One day, she would tell her children, and they would tell theirs, and long after he was gone, long after this moment had become history, the world would still turn, still reach, still hunger for the beyond.

He closed his eyes, let the night wrap around him, let the wonder of it all settle into his skin.

America had reached the moon.

And so had he.

Fifty-Four

Parking Lot Test

Jerzy was sporting some gray highlights. He had spent years working for himself, designing medals, service awards, and insignia with the same meticulous care he had once given to operating factory machines. His work had taken him into the homes and offices of men who needed unique and original symbols to mark achievements, to recognize sacrifice, to bestow honor. He had built a name for himself —not famous, but respected, steady, dependable. A man who knew how to take an idea and shape it into something permanent, something that could be held, displayed, passed down.

But now, the ground beneath him was shifting. The work volume had changed. Not all at once, but slowly, steadily, like water wearing away at stone. Jerzy had been freelancing for years, providing emblematic designs for a variety of clients, but the writing on the wall had been becoming clearer each day. The factory work was drying up. His regular clients were tightening their belts, sending their orders overseas where labor was cheaper, where things could be produced faster and at a fraction of the cost. The signs were there, if he was honest with himself. The work that once flowed in steady streams was now sporadic at best. A freelance artist without clients was no different than a bird without wings.

Some of the companies he had designed for, companies he had served faithfully, were shutting down or—worse—moving. Not to another city. Not even to another state. But across the ocean, where labor cost pennies, where men like him, men with families, with pride, were not needed.

It wasn't that the work had dried up entirely. Orders still came in, though less frequently than before. It was the way things were changing. Companies were consolidating, cutting costs, streamlining. Some of his oldest clients had retired or sold their businesses, and the new owners—young, sharp-eyed, numbers-driven—saw his work not as an art but as an expense to be reduced, outsourced, even eliminated.

And so, the phone rang less. The orders became smaller. He still had enough to live on—for now. But he could see where this was going, as clearly as he could see the fine lines in Ekaterina's face, the way the house creaked louder in the mornings, the way time moved forward with or without his consent.

He needed stability. A regular paycheck. Something that would allow him to plan ahead instead of waiting for the next commission, hoping it would come. And he could always continue to freelance on the side. So, with the weight of this quiet realization pressing against his shoulders, Jerzy decided it was time for a change. But how? How could a man who had thrived as a lone wolf suddenly fit into a corporate structure? How could he trust that, as a salaried employee, his skills would still be valued the way they were when he was the master of his own domain?

That was why, for the first time in decades, Jerzy found himself looking for a job—not just any job, but one that would pay well enough to make the effort worthwhile. He had never been the kind of man to ask outright what a company paid. It felt cheap, desperate. But he wasn't without his methods.

He had built his life here, in this country, with these hands, and he would not sit idly by, waiting for someone to tell him he was no longer needed. He would find a place, a company that understood his worth, one that would see him not merely as another name on a payroll, but as something more.

So, with the weight of this quiet realization pressing against his shoulders, Jerzy decided this was the time for a change. But how? How could a man who had thrived as a lone wolf suddenly fit into a corporate structure? How could he trust that, as a salaried employee, his skills would still be valued the way they were when he was the master of his own domain?

And how to find such a company?

The newspapers were useless. The few ads were for junior positions, for young men just starting out, eager to take whatever they could get. Jerzy needed more. He needed a place that would pay him what he was worth, a place that wasn't shrinking, wasn't closing its doors in the dead of night and leaving its workers stranded.

Then, one evening, as he sat with his coffee, staring out at the cars passing by, he had an idea.

New cars.

It was simple. A company that was doing well, that was thriving, paid its employees enough to afford new cars. And a company that paid well would not need to advertise for help—the men there would stay, because they had no reason to leave.

The next morning, he took out a notebook, sat at the kitchen table, and wrote down the names of every company he had ever heard of, every factory, every plant, every business in his industry that seemed like it might be the right fit. Then, he got into his car and started driving.

He did not go inside. He did not ask questions. He did not waste his time with managers who would give him the runaround.

Instead, he merely went to their parking lots.

He sat across the street, watched as the workers arrived in the morning, as they left in the evening. He took note of the cars—how many were old and rusting, how many were new, how many still had their dealership plates. And slowly, as the days passed, a pattern emerged.

Some lots were filled with battered old sedans, cars that had seen too many winters, their paint peeling, their tires balding.

But others—others were different.

New Buicks. Freshly washed Fords. A Cadillac or two, parked near the entrance.

By the end of the week, he found that company in an unassuming manufacturing plant.

Their specialty was badges. Police, fire, and private security badges, shipped all over the world. A business that had been going strong for almost a century, with clients all over the world, but oddly enough—despite the significance of their products—they had no art department. They didn't think they needed one. They'd been using the same tired designs for so long that no one thought to question it. It was the sort of complacency Jerzy had come to know in his younger years, back in Poland, a stifling environment that slowly suffocated creativity.

So, Jerzy did what Jerzy did best. He researched. He studied the company's catalogue, its existing designs. He examined every line, every curve, every emblem, and he created something new. Fresh, vibrant, and uniquely his own, while still keeping in mind the tradition these badges carried. He put together a portfolio of his ideas—sample badges, concepts, each one a modern, meaningful take on a symbol that had carried decades of history. And then, with a quiet confidence, he walked into their office.

The reception he received was not immediate excitement but a guarded curiosity. When Jerzy laid out his work, however, the silence in the room was deafening. But after a few moments, it happened—he saw the spark in their eyes. These weren't just badges. They were representations of pride, honor, and service, and Jerzy's designs, brimming with new life, originality, and made it clear that the company's image was about to evolve into something far more dynamic. They needed him. There was no denying it.

Negotiations were tougher than Jerzy had anticipated. The company balked at his initial salary request, but Jerzy knew he had them cornered. With a calm smile, he dropped the name of a competitor of theirs—a rival company that had a well-established art department. Their clients had always looked to them for custom designs, and they were starting to steal the kind of attention Jerzy knew this company needed to keep its edge. It wasn't long before they agreed to his terms, and Jerzy knew they had made the right decision.

His first year with the company proved him right. As soon as they began offering customized badges—something they had never done before—requests came flooding in from all over the world. Clients loved the unique, personalized designs, and soon the company was booming bigger than ever. Jerzy was in his element, designing with more freedom than he'd had in years, contributing in ways he had only dreamed of.

That first year, at the company's Christmas party, Jerzy had an epiphany. He saw the depth of the company's culture, the loyalty and respect it commanded from its employees. The most telling moment came when a woman who had worked in the factory for thirty-five years was retiring. The management had a special gift for her—$1,000 for every year she had spent with the company. She could buy herself a new house with that kind of money, Jerzy thought, blinking in disbelief.

It was then that Jerzy knew he had made the right decision. This wasn't just a job—it was a family. And for the first time in years, Jerzy felt a part of something that truly valued him. He wasn't just a cog in a machine; he was an integral piece of the company's future. The same way he had put his heart into every piece of art he created, this company had put its heart into its people. Jerzy knew, without a doubt, that he had found a home.

Fifty-Five

Inside the Cell

Time had a way of grinding a man down, smoothing the sharp edges, tempering the fire, but never quite extinguishing it, though it whispered that it would, that it should, that a man, past the years where hunger was the engine that drove him forward, ought to settle, ought to bow his head and accept that he was no longer the force he once was, that the world belonged now to younger men with faster hands, with brighter ideas, with no memory of what it was to build something from nothing, to scrape and claw and will a life into existence with nothing but the strength in his fingers and the stubborn belief that it was possible. The years had moved over him like water over stone, relentless, inevitable, shaping him, carving into his body new rivers of pain, etching into his skin the map of where he had been, what he had endured—lines across his forehead from the long hours bent over a drafting table, the silver threading through his hair like winter creeping into autumn, the stiffness in his joints, the way he had to ease into movement now, slow in the mornings, slow when rising from his chair after too many hours still, the weight of the years pressing into his bones, whispering of all the ways he had changed, all the ways he had stayed the same.

And yet, the fire remained. Smaller, perhaps, tempered, no longer the reckless blaze of a young man with something to prove, but steady, smoldering, waiting for the right moment to burn again. He had seen the world shift around him, seen the factories he once designed for close their doors, seen the faces of men who had worked their whole lives for something solid, something stable, turn hollow when they were told their jobs no longer existed, that the world had moved on, that machines and cheaper hands half a world away could do the same work for a fraction of the cost. He had watched, but he had never accepted, never surrendered to the quiet resignation of men who let time steal their fight.

Sixty now. Sixty and watching the veins in his hands rise beneath his skin like the roots of an old tree, watching the way his fingers curled a little slower around a pencil, the way his grip ached after hours of drawing. Sixty and feeling, in some distant part of himself, the pull of rest, of slowing down, of letting go—but no, not yet, not while there was still something in him that refused to be counted out. The world had long since decided that men like him were supposed to be too old, too tired, too quiet to resist, to demand, to stand their ground. But Jerzy had spent a lifetime defying what the world expected of him, and he had no intention of stopping now.

* * *

The accident was not his fault. He had seen it all as it happened, the way she had changed lanes without looking, how the sharp tilt of her head suggested she had seen exactly what was happening, and had cut in front of him—and he had braked, had turned the wheel as far as he could without flipping the car, but the impact had come anyway, the jarring, sickening sound of metal folding in on itself, the lurch of his body against the restraints. And then, the woman, stepping out of her car, her hands already clutching at her neck, her voice rising into an indignant, pained wail before he had even gotten out of his car. He should have known then how it would go.

The judge was old, though younger than Jerzy, with the sort of face that never softened, a mouth drawn tight like a knot that would never be undone. His eyes, when they flicked to Jerzy, were already full of dismissal. The court was not a place for men like him, men with names that did not roll easily off American tongues, men whose voices carried the weight of other languages, other histories, men who had lived through war, through displacement, only to find themselves still fighting, still justifying their right to stand where they stood.

The lawyer, a young man with a cheap suit and a habit of shuffling papers without ever seeming to read them, was failing him, speaking in hesitant half-statements, never pressing, never pushing, letting the woman's exaggerated claims stand uncontested. Jerzy clenched his fists, felt the words building in his chest, words sharpened by anger, by truth, and when the lawyer stammered again, Jerzy could not hold them back.

"You are not listening!" His voice rang through the courtroom. "I did not hit her. She swerved into me!"

The judge's gavel slammed down. "You'll speak when spoken to, Mr. Czaplicki."

Jerzy could feel the heat rising to his face, the pulse pounding in his temple. He tried again, his voice harder now, the accent thickening, not with uncertainty but with force, with years of knowing that a man had to speak for himself or be trampled. "This is not justice. Even the Nazis let me speak."

A hush fell over the courtroom. The judge's face twisted, and then his voice came low and dangerous. "Do you want to go to jail for contempt, Mr. Czaplicki? Think about it overnight, and give me an answer tomorrow when you are back in this courtroom. Court dismissed!" The gavel came down even harder this time.

The next day, as soon as court began, Jerzy was immediately told to approach the bench. "Have you thought about my question from yesterday, Mr. Czaplicki? Do you really want to go to jail?"

This was the moment where he was meant to retreat, to lower his head, to apologize, to yield. The air was thick with waiting.

Instead, Jerzy held the judge's gaze, slow and deliberate, reached into his back pocket, pulled out his toothbrush, and held it up at arm's length to the judge, like an offering. "I am all packed."

The sentence was swift—three days in jail. Enough to teach him a lesson. Enough to remind him of his place.

* * *

Life is always fluid, shifting, and in the jail cell, Jerzy found himself in the company of two men hunched over a chessboard, the board worn into the surface by years of use, the pieces chipped, the edges smoothed by countless hands. One man sighed, pushing his chair back. "I'm done," he said. "No way out of this."

"Wait!" Jerzy said, He studied the board. The losing side had only a single pawn and his king, the other man still had most of his pieces, but there was something there, something left, and Jerzy knew better than to surrender before the end. He gestured to the chair. "Can I finish the game for him?"

The game unfolded in silence, the steady movement of hands, a quiet rhythm of thought and strategy. The winning man smirked at first, amused, then frowning, then leaning in, then shaking his head as his advantage crumbled. Jerzy had managed to somehow move his pawn, protected by his king, all the way to the last row, and exchanged it for a queen. And then, the final move. Jerzy sat back, satisfied. "Thank you for letting an old man win," he said loudly enough for everyone to hear, even thought that was not true. Sometimes a man's dignity was more important than the truth. Jerzy had just gained another friend.

On the third day, his lawyer arrived, his face flushed with something like triumph. "We got her," he said. "Your little vacation in here gave us three extra days, so I hired a private eye to follow her. Got pictures of her bringing out her trash without the neck brace on. And not only that, but I found an eyewitness—someone who saw what really happened."

The next day in court, the lawsuit was dismissed, and the woman ordered to pay all of his court costs. When asked if he wanted to countersue, Jerzy looked deeply at the woman, and saw something in her eyes. Pain. Suffering. "No," was all he said.

Jerzy walked out of the courthouse and into the crisp afternoon air, stretching his arms, tilting his head back to the sky. There were battles in life, some big, some small, and while this one had been absurd in its own way, it had also been necessary. Because a man did not roll over when the world tried to crush him. He stood. He fought. And, sometimes, he even won.

Fifty-Six

The Porch

Time was now Jerzy's constant companion. It was with him from the time he arose in the early morning hours until the time he went to bed, constantly reminding him of its presence. And Jerzy—now sixty-five, now stiff in the mornings, now tracing the veins in his hands with something like disbelief—still carried enough of that fire to know when he was being wronged. It wasn't just a matter of stubbornness, though there was that, too. It was memory, deep and ingrained, the kind that lived in his hands as much as in his mind.

They told him it couldn't be done.

The first contractor took one look at the back of the house, crossed his arms, and shook his head. "Not possible," he said, like a man delivering a funeral notice. "There's nothing to support it."

The second one sighed before Jerzy even finished explaining. "It's a nice idea," he said, "but structurally, it won't hold."

Jerzy thanked them, but he didn't believe them. He had never believed in the words *it can't be done*. He knew better.

Because he had seen impossible things done before.

Growing up in Poland had taught him that.

Long before he came to America, before he ever laid eyes on a factory or sketched his first design, he had seen individuals raise walls without help, set roofs atop beams with nothing but their own will to keep them standing. The village had burned—how many times? Too many to count. A chimney not properly damped, a gust of wind catching at the thatch, a careless ember finding a wooden beam, and then it was all gone. Fire didn't discriminate; it took everything. But the people never sat in the ashes. They built again.

Jerzy had been a boy the first time he helped. There was no blueprint, no architect with his neat little drawings. The knowledge lived in the hands of the men who had done it before, passed from father to son, neighbor to neighbor. He had learned by watching, by doing. How to drive a wooden peg home so it wouldn't split the beam. How to set a post so it wouldn't shift in the spring thaw. How to brace against the weight of the world itself. All done in a time without blueprints

And he learned, too, that anything could be made stronger than before.

The trick wasn't to work *around* the limits. It was to *use* them.

So, when the contractors told him *it can't be done,* what he heard was, *they don't know how to do it.*

But *he* did.

The problem wasn't the upper-story deck itself; it was the attachment. The weight had to be carried through the house, not just against it. That was the key. So, he wouldn't just bolt the ledger board to the house—he would make the house itself part of the deck's frame.

The first step was finding the studs inside the back wall. Not just the obvious ones—the deep ones, the structural ones, the bones of the house itself. Then he measured, marked, and drilled straight through. Long steel rods went in next, sliding clean through the wall, past the insulation, past the layers of plaster and paint, through the framing inside.

On the other side, inside the house, he bolted them into place, securing them to the floor joists. The deck wouldn't just *cling* to the house—it would *anchor* inside of it.

Then came the braces. He ran two diagonal supports down from the deck's frame, meeting the steel rods where they passed through the wall. The whole thing locked together in a perfect triangle, unyielding, distributing the force evenly.

And the best part? The back wall, instead of being a weak point, became a *load-bearing* wall for the deck itself.

By the time he finished, it looked as though it had been built *with* the house, not added after. It was solid. Permanent.

Three weeks later, he invited the first contractor over to see it.

The man stepped onto the deck, shifted his weight experimentally, gave a reluctant nod. "Seems solid," he admitted.

"It is." Jerzy crossed his arms. "And it *was* possible."

The man sighed. "You know, if it fell down, I was gonna say I told you so."

Jerzy smiled. "And now?"

"Now I have no idea how you pulled this off."

Jerzy just shrugged. "I do."

Fifty-Seven

The Return

The seasons flowed on, gaining speed with each passing year, the world's edges drawing in, its horizons folding closer, the grand adventure of youth distilled into the repetition of days, meals at the same table, conversations circling back on themselves like a needle stuck in an old groove. Jerzy felt it, the creeping sameness, the slow tightening of life's once-endless possibilities into something smaller, narrower, more predictable. But if time thought it could tame him, thought it could whittle him down into just another old man shuffling toward the inevitable, well—time had another thing coming.

While his body might have started its slow betrayal—his knees complaining on cold mornings, his hands stiffening just enough to remind him that they had once built and shaped and created with ease —his tongue, oh, his tongue had only sharpened with age. It slipped between the cracks of conversation like a knife, cutting through the mundane, livening up the dull, turning even the smallest moments into performances. He was a man of stories now, of embellishments and exaggerations so well-crafted that even he, at times, half-believed them.

He had always loved a good challenge, had never been able to resist the spark of competition, and now, as the years stacked up behind him, he found new ways to stir the pot. He would eye some wiry young man, some sprinter-legged, hot-blooded fool brimming with the invincibility of youth, and lay down his challenge.

"Fifty dollars," he would say, stretching his back as if preparing for the race of his life, "says I can beat you to that lamppost. Want to bet?"

The kid would laugh, shake his head, wave it off—but there was something in Jerzy's eyes, something in the curl of his lips, that made them hesitate. What did the old man know? What trick was he hiding? Did he have some hidden speed, some secret reserve of strength waiting to be unleashed? Jerzy never had to race a single person. Not one. They always backed down, unwilling to risk the humiliation of losing to him, no matter how impossible it seemed. And that, of course, was the win.

Then there were the young women—shopkeepers, waitresses, cashiers—girls with their whole lives ahead of them, moving too fast, not yet understanding that someday they, too, would slow down. He would flatter them outrageously, like a big overaged flirt, watching the way they blinked, their expressions caught between amusement and suspicion.

"You must be an angel," he would say, tapping his temple as if just now realizing something profound. "No, really. It explains everything —why the sun seems to follow you, why the air feels lighter when you walk past. I should have seen it sooner."

Some of them blushed, some of them laughed outright, but the best ones played along, batting their lashes and saying, "Ah, but if I were an angel, wouldn't I have wings?"

And he would shake his head gravely. "No, no. The other angels were jealous, so they clipped them to keep you here."

Ekaterina, standing nearby, would smirk over the top of her grocery list, never interfering, never scolding. She had long since accepted that Jerzy was a performer at heart, a magician with words, a man who spun the ordinary into something worth remembering.

But it was Dorota's boyfriend, Mark, the quiet, well-mannered guy with the careful handshake, who got one of Jerzy's finest lines. They had been sitting in the living room, Jerzy sizing him up the way a father does, weighing the worth of the man who had somehow captured his daughter's affection.

"You know, my wife loves me very much," Jerzy said, his voice just low enough to make the guy lean in, unsure of where this was going.

Mark nodded quickly, eager to agree, to say the right thing. "Yes, sir. That's clear."

Jerzy tilted his head, took a slow sip of his drink, then said, "You know how I know?" He tugged at the cuff of his shirt just enough to draw attention to it, then let it drop again. "She lets me wear long sleeve shirts to hide the bruises."

For a moment, there was only silence. Then Mark's eyes widened, his mouth opening and closing like a fish caught too far from the water. Ekaterina, passing through with a tray of tea, sighed. "Don't believe a word he says, Mark," she said, setting down the cups. "If anything, I should be the one hiding my bruises from having to drag his stubborn self around all these years."

Jerzy grinned, watching Mark's shoulders relax, his nervous laughter finally spilling out. Later, when they were alone, Mark complimented his girlfriend's father about his amazingly creative sense of humor.

"You are just saying that because it is true," responded Jerzy, as though it was a sincere response. Neither man knew what to say over that, so they just stared at each other, then broke out in simultaneous laughter.

It was a game, a dance, a way of filling the spaces left by time, of refusing to be reduced to an old man with only memorie to keep him company. If the world insisted on slowing him down, he would at least make sure it did so while laughing.

And if the stories got a little taller with each telling, well—wasn't that the privilege of age?

* * *

When the end finally came, as it always must, the room was quiet, save for the slow, measured breaths that barely stirred the air. The world outside continued, indifferent—cars rolling down distant streets, birds creating patterns in the late afternoon sky—but here, in this small, dim-lit space, time had narrowed to the width of a single bed, to the clasp of two hands, to the fading light in Jerzy's eyes.

Ekaterina sat beside him, her fingers wrapped gently around his, as though she could hold him here just a little longer. He had been speaking, though now his voice was thin, a whisper that flickered like a candle in a breeze.

"I was five when Mama died," he murmured. "I don't think I ever really understood it then. Just that she was there, and then she wasn't. And nothing was ever quite as warm after that."

She squeezed his hand, offering what little warmth she could now.

"Boguslaw," he said after a pause, the name like a shadow across his breath. "The way he looked at me... like I was nothing." His mouth curled, just slightly. "But I wasn't nothing. I wasn't."

She shook her head. "No, you were not," she whispered.

"Then the bombing," he said, his gaze unfocused, drifting somewhere beyond the room. "I was sixteen. The sky was black with planes. And the streets—God, the streets were burning. So many—" His breath hitched, and he let the words dissolve.

Ekaterina swallowed against the lump rising in her throat. She had heard these stories before, all of them, but never like this—not as a farewell, not as a summation of an entire life.

He was quiet for a long moment before his lips twitched again in a ghost of a smile. "The chemical factory," he said, shaking his head weakly. "Never thought I'd live to see thirty, after that place." His gaze flickered toward her, clearer now, more present. "And you... you with your glasses."

She let out a small, shaky laugh, remembering.

"Remember? We lost them when I kissed you," he went on, as though they were once again in that moment, two young lovers in the rubble of a broken world, where even hunger and cruelty could not dampen the fire of youth.

"The constant hunger," he murmured, the smile fading. "God, we were so thin. It was your love that kept me alive." His hand trembled slightly in hers. "The end of the war, the camp, the group marriage…" He exhaled slowly.

Then another pause, a heavier one. He closed his eyes for a moment before opening them again.

"Our son," he said, barely audible now.

Ekaterina shut her eyes against the sting, against the way that loss never dulled, only settled deep, like a buried coal still burning.

"Dorota's polio."

He was unraveling it all, every sorrow, every hardship, as though laying down each stone he had carried.

"The immigration, with nothing but the clothes on our backs" A breath. "Jail."

Another pause. Longer this time. And then nothing.

Ekaterina felt the silence stretch, and the weight of it filled her chest like lead. She knew. She *knew*.

She had thought she was ready, thought she had spent all her grief long ago, preparing for this moment. But still, it came for her, silent, unseen, a tide rising in her throat. She would not let him hear it. Not now, not when he had fought so hard, endured so much. She wept quietly, tears slipping down her cheeks in silence, unseen by the man whose eyes had always seen everything.

Then, suddenly, his fingers pressed against hers, the smallest movement, the last of his strength. His gaze found hers, soft, full of everything words could not hold.

"It was a good life, wasn't it?" he asked, his voice as light as breath itself.

Ekaterina could only nod, could only press his hand to her lips.

And then he smiled. A small, contented smile. And closed his eyes.

And this time, he did not open them again.

The last breath left him like a whisper. A sigh that belonged not just to this moment but to the whole of him, to everything he had been and done and fought for.

Ekaterina sat there, her fingers still curled around his, staring at the face that had aged beside hers, the man who had held her heart through war and exile and hunger and joy. She thought she had nothing left, that her grief had already spent itself in quiet tears, but the finality of it struck like a bell, deep and resonant.

And so, she wept. The last of her tears, the final surrender.

And when all the tears were gone, when the weight of it had passed through her, she laid down beside him and followed, as always.

They were inexorably linked, after all.

Author's Note

The early portion of this story was inspired by real-life memories shared with me by a dear friend—an older Polish immigrant whose strength and vision shaped much of the character of Jerzy. Before his passing, he gave me permission to use elements of his story in fictional form, with all names and personal details changed.

Though fictionalized, I remain grateful for the gift of his trust and for the human truths he so generously shared.

Acknowledgments

To *Pinky*, whose quiet brilliance and generous spirit brought order to the chaos.

Your careful hands shaped this manuscript into its final form, meeting every unseen requirement with grace and precision.

You asked for no credit—but you have it here, with all my gratitude.

Thank you.

* * *

I also extend a huge thank you to you, Alicia Haske Wojtkowiak, for your diligence and eagle-eyed care in proofreading this manuscript.

Your sharp focus and steady commitment brought clarity to the pages and confidence to the final draft.

Thank you, Al.

Thank you for reading this. I've spent most of my life reading, thinking, and trying to understand what's underneath this daily drama—what really matters, what's lasting, and what it means to be alive, and human. This novel grew from that search.

Much of the material was inspired by the lives of a few dear friends, and relatives, many from my parents' generation, all of them gone now, but not forgotten. I miss their energy and enthusiasm.

At the moment, I live quietly, surrounded by books, silence, and a long echo of ideas that still won't leave me alone. Being on the far side of 77, I would assume that my days ahead number far fewer than those left behind, yet there is at least one more novel still marinating on the back burner, and I hope to get it out while I am still kicking.

In the meantime, I really would love to hear from you. You can reach me through my website at rickburrauthor.com, or stop by my Facebook site, *Beyond the Page*, and say hello.

Rick